"Sarah."

There was an ache in Damon's voice.

Her heart did a funny little jump in her chest and she turned her head to look at him. Her gaze collided with his. Stark hunger was in his eyes. Raw need. Desire. He reached for her, caught the nape of her neck, and slowly lowered his head to hers. His mouth fastened to hers. They simply melted together. Merged.

Fireworks might have burst in the air around them. Or maybe it was the stars scattering across the sky, glittering like gems. Fire raced up her skin, heat spread through her body. He claimed her. Branded her. And he did a thorough job of it. They fed on one another. Were lost in smoky desire. His mouth was perfect, hot and hungry and demanding and possessive.

No one had ever kissed her like that. She had never thought it would be like that . . .

—from Christine Feehan's "Magic in the Wind"

Please turn to the back of this book for a
special preview of Christine Feehan's

SHADOW GAME

Now available from Jove Books!

Lover BEWARE

CHRISTINE FEEHAN 91
KATHERINE SUTCLIFFE 71
FIONA BRAND 64
EILEEN WILKS 105

BERKLEY BOOKS, NEW YORK

THE BERKLEY PUBLISHING GROUP
Published by the Penguin Group
Penguin Group (USA) Inc.
375 Hudson Street, New York, New York 10014, USA
Penguin Group (Canada), 90 Eglinton Avenue East, Suite 700, Toronto, Ontario M4P 2Y3, Canada
(a division of Pearson Penguin Canada Inc.)
Penguin Books Ltd., 80 Strand, London WC2R 0RL, England
Penguin Group Ireland, 25 St. Stephen's Green, Dublin 2, Ireland (a division of Penguin Books Ltd.)
Penguin Group (Australia), 250 Camberwell Road, Camberwell, Victoria 3124, Australia
(a division of Pearson Australia Group Pty. Ltd.)
Penguin Books India Pvt. Ltd., 11 Community Centre, Panchsheel Park, New Delhi—110 017, India
Penguin Group (NZ), Cnr. Airborne and Rosedale Roads, Albany, Auckland 1310, New Zealand
(a division of Pearson New Zealand Ltd.)
Penguin Books (South Africa) (Pty.) Ltd., 24 Sturdee Avenue, Rosebank, Johannesburg 2196,
South Africa

Penguin Books Ltd., Registered Offices: 80 Strand, London WC2R 0RL, England

This is a work of fiction. Names, characters, places, and incidents either are the product of each author's imagination or are used fictitiously, and any resemblance to actual persons, living or dead, business establishments, events, or locales is entirely coincidental. The publisher does not have any control over and does not assume any responsibility for author or third-party websites or their content.

LOVER BEWARE

A Berkley Book / published by arrangement with the authors

PRINTING HISTORY
Berkley edition / July 2003

ISBN: 978-0-425-18905-4

BERKLEY®
Berkley Books are published by The Berkley Publishing Group,
a division of Penguin Group (USA) Inc.,
375 Hudson Street, New York, New York 10014.
BERKLEY is a registered trademark of Penguin Group (USA) Inc.
The "B" design is a trademark belonging to Penguin Group (USA) Inc.

PRINTED IN THE UNITED STATES OF AMERICA

20   19   18   17   16

Magic in the Wind

CHRISTINE FEEHAN

For my sisters. . . . Thank you for the magic and the love that has always been in my life.

Chapter 1

⁓

"SARAH'S BACK. SARAH'S come home." The whisper was overly loud and tinged with something close to fear. Or respect. Damon Wilder couldn't decide which. He'd been hearing the same small-town gossip for several hours and it was always said in the same hushed tones. He hated to admit to curiosity and he wasn't about to stoop to asking, not after he had made such a point of insisting on absolute privacy since he arrived last month.

As he walked down the quaint narrow sidewalk made of wood, the wind seemed to whisper, "Sarah's back." He heard it as he passed the gas station and burly Jeff Dockins waved to him. He heard it as he lingered in the small bakery. *Sarah*. The name shouldn't carry mystery, but it did.

He had no idea who Sarah was, but she commanded such interest and awe from the townspeople he found himself totally intrigued. He knew from experience the people in the sleepy little coastal town were not easily impressed. No amount of money, fame, or title earned one deference. Everyone was treated the same, from the poorest to the richest, and there seemed to be no prejudice against religion or any other preferences. It was why he had chosen the town. A man could be anybody here and no one cared.

All day he had heard the whispers. He'd never once caught a glimpse of the mysterious Sarah. But he'd heard she'd once climbed the sheer cliffs above the sea to rescue a dog. An impossible task. He'd seen those crumbling cliffs and no one could climb them. He found himself smiling at the idea of anyone attempting such an impossible feat, and few things amused him or intrigued him.

The only grocery store was in the center of town and most of the gossip originated there and then spread like wildfire. Damon decided he needed a few things before he went home. He hadn't been in the store for more than two minutes when he heard it again. "Sarah's back." The same hushed whisper, the same awe and respect.

Inez Nelson, owner of the grocery store, held court, spilling out gossip as she normally did, instead of ringing up the groceries on the cash register. It usually drove him crazy to have to wait, but this time he lingered by the bread rack in the hope of learning more of the mysterious Sarah who had finally returned.

"Are you sure, Inez?" Trudy Garret asked, dragging her four-year-old closer to her and nearly strangling the child with her hug. "Are her sisters back, too?"

"Oh, I'm certain, all right. She came right into the store as real as you please and bought a ton of groceries. She was back at the cliff house, she said. She didn't say anything about the others, but if one shows up the others aren't far behind."

Trudy Garret looked around, lowered her voice another octave. "Was she still . . . Sarah?"

Damon rolled his eyes. Everyone always annoyed the hell out of him. He thought moving to a small town would allow him to find a way to get along to some extent but people were just plain idiots. Of course Sarah was still Sarah. Who the hell else would she be? Sarah was probably the only one with a brain within a fifty-mile radius so they thought she was different.

"What could it mean?" Trudy asked. "Sarah only comes back when something is going to happen."

"I asked her if everything was all right and she just smiled in that way she has and said yes. You wouldn't want me to pry into Sarah's business, now would you, dear," Inez said piously.

Damon let his breath out in a hissing rush of impatience. Inez made it her life's work to pry into everyone's business. Why should the absent Sarah be excluded?

"Last time she was here Dockins nearly died, do you remember that?" Trudy asked. "He fell from his roof and Sarah just happened to be walking by and . . ." She trailed off and glanced around the store and lowered her voice to a conspirator's whisper. "Old Mars at the fruit stand said Penny told him Sarah . . ."

"Trudy, dear, you know Mars is totally unreliable in the things he says. He's a dear, sweet man, but he sometimes makes things up," Inez pointed out.

Old man Mars was crotchety, mean, and known to throw fruit at cars if he was in a foul enough mood. Damon waited for lightning to strike Inez for her blatant lie, but nothing happened. The worst of it was, Damon wanted to know what old Mars had said about Sarah, even if it was a blatant lie. And that really irritated him.

Trudy leaned even closer, looked melodramatically to the right and left without even noticing he was there. Damon sighed heavily, wanting to shake the woman. "Do you remember the time little Paul Baily fell into that blowhole?"

"I remember that, now that you say. He was wedged in so tight and no one could get to him, he'd slipped down so far. The tide was coming in."

"I was there, Inez, I saw her get him out." Trudy straightened up. "Penny said she'd heard from her hairdresser that Sarah was working for a secret agency and she was sent to some foreign country undercover to assassinate the leader of a terrorist group."

"Oh, I don't think so, Trudy. Sarah wouldn't kill anything." The store owner's hands fluttered to her throat in protest. "I just can't imagine."

Damon had had enough of gossip. If they weren't going to say anything worth hearing, he was going to get the hell out of there before Inez turned her spotlight on him. He plunked his groceries down on the counter and looked as bored as he could manage. "I'm in a hurry, Inez," he said, hoping to facilitate matters and avoid Inez's usual attempts at matchmaking.

"Why, Damon Wilder, how lovely to see you. Have you met Trudy Garret? Trudy is a wonderful woman, a native of our town. She works over at the Salt Bar and Grill. Have you been there to eat yet? The salmon is very good."

"So I've heard," he muttered, barely glancing at Trudy to acknowledge the introduction. It didn't matter. They'd all made up their minds about him, making up the history he refused to provide. He felt a little sorry for the returning Sarah. They were making up things about her as well. "You might tell me about that beautiful old house on the cliffs," he said, shocking himself. Shocking Inez. He never gave anyone an opening for conversation. He wanted to be left alone. Damn Sarah for being so mysterious.

Inez looked as if she might faint and for once she was speechless.

"You must know the one I'm talking about," Damon persisted, in spite of himself. "Three stories, balconies everywhere, a round turret. It's grown over quite wild around the house, but there's a path leading to the old lighthouse. I was walking up there and with all the wild growth, I expected the house to be in bad shape, dilapidated like most of the abandoned homes around here, but it was in beautiful condition. I'd like to know what preservatives were used."

"That's private property, Mr. Wilder," Inez said. "The house has been in the same family for well over a hundred years. I don't know what they use in the paint, but it does weather well. No one lurks around that house." Inez was definitely issuing a reprimand to him.

"I was hardly lurking, Inez," he said, exasperated. "As you well know, the sea salt is hard on the paint and wood of the houses. That house is in remarkable condition. In fact, it looks newly built. I'm curious as to what was used. I'd like to preserve my house in the same way." He made an effort to sound reasonable instead of annoyed. "I'm a bit of a chemist and I can't figure out what would keep a house so pristine over the years. There's no sign of damage from the sea, from age, or even insects. Remarkable."

Inez pursed her lips, always a bad sign. "Well, I'm certain I have no idea." Her voice was stiff, as if she were highly offended. She rang up his groceries in remarkable time without saying another word.

Damon gathered the bags into one arm, his expression daring Inez to ask him if he needed help. Leaning heavily on his cane, he turned to Trudy. "The hairdresser's dog walker told the street cleaner that he saw Sarah walk on water."

Trudy's eyes widened in shock, but there was belief on her face. Inez made some kind of noise he couldn't identify. Disgusted, Damon turned on his heel and stalked out. Ever since the first whisper of Sarah's name he had been unsettled. Disturbed. Agitated. There was something unfamiliar growing inside of him. Anticipation? Excitement? That was ridiculous. He muttered a curse under his breath at the absent Sarah.

He wanted to be left alone, didn't he? He had no interest in the woman the townspeople gossiped about. Sarah might not walk on water but her house was a mystery. He saw no reason why he shouldn't pay her a neighborly visit and ask what preservatives were used in the wood to achieve the nearly impossible results.

Damon Wilder was a man driven to the edge of sanity. Moving to this tiny town on the coast was his last effort to hang onto life. He had no idea how he was going to do it, or why he had chosen this particular town with all its resident eccentrics, but he had been drawn here. Nothing else would do. He had stepped on the rich soil and knew either this place would be home or he had none. It was hell trying to fit in, but the sea soothed him and the long walks over million-year-old rocks and cliffs occupied his mind.

Damon took his time putting his groceries away. The knowledge that this town, this place, was his last stand had been so strong he had actually purchased a house. His home was one of the few things that gave him pleasure. He loved working on it. He loved the wood. He could lose himself in the artistry of reshaping a room to suit his exact needs. For hours at a time the work occupied him such that nothing else could invade his brain and he was at peace for a time.

He stared out his large bay window, the one that looked out over the sea. The one that had an unobstructed view of the house on the cliff. Damon had spent more hours than he cared to think about staring up at the dark silent windows and the balconies and battlements. It was a unique house from another

century, another time and place. There were lights on for the
first time. The windows shone a bright welcome.

His leg hurt like hell. He needed to sit and rest, not go
traipsing around the countryside. Damon stared at the house,
drawn to the warmth of it. It seemed almost alive, begging
him to come closer. He went outside onto his deck, intending
to sit in the chair and enjoy his view of the sea. Instead he
found himself limping his way steadily up the path toward the
cliffs. It was nearly a compulsion. The path was narrow and
steep and rocky in places, almost no more than a deer trail and
overgrown at that. His cane slipped on the pebbles and twice
he nearly fell. He was swearing by the time he made it to the
edge of the private property.

He stood there staring in shock. Damon had been there not
two days before, walking around the house and the grounds.
It had been wildly overgrown, the bushes high and weeds
everywhere. The shrubbery and trees had drooped with winter
darkness on the leaves. A noticeable absence of sound had
given the place an eerie, creepy feeling. Now there were flowers, as if everything had burst into blossom overnight. A riot
of color met his eyes, a carpet of grass was beneath his feet.
He could hear the insects buzzing, the sound of frogs calling
merrily back and forth as if spring had come instantly.

The gate, which had been securely locked, stood open in
welcome. Everything seemed to be welcoming him. A sense
of peace began to steal into his heart. A part of him wanted
to sit on one of the inviting benches and soak in the atmo-
sphere.

Roses climbed the trellis and rhododendrons were everywhere, great forests of them. He'd never seen such towering
plants. Damon started up the pathway, noting every single
weed was gone. Stepping stones led the way to the house. Each
round of stone held a meticulously carved symbol. Great care
had been taken to etch the symbol deep into the stone. Damon
leaned down to feel the highly polished work. He admired the
craftsmanship and detail. The artisans in the small town all
had that trait, one he greatly respected.

As he neared the house, a wind rose off the sea and carried
sea spray and a lilting melody. *"Sarah's back. Sarah's home."*
The words sang across the land joyously. It was then he heard
the birds and looked around him. They were everywhere, all

kinds of birds, flitting from tree to tree, a flutter of wings overhead. Squirrels chattered as they rushed from branch to branch. The sun was sinking over the ocean, turning the sky into bright colors of pink and orange and red. The fog was on the far horizon, meeting the sea to give the impression of an island in the clouds. Damon had never seen anything so beautiful. He simply stood there, leaning on his cane and staring in wonder at the transformation around him.

Voices drifted from the house. One was soft and melodious. He couldn't catch the words but the tone worked its way through his skin into his very bones. Into his vital organs. He moved closer, drawn by the sound, and immediately saw two dogs on the front porch. Both were watching him alertly, heads down, hair up, neither making a sound.

Damon froze. The voices continued. One was weeping. He could hear the heartbreaking sound. A woman's voice. The melodious voice soothed. Damon shifted his weight and took a two-handed grip on his cane. If he had to use it as a weapon, that would give him more leverage. Concerned though he was with the dogs, he was more centered on the voice. He strained to listen.

"Please, Sarah, you have to be able to do something. I know you can. Please say you'll help me. I can't bear this," the crying voice said.

Her sorrow was so deep Damon ached for her. He couldn't remember the last time he'd felt someone's pain. He couldn't remember how to feel anything but bored or frustrated. The dogs both sniffed the air and, as if recognizing him, wagged their tails in greeting and sat down, hair settling to make them appear much more friendly. Keeping one eye on the dogs, he strained to catch the words spoken in that soft lilting tone.

"I know it's difficult, Irene, but this isn't something like putting a Band-Aid on a scraped knee. What do the doctors say?"

There was more sobbing. It shook him, hurt him, tore up his insides so that his gut churned and a terrible weight pressed on his chest. Damon forgot all about the dogs and pressed his hand over his heart. Irene Madison. Now he recognized the voice, knew from Inez at the grocery store that her fifteen-year-old son, Drew, was terminally ill.

"There's no hope, Sarah. They said to take him home and

make him comfortable. You know you can find a way. Please do this for us, for me."

Damon edged closer to the house, wondering what the hell she thought Sarah could do. Work a miracle? There was a small silence. The window was open, the wind setting the white lacy curtains dancing. He waited, holding his breath. Waited for Sarah's answer. Waited for the sound of her voice.

"Irene, you know I don't do that sort of thing. I've only just come back. I haven't even unpacked. You're asking me . . ."

"Sarah, I'm begging you. I'll do anything, give you anything. I'm begging on my knees . . ." The sobs were choking Damon. The pain was so raw in the woman.

"Irene, get up! What are you doing? Stop it."

"You have to say you'll come to see him. Please, Sarah. Our mothers were best friends. If not for me, do it for my mother."

"I'll come by, Irene. I'm not promising anything, but I'll stop by." There was resignation in that gentle voice. Weariness. "My sisters will be coming in a day or so and as soon as we're all rested we'll stop by and see what we can do."

"I know you think I'm asking for a miracle, but I'm not, I just want more time with him. Come when you're rested, when the others have come and can help." The relief Irene felt spilled over to Damon and he had no clue why. Only that the weight pressing on his chest lifted and his heart soared for a moment.

"I'll see what I can do."

The voices were traveling toward him. Damon waited, his heart pounding in anticipation. He had no idea what to expect or even what he wanted, but everything in him stilled.

The door opened and two women emerged to stand in the shadow of the wide, columned porch. "Thank you, Sarah. Thank you so much," Irene said, clutching at Sarah's hands gratefully. "I knew you would come." She hurried down the stairs, straight past the dogs, who had rushed to their mistress. Irene managed a quick smile for Damon as she passed him, her tearstained face bright with hope.

Damon leaned on his cane and stared up at Sarah.

Chapter 2

SARAH STOOD ON the porch, her body in the shadows. Damon had no idea of her age. Her face seemed timeless. Her eyes were old eyes, filled with intelligence and power. Her skin was smooth and flawless, giving her the appearance of extreme youth, very much at odds with the knowledge in her direct gaze. She simply stood there quietly, her incredible eyes fixed on him.

"How did you get through the gate?"

It wasn't what he expected. Damon half turned to look back at the wrought-iron masterpiece of art. The gate was six feet high and an intricate piece of craftsmanship. He had studied it on more than one occasion, noting the symbols and depictions of various animals and stars and moons. A collage of creatures with raw power mixed with universal signs of the earth, water, fire, and wind. Always before when he had come to stare at the house and grounds the gate had been firmly locked.

"It was open," he replied simply.

Her eyebrow shot up and she looked from him to the gate and back again. There was interest in her gaze. "And the dogs?" Her hand dropped to one massive head as she absently scratched the ears.

"They gave me the once-over and decided I was friendly," he answered.

A faint frown touched her face, was gone in an instant. "Did they? You must get along well with animals."

"I don't get along well with anything," he blurted out before he could stop himself. He was so shocked and embarrassed at the admission he couldn't find a way to laugh it off, so it remained there between them.

Sarah simply studied his face for a long while. An eternity. She had a direct gaze that seemed to see past his physical body and delve straight to his soul. It made Damon uncomfortable and ashamed. "You'd better come in and sit down for a while," she said. "There's a blackness around your aura. I can tell you're in pain, although I can't see why you've come yet." She turned and went into the house, clearly expecting him to follow her. Both dogs did, hurrying after her, pacing at her heels.

Damon had been acting out of character ever since he heard that first whisper of gossip. He stood, leaning on his cane, wondering what had gotten into him. He'd seen the mighty Sarah. She was just a woman with incredible eyes. That was all. She couldn't walk on water or move mountains. She couldn't scale impossible cliffs or assassinate heads of terrorist organizations. She was just a woman. And probably as loony as hell. His aura was black? What the hell did that mean? She probably had voodoo dolls and dead chickens in her house.

He stared at the open door. She didn't come back or look to see if he was following. The house had swallowed her up. Mysterious Sarah. Damon lifted his eyes to the gathering darkness, to the first stars and the floating wisps of clouds. It irritated him but he knew he was going to follow her into that house. Just like her damn dogs.

Damon consoled himself with the fact that he was extremely interested in the preservation of wood and paint. He had been interested in her house long before she arrived back in town. He couldn't pass up a genuine opportunity to study it up close, even if it meant trying to make small talk with a crazy stranger. He raked his hand through his dark hair and glared at the empty doorway. Muttering curses beneath his breath, he stalked after her as best he could with his cane and his damaged hip and leg.

The porch stairs were as solid as a rock. The verandah itself was wide and beautiful, wrapping around the house, an invitation to sit in the shade and enjoy the view of the pounding sea. Damon wanted to linger there and continue to feel the peace of Sarah's home, but he stepped inside. The air seemed cool and scented, smelling of some fragrance that reminded him of the forests and flowers. The entryway was wide, tiled with a mosaic design, and it opened into a huge room.

With a sense of awe, Damon stared down at the artwork on the floor. There was a feeling of falling into another world when he looked at it. The deep blue of the sea was really the ocean in the sky. Stars burst and flared into life. The moon was a shining ball of silver. He stood transfixed, wanting to get on his knees and examine every inch of the floor. "I like this floor. It's a shame to walk on it," he announced loudly.

"I'm glad you like it. I think it's beautiful," she said. Her voice was velvet soft, but it carried through the house back to him. "My grandmother and her sisters made that together. It took them a very long time to get it just right. Tell me what you see when you look into the midnight sky there."

He hesitated but the pull of the floor was too much to resist. He examined it carefully. "There are dark shadows in the clouds across the moon. And behind the clouds, a ring of red surrounds the moon. The stars connect and make a bizarre pattern. The body of a man is floating on the sea of clouds and something has pierced his heart." He looked up at her, a challenge on his face.

Sarah merely smiled. "I was about to have tea; would you care for a cup?" She walked away from him into the open kitchen.

Damon could hear the sound of water as she filled the teakettle. "Yes, thank you, that sounds good." And it did, which was crazy. He never drank tea. Not a single cup. He was losing his mind.

"The pictures of my grandmother and her sisters are to your left, if you'd like to see them."

He had always considered looking at pictures of people he didn't know utterly ridiculous, but he couldn't resist looking at the photographs of the women who had managed to create such beauty on a floor. He wandered over to the wall of memories. There were many photographs of women, some black-

and-white, others in color. Some of the pictures were obviously very old, but he could easily see the resemblance among the women. Damon cleared his throat. He frowned when he noticed a strange pattern running through every grouping. "Why are there seven women in each family picture?"

"There seems to be a strange phenomenon in our family," Sarah answered readily. "Every generation, someone produces seven daughters."

Startled, Damon leaned on his cane and studied each group of faces. "One out of the seven girls has always given birth to seven daughters? On purpose?"

Sarah laughed and came around the corner to join him in front of the wall of photographs. "Every generation."

He looked from her to the faces of her sisters in a picture near the center of the wall. "Which one carries the strain of insanity?"

"Good question. No one's ever thought to ask it before. My sister Elle is the seventh daughter so she inherits the mantle of responsibility. Or insanity, if you prefer." Sarah pointed to a girl with a young face, vivid green eyes, and a wealth of red hair pulled carelessly into a ponytail.

"And where is poor Elle right now?" Damon asked.

Sarah inhaled, then let her breath out slowly, her long lashes fluttering down. At once her face was in repose. She looked tranquil, radiant. Watching her did something funny to Damon's heart, a curious melting sensation that was utterly terrifying. He couldn't take his fascinated gaze off of her. Strangely, for just one moment, he felt as if Sarah was no longer in the room with him. As if her physical body had separated from her spirit, allowing her to travel across time and space. Damon shook himself, trying to get rid of the crazy impression. He wasn't an imaginative person, yet he was certain Sarah had somehow touched her sister Elle.

"Elle is in a cave of gems, deep under the ground where she can hear the heartbeat of the earth." Sarah opened her eyes and looked at him. "I'm Sarah Drake."

"Damon Wilder." He gestured toward his house. "Your new neighbor." He was staring at her, drinking her in. It didn't make sense. He was certain she wasn't the most beautiful woman in the world but his heart and lungs were insisting she was. Sarah was average height, with a woman's figure. She wore faded, worn blue jeans and a plaid flannel shirt. She certainly was not at all glamorous, yet his lungs burned for air and his heart accelerated. His body hardened painfully when she wasn't even trying to be a sexy siren, simply standing there in her comfortable old clothes with her wealth of dark hair pulled back from her pale face. It was the most infuriating and humiliating thing it was his misfortune to endure.

"You bought the old Hanover place. The view is fantastic. How did you come to find our little town?" Her cool blue gaze was direct and far too assessing. "You look like a man who would be far more comfortable in a big city."

Damon's fist tightened around his cane. Sarah could see his knuckles were white. "I saw it on a map and just knew it was the place I wanted to live in when I retired." She studied his face, the lines of suffering etched into his face, the too old eyes. He was surrounded with the mark of Death, and he read Death in the midnight sky, yet she was strangely drawn to him.

Her eyebrow went up, a perfect arch. "You're a little young to retire, I would have thought. There's not a lot of excitement here."

"I'll have to disagree with that. Have you hung out around the grocery store lately? Inez provides amazing entertainment." There was a wealth of sarcasm mixed with contempt in his voice.

Sarah turned away from him, her shoulders stiffening visibly. "What do you actually know about Inez to have managed to form an opinion in your month of living here?" She sounded sweet and interested but he had the feeling he had just stepped hard on her toes.

Damon limped after her like a puppy dog, trying not to mutter foul curses under his breath. It never mattered to him what other people thought. Everyone had opinions and few actually had educated ones. Why the hell did Sarah's opinion of him matter? And why did her hips have to sway with mesmerizing invitation?

The kitchen was tiled with the same midnight blue that had formed the sky in the mosaic. A long bank of windows looked out over a garden of flowers and herbs. He could see a three-tiered fountain in the middle of the courtyard. Sarah waved him toward the long table while she fixed the tea. Damon couldn't see a speck of dust or dirt anywhere in the house. "When did you arrive?"

"Late last night. It feels wonderful to be home again. It's been a couple of years since my last visit. My parents are in Europe at the moment. They own several homes and love Italy. My grandmother is with them, so the cliff house has been empty."

"So this is your parents' home?" When she shook her head with her slight, mysterious smile he asked, "Do you own this house?"

"With my sisters. It was given to us through our mother." She brought a steaming mug of tea and placed it on the table beside his hand. "I think you'll like this. It's soothing and will help take away the pain."

"I didn't say I was in pain." Damon could have kicked himself. Even to his own ears he sounded ridiculous, a defiant child denying the truth. "Thank you," he managed to mutter, trying to smell the tea without offending her.

Sarah sat across from him, cradling a teacup between her palms. "How can I help you, Mr. Wilder?"

"Call me Damon," he said.

"Damon then," she acknowledged with a small smile. "I'm just Sarah."

Damon could feel her penetrating gaze. "I've been very interested in your house, Sarah. The paint hasn't faded or peeled, not even in the salt air. I was hoping you would tell me what preservative you used."

Sarah leaned back in her chair, brought the teacup to her mouth. She had a beautiful mouth. Wide and full and curved as if she laughed all the time. Or invited kisses. The thought came unbidden as he stared at her mouth. Sheer temptation. Damon felt the weight of her gaze. Color began to creep up the back of his neck.

"I see. You came out late in the evening even though you were hurting because you were anxious to know what kind of preservative I use on my house. That certainly makes perfect sense."

There was no amusement in her voice, not even a hint of sarcasm, but the dull red color spread to his face. Her eyes saw too much, saw into him where he didn't want to be seen, where he couldn't afford to be seen. He wanted to look away but he couldn't seem to pull his gaze from hers.

"Tell me why you're really here." Her voice was soft, inviting confidence.

He raked both hands through his hair in frustration. "I honestly don't know. I'm sorry for invading your privacy." But he wasn't. It was a lie and they both knew it.

She took another sip of tea and gestured toward his mug. "Drink it. It's a special blend I make myself. I think you'll like it and I know it will make you feel better." She grinned at him. "I can promise you there aren't any toads or eye of newt in it."

Sarah's smile robbed him of breath immediately. It was a strange thing to feel a punch in the gut so hard it drove the air out of one's lungs just with a simple smile. He waited several heartbeats until he recovered enough to speak. "Why do you think I need to feel better?" he asked, striving for nonchalance.

"I don't have to be a seer for that, Damon. You're limping. There are white lines around your mouth and your leg is trembling."

Damon raised the cup to his mouth, took a cautious sip of the brew. The taste was unique. "I was attacked awhile back." The words emerged before he could stop them. Horrified, he stared into the tea mug, afraid her brew was a truth serum.

Sarah put her teacup carefully on the table. "A person attacked you?"

"Well, he wasn't an alien." He swallowed a gulp of tea. The heat warmed him, spreading through his body to reach sore, painful places.

"Why would one man want to kill another?" Sarah mused aloud. "I've never understood that. Money is such a silly reason really."

"Most people don't think so." He rubbed his head as if it hurt, or maybe in memory. "People kill for all sorts of reasons, Sarah."

"How awful for you. I hope he was caught."

Before he could stop himself, Damon shook his head. Her vivid gaze settled on his face, looked inside of him again until he wanted to curse. "I was able to get away, but my assistant"—he stopped, corrected himself—"my friend wasn't so lucky."

"Oh, Damon, I'm so sorry."

"I don't want to think about it." He couldn't. It was too close, too raw. Still in his nightmares, still in his heart and soul. He could hear the echoes of screams. He could see the pleading in Dan Treadway's eyes. He would carry that sight to his death, forever etched in his brain. At once the pain was almost too much to bear. He wept inside, his chest burning, his throat clogging with grief.

Sarah reached across the table to place her fingertips on his head. The gesture seemed natural, casual even, and her touch was so light he barely felt it. Yet he felt the results like shooting stars bursting through his brain. Tiny electrical impulses that blasted away the terrible throbbing in his temples and the back of his neck.

He caught her wrists, pulled her hands away from him. He was shaking and she could feel it. "Don't. Don't do that." He released her immediately.

"I'm sorry, I should have asked first," Sarah said. "I was only trying to help you. Would you like me to take you home? It's already dark outside and it wouldn't be safe for you to try to go down the hill without adequate light."

"So I take it the paint preservative is a deep dark family secret," Damon said, attempting to lighten the situation. He drained the tea mug and stood up. "Yes, thanks, I wouldn't mind a ride." It was hard on the ego to have to accept it but he wasn't a complete fool. Could he have behaved any more like an idiot?

Sarah's soft laughter startled him. "I actually don't know whether the preservative is a family secret or not. I'll have to do a little research on the subject and get back to you."

Damon couldn't help smiling just because she was. There was something contagious about Sarah's laughter, something addictive about her personality. "Did you know that when you came home, the wind actually whispered, 'Sarah's back. Sarah's home.' I heard it myself." The words slipped out, almost a tribute.

She didn't laugh at him as he expected. She looked pleased. "What a beautiful thing to say. Thank you, Damon," she said sincerely. "Was the gate really open? The front gate with all the artwork? Not the side gate?"

"Yes, it was standing wide open welcoming me. At least that's how it felt."

Her sea blue eyes drifted over his face, taking in every detail, every line. He knew he wasn't much to look at. A man in his forties, battered and scarred by life. The scars didn't show physically but they went deep and she could clearly see the tormented man. "How very interesting. I think we're destined to be friends, Damon." Her voice wrapped him up in silk and heat.

Damon could see why the townspeople said her name with awe. With respect. Mysterious Sarah. She seemed so open, yet her eyes held a thousand secrets. There was music in her voice and healing in her hands. "I'm glad you've come home, Sarah," he said, hoping he wasn't making more of a fool of himself.

"So am I," she answered.

Chapter 3

"SARAH!" HANNAH DRAKE threw herself into her sister's arms. "It's so good to see you. I missed you so much." She drew back, stretching her arms to full length, the better to examine Sarah. "Why, Sarah, you look like a cat burglar, ready to rob the local museum. I had no idea Frank Warner's paintings had become valuable." She laughed merrily at her own joke.

Sarah's soft laughter merged with Hannah's. "I should have known you'd come creeping in at two A.M. That's so you, Hannah. Where were you this time?"

"Egypt. What an absolutely beautiful country it is." Hannah sat on the porch swing wearily. "But I'm wiped out. I've been traveling forever to get back home." She regarded Sarah's sleek black outfit with a slight frown. "Interesting set of tools you're sporting there, sister mine. I'm not going to have to bail you out of jail, am I? I'm really tired and if the police have to call, I might not wake up."

Sarah adjusted the belt of small tools slung low on her waist without a hint of embarrassment. "If I can't charm a police officer out of booking me for a little break-in, I don't deserve the name Drake. Go on in, Hannah, and go to bed. I'm worried about our neighbor and think I'll just go scout around and make certain nothing happens to him."

Hannah's eyebrow shot up. "Good heavens, Sarah. A man? There's an honest-to-God man in your life? Where is he? I want to go with you." She clasped her hands together, her face radiant. "Wait until I tell the others. The mighty Sarah has fallen!"

"I have *not* fallen—don't start, Hannah. I just have one of my hunches and I'm going to check it out. It has nothing to do with Damon at all."

"Ooh, this is really getting interesting. Damon. You remember his name. How did you meet him? Spill it, Sarah, every last detail!"

"There's nothing to spill. He just waltzed in asking about paint and wood preservatives." Sarah's tone was cool and aloof.

"You want me to believe he walked in on his own without an invitation? You had to have asked him to the house."

"No, I didn't," Sarah denied. "As a matter of fact the gate was open and the dogs allowed him in."

"The gate was open on its own?" Hannah was incredulous. She jumped to her feet. "I'm going with you for certain!"

"No, you're not, you're exhausted, remember?"

"Wait until I tell the others the gate opened for him." Hannah raised her arms to the heavens and stars. "The gate opens for the right man, doesn't it? Isn't that how it works? The gate will swing open in welcome for the man who is destined to become the love of the eldest child's life."

"I don't believe in that nonsense and you know it." Sarah tried to glare but found herself laughing. "I can't believe you'd even think of that old prophecy."

"Like you didn't think of it yourself," Hannah teased. "You're just going off to do the neighborly thing in the middle of the night and just sort of scout around his house. If you say so, of course I'll believe it. Is that telescope up on the battlement directed toward his bedroom?"

"Don't you dare look," Sarah ordered.

Hannah studied her face. "You're laughing but your eyes aren't. What's wrong, Sarah?" She put her hand on her sister's shoulder. "Tell me."

Sarah frowned. "He carries Death on him. I've seen it. And

he read it in the mosaic. I don't know whose death, but I'm drawn to him. His heart is broken and pierced through, and the weight of carrying Death is slowly crushing him. He saw a red ring around the moon."

"Violence and death surround him," Hannah said softly, almost to herself. "Why are you going alone?"

"I have to. I feel . . ." Sarah searched for the right word. "Drawn. It's more than a job, Hannah. It's him."

"He could be dangerous."

"He's surrounded by danger, but if he's dangerous to me, it isn't in the way you're thinking."

"Oh my gosh, you really do like this guy. You think he's hot. I'm telling the others and I'm going up to the battlement to check him out!" Hannah turned and raced into the house, banging the screen door so Sarah couldn't follow her.

Sarah laughed as she blew a kiss to her sister and started down the stairs. Hannah looked wonderful as always. Tall and tanned and beautiful even after traveling across the sea. If her wavy hair was tousled, she just looked in vogue. Other women paid fortunes to try to achieve her natural wind-blown style. Sarah had always been uncommonly proud of Hannah's genuine elegance. She had a bright spirit that shone like the stars overhead. Hannah had a free spirit that longed for wide-open spaces and the wonders of the world. She spoke several languages and traveled extensively. One month she might be found in the pages of a magazine with the jet-setters, the next she was on a dig in Cairo. Her tall slender carriage and incredibly beautiful face made her sought after by every magazine and fashion designer. It was her gentle personality that always drew people to her. Sarah was happy she was home.

Sarah made a little sound as she made her way down the small deer path that cut through her property to Damon Wilder's. She knew every inch of her property. And she knew every inch of his. Her hair was tightly braided to keep it from being snagged on low branches or brambles. Her soft-soled shoes were light, allowing her to feel her way over twigs and dried leaves. She wasn't thinking about Damon's broad shoulders or his dark, tormented eyes. And she didn't believe in romance. Not for Sarah. That was for elegant Hannah or beautiful Joley. Well, maybe not the beautiful, *wild* Joley, but definitely for most of her other sisters. Just not Sarah.

Damon Wilder was in trouble in more ways than he knew. Sarah didn't like complications. Ancient prophecies and broad shoulders and black auras were definite complications. Moonlight spilled over the sea as she made her way along the cliffs, following the narrow deer path that eventually wound down the back side of Damon's property. The powerful waves boomed as they rushed and ebbed and collapsed in a froth of white. Sarah found the sound of the sea soothing, even when it raged in a storm. She belonged there, had always belonged, as had her family before her. She didn't fear the sea or the wilds of the countryside, yet her heart was pounding in sudden alarm. Pounding with absolute knowledge.

She was not alone in the night. Instinctively she lowered her body so she wouldn't be silhouetted against the horizon. She used more care, blending into the shadows, using the foliage for cover. She moved with stealth. She was used to secrecy, a highly trained professional. There was no sound as the branches slid away from her tightly knit jumpsuit and her crepe-soled shoes eased over the ground.

Sarah made her way to the outskirts of the house. She knew all about Damon Wilder. One of the smartest men on the planet. A government's treasure. The one-man think tank that had come up with one of the most innovative defense systems ever conceived. His ideas were pure genius, far ahead of their time. He was a steady, focused man. A perfectionist who never overlooked the smallest detail.

When she read about him, before accepting her watchdog assignment, Sarah had been impressed with the sheer tenacity of his character. Now that she had met him, she ached for the man, for the horror of what he had been through. She never allowed her work to be personal, yet she couldn't stop thinking about his eyes and the torment she could see in their dark depths. And she couldn't help but wonder why Death had attached itself to him and was clinging with greedy claws.

Sarah rarely accepted such an assignment, but she knew her cover couldn't have been more perfect. Meant to be. That gave her a slight flutter of apprehension. Destiny, fate, whatever one wanted to call it, was a force to be reckoned with in her family and she had managed to avoid it carefully for years. Damon Wilder had chosen her hometown to settle in. What did that mean? Sarah didn't believe in such close coincidence.

She had no time to circle the house or check the coastal road. As she approached the side of the house facing her home, she heard a muffled curse coming from her left. Sarah inched that way, dropped to her belly, lying flat out in the darker shadows of the trees. She lifted her head cautiously, only her eyes moving restlessly, continually, examining the landscape. It took a few moments to locate her adversaries. She could make out two men not more than forty feet from her, on the downhill, right in the middle of the densest brush. Sarah had the urge to smile. She hoped for their sakes they were wearing their dogs' tick collars.

Lying in the shrubs, she began a slow, complicated pattern with her hands, a flowing dance of fingers while the leaves rustled and twigs began to move as if coming alive. Tiny, silent creatures dropped from branches overhead, fell from leaves, and pushed up from the ground to migrate downhill toward the thickest brush.

Sarah knew that the one window lit up in Damon's house was a bedroom. If the telescope set up on the battlements of her house happened to be pointed in that direction, it was only because it was the last room she had investigated. It just so happened that it was Damon's bedroom, a complete coincidence. Sarah glanced back at her house overlooking the pounding waves, suddenly worried that Hannah might have her eye glued to the lens.

She hissed softly, melodiously, an almost silent note of command the wind caught and carried skyward toward the sea, toward the house on the cliff. The brush of material against wood and leaves attracted her immediate attention. She watched one of the men scuttle like a crab down the hill toward Damon's house. He crouched just below the lit window, then cautiously raised his head to look inside.

The window was raised a few inches to allow the ocean air inside. The breeze blew the kettle cloth drapes inward so that they performed a strange ghoulish dance. With the fluttering curtains it was nearly impossible to get a clear glimpse of the interior. The man half stood, flattening his body against the wall, tilting his head to peer inside.

Sarah could make out the second man lying prone, his rifle directed at the window. She inched her way across the low grasses, moving with the wind as it blew over the land. The man with his rifle trained on the window never took his gaze from his target. Never flinched, the gun rock steady. A pro, then; she had expected it but had hoped otherwise. She could see the tiny insects crawling into his clothing.

Above her head the clouds were drifting away from the moon, threatening to expose her completely. She wormed her way through the grass and brambles, gaining a few more feet. Sarah pulled her gun from her shoulder holster.

Hearing a slight noise from inside the room, the assailant at the window put up his hand in warning. He peered in the window in an attempt to locate Damon. A solid thunk sounded loud as Damon's cane landed solidly on his jaw. At once the man screamed, the high-pitched cry reverberating through the night. He fell backward onto the ground, holding his face, rolling and writhing in pain.

Sarah kept her gaze fixed on the partner with the rifle. He was waiting for Damon to expose himself at the window. Damon was too smart to do such an idiotic thing. The curtains continued their macabre dancing but nothing else stirred in the night. The moans continued from beneath the window but the assailant didn't get to his feet.

The rifleman crawled forward on his belly, slipping in the wet grass so that he rolled, protecting his rifle. It was the slip Sarah was waiting for. She was on him immediately, pressing her gun into the back of his neck.

"I suggest you remain very still," she said softly. "You're trespassing on private property and we just don't like that sort of thing around here." As she spoke, she kept a wary eye on the man by the window. She raised her voice. "Damon, have you called the sheriff? You've got a couple of night visitors out here that may need a place to stay for a few days and I heard the jail was empty tonight."

"Is that you, Sarah?"

"I was taking a little stroll and saw a high-powered rifle kind of lying around in the dirt." She kicked the rifle out of the captured man's hands. "It's truly a thing of beauty; I just couldn't pass up the opportunity to get a good look at it." There was a hint of laughter in her voice, but the muzzle of her gun remained very firmly pressed against her captive's neck. "You should stay right there, Damon. There's two of them out here and they look a bit aggravated." She leaned close to the man on the ground, but kept her eyes on his partner by the window. "You might want to check yourself the minute you're in jail. You're probably crawling with ticks. Nasty little bugs, they burrow in, drink your blood, and pass on all sorts of interesting things, from staph to Lyme disease. That bush you were hiding in is lousy with them."

Her heart was still pounding out a rhythm of warning. Then she knew. Sarah flung herself to her right, rolling away, even as she heard the whine of bullets zinging past her and thudding into the ground. Of course there had to be a third man, a driver waiting in the darkness up on the road. She had been unable to scout out the land properly. It made perfect sense they would have a driver, a backup should there be need.

The man next to her scrambled up and dove on top of her, making a grab for her gun. Sarah managed to get one bent leg into his stomach to launch him over her head. She felt the sting of her earlobe as her earring, tangled in his shirt, was jerked from her ear. He swore viciously as he picked himself up and raced away from her toward the road. The one closest to the house was already in motion, staggering up the hill, still holding his jaw in his hands. The driver provided cover, pinning her down with a spray of bullets. The silencer indicated the men had no desire to announce their presence to the townspeople.

"Sarah? You all right out there?" Damon called anxiously. Even with the silencer, he couldn't fail to hear the telltale whine of bullets.

"Yes." She was disgusted with herself. She could hear the motor of the car roar to life, the wheels spinning in dirt for a moment before they caught and the vehicle raced away down the coastal highway. "I'm sorry, Damon, I let them get away."

"*You're* sorry! You could have been killed, Sarah. And no, I didn't call the sheriff. I was hoping they were neighborhood kids looking to do a prank."

"And I took you for such a brilliant man, too," she teased, sitting up and pulling twigs out of her hair. She touched her stinging ear, came away with blood on her fingers. It was her favorite earring, too.

The drapes rustled and Damon poked his head out the window. "Are we going to call back and forth or are you going to come in here and talk with me." There was more demand than question in his voice.

Sarah laughed softly. "Do you think that's such a good idea? Can you imagine what Inez would say if she knew I was visiting you in the middle of the night?" She reached for the rifle, taking care to pick it up using a handkerchief. "She'd ask you your intentions. You'd have to deny you had any. The word would spread that you'd ruined me and I'd be pitied. I couldn't take that. It's better if I just slink home quietly."

Damon leaned farther out the window. "Damn it, Sarah, I'm not amused. You could have been killed. Do you even understand that? These men were dangerous and you're out taking a little stroll in the moonlight and playing neighborhood cop." His voice was harsher than he intended, but she'd scared the hell out of him. He rubbed a hand over his face, feeling sick at the thought of her in danger.

"I wasn't in any danger, Damon," Sarah assured him. "This rifle, in case you're interested, has tranqs in it, not bullets. At least they weren't trying to kill you, they wanted you alive."

He sighed. She was just sitting there on the ground with the sliver of moonlight spilling over her. The rifle was lying across her knees and she was smiling at him. Sarah's smile was enough to stop a man's heart. Damon took a good look at her clothes, at the gun still in her hand. He stiffened, swore softly. "Damn you anyway, Drake. I should have known you were too good to be true!"

"Were you believing all the stories about me, after all, Damon?" she asked. But dread was beginning even though it shouldn't matter what he thought of her. Or what he knew. She had a job. It shouldn't matter, yet she felt the weight in her chest, heavy like a stone. She felt a sudden fear crawling in her stomach of losing something special before it even started.

"Who sent you, Sarah? And don't lie to me. Whom do you work for?"

"Did you really think they were going to let you walk away without any kind of protection after what happened, Damon?" Sarah kept the sympathy from her voice, knowing it would only anger him further.

He swore bitterly. "I told them I wasn't going to be responsible for another death. Get the hell off my property,

Sarah, and don't you come back." Something deep inside of him unexpectedly hurt like hell. He had just met her. The hope hadn't even fully developed, only in his heart, not his mind, but he still felt it. It was a betrayal and his Sarah, mysterious Sarah with her beautiful smile and her lying eyes, had broken him before he'd even managed to find himself.

"I can assure you, Mr. Wilder, despite the fact that I'm a woman, I'm very capable of doing my job." Deliberately she tried to refocus the argument, putting stiff outrage in her tone.

"I don't care how good you are at your damned job or anything else. Get off my property before I call the sheriff and have you arrested for trespassing." Damon slammed the window closed with a terrible finality. The light went off as if somehow that would cut all communication between them.

Sarah sat on the ground and stared at the darkened window with a heavy heart. The sea rolled and boomed with a steadiness that never ceased. The wind tugged at her hair and the clouds drifted above her head. She drew up her knees and contemplated the fact that old prophecies should never be passed from generation to generation. That way, one could never be disappointed.

Chapter 4

SARAH DIDN'T BOTHER to knock politely on the locked door. Damon Wilder was hurt and angry and she didn't really blame him. She was nearly as confused as he was. Curses on old prophecies that insisted on messing up lives. If they'd been two people meeting casually everything would have been all right. But no, the gate had to stand open in welcome. It was neither of their faults, but how was she going to explain a two-hundred-year-old foretelling? How was she going to tell him her family came from a long line of powerful women who drew power from the universe around them and that prophecies several hundreds of years old *always* came true?

Sarah did the only thing any self-respecting woman would do in the middle of the night. She pulled out her small set of tools and picked the front door lock. She made a mental note to install a decent security system in his house and lecture him about at least buying a dead bolt in the interim.

As a child she had often played in the house and she knew its layout almost as well as she knew her own. Sarah moved swiftly through the living room. She saw very little furniture although Damon had moved in well over a month earlier. No pictures were on the wall, nothing to indicate it was a home, not just a temporary place to dwell.

Damon lay on his bed staring up at the ceiling. He had started out seething, but there was too much fear to sustain it. Sarah had nearly walked into an ambush. It didn't matter that she had been sent to be his watchdog, she could have been killed. It didn't bear thinking about. Sarah. Shrouded in mystery. How could he fixate on a woman so quickly when he rarely noticed anyone? If he closed his eyes he could see her. There was a softness about her, a femininity that appealed to him on every level. She would probably laugh if she knew he had an unreasonable and totally mad desire to protect her.

Damon bit out another quiet oath, not certain he could force himself to pick up and leave again. Where could he go? This was the end of the earth and yet somehow they had found him after all these months. No one would be safe around him.

"Do you always lie in the dark on your bed and swear at the ceiling?" Sarah asked quietly. "Because that could become a real issue later on in our relationship."

Damon opened his eyes to stare up at her. Sarah. Real. In his bedroom dressed in a skintight black suit that clung to every curve. His mouth watered and every cell in his body leapt to life in reaction. "It happens at those times I've been betrayed. I don't know, really, a knee-jerk reaction I can't seem to stop."

Sarah looked around for a chair, couldn't find one, and shoved his legs over to make room on the bed. "Betrayal can be painful. In all honesty I haven't had the experience. My sisters guard my back, so to speak." She turned the full power of huge blue eyes on him. "Do you believe that having friends insist on your protection is a betrayal?"

He could hear the sincerity in her voice. "You don't understand." How could she? How could anyone? "They had no right to hire you, Sarah. I quit my job, retired, if you want it neat and tidy. I have no intention of ever going back again. I cut all ties with that job and every branch of the military and the private sector."

"You tried to keep everyone around you safe by leaving." It was a statement of fact. He would think she was crazy if she told him he carried Death with him. "What happened, Damon?"

"Didn't they give you a three-inch-thick file to read on me before they sent you here?" he demanded, trying to sustain his anger with her.

Sarah simply waited, allowing the silence to lengthen and stretch between them. Sometimes silence was more eloquent than words. Damon was tense, his body rigid next to hers. His fingers were curled into a tight fist around the comforter. Sarah laid her hand gently over his.

He could have resisted most anything, but not that silent gesture of camaraderie. He twisted his hand around until his fingers laced through hers. "They hit us about five blocks from work. Dan Treadway was with me. We planned to have dinner and go back to work. We both wanted to see if we could work out a glitch with a minor problem we were having with the project." He chose his words carefully. He no longer worked for the government but his work had been classified.

"They beat us both nearly unconscious before they threw us in the trunk. They didn't even pretend to want our money. They drove to a warehouse, an old paint factory, and demanded information on a project we just couldn't safely give them."

Sarah felt his hand tremble in hers. She had read the hospital report. Both men had been tortured. She knew Damon carried the scars from numerous burns on his torso. "I couldn't give them what they wanted and poor Dan had no idea what they were even talking about." He pressed his fingertips to his eyes as if the pressure would stop the pain. Stop the memory that never left him. "He never even worked on the project they wanted information about."

Sarah knew Dan Treadway had been shot in the knee and then again in the head, killing him. Damon had refused to turn over classified information that could have resulted in the deaths of several field agents. And he had steadfastly refused to give up the newest defense system. Damon started a fire with paint thinners, nearly blowing up the building. In his escape attempt he was crushed between the wall of the warehouse and the grille of a car, severely damaging his hip and leg.

"I don't want friends, Sarah. No one can afford to be my friend."

Sarah knew he spoke the truth. Death clung and searched

for victims. She wouldn't tell him, but often Death felt cheated. If that were the case, it would demand a sacrifice before it would be appeased. "Does the company know who these people are?" Sarah prompted.

His dark gaze was haunted. "You would know that better than I would. Enemies of our country. Mercenaries. Hell, who cares? They wanted something my brain conceived, bad enough to kill an innocent man for it. I don't want to think up anything worth killing over again. So here I am."

"Did you talk to anyone, a doctor?"

He laughed. "Of course I did. The company made certain I talked to one, especially after I announced my retirement. There were a few loose ends and they didn't want me leaving. I didn't much care what they wanted." He turned his head. Edgy. Brooding. "Is it part of your job to try to get me to go back?"

Sarah shook her head. "I don't tell people what to do, Damon. I don't believe in that." Her mouth curved. "Well," she hedged, "I guess that's not altogether true. There is the exception of my sisters. They expect me to boss them around, though, because I'm the oldest and I'm very good at bossing."

"Did you want to come back here, Sarah?" The sound of the sea was soothing. It did sound like home.

"More than anything. I've felt the pull of the ocean for a while now. I've always known I'd come back home and settle here. I just don't know when I'm going to manage it. Damon, your house has no security whatsoever. Did it occur to you they could waltz in here and grab you again?"

Damon tried not to read too much into that worried note in her voice. Tried not to think that it was personal. "It's been months. I thought they would leave me alone."

Sarah whistled softly. "You even lie with that straight face and those angelic eyes. I'm taking notes. That one is right up there with swearing at the ceiling. You wanted them to come after you, didn't you?" It was a shrewd guess. She hadn't known him long enough to judge his character yet, but she'd read the files thoroughly and every word portrayed a relentless, tenacious man, focused on his goals at all times.

"Wouldn't you? They forced me to make a choice between information that is vital to our nation and my friend's life. He was looking at me when they shot him, Sarah. I'll never forget the way he looked at me." He rubbed his throbbing temple. The vision haunted his dreams and brought him out of a sound sleep so that he sat up, heart pounding, screaming a denial to the uncaring night.

"What kind of a plan do you have?"

Damon felt his stomach knot up. Her tone was very interested. She expected a plan. He had the reputation of being a brain. He should have a plan. His plan had been to draw his enemies to him and dispose of them, first with his cane and then he'd call the sheriff. He doubted if Sarah would be impressed.

She sighed. "Damon, tell me you did have a plan."

"Just because you walk on water doesn't mean everyone else does," he muttered.

"Who told you I walked on water?" Sarah demanded, annoyed. "For heaven's sake, I only did it once and it was just showing off. All my sisters can do the same thing."

He gaped at her, his eyes wide with shock. She kept a straight face, but the laughter in her eyes gave her away. Damon did the noble thing and shoved her off the bed. Sarah landed on the floor, her soft laughter inviting him to join in.

"You so deserved that," she said. "You really did. Walk on water. That's a new one. Where did you hear that? And you believed it, too."

Damon turned on his side, propped up on one elbow to look down at her. "I started the rumor myself at Inez's store. For a minute there I thought I was psychic."

"Oh, thank you so much; now all the kids will be asking me to show them. The next time you come calling I'm going to sic the dogs on you."

"What makes you think I'm going to come calling?" he asked curiously.

"I never told you about the paint preservative. You're a persistent man." She leaned her head against the bed. "Do you have a family anywhere, Damon?"

"I was an only child. My parents died years ago, first my father, then six months later my mother. They were wild about each other."

"How strange that would be, to grow up alone. I've had my sisters always and can't imagine life without them."

His fingers crept of their own accord to find the thick mass of her hair. She was wearing it in a tight braid, but he managed to rub the silky strands between his thumb and finger. How the hell did she manage to get her hair so soft? Mysterious Sarah. He was fast beginning to think of her as *his* Sarah. "Do you like them all?"

Sarah smiled there in the darkness. She loved her sisters. There was no question about that, but no one had ever thought to ask if she liked them. "Very much, Damon. You would, too. Each of them is unique and gifted in her own way. All of them have a great sense of humor. We laugh a lot at our house." He was tugging at her hair. It didn't hurt, in fact it was a pleasant sensation, but it was causing little butterfly wings to flutter in the pit of her stomach. "What are you doing?"

"I snagged my watch in your braid and thought I'd just take it out," he answered casually. He was lying and he didn't even care that it was a lie and that she knew it was a lie. Any excuse to see her hair tumbling down in a cloud around her face.

Sarah laughed softly. "My braid? Or your watch?" He was definitely tugging her hair out of its tight arrangement. "It took me twenty minutes to get my hair like that. I've never been good at hair things."

"A wasted twenty minutes. You have beautiful hair. There's no need to be good at hair things."

Sarah was absurdly pleased that he'd noticed. It was her one call to glory. "Thank you." She tapped her fingers on her knee, trying to find a way to get him to agree with her on his protection. "Damon, it's important to protect your house. I could set up a good security system for you. I'll let the sheriff know we have a problem and they'll help us out."

"Us? Sarah, you need to be as far away from me as possible." Even as he said it, his hands were tunneling in the rich wealth of her hair, a hopeless compulsion he couldn't prevent. He wanted to feel that silky softness sliding over his skin.

"I thought you were supposed to be brilliant, Damon. Didn't I read in your file that you were one of the smartest men on the face of the earth? Along with your swearing issues and your hair issues, please tell me you don't have idiot macho tendencies, too. If that's the case, I'm going to have to seriously study this gate prophecy. I can live with the other things but idiocy might be stretching my patience."

He tugged on her hair to make certain she was paying attention. "*One* of the smartest men? Is that what that report said? I should read the file over for you and weed out the blatant lies. I'm certain I'm *the* smartest, not *one* of the smartest. You don't have to insult me by pretending the report said otherwise. And what is the gate prophecy?"

She waved away his inquiry. "I'll have to tell you about the Drake history sometime, but right now, I think you might clear up the idiot macho issue for me," she insisted. "Brainy men tend to be arrogant but they shouldn't be stupid. I'm a security expert, Damon."

He sighed loudly. "So I'm supposed to tell all my friends that my lady friend is the muscle in our relationship."

"Do we have a relationship?" She tilted her head to look back at him. "And surely the smartest man on earth would have a strong enough ego to be fine with his lady friend being the muscle. Relationship or no."

"Oh, if there's no relationship, I doubt if any man could take that big a blow to his ego, Sarah. We need to call in an expert on this subject, consult a counselor before we make a decision. And it never hurts to get a second opinion if we don't like the first one."

Damon couldn't help the grin that spread across his face. It felt good to smile. She had thrown his life into complete confusion, but she made him smile. Made him want to laugh. Intrigued him. Turned him inside out. Gave him a reason to live. And the heavy weight that seemed to be pressing down on his shoulders and chest was lifted for just a few moments.

"You won't have to worry on that score, Damon. We'll have six very loud and long-winded second opinions. My sisters will have more to say than you'll ever want to hear on the subject. For that matter, on every subject. You won't need a counselor for anything; they'll all be happy to oblige, absolutely free of charge."

Sarah glanced toward the cliff house. Through the bedroom window that should have had the drapes closed. The curtains were parted in the middle, pushed to either side by an unseen hand.

"Sarah." There was an ache in Damon's voice.

Her heart did a funny little jump in her chest and she turned her head to look at him. Her gaze collided with his. Stark hunger was in his eyes. Raw need. Desire. He reached for her, caught the nape of her neck, and slowly lowered his head to hers. His mouth fastened onto hers. They simply melted together. Merged.

Fireworks might have burst in the air around them. Or maybe it was the stars scattering across the sky, glittering like gems. Fire raced up her skin, heat spread through her body. He claimed her. Branded her. And he did a thorough job of it. They fed on one another. Were lost in smoky desire. His mouth was perfect, hot and hungry and demanding and possessive.

No one had ever kissed her like that. She had never thought it would be like that. She wanted to just stay there all night and kiss.

Damon shifted his weight on the bed, deepening the kiss. He tumbled over the edge, sprawling on the floor, pulling her over so that she collapsed on top of him. Instantly his arms circled her and held her to his chest.

Sarah could feel the laughter start deep inside him, where it started in her. They lay in a tangle of arms and legs, laughing happily. She lifted her head to look at him, to trace his wonderful mouth with her fingertip. "Sheer magic, Damon. That's what you are. Does this happen every time you kiss a woman?"

"I don't kiss women," he admitted, shaken to his very core. His fingers were tunneling in her wealth of hair, her thick silky hair that he wanted to bury his face in.

"Well, men then. Does it happen all the time? Because quite frankly it's amazing. You're truly amazing."

The laughter welled up all over again. Damon helped her to sit up, her back against the bed. He sat next to her. Both of them stared out the window toward the cliff house.

"I could have sworn I closed those drapes," he commented.

"You probably did," Sarah admitted with a small sigh. "It's the sisters. My sisters. They're probably watching us right this minute. Hannah came home right before I left and Kate and Abigail arrived about the time the driver was shooting at me. You could wave at them if you felt up to it."

"How are they watching us?" Damon asked, interested.

"The telescope. I use it to watch the sky." She used her most pious voice. "And sometimes the ocean, but my sisters are notoriously and pathetically interested in *my* business. I shall have to teach them some manners.' She waved her hand casually, murmuring something he couldn't quite catch, but it sounded light and airy and melodious.

Shadows entered the room. Moved. The drapes swayed gently, blocked the sliver of moon, the faint light reflected by the pounding sea. Damon blinked; in that split second the curtains were drawn firmly across the window.

Chapter 5

"YOU WERE KISSING that man," Hannah accused gleefully. "Sarah Drake, you hussy. You were kissing a perfect stranger."

Sarah looked as cool as possible under fire. "I don't know what you thought you saw with your eye glued to the telescope lens, but certainly not that! You ought to be ashamed of yourself spying that way. And using . . ." She trailed off to motion in the air with her fingers, glaring at all three of her sisters as she did so. "To open the curtains in a private bedroom is an absolute no-no, which we all agreed on when we set down the rules."

"There are exceptions to the rules," Kate pointed out demurely. She was curled up in a straight-backed wooden chair at the table, her knees drawn up, with a wide, engaging grin on her face as she painted her toenails.

"What exceptions?" Sarah demanded, her hands on her hips.

Kate shrugged and blew on her toenails before answering. "When our sister is hanging out with a man with a black aura around him." She raised her head to look at Sarah, her gaze steady. "That's very dangerous and you know it. You can't play around with Death. Not even you, Sarah."

Sarah turned to glare at Hannah. She didn't want to talk about it, or even name Death, afraid if she gave it substance she would increase its power, so she remained silent.

Hannah shook her head. "It wasn't me ratting you out. You left the tea leaves in the cup and it was there for everyone to read."

"You still had no right to go against the rules without a vote." Sarah was fairly certain she'd lost the argument, but she wasn't going down without a fight. They were right about Death. Just the idea of facing it made her shiver inside. If she wasn't so drawn to Damon, she would have backed away and allowed nature to take its course. For some unexplained reason, she couldn't bear the thought of Damon suffering.

Kate smirked. "Don't worry, we made certain to convene a hasty meeting and vote on whether or not the situation called for the use of power. It was fully agreed upon that it was wholly warranted."

"You convened a meeting?" Sarah glared at them all with righteous indignation. "Without me? Without the others? The three of you don't make up the majority. Oh, you are in so much trouble!" she said triumphantly.

Hannah blew her a kiss, sweetly reasonable. "Of course we didn't do that, Sarah. We contacted everyone on the spot. It was perfectly legit. We told them about the gate and how it opened on its own for him. And how the dogs greeted him. Elle sent hugs and kisses and says she misses you. Joley wanted to come home right away and get in on the fun but she's tied up." She frowned. "I hope not literally, I didn't think to ask and you never know with Joley. And Libby is working in Guatemala or some other place she's discovered with no bathroom and probably leeches, healing the sick children as usual."

"I thought she was in Africa investigating that crawlie thing that was killing everyone when they tried to harvest their crops," Kate said. "She was sending me some research material for my next book."

"Wherever she is, Libby agreed totally we needed to make certain Sarah was safe." Hannah looked innocent. "That's all we were doing, Sarah. Everyone agreed that for your safety we needed to see into that bedroom immediately."

Kate and Abbey burst into laughter again. "I was a bit worried when he got so exuberant he fell on the floor," Abbey said. "But clearly you weren't in a life-threatening situation so we left you to it."

"And boy, did you go to it," Kate added. "Really, Sarah, a little less enthusiasm on your part might have gone a long way toward giving some credence to our chasing-men theory." The three sisters exchanged nods as if research were very important.

Struggling not to laugh, Sarah tapped her foot, hands on hips, looking at their unrepentant faces. "You knew I wasn't in any danger, you peeping Thomasinas. Shame on the lot of you! I'll have you know I was *working* last night."

That brought another round of laughter that nearly tipped Kate right out of the chair. "A *working* girl!"

"Is that what you call it? You were working at *something,* Sarah," Hannah agreed.

"She's a *fast* worker," Abbey added.

Sarah's mouth twitched with the effort to remain straight-faced. "I do security work, you horrible hags. I'm his bodyguard!"

Kate did fall off the chair laughing. Hannah slumped over the table, her elegant body gracefully posed. "You were guarding his body all right, Sarah," Abbey said, just managing to get the words out through the shrieks of laughter.

"*Closely* guarding his body," Kate contributed.

"Locked up those lips nice and safe," Hannah agreed. "Ooh, Sarah, baby, you are *great* at that job."

Sarah's only recourse was to fall back on dignity. They weren't listening to their big sister's voice of *total authority* at their antics. She drew herself up, looked as haughty as she could with the three of them rolling around together, laughing like hyenas. "Go ahead and howl, but the three of you just might want to read that old prophecy. Read the *entire* thing, not just the first line or two."

The smile faded from Hannah's face. "Sarah's looking awfully smug. Where is that old book anyway?"

Abbey sat up straight. "Sarah Drake, you didn't dare cast on us, did you?"

"I don't cast," Sarah said, "that's Hannah's department. Damon is coming over. I wanted him to meet you." She looked suddenly vulnerable. "I really like him. We talked all night about everything. You know those uncomfortable silences with strangers who can't possibly understand us? We didn't have one of them. He's so worn out from carrying Death. Of course, he doesn't know that's what he's doing and if he did, he would have sent me away immediately."

"Oh, Sarah." Hannah's voice was filled with compassion.

"I have to find a way to help him. He couldn't bear another death on his hands. His friend was killed, but he managed to save himself." She swept a hand through her hair and looked at her sisters with desperation in her eyes. "I liked everything about him. There wasn't a subject we skipped. And we laughed together over everything." She lifted her gaze to her sisters. "I really, really liked him."

"Then we'll like him, too," Kate reassured her. "And we'll find a way to help him." She opened the refrigerator and peered in, pulling at drawers. "Did you get fresh veggies?"

"Of course, and plenty of fruit. By the way, congratulations on your latest release. I read it cover to cover and it was wonderful. As always, Katie, your stories are fantastic," Sarah praised sincerely. "And thanks, Kate."

Abbey hugged Kate. "My favorite memories are when we were little and we used to lie on the balcony looking up at the stars, with you telling us your stories. You deserve all those bestseller lists."

Kate kissed her sister. "And you aren't prejudiced at all."

"Even if we were," Hannah said, "you're still the best storyteller ever born and deserve every award and list you get on."

Kate blushed, turning nearly as red as the highlights in her chestnut hair. She looked pleased. "How did the spotlight get turned on me? Sarah's the one who spent the night with a perfect stranger."

"I had to spend the night with him," Sarah insisted. "There's no security at his house. And I've asked Jonas Harrington to drop by this morning to meet Damon."

All three women groaned in unison. "How could you invite that Neanderthal to our home, Sarah?" Hannah demanded.

"He's the local sheriff," Sarah pointed out. "Come on, all that was a long time ago—we were kids."

"He was a total jerk to me and he still is," Hannah said.

The mug, filled with coffee, on the table in front of her began to steam. Hannah looked down and saw the liquid was beginning to boil. Hastily she blew on the surface.

There was a small silence. "Fine!" Hannah exploded. "I'll admit he still makes me mad if I just think about him. And if he calls me Baby Doll or Barbie Doll, I'm turning him into a big fat toad. He already is one, he may as well look like it."

"You can't turn the sheriff into a toad, Hannah. It's against the rules," Abbey reminded her. "Give him a doughnut gut or a nervous twitch."

"That's not good enough," Kate chimed in. "You need imagination to pay that man back. Something much more subtle—like every time he goes to lie to a woman to get her in bed, he blurts out the truth or tells them what a hound dog he is."

"I'll do worse than that," Hannah threatened, "I'll make it so he's lousy in bed! Mister Macho Man, the bad boy who couldn't do anything but make fun of me in school. He thinks he's such a lady's man."

"Hannah." Sarah heard the pain in her sister's voice and spoke gently. "You were then, and still are now, so incredibly beautiful and brainy. No one could ever conceive of you being so painfully shy. You hid it well. No one knew you threw up before school every day or that we had to work combined spells to keep you functioning in public situations. They wouldn't know you still have problems. You've faced those ears by doing the things that terrify you and you're always successful. Outsiders see your beauty and brains and success. They don't see what you're hiding in private."

"Someone's coming up the path," Kate said without looking away from Hannah. She held out her hand to her sister. "We're all so proud of you, Hannah. Who cares what Jonas Harrington thinks?"

"It's not Harrington, although he's close by somewhere," Abbey said. "I think it's Sarah's gate crasher. You know, the one she spent the night with. I still can't get over that, and Elle says she wants every intimate detail the minute you get a chance."

"There are no intimate details," Sarah objected, exasperated. "I'm going to install a security system for him. Kate, don't let them read your books anymore, you're giving them wild imaginations."

"It wasn't our imaginations that he was kissing you," Hannah pointed out gleefully. "We *saw* you!"

"And you were kissing him back," Abbey added.

"Well, that part wasn't altogether my fault!" Sarah defended. "He's a *great* kisser. What could I do but kiss the man back?"

The sisters looked at one another solemnly and burst out laughing simultaneously. The dog curled up in the corner lifted his head and whined softly to get their attention.

"He's here, Sarah, and the gate must have opened for him a second time," Kate said, intrigued. "I really have to take a long look at the Drake history book. I want to see *exactly* what that prophecy says. How strange that something written hundreds of years ago applies to us even in this modern day and age."

"Kate, sweetie," Abbey said, "every age thinks it's progressive and modern but in reality we're going to be considered backward someday."

"He's on the verandah," Kate announced and hurried to the front door.

Her sisters trailed after her. Sarah's heart began to race. Damon was not the kind of man she had ever considered she'd be attracted to, yet she couldn't stop thinking about him. She thought a lot about his smile, the way two small dents appeared near the corners of his mouth. Intriguing, tempting little dents. He had the kind of smile that invited long drugging kisses, hot, melting together. . . .

"Sarah!" Hannah hissed her name. "The temperature just went up a hundred degrees in here. You know you can't think like that around us. Sheesh! One day with this man and your entire moral code has collapsed."

Sarah considered arguing, but she didn't have much of a defense. If Damon hadn't been such a gentleman and stopped at just kissing, she might have made love to him. All right, she *would* have made love to him. She *should* have made love to him. She lay awake all night, hot and bothered and edgy with need. Darn the man for having chivalrous manners anyway. She smiled and touched her mouth with a feeling of awe.

He had kissed her most of the night. Delicious, wonderful, sinfully rich kisses . . .

"Sarah!" All three of her sisters reprimanded her at once.

Sarah grinned at them unrepentantly. "I can't help it, he just affects me that way."

"Well, try not to throw yourself at him," Abbey urged. "It's so unbecoming in a Drake. Dignity at all times when it comes to men."

Hannah was looking out the window. She wrinkled her nose. "Kate, when you open the door for Damon, do let the dogs out for their morning romp. They've been cooped up all night, the poor things."

Kate nodded and obediently waved the dogs through as she greeted Damon. "How nice to see you, Mr. Wilder. Sarah has told us so much about you."

The dogs rushed past Damon. He leaned heavily on his cane, watching the large animals charge the sheriff, who was making his way up the path. Just as the man reached the gate, it swung closed with a loud bang. The dogs hit it hard, growling, baring their teeth, and digging frantically in an effort to get at their prey.

"This isn't funny, Hannah!" Jonas Harrington yelled. "I was *invited* by your sister and I showed up as a favor. Stop being so childish and call off your hounds."

Hannah smiled sweetly at Damon and held out her hand. "Pay no attention to the toad, Mr. Wilder, he comes around every now and then playing with his little gun, thinking he's going to impress the natives." She yawned, covering her mouth delicately. "It's so boring and childish but we have to humor him."

Sarah whistled sharply and the dogs instantly ceased growling, backing away from the fence to return to the house. When the animals were safely by her side, the gate swung open invitingly and the sheriff stalked through, his face a grim mask, his slashing gaze fixed on Hannah.

"What happens if you don't humor him?" Damon asked.

"Why, he throws his power around harassing us with tickets for speeding," Hannah said, holding her ground, her chin up.

"You *were* speeding, Hannah. Did you think I was going to let you off just because you're beautiful?" The sheriff shook hands with Damon. "Jonas Harrington, the only sane one when it comes to Baby Doll's true character."

Hannah flashed him a brilliant smile. Her sisters moved closer to her, protectively, Damon thought. "Why not, Sheriff? All the other cops *always* let me off." She turned on her heel and walked away.

Kate and Abbey let out a collective soft sigh.

"You gave my sister a ticket?" Sarah asked, outraged. "Jonas, you really are a self-centered toad. Why can't you just leave her alone? It's so high school to keep up grudges. Get over it."

"She was the one speeding like a teenager," Jonas pointed out. "Aside from feeding me to your dogs, did you have a real reason for inviting me up here?"

Taunting laughter floated back to them. "Don't flatter yourself, Harrington; nobody *wants* you here."

As Jonas Harrington stepped into the house, the ivy hanging from the ceiling swayed precariously and a thick ropy vine slapped him in the back of his head. Jonas spun around, his hands up as if to fight. He shoved the plant away from him and stormed into the living room, muttering foul curses beneath his breath.

Damon was behind him and stopped immediately, looking warily around the room, then back to the ivy. "Do your plants eat your visitors often?" he asked with grave curiosity as he pushed the vine away from him with his cane. Gingerly he walked around the masses of greenery.

"Only the ones who are mean to my sisters," Sarah replied.

Without warning, startling both of them, Damon suddenly reached out, caught Sarah by the nape of her neck, and dragged her to him. His mouth fastened on hers hungrily. Sarah melted into him. Merged. Became liquid fire. Went up in flames. Her arms crept around his neck. The cane dropped on the floor and they were devouring each other. The world fell away until there was only Damon and Sarah and raging need.

"*Sarah!*" The name shimmered in the air, breaking them apart so that they just stood, clinging, staring into each other's eyes, drowning. Shocked.

Sarah blinked, trying to focus, then looked around and blushed when she saw Jonas Harrington gaping. "Close your mouth, Jonas," she commanded, her tone daring him to make a comment. She'd known Jonas all of her life. Of course he couldn't pass up the opportunity. She waited, cringing.

"Holy smoke." Jonas held out his hand to Damon. "You're a god. Kissing a Drake woman is dangerous, kind of like taking a chance on kissing a viper. You just dove right in and went for it." He pumped Damon's hand with great enthusiasm.

"Ha ha." Sarah glared at the sheriff. "Don't you start, and don't you spread any rumors either, Jonas. I'm already annoyed with you for giving Hannah a ticket."

The smile faded from the sheriff's face. "I don't think because a woman is drop-dead gorgeous she should be treated any differently. She has everything too easy, Sarah. You all treat her like a little baby doll."

"You don't know Hannah at all, Jonas, and you don't deserve to know her. She wouldn't expect you to let her slide because of her looks, you idiot." Sarah threw her hands into the air. "Forget it, I'm finished trying to explain anything to you. If you don't understand friendship by now you never will. Let's get on with this. Damon and I have a busy schedule today." She gestured toward a chair.

Harrington was looking toward the stairs.

"Sit!" Sarah demanded. "This is business. Murder. Right up your alley, Jonas."

Chapter 6

⁓

JONAS HARRINGTON LISTENED calmly while Sarah told him the events that had taken place the night before. His dark features hardened perceptibly while she talked. He flicked a smoldering glare toward Kate and Abbey. "Why wasn't I called last night? I might have been able to do something last night. Damn it, Sarah, where's your head? You could have been killed!"

"Well, I wasn't. I saved the rifle for you, hoping you might get prints off of it, but I doubt it." Sarah smiled at him.

Jonas shook his head. "Don't do that; you've been giving me that same smile since kindergarten and it always gets you out of trouble." He gestured toward her face. "Take a long look at her, Damon, because that's going to be her answer every time she does something you don't like." He leaned forward in his chair, his eyes slashing at her. "What about your sisters? Did it even occur to you that you might bring these people down on your own house?"

Furious, he rose, a big man, moving like a jungle cat, pacing restlessly through the long living room. "These men are professionals. You both know that. Whatever you did to bring this on . . ."

"He worked in a high-security job, Jonas, nothing illegal. It isn't drug related so get that right out of your head."

Damon leaned back in his chair, torn between worry that he'd placed the Drake family in danger and feeling pleased that Sarah had turned protective. She immediately had become a fierce tigress ready to spring if the sheriff continued to cast aspersions on his character.

"I want to know what we're up against. And don't start throwing words around like security clearance to me. If we have a couple of men willing to break into a house with a high-powered rifle—"

"They had a tranq dart in it," Sarah interrupted hastily.

"I was kidnapped, along with my assistant, nearly a year ago. My assistant was killed and I barely escaped with my life." As Damon spoke, a dark shadow fell across the room. Outside, the ocean waves thundered and sprayed into the air. "They wanted information that could have affected the security of our nation and I refused to give it to them." Damon passed a hand over his face as if wiping away a nightmare. "I know that sounds melodramatic, but . . ." He slowly unbuttoned his shirt to expose his chest and the whorls and scars left behind. "I want you to know what these people are like."

The shadow lengthened and grew along the wall behind Damon. The shadow began to take shape, gray, translucent, but there all the same, growing in form until a faceless ghoul emerged with outstretched arms and a long thin body. The mouth yawned open wide, a gesture of greed and craving for the addiction Death had developed. The arms could have been reaching for either Jonas or Damon.

Damon hunched away from Jonas, pain flickering across his face, his shoulders stiffening as if under a great load.

Alarmed, Hannah reached out and jerked Jonas halfway across the room out of harm's way. Jonas swore under his breath and planted his feet firmly, thinking she was attempting to throw him out of the house.

Sarah adjusted the blinds at the window, filtering out the light, and returned to Damon's side, touching him gently. That was all. The lightest of touches. She simply laid her hand over his, yet peace stole into him as he buttoned his shirt. The terrible weight that always seemed to be pressing him into the ground lightened.

Kate's eyes filled with tears and she pressed her fingers to her mouth.

Abbey left the room to return with a cup of tea. "Drink this, Damon," she said. "You'll enjoy the taste."

The aroma alone added to the soothing touch Sarah had provided. He didn't think to ask how she had managed to make hot tea in a matter of seconds.

"I could use a cup of tea," Jonas said, "if anyone's asking. And a touch of sanity in the house would be nice, too. Baby Doll was going to huck me right out the door and you all just stood there watching."

"I'll make it for you." Hannah leaned against the door frame and looked up at the sheriff. Her fingers twisted together, the only sign of her agitation. "Do you like it sweet? I'm certain I can come up with an appropriate concoction."

"I think I'll pass altogether. One of these days I'm going to retaliate, Hannah."

She made a face at him as he crossed to the sliding-glass door to stare outside at the pounding waves. "I have a bad feeling about this, Sarah. I know you're used to doing things differently and people have no idea how you do it. Maybe you don't know either, I certainly don't, but I believe in you. I sometimes just feel things. It's one of the things that makes me good at my job." He turned to look at her. "I have a *very* bad feeling about this. Frankly, I'm afraid for all of you."

There was a small silence. "I believe you, Jonas," Sarah said. "I've always known you had a gift."

His gaze moved around the room, restlessly touching on each woman. "I've known this family since I was a boy. Feuds"—his smoldering gaze went to Hannah—"are petty when it comes to your safety. I'm not losing any of you over this. I want to be called if one of you stubs your toe. If you see a stranger or you hear a funny noise. I'm not kidding around with you over this issue. I want your word that you'll call me. You have my private number as well as the number to the office and 911."

"Jonas, don't worry, we'll be fine. I'm very good at what I do," Sarah said with complete confidence.

Jonas took a step toward her, very reminiscent of a stalking panther. Damon was grateful he was too old to be intimidated. "I want your word. Every one of you."

Damon nodded. "I have to agree with Harrington. These men tortured us. They don't play around. I'll admit when I'm around you, I feel magic in the air, but these men are evil and capable of torture and murder. I have to know you're all safe or I'll have to leave this town."

"Damon!" Sarah looked stricken. "They'll just follow you." Worse, he would carry Death with him wherever he chose to go.

"Then cooperate with the sheriff. Give him whatever he needs to stop these men." As ridiculous as it seemed when he'd just met her, Damon couldn't bear the thought of leaving Sarah, but he wasn't about to risk her life.

"I don't mind calling you, Jonas," Kate said readily.

Abbey held up her hand. "I'm in."

Sarah nodded. "I'm always grateful for help from the local law."

All eyes turned to Hannah. She shrugged indifferently. "Whatever helps Damon, I'm willing to do."

Jonas ignored the grudge in her voice and nodded. "I want all of you to watch your step. Be aware of your surroundings and any strangers. Keep those dogs close and lock up the house!"

"We're all over it," Sarah agreed. "Really, Jonas, we don't want any part of men with guns. We'll call you even if the cat meows."

He looked a little mollified. "I'll want extra patrols around here as well as around Damon's house, Sarah."

"Well, of course, Jonas," Sarah agreed.

"It will give me every opportunity to make friends with them," Hannah said. "I don't know many of the new people in town."

Jonas glared at her. "You and your slinky body can just stay away from my deputies."

Hannah made a face at him, raised her hand to push at the hair spilling across her face. An icy wind rushed through the room, giving life to the curtains, so that they danced in a macabre fashion, fluttering, reaching toward Jonas as if to bind him in the thick folds.

Sarah glimpsed a dark shadow moving within the drapes. Her hands went up in a casual, graceful wave. Kate and Abbey followed the gentle movements with their own. The wind died abruptly and the curtains dropped into place.

Damon cleared his throat. "Does someone want to tell me what happened?"

Jonas shook his head. "Never be dumb enough to ask for an explanation from any of them, Damon. You might get it and your hair will turn gray." His gaze swung to Hannah. "Don't even think about it. Ladies, I can find my own way out."

Damon didn't take his eyes from Sarah. She was looking at Hannah and there was accusation in her gaze. Out of the corner of his eye, he could see Abbey and Kate doing the same thing.

Hannah threw her hands into the air. "I wasn't thinking, okay? I'm sorry."

The silence lengthened, disapproval thick in the room.

Hannah sighed. "I really am sorry. I forgot for just a moment about Dea—" She broke off abruptly, her gaze shifting to Damon. "About the other thing we're dealing with. It won't happen again."

"It better not," Sarah said. "You can't afford to forget for one moment. This is too dangerous, Hannah."

"Wait a minute," Damon interrupted. "If you're talking about me and those men the other night, I don't want your family involved in any way."

"The men?" Kate raised her eyebrow. "Not in the least, Damon, didn't give them a thought. There are things far more dangerous than human beings."

He watched the four women exchange long knowing looks and was exasperated. They knew something he didn't. Something regarding him. "I can understand why poor Harrington gets so frustrated with you."

Sarah rose and blew him a kiss. "He loves all seven of us. He just likes to puff out his chest."

"He was genuinely worried," Damon said. "And I am, too. The things he said make sense. It's bad enough to think of you in danger, let alone all your sisters." He raked a hand through his hair in agitation. "I can't be responsible for that."

To his shock they all laughed. "Damon." Sarah's voice was a mixture of amusement and tenderness. "We accepted responsibility for our own decisions a very long time ago. We're

grown women. When we choose to involve ourselves in problems, we accept the consequences." She leaned toward him.

Abbey groaned dramatically. "She's going to do it. She's
going to kiss him right in front of us."

"That is so not fair, Sarah," Hannah protested.

"Go ahead," Kate encouraged. "I need to write a good love
scene."

When Sarah hesitated, her gaze lost in his, Damon took
advantage and did the job thoroughly, not wanting to let Kate
down.

Chapter 7

"SO, SARAH," DAMON said, putting down his glass of iced tea as they sat on his porch. Damon and Sarah spent every minute they could find together. Taking walks on the beach. Working on a security system for his house. Lazy days of laughter and whispered confidences. Damon enjoyed every moment spent in her home, getting to know her sisters. He never ran out of things to say to Sarah and he loved her stories and open personality. There was sunshine in his life and its name was Sarah.

She took a handful of his chips and smiled at him. Overhead the seagulls circled, looking down with hopeful eyes. Damon had had no more unwelcome nighttime visitors and appreciated the regularity of the sheriff driving by to check the neighborhood.

Damon shook his head, dazzled by her smile. She could take every thought out of his head with that smile. "Sarah, are you afraid for me or for everyone else? It's occurred to me that there's always this buffer between everyone we run across and me. I didn't really notice at first, but last night I was thinking about it. I'm getting to know you and I think you prefer that your friends don't see you with me."

Sarah's breath caught in her throat at the hint of pain in his voice. The more time she spent with him, the more she wanted to be with him. And the dark shadow surrounding him gripped him all the harder. "I don't mind anyone seeing us together. You're the one worried about gossip. I'm used to it and it doesn't bother me."

"Then we'll go into town together." It was a challenge.

Sarah let out her breath. The early morning fog had burned off, leaving the sky an amazing shade of blue. She could see clouds gathering far out over the sea. She looked carefully at Damon, inspecting every inch of him. There was no dark shadow around him and his shoulders weren't hunched as if carrying a great weight. "Sounds great, if you're really certain you want to brave it."

He stood up and held out his hand to her. "Come on."

"Right now?" She hadn't expected he would really want to go, but she obediently took his hand and allowed him to help her up.

"Yes, while I have my courage up. Walking with you through town should set a match to the gossips. The story will spread like wildfire."

Sarah laughed softly, knowing it was true. Once they had walked the short distance to the town, she started in the direction of the grocery store, determined to get it over with.

"I feel a little sorry for Harrington," Damon said as he walked with Sarah along the main street of town. "He drops by the house sometimes and he's very nice." He reached out and tangled his fingers with Sarah's.

"Are you certain you want to do this?" Sarah's voice was skeptical. "Holding my hand in public is going to bring the spotlight shining very brightly on you. Rumors are going to race through town faster than a seagull flies. I know how much your privacy means to you."

"That was before I retired. When I worked from morning until night and had no life." Damon laughed softly. He was happy. Looking at her made him happy. Walking with her, talking with her. It was ridiculous how happy he was when he was in her company. It made no sense but he wasn't going to question a gift from the heavens. "We may as well give them something real to gossip about."

Sarah's laugh floated on the breeze, a melodious sound that

turned heads. "Not 'gossip,' Damon, it's 'news.' No one gossips here. You have to get it straight."

Damon listened to the sound of their shoes on the wooden walkway. Everything was so different with Sarah. He felt as if he'd finally come home. He looked around him to the picturesque homes, so quaint and unique. It no longer felt alien or hostile to him; the people were eccentric, but endearing. How had Sarah done that? Mysterious Sarah. Even the wind welcomed her back home. His fingers tightened around hers, holding her to him. He wasn't altogether certain Sarah was human and he feared she might fly away from him without warning, joining the birds out over the sea.

She waved to a young woman on a porch. "They're good people, Damon. You won't find more accepting people in your life than the ones living here."

"Even Harrington?" he teased.

"I feel a little sorry for him, too," Sarah answered seriously. "Most of the time, Jonas is a caring, compassionate man and very good with everyone, but he just refuses to see the truth about Hannah. He looks at her and only sees what's on the outside. She's always been beautiful. He was very popular with the girls in school, an incredible athlete, tons of scholarships, the resident dreamboat. He thought Hannah was stuck up because she never spoke to him. He made her life a living hell, teasing her unmercifully all through school. She's never forgiven him and he'll never understand why. He's a good man and he wasn't being malicious in school. From his perspective, he was just teasing. He has no idea Hannah is painfully shy and he never will."

Damon made a dissenting noise in his throat. "She's a supermodel, Sarah—on the cover of every magazine there is. She travels all over the world. And, I have to say, she appears very confident on every television and news interview and talk show I've seen her on. I would never associate her with the word 'shy.' "

"She hyperventilates before speaking in public; in fact, she carries a paper bag with her. Most of the talk show hosts and interviewers are careful with her. Because she's painfully shy doesn't mean she allows it to affect her life."

"Why wouldn't you just clue Harrington in?"

"Why should he judge Hannah so harshly, just because she

looks the way she does? My sister Joley is striking as well, although not in exactly the same way. Jonas would never dare torment her. All of my sisters are good-looking and he doesn't use that sarcastic tone on them. He only does it to Hannah and in front of everyone."

Damon heard the fierce protective note in her voice and smiled. He drew her closer beneath his broad shoulder. His Sarah. Without warning, fear struck, deep, haunting, sharp like a knife. His breath left his lungs. "Sarah? Are we thinking the same thing? I've never wanted someone in my life before. Not once. I've only just met you and can't imagine the rest of my life without you." He raked his fingers through his hair, his cane nearly hitting his head. "Do you know what I sound like? An obsessed stalker. I'm not like this with women, Sarah."

Her eyes danced. "That leaves wide-open territory, Damon. You're talking about a family with six sisters and a billion cousins. I have a million aunts and uncles. You can't leave yourself open like that or they're going to tease you unmercifully."

They halted in front of the grocery store. Damon faced her, catching her chin in his hand to tilt her face up to his. "I'm serious, Sarah. I know I want a future with you in it. I have to know we're on the same page."

Sarah went up on her toes to press a kiss to his mouth. "Here's a little news flash for you, Damon. I don't compromise my jobs by getting involved with my clients. I don't, as a rule, kiss strange men and spend the night wishing they'd make the big move."

"You want me to make a move on you?"

Sarah laughed, tugged at his hand, dragging him into the store. "Of course I do."

"Well, this is a hell of a time to tell me."

Inez was at the store window with three of her customers, staring at Sarah and Damon with their mouths open. Damon scowled at them. "Is it fly-catching season?"

Sarah squeezed his hand tightly in warning. All the while she was smiling serenely. "Inez! We just dropped in for a quick minute. Kate and Hannah and Abigail are in town for a few days and they can't wait to see you! Joley and Elle and Libby send their love and told me to tell you they hope to get back soon." Her voice was bright and cheerful, dispelling an air of gloom in the store. "You do know Damon, of course."

Inez nodded, her hawklike gaze narrowing in shock on their linked hands. Her throat worked convulsively. "Yes, of course I do. I didn't know you two were *intimate* friends."

Damon glared at her, daring the woman to imply anything else. Sarah simply laughed. "I snagged him the minute I saw him, Inez. You always told me to settle down with a good man and, well . . . here he is."

"I never guessed, and Mr. Wilder didn't say a single word," Inez said.

Damon forced a smile under the subtle pressure of Sarah's grip. Her nails were biting into his hand. "Call me Damon, Inez. I never managed to catch you alone." It was the best excuse he could come up with and sound plausible. It must have worked because Inez beamed at him, bestowing on him a smile she reserved for her closest friends. In spite of himself, Damon could feel a tiny glow of pleasure at the acceptance.

"How is everything lately?" Sarah asked before Damon could warn her it was a bad idea to get Inez started.

"Honestly, Sarah, Donna over at the gift shop is a lovely woman but she just doesn't understand the importance of recycling. Just this morning I saw her dump her papers right in with plastic. I've sorted for her many times and showed her the easiest way to go about it but she just can't get the hang of it. Be a dear and do something about it, won't you?"

Damon's mouth nearly fell open at the request. What did Inez want Sarah to do? Separate the woman's garbage for her?

"No problem, Inez. I'll go over there now. Damon and I are hoping some of our friends will help us with a small problem. There are some strangers who have been in town, probably for a week or two—three men. We'd like to know their whereabouts, their movements, that sort of thing. Unfortunately we don't have a clear description but one of them has a facial injury, most likely around his jaw. I'm hoping another might have gotten bitten by a tick." She paused, a wicked little grin playing around the corners of her mouth. "Maybe a lot of ticks."

"What have they done?" Inez asked, lowering her voice as if she'd joined a conspiracy.

"They tried to break into Damon's house. Jonas has all the information we could give him. He was going to check the hospital and clinic." She'd turned over the tranquilizer gun to him, too. "If someone spots them, or mentions them to you, would you mind giving me a call? And maybe it would be good to call Jonas, too."

"Now, dear, you know I don't believe in sticking my nose into anyone's business, but if you really need me to help you, I'll be more than happy to oblige," Inez said. "There are always so many tourists but we should be able to spot a man with something wrong with his jaw."

Sarah leaned over to kiss Inez affectionately. "You're such a good friend, Inez. I don't know what we'd all do without you." She turned to look at the three customers. "Irene, I hope you don't mind me bringing Damon when I call on you and Drew this afternoon." She wanted to assess Drew's condition before she brought her sisters over and raised Irene's hopes further. "We just want to visit with him a few minutes," she added hastily. "We won't tire him."

Irene's expression brightened considerably. "Thank you, Sarah; of course you can bring anyone you want with you. I told Drew you might be dropping by and he was so excited. He'll love the company. He rarely sees even his friends anymore."

"Good, I can't wait to see him again. Now don't go to any trouble, Irene. Last time I came to visit, you had an entire luncheon waiting." Sarah rubbed Damon's arm. "Irene is such a wonderful cook."

"Oh, she is," Inez agreed readily. "Her baked goods are always the first to go at every fundraiser."

Irene broke into a smile, looking pleased.

The warmth in Damon's heart rushed to his belly, heated his blood. Sarah spread sunshine. That had to be her secret. Wherever she went, she just spread goodwill to others because she genuinely cared about them. It wasn't that she was being merely tolerant; she liked her neighbors with all their idiosyncrasies. He couldn't help the strange feeling of pride sweeping through him. How had he gotten so lucky?

Damon pushed his sunglasses onto his nose as they meandered across the street. He saw they were heading toward the colorful gift shop. "Are you really going to sort some woman's garbage, Sarah?"

"Of course not, I'm just popping in to say hello. Maybe

our intruders will buy a memento of their stay or possibly a gift for someone. You never know, we may as well cover all the bases," Sarah replied blithely.

Damon laughed. "Sarah, honey, I hardly think kidnappers are going to take the time to buy a memento of their stay. I could be wrong, but it seems rather unlikely."

Sarah simply grinned at him. She took his breath away with her smile. She should have always been in his life. By his side. All those years working, never thinking about anything else, and Sarah had been somewhere in the world. If he had met her earlier, he might have retired sooner and . . .

"Do you have any idea how perfectly tempting your mouth is, Damon?" Sarah interrupted his thoughts, her voice matter-of-fact, intensely interested.

"Sarah! Sarah Drake! Yoo-hoo!" A tall woman of Amazonian proportions and extraordinary skin waved wildly, intercepting them. An older man, obviously her father, and a teenage boy followed her at a much more sedate pace.

The clouds, gathering ominously over the sea, so far away only minutes earlier, moved inward at a rapid rate. The wind howled, blowing in from the sea, carrying something dark and dangerous with it. Icy fingers touched Sarah's face, almost a caress of delight . . . or challenge. She watched Damon's face, his body, as he accepted the weight, a settling of his shoulders, small lines appearing near his mouth. He didn't appear to notice, already far too familiar with his grim companion.

She moved closer to Damon, a purely protective gesture as the two men approached them in the wake of the woman. The welcoming smile faded from Sarah's face. A shadow moved on the walkway, slithering along the ground, a wide dark net casting for prey. "Patsy, it's been a long time." But she was looking at the older man. "Mr. Granger. How nice to see you again. And Pete, I'm so glad we ran into you. I'm visiting Drew soon. I'll be able to tell him I saw you. I'll bet he'll be happy to hear from you."

Pete Granger scuffed the toe of his boot on the sidewalk. "I should go see him. It's been awhile. I didn't know what to say."

Sarah placed her hand on his shoulder. Damon could see she was worried. "You'll find the right thing to say to him. That's what friendship is, Pete, to be there in good and bad

times. The good is easy, the bad, well"—she shrugged—
"that's a bit more difficult. But you've always been incredibly
tough and Drew's best friend. I know you'll be there for him."

Pete nodded his head. "Tell him I'll be over this evening."

Sarah smiled her approval. "I think that's a great idea,
Pete." She touched the elder Granger with gentle fingers.
"How did your visit to the cardiologist go?"

"Why, Sarah," Patsy answered, "Dad doesn't have a cardiologist. There's nothing wrong with his heart."

"Really? It never hurts to be safe, Mr. Granger. Checkups
are always so annoying but ultimately necessary. Patsy, do you
remember that cardiologist my mother went to when we were
in our first year of college? In San Francisco?"

Patsy exchanged a long look with her father. "I do remember, Sarah. Maybe we could get him in next month when
things settle down at the shop."

"These things are always better if you insist on taking care
of them immediately," Sarah prompted. "This is Damon Wilder, a friend of mine. Have you three met yet?"

Damon was simply astonished. Pete was going to go visit
his very ill friend and Mr. Granger was going to see a cardiologist, all at Sarah's suggestion. He looked closer at the older
man. He couldn't see that Granger looked sick. What had
Sarah seen that he hadn't? There was no doubt in his mind
that the cardiologist was going to find something wrong with
Mr. Granger's heart.

Sarah asked the three of them to keep an eye out for strangers with bruises on their face or jaw and the trio agreed before
hurrying away.

"How do you do that?" Damon asked, intrigued. She was
doing something, knew things she shouldn't know.

"Do what?" Sarah asked. "I have no idea what you're talking about."

Damon studied her face there on the street with the sunlight
shining down on them. He couldn't stop looking at her,
couldn't stop wanting her. Couldn't believe she was real. "You
see something beyond the human eye, Sarah, something science can't explain. I believe in science, yet I can't find an
explanation for what you do."

Damon was looking at her with so much hunger, so much
stark desire in his expression, Sarah's heart melted on the spot

and her body went up in flames. "It's a Drake legacy. A gift." Wherever she had been going was gone out of her head. She couldn't think of anything but Damon and the need on his face, the hunger in his eyes. Her fingers tangled in the front of his shirt, right outside the gift shop in plain sight of the interested townspeople.

"The Drake gate prophecy forgot to mention the intensity of the physical attraction," she murmured.

A man could drown in her eyes, be lost forever. His hands tightened possessively, brought her closer to him, right up against his body. Every cell reacted instantly. Whips of lightning danced in his bloodstream while tongues of fire licked his skin, at the simple touch of her fully clothed body. What was going to happen when she was naked, completely bare beneath him? "I might not survive," he whispered.

"Would we care?" Sarah asked. She couldn't look away from him, couldn't stop staring into his eyes. She wanted him. Ached for him. Wanted to be alone with him. It didn't matter where, just that they were alone.

"You can't look at me like that," Damon said. "I'm going up in flames and I'm too damned old to be acting like a teenager."

"No, you're not," Sarah denied. "By all means, I don't mind at all." She half-turned toward the street, still in his arms. "I think Inez is falling out of her window. Poor thing, she's bound to lose her eyesight if she keeps this up. I should have suggested she get a new pair of glasses. I'll let Abigail suggest it. You have to be careful with Inez because she's so sensitive."

It was the way Sarah said it, so absolutely sincere, that tugged at his heartstrings. "I never could get along with people. Ever. Not even in college. Everyone always annoyed me. I preferred books and my lab to talking with a human being," he admitted, wanting her to understand the difference she'd made. He was actually beginning to care about Inez and that was plain damned scary. He was finding the townspeople interesting after seeing them through her eyes.

"Let's go back to my house," he suggested. "Didn't you say there could be bugs in that security system you installed?"

"I'm certain I need to check it over," Sarah agreed, "but I do have to make this one stop first. I promised Inez."

Chapter 8

THE SMALL GIFT shop was cheerful and bright. Celtic music played softly. New Age books and crystals of all colors occupied one side of the store while fairies and dragons and mythical creatures reigned supreme on the other. Damon had been prepared for clutter after the comments on the shop owner's lack of recycling education, but the store was spotless.

"I think Donna knows her recycling stuff," Damon whispered against Sarah's ear. "She probably brushed up after she saw Inez peering at her through the store window with her lips pursed and her hands on her hips." His teeth nibbled for just a moment, sending a tremor through her. "Let's get out of here while we have the chance."

Sarah shook her head. "I have an especially strong feeling we should talk with Donna today." She was frowning slightly, a puzzled expression on her face.

Damon felt something twist and settle around his heart. Knowledge blossomed. Belief. He was a man of logic and books, yet he knew Sarah was different. He knew she was magic. Mysterious Sarah was back home and with her, some undefined power that couldn't be ignored. He felt it now for himself, after having been in her presence. It was very real, something he couldn't explain but knew was there, deep inside of her.

His knowledge made it much easier to accept the amazing intensity of the chemistry between them. More than that, it helped him to believe in the powerful emotions already surfacing for her. How did one fall in love at first sight? He'd always scoffed at the idea, yet Sarah was wrapped securely around his heart and he had known her for only a few days.

"If you feel we should talk to Donna, then by all means, let's find the woman," he agreed readily. She had changed him for all time. *He* was different inside and he preferred the man he was becoming to the man he had been. If he spent too much time thinking about it, his feelings made no sense, but he didn't want to think about it. He simply accepted it, embraced the opportunity destiny had given him.

Sarah called out, moving through the store with the natural grace Damon had come to associate with her. "Donna's daughter went to school with Joley. Donna is a sweetheart, Damon—have you met her?" She peeked around the bead-curtained doorway leading to the back of the store.

"I've seen her," Damon said, "in Inez's store. She and Inez like to exchange sarcasm."

"They've been friends for years. When Inez was sick a few years ago, Donna moved into Inez's house and cared for her, ran her own gift shop and the grocery store. They just like to grouse at one another, but it's all in fun. The back screen is open. That's strange. Donna has a phobia about insects. She never leaves doors open." There was concern in her voice.

Damon followed Sarah through the beaded curtain, noting the neatly stacked paper tied with cord and the barrel of plastic labeled with inch-high letters. "I'd have to say Donna knows more about recycling than most people."

"Of course she does." Sarah's tone was vague, as if she wasn't paying much attention. "She just likes to give Inez something to say."

"You mean she does it on purpose?" Damon wanted to laugh but Sarah's behavior was making him uneasy. They stepped out of the shop onto a back porch.

The wind rushed them, coming at them from the sea. Coming from the direction of the cliff house. Sarah raised her face to the wind, closed her eyes for a moment. Damon watched her face, watched her body. There was a complete stillness about her. She was there with him physically, but he had the impression her spirit was riding on the wind. That mentally she was with her sisters in the cliff house.

The wind chilled him, raised goose bumps on his arms, sent a shiver of alarm down his back. Something was wrong. Sarah knew something was wrong and he knew it now as well.

Sarah opened her eyes and looked at him with apprehension. "Donna." She whispered the name.

The wind whipped leaves from the trees and whirled them in small eddies of chaos and confusion. Sarah watched the whirling mass of leaves intently. Her fingers closed around his wrist. "I don't think she's far but we have to hurry. Call the sheriff's office. Tell them to send an ambulance and to send a car over. I think one of your kidnappers did decide to shop at Donna's."

She started away from him, toward the small house that sat behind the gift shop. It was overgrown with masses of flowers and bushes, a virtual refuge in the middle of town. "Wait a minute!" Damon hesitated, torn between making the phone call and following Sarah. "What if someone's still there, and what if the sheriff thinks I'm a nut?"

"Someone is still there and just say I said hurry." Sarah flung the words back over her shoulder. She was moving fast, yet silently, lithely, so graceful she reminded him of a stalking animal.

Damon swore under his breath and hurried back inside the store. Inez was standing just inside the beaded curtain. Her face was very pale. "What is it?" she demanded, her hand fluttering to her heart.

"Sarah said to call the sheriff and tell them to hurry. She also said to call an ambulance. Would you do that so I can make certain nothing happens to Sarah?" Damon spoke gently, afraid the older woman might collapse.

Inez lifted her chin. "You go, I'll have a dozen cops here immediately."

Damon breathed a sigh of relief and hurried after Sarah. She was already out of his sight, lost behind the rioting explosion of flowers. He silently cursed his bum leg. He could go anywhere if he went slowly enough but he couldn't run and even walking fast was dangerous. His leg would simply give out.

His heart was pounding so hard in his chest he feared it would explode. Sarah in danger was terrifying. He had thought there was nothing left for him, yet she had come into his life at his darkest hour and brought hope and light. Laughter and compassion. She was even teaching him to appreciate Inez. Damon swore again, pressing his luck, using his cane to hold back the bushes while he tried to rush over the cobblestones Donna had so painstakingly used to build the pathway between her house and her shop.

A soft hiss to his left gave Sarah's position away. She was inching her way toward the door of Donna's house, using several large rhododendrons as cover. Her hand signal was clear: she wanted him to crouch low and stay where he was. A humiliating thought. Sarah racing to the rescue while he hid in the bushes. The worst of it was, he could see that she was a professional. She moved like one, and she had produced a gun from somewhere. It fit into her hand as if she were so familiar with it, the gun was a part of her.

Damon realized, for all their long talks together, he didn't know Sarah very well at all. His heart and mind and soul wanted and needed her, but he didn't know her. Enthralled, he watched as she gained the porch. Even the wind seemed to have stilled, holding its breath.

Sarah turned back to look up at the sky, to lift her arms toward the clouds. Her face was toward the cliff house. Damon had a sudden vision of her sisters standing on the battlements in front of the rolling sea, raising their arms in unison with Sarah. Calling on the wind, calling on the elements to bind their wills together.

The wind moaned softly, carrying the sound of a melodious song, so faint he couldn't catch the words but he knew the voices were female. Dark threads spun into thick clouds overhead and the wind rushed at the house, rattling the windows and shaking the doors. The sky darkened ominously, fat drops of rain splattered the roof and yard. Damon tasted salt in the air. The rain seemed to come from the ocean itself, as if the wind, in answer to some power, had driven the salt water from the sea and spread it over the land.

The wind pulled back, reminiscent of a wave, then rushed

again, this time with a roar of rage, aiming at the entry. Under the assault, the door burst inward, allowing the chilling wind into the house. Sarah rolled in behind it, as papers and magazines flew in all directions, providing a small distraction. She was already up on one knee in a smooth motion, tracking with her gun.

"I don't want to have to shoot you, but I will," she said. The words carried clearly to Damon although her voice was very low. "Put the gun down and kick it away from you." Damon hurried up the porch steps. He could see that Sarah's hand was rock steady. "Donna, don't try to move, an ambulance is on the way." Her gaze hadn't shifted from the man standing over Donna's body.

Damon could see the lump on Donna's head, the blood spilling onto the thick carpet. His fingers tightened around his cane until his knuckles turned white. He transferred his hold to a two-handed grip. Fury shook him at the sight of the woman on the floor and the man he recognized standing over her.

"Damon." Sarah's voice was gentle but commanding. "Don't."

He hadn't realized he had taken an aggressive step forward. Sarah hadn't turned her head, hadn't taken her alert gaze from Donna's attacker, but she somehow knew his intention. He forced himself back under control.

"Why would you attack a helpless woman?" Damon asked. He was shaking with anger, with the need to retaliate.

"Don't engage with him," Sarah counseled. "I hear a siren. Will you please see if it's the sheriff?"

Damon turned and nearly ran over Inez. He caught her as she tried to rush to Donna's side. "You can't get between Sarah and the man who attacked Donna," he said. Inez felt light and fragile in his hands. She never seemed old, yet now he could see age lined her face. She looked so anxious he was afraid for her. Very gently he drew her away from the entrance, pulling her to one side.

The wind whipped through the room, sent loose papers once more into the air. Inez shivered and reached to close the door on the chilling sea breeze.

"No!" Sarah's voice was sharp this time, unlike her.

It was enough to stimulate Damon into action. He held the

door open to the elements. It was only then that he felt the subtle flow of power entering with the wind. Faintly he could hear, or imagined that he heard, the chanting carried from the direction of the ocean . . . or the cliff house.

He studied Donna's assailant, one of the men who had tortured him. The man who had pressed a gun to Dan's head and pulled the trigger. Why was he simply standing there motionless? Was it really the threat of Sarah's gun?

Damon had no doubt that she would shoot, but would that be enough to intimidate a man like this one? He doubted it. There was something else in the room, something holding the killer.

A sense of rightness stole into his heart, carried with it a sense of peace. Sarah was a woman of silk and steel. She was magnificent.

"Jonas is coming," Inez whispered to Damon. "Sarah's going to have a problem. She'll be weak and sick after this. She won't want anyone to see her like that."

Damon could see the acceptance of his relationship with Sarah in Inez's expression. It made him feel as if he truly belonged. Inez's approval meant more to him than it should have, made him feel a part of the close-knit community instead of the outsider he always seemed to be wherever he went.

He nodded his head, pretending to understand, determined to be there for Sarah the way she seemed to be for everyone else.

Jonas Harrington came through the door first, his eyes hard and unflinching. He had Donna's assailant in handcuffs immediately. Sarah sank back on her haunches, her head bowed. She wiped sweat from her brow with the back of a trembling hand. Damon went to her immediately, helping her up, forcing her to lean on him when she didn't want to, when she was worried about his hip and leg.

Sarah went down the hall with Damon's help, found a chair in the kitchen where she could sit. She looked up at him and smiled her appreciation. That was all. And it was everything. He got her a glass of water, helped her steady her hands enough to drink it. She recovered fairly quickly, but she remained pale.

"Are your sisters feeling the same effects?" he asked.

Sarah nodded. "It isn't the same as casting. It takes a tremendous amount of our energy to hold someone against his or her will. It wasn't in his nature to be passive." She held out her hand. "I'm doing better. I need to eat something and sleep for a little while." She sighed. "I promised Irene I'd go visit Drew tonight but I don't have any strength left after this, not the kind I'd need to help them." She pressed her fingertips to her temples. "I can't really do anything for Drew and Irene knows that. Extending his life might not be the best thing. If only Libby were here."

"Sarah." He spoke in his most gentle tone. "Leave it alone for now. Let me take you home; I'll fix you a good meal and you can sleep. I'll talk to Irene myself. She'll understand."

"How did you know my sisters were helping me?"

"I felt them," he replied. "Are you steady enough to talk with the sheriff?"

She nodded. "And I want to make certain Donna's all right."

When they returned to the living room, Harrington already had Donna's assailant in the squad car. Donna burst into tears, clinging to Sarah and Inez, making Damon feel helpless and useless but filled with a deep sense of pride in Sarah and her sisters.

"Why did he attack you, Donna?" Sarah asked.

"I noticed he had your earring, Sarah. The one Joley made for you. He was wearing it. It's one of a kind and I thought you must have lost it. So I asked him about it. He hit me hard and dragged me out of the store back into my house. He kept asking me questions about you and about Mr. Wilder."

Sarah pressed her hand against Donna's wound, just for a moment. Damon watched her face carefully, watched her skin grow paler until she swayed slightly with weariness. Sarah leaned down and kissed Donna's cheek. "You'll be fine. Don't worry about the store, we'll lock up for you."

"I'm going to the hospital with her," Inez said, glaring at the paramedics as if daring them to deny her. She held Donna's hand as they took her out.

"Sarah?" Jonas Harrington stood waiting against the wall. "You have a permit to carry that gun?"

"You know I do, Jonas," she replied. "You've seen it more than once. Yes, it's up-to-date. And I didn't shoot the man, although I was inclined to with Donna lying on the floor bleeding. And he is wearing my earring. I want it back."

"I'll get it back for you," Jonas was patient. "I know you're tired, but I need you to answer a few questions."

"That's one of the men who kidnapped me. He's the one who killed my assistant," Damon explained. "The other two must be staying somewhere in town. It shouldn't be that hard to find them now that we have him."

"I'll find them." Jonas's voice was grim. "Sarah, will you come by the office later and give me a full statement? I've sent the perp in the squad car down to the office. There's already an outstanding warrant for his arrest and the feds are going to be swarming all over this place as soon as we notify them. They're going to want to talk to the two of you, so you'd better go rest while you can."

Damon circled Sarah's shoulders with his arm. "Can you give us a ride to my place, Sheriff?"

"Sure. Let's lock up and get out of here before Sarah keels over and her sisters haul us both over the coals. You've never seen them en masse, coming after you." He shuddered. "It's a scary sight, Wilder."

"You're the only one it's ever happened to so far," Sarah pointed out.

Chapter 9

DAMON STARED DOWN into Sarah's sleeping face. She was beautiful lying there in the middle of his bed. He had been standing there, leaning against the wall, for some time just watching over her. Guarding her. It seemed rather silly and melodramatic when she was the one with the gun and the training, but it felt as necessary to him as breathing.

Where had such a wealth of feeling come from nearly overnight? Could a man fall deeply in love with a woman so quickly? She was everything and more than he'd ever thought of or dreamed about. How could anyone not love Sarah with her compassion and tolerance and understanding? She genuinely cared about the people in her town. Somehow that deep emotion was rubbing off on him.

She could have been killed. The thought hit him hard. A physical blow in the pit of his stomach. How was it possible to feel so much for one person when he'd just met her? His entire life he'd barely noticed people, let alone cared about their lives. From the moment he'd heard her name whispered on the wind, he knew, deep down where it counted, that she would change his life for all time.

Their walks together, all the times on the beach, whispering in his house, or hers, even spending time with her family had only strengthened his feelings for her.

Sarah opened her eyes and the first thing she saw was Damon's face. He was leaning against the far wall, simply watching her. She could see his expression clearly, naked desire, mixed with knowledge of their future. His emotions were stark and raw and so real it brought tears to her eyes. Damon hadn't expected to like her, let alone feel anything else for her.

She held out her hand to him. "Don't stand over there all alone. You aren't alone anymore and neither am I."

He heard the invitation in her voice and his body began to stir in anticipation. But he stood there drinking her in. Wanting her in so many ways that weren't just physical.

"You weren't, you know, Sarah. You've never been alone. You don't need me in the same way I need you. You have a family and they wrap you up in love and warmth and support. I never considered the value of family and love. Sharing a day with someone you care about is worth all the gold in the world. I didn't know that before I met you."

She sat up, studying him with her cool gaze. Assessing. Liking what she saw. Damon didn't know why but he could see it on her face. "I'm glad then, Damon, if I gave you such a gift. My family is my treasure."

He nodded. What would it be like to wake up every morning and hear her voice? There was always a caress in her voice, a stroking quality that he felt on his skin. Deep in his body. "And you're my treasure, Sarah. I had no idea I was even capable of feeling this way about anyone."

Sarah smiled. The smile she seemed to reserve for him. It lit up her face and made her eyes shine, but more, it lit up his insides so that he burned with something indefinable. "You brought me life, Sarah. You handed me my life. I existed before I met you, but I wasn't living."

"Yes, you were, Damon. You're a brilliant man. The things you created made our world safer. I watch your face light up when you tell me about other ideas you have and what the possibilities are. That's living."

"I had nothing else but my ideas." He straightened suddenly, coming away from the wall, walking toward her, confidence on his face. "That was how I escaped, into my brain and the endless ideas I could find there." He traced the classic lines of her face, her cheekbones. Her generous mouth. "Take off your blouse, Sarah. I want to see you."

A faint blush stole into her cheeks but her hands went to the tiny pearl buttons on her blouse and slowly began to slide the edges apart. His breath caught in his throat as he watched her. Sarah didn't try to be sexy, there was never anything affected about her, yet it was the sexiest thing he'd ever seen. The edges of her blouse slowly gaped open, to reveal her lush creamy flesh beneath it. She had a woman's body, shaped to please a man with soft curves and lines.

Her breasts were covered with fine white lace. Sarah stood up, her body very close to his. Damon felt a rush of heat take him, a whip of lightning dance through his body. His blood thickened and pooled. His body hardened almost to the point of pain. He embraced it, reveled in the intensity of his need for her.

"You're so beautiful, Sarah. Inside and out. I still can't believe I could go from living in hell straight to paradise."

She reached for him. "I'm not like that at all, Damon. I'm not truly beautiful, not by any stretch of the imagination. I'm not even close. And living with me would not be paradise. I'm outspoken and like my way."

With exquisite tenderness, he bent his head to find her mouth with his. For a moment they were lost together, transported out of time by the magic flowing between them. When Damon lifted his head to look down at her, his gaze was hungry. Needy. Possessive. "You're beautiful to me, Sarah. I will never see you any other way. And lucky for you, I'm stubborn and very outspoken myself. I think those are admirable traits."

"That is lucky," she murmured, allowing her eyelashes to drift down and her head to fall back as he pulled her closer, his mouth breathing warm, moist air over her nipple right through the white lace. Her arms cradled his head as she arched her body, offering temptation, offering heaven.

His mouth was hot and damp as it closed over her breast. Fire raced through her, through him. Sarah gave herself up to sensual pleasure as his tongue danced and teased and his mouth suckled strongly right through the lace. He took his time, a lazy, leisurely exploration, his hands shaping her body, using the pads of his fingers as a blind man would to trace every curve and hollow. Memorizing her. Worshipping her.

Sarah was lost in sensation. Drowning in it. She couldn't remember him unsnapping her jeans, or even unzipping them. But her lacy bra had long ago floated to the floor and somehow he managed to push denim from her hips. In a haze of need and heat she stepped out of the last of her clothes.

He was never hurried, even as his mouth fused once more with hers and she was trying to drag his shirt from his broad shoulders so she could be skin to skin with him. He was patient and thorough, determined to know her body, to find every hidden trigger point that had her gasping in need. His hands moved over her, finding the shadows and hollows, tracing her ribs lovingly. He allowed Sarah to drag his clothes from his body, not appearing to notice or care, so completely ensnared by the wonders of giving her pleasure. He loved the little gasps and soft cries that came from deep in her throat.

Sarah. So responsive and giving. He should have known she would be a generous lover, merging with him so completely, giving of herself endlessly. Her selfless gift only made him want to be equally generous. For the first time his scars weren't shameful and something he hid. When her fingertips traced them, there was no reluctance, no shrinking away from the ugly memories of torture and murder. She soothed his body, caressing his skin, arousing him further, eager to touch him, wanting him with the same urgency he wanted her.

He lowered her slowly to the sheets, following her down, settling his body over hers. Her face was beautiful as she stared up at him. He kissed her eyes, the tip of her nose, the corners of her mouth.

Everywhere he touched her he left flames behind. Sarah was astonished at the sheer intensity of the fire. He was so unhurried, taking his time, but she was going up in flames, burning inside and out, needing his body in hers. She heard her own voice, a soft plea for mercy as his lips nipped over her navel, went lower. His hands moved with assurance, finding the insides of her thighs, the damp heat waiting for him at the junction of her legs.

"Damon." She could barely breathe his name. Her breath seemed to have permanently left her body. There wasn't enough air in the room.

His finger pushed deep inside her, a stroke of sensuality that drove her out of her mind. Every sane thought she'd ever had was gone. There was a roaring in her head when his mouth found her, claimed her, branded her his. She couldn't keep her hips still, writhing until his arms pinned her there, while his hot mouth ravaged her and wave after wave of pleasure rippled through her body with the force of the booming ocean. Her fingers tangled in his hair, her only anchor to hold her to earth while she soared free, gasping out his name.

Damon moved then, blanketing her completely, his hips settling into the cradle of hers. He was thick and hard and throbbing with his own need. He pushed deep inside of her, his voice hoarse as he cried out as the sweeping pleasure engulfed him. She was hot and slick and tight, a velvet fist closing around him, gripping with a fire he'd never known. Sarah. Magical Sarah.

He began to move. Never hurried. Why would he hurry his first time with Sarah? He wanted the moment to last forever. To be forever for both of them. He loved watching her face as he moved with her. As his body surged deep and her body took him in, her secret sanctuary of heat and joy. Her hips rose to join him, matching his rhythm, tilting to take him deeper and deeper with every stroke, wanting every inch of him. Wanting his possession as much as he wanted her.

The fire just kept building. He was in complete control one moment, certain of it, reveling in it, and then the pleasure was almost too much to bear, hitting him with the force of a freight train, starting in his toes and blowing out the top of his head. His voice was lifted with hers, merged and in perfect unison.

He could feel the aftershocks shaking her, tightening around him, drawing them ever closer. They lay together, not daring to move, unable to move, their hearts wild and lungs starving for air, their arms wrapped tightly around one another. The ocean breeze was gentle on the window, whispering soothing sounds while the sea sang to them with rolling waves.

Damon found peace. She lay in his arms, occasionally rousing herself enough to kiss his chest, her tongue tracing a scar. Each time she did so, his body tightened in answer and hers responded with another aftershock. They were merged so completely, so tightly bound together he couldn't tell where he started or left off.

"Stay with me the rest of the day, Sarah. All night. We can do anything you like. Just be with me." He propped himself up on his elbows to take most of his weight off of her. He wanted to be locked together, one body, sharing the same skin, absorbing her.

She reached up to trace the lines of his face. "I can't think of anywhere I'd rather be or who I'd rather be spending time with."

"Do you wonder why you chose me? I stopped asking myself that question and just accept it. I'm grateful, Sarah."

"I look at you and I just know. Who can say why one heart belongs to another? I don't ask myself that question either, Damon. I'm just grateful the gate opened for you." She laughed with sudden amusement. "It has occurred to me you might be seducing me to try to get the secret of paint preservation."

He tangled his fingers with hers, stretched her arms above her head. "It did seem a good idea. Maybe one of these days I'll be able to speak when I'm making love to you and I'll be able to pry the secret out of you."

"Good plan; it might work, too, if I could manage to speak when you're making love to me." She gasped as he lowered his head to her breast. "Damon." Her body was hypersensitive, but she arched into the heat of his mouth.

"I'm sorry, you looked so tempting, I couldn't help myself. How do you feel about just lying here without a stitch on while I build a fire and cook something for you to eat? I'm not certain I can bear for you to put your clothes back on." His teeth scraped back and forth over her breast. His tongue laved her nipple.

Sarah's entire body tightened, every muscle going taut. "You just want me to be lying here waiting for you?"

"Waiting *eagerly* for me," he corrected. "Needing me would be good. I wouldn't mind if you just lay here on my bed thinking of my body buried inside you."

"I see. I thought it might be better if I just followed you around, looking at you, touching you while you worked. Inspiring you. I have my ways, you know, of inspiring you."

There was a wicked note in her voice that made his entire body aware of how receptive and pliant she was. He was all at once as hard as a rock, thick with need. Damon watched her eyes widen in pleased surprise. Desire spread through both of them, sheer bliss. "I've never felt this way with any other woman, Sarah. I know it isn't possible. I think you really could walk on water."

"For a man who spent a lot of time in a laboratory, you know your way around women," she pointed out. He was moving with that exquisite slowness he used to drive her straight up the wall. The friction on her already sensitive body was turning her inside out. It didn't matter how many times she went over the edge, Damon moved with almost perfect insight, perfect knowledge of what she needed. What she wanted.

"I can read your face and your body," he said. "I love that, Sarah. You don't hold anything back from me."

"Why should I?" Why would she want to when the rewards were so great? If Damon was the man destiny insisted would be the love of her life, her best friend and partner, she was willing to accept whatever he had to give.

Sarah loved the sound of his voice, the thoughtful intelligent way he approached every subject. And she loved his complete honesty. There was that same raw honesty in his lovemaking. He gave himself to her, even as he took her for his own. She *felt* his possession deep in her soul, branded into her very bones.

There was that patient thoroughness and then, when he was fully aroused, his body was a driving force, each stroke hard and fast and insistent, taking them both soaring out over the sea, free-falling through time and space until neither could move again.

Damon held her in his arms, curled next to her, not wanting to end the closeness between them. They were completely sated for the moment, exhausted, breathing with effort, yet there was the same sense of absolute peace. "Sarah." He whispered her name, a tribute more than anything else.

"All those things you feel about me," she said, snuggling closer to him, "I feel about you. I didn't want anyone in my life any more than you did. I sometimes tire of giving pieces of myself to other people, yet I can't help myself. I find places I'm safe, places where I'm alone and can crawl into a hole and disappear for a while."

"Now you have me. I'll be your sanctuary, Sarah. I don't mind running interference in the times you need to regroup." His smile was against her temple. "I've never had a problem bossing people. I've always had a difficult time communicating with people. They never understood what I was talking about and it drove me crazy. Sometimes when you have an idea and it's so clear and you know it's right, you just have to share it with someone. But no one has ever been there."

Sarah kissed his fingertips. "You can tell me any idea that comes into your head, Damon. I admire you." Her smile was in her voice. "And I'm *very* good at communicating so you'll never have to worry about that."

"I noticed," he said. "Speaking of communication, I made certain the curtains couldn't creep open. I safety-pinned them together just in case any of your sisters decided to go up on the battlements to look through the telescope."

Sarah laughed just as he knew she would. "They know I'm with you. They wouldn't invade our privacy when we're really making love. They simply love to tease me. You'll have a lot of that come morning."

Damon didn't mind at all. He tightened his arms around her and found he was looking forward to anything her sisters might want to dish out.

Chapter 10

"OKAY, HAVE ANY of you really read this prophecy?" Kate demanded as they walked along the sidewalk toward Irene's house. The fog was thick and heavy, lying over the sea and most of the town like a blanket. "Because I have and it isn't good news for the rest of us."

"I don't like the sound of that," Hannah said. "Maybe we shouldn't ask. Can ignorance keep us safe?"

"What prophecy?" Damon asked curiously. They had spent the morning together over breakfast, teasing him unmercifully, making Sarah blush and hide her face against his chest. He had felt just as he anticipated—part of a family—and the feeling was priceless.

Sarah laughed in wicked delight. "You all thought it was so funny when it was happening to me, but *I* had read the entire thing. I know what's in store for the rest of you. One by one you'll fall like dominoes."

Abbey made a face at Sarah. "Not all of us, Sarah. I don't believe in fate."

The other girls roared with laughter. Sarah slipped her hand into Damon's. "The prophecy is this horrible curse put on the seven sisters. Well, we thought it was a curse. I'm not so certain now that I've met you."

His eyebrow shot up. "Now I'm really curious. I'm involved with this prophecy in some way?"

The four women laughed again. The sound turned heads up and down the street. "You are the prophecy, Damon," Kate said. "The gate opened for you."

Sarah gave a short synopsis of the quote. "Seven sisters intertwined, controlling elements of land, sea, and air, cannot control the fate they flee. One by one, oldest to last, destiny will find them. When the locked gate swings open in welcome, the first shall find true love. There's a lot more, but basically it goes on to say, one by one all the other sisters shall be wed."

Sarah's three sisters muttered and grumbled and shook their heads. Damon burst out laughing. "You have to marry me, don't you? I've been wondering how I was going to manage to keep you, but you don't have a choice. I like that prophecy. Does it say anything about waiting on me hand and foot?"

"Absolutely not," Sarah replied and glared at her laughing sisters. "Keep it up—the rest of you, even you, Abbey, are going to see me laughing at you." She tightened her fingers around Damon's hand. "We all made a pact when we were kids to keep the gate padlocked and never really date so we could be independent and free. We've always liked our life together . . . and poor Elle—the thought of seven daughters is rather daunting."

"Thank heavens Elle gets all the kids," Abbey said. "I am going to have one, and only because if I don't the rest of you will drive me crazy."

"Why does Elle have to have the seven daughters?" Damon asked.

"The seventh daughter always has seven daughters," Kate explained. "It's been that way for generations. I've been reading the history of the Drake family and I've found over the years, from all the entries made, we at least have a legacy of happy marriages." She smiled at Damon. "So far I haven't seen anything that indicated waiting on the man hand and foot but I'll keep looking."

"While you're at it, will you also keep an eye out for the traditional obey-the-husband rule?" Damon asked. "I've always thought that word was crucial in the marriage ceremony. Without it, a man doesn't stand a chance."

"Dream on," Sarah said. "That will never happen. The problem with being locked up in a stuffy lab all of your life is becoming evident. Delusions start early."

They were passing a small, neat home with a large front yard surrounded by the proverbial white picket fence. An older couple was working on a fountain in the middle of a bed of flowers. Sarah suddenly stopped, turned back to look at the house and the couple. A shadow slithered across the roof. A hint of something seen, then lost in the fog. "I'll just be a minute." She waved to the older couple and both stood up immediately and came over to the fence.

Sarah's sisters looked at one another uneasily. Damon followed Sarah. "It isn't necessary to speak to every citizen in town," he advised Sarah's back. She ignored his good judgment and struck up a conversation with the older couple anyway. Damon sighed. He had a feeling he was going to be following Sarah and talking to everyone they met for the rest of his life.

"Why, Sarah, I'd heard you were back. Is everything all right? I haven't seen you for what is it now? Two years?" The older woman spoke as she waved to the sisters.

"Mrs. Darden, I was admiring your yard. Did you remodel your house recently?"

The Dardens looked at one another then back to Sarah. Mr. Darden cleared his throat. "Yes, Sarah, the living room and kitchen. We came into a little money and we always wanted to fix up the house. It's exactly the way we want it now."

"That's wonderful." She rubbed the back of her neck and looked up at the roof. "I see you've got ladders out. Are you re-roofing?"

"It was leaking this winter, Sarah," Mr. Darden said. "We lost a tree some months ago and a branch hit the house. We've had trouble ever since."

"It looks as if you're doing the work yourself," Sarah observed and rubbed the back of her neck a second time.

Damon reached out to massage her neck with gentle fingers. The tremendous tension he felt in her neck and shoulders kept him silent. Wondering.

"I hear Lance does wonderful roofing, Mr. Darden. He's

fast and guarantees his work. Rather than you climbing around on the roof, wasting your time when you could be gardening." She turned her head slightly to look at Damon. "Mr. Darden is renowned for his garden and flowers. He wins every year at the fair for his hybrids."

Damon could see shadows in her eyes. He smiled at her, leaned forward to brush a gentle kiss on the top of her head when she turned back to the Dardens. "Lance probably needs the work and you'd be doing him such a favor."

Mrs. Darden tugged at her husband's hand. "Thank you, Sarah, it's good advice and we'll do that. I've been worrying about Clyde up there on that roof but . . ." She trailed off.

"I think you're right, Sarah," Mr. Darden suddenly agreed. "I think I'll call Lance straightaway."

Sarah shrugged with studied casualness but Damon felt her shoulders sag in relief. "I can't wait for the fair this year to see your beautiful entries. I really wanted you to meet Damon Wilder, a friend of mine. He bought the old Hanover place." She smiled sweetly at Damon to include him. "I know you're often in the garden and working on your lovely yard—have you noticed any strangers around that were asking questions or making you feel uncomfortable?"

The Dardens looked at one another. "No, Sarah, I can't say that we have," Mrs. Darden answered, "but then we strictly mind our own business. You know I've always believed in staying out of my neighbors' affairs."

"It's just that with you working outdoors so much I thought you might be able to keep an eye out for me and give me a call if anything should look suspicious," Sarah said.

"You can count on us, Sarah," Mr. Darden said. "I just bought myself a new pair of binoculars and sitting on my front porch I have a good view of the entire street!"

"Thank you, Mr. Darden," Sarah said. "That would be wonderful. We're just on our way to visit Irene and Drew."

The smile faded from Mrs. Darden's face. "Oh, that's so sad, Sarah, I hope you can help them. When is Libby going to come home? She would be such a help. How's she doing these days?"

"Libby's overseas right now, Mrs. Darden," Sarah said. "She's doing fine. Hopefully she'll be able to get home soon. I'll tell her you were inquiring about her."

"I heard the awful news on Donna," Mrs. Darden continued. "Are these strangers involved in her attack? I heard you shot one of them. I don't believe in violence as a rule, Sarah, now, you know that, but I hope you did enough damage that he'll think twice before he attacks another woman."

"Donna's going to be fine," Sarah assured her, "and I didn't shoot him."

Mrs. Darden patted Sarah's shoulder. "It's all right dear, I understand."

Sarah turned away with a cheery wave. The sisters erupted into wild laughter. Damon shook his head incredulously. "She thinks you shot that man. Even now, with you denying it, she thinks you shot him."

"True." Sarah pinned him with a steely gaze. "She also believes someone saw me walk on water. Now who could have started that rumor?"

Hannah tugged at Damon's sleeve in a teasing way, a gesture of affection for her. "That was a good one, Damon, I wish I'd thought of it."

Kate threw back her head and laughed, her wild mane of hair blowing around her in the light breeze. "That was priceless. And you should hear what they're saying about you. The whisper is, you're some famous wizard Sarah's been studying under."

"Now really," Sarah objected, "at least they could have said *he's* been studying under *me*. I swear chauvinism is still rearing its ugly head in this century."

Damon could feel a glow spreading. He felt a part of their family. He belonged with them, in the midst of their laughter and camaraderie. He didn't feel on the outside looking in, as he had most of his life. Sarah's sisters seem to accept him readily into their lives and even their hearts. Tolerance and acceptance seemed a big part of Sarah's family. It suddenly occurred to him, even with a threat hanging over his head, that he'd spent less time thinking of past trauma and more about the present and future than he had in months.

"I think I like being thought of as a wizard," Damon mused.

"Sarah says you're a brain." Kate waved at Jonas Harrington as he cruised by them in his patrol car.

"What are you doing?" Hannah hissed, smacking Kate's

hand down. "Don't be nice to that idiot. We should make him drive into a ditch or something."

"Don't you dare," Sarah told her sister sternly. "I mean it, Hannah, you can't use our gifts for revenge. Only for good. Especially now."

"It would be for good," Hannah pointed out. "It would teach that horrible man some manners. Don't look at him. And Damon, stop smiling at him. We don't want him stopping to talk." She made a growling noise of disgust in the back of her throat as the patrol car pulled to the sidewalk ahead of them. "Now see what you've done?" She threw her hands into the air as Harrington got out of his car. A sudden rush of wind took his hat from his head and sent it skittering along the gutter.

"Very funny, Baby Doll," Harrington said. "You just have to show off, don't you? I guess that pretty face of yours just doesn't get you enough attention."

Kate and Sarah both put a restraining hand on Hannah's arm. Sarah stepped slightly between the sheriff and her sister. "Did you get anything out of your prisoner, Jonas?" Her voice was carefully pleasant.

Jonas continued to pin Hannah with his ice cold gaze. "Not much, Sarah, and we still haven't located the other two men you say were at Wilder's house the other night. You might have called me instead of charging in on your own."

Hannah stirred as if she might protest. Damon could see the fine tremor that ran through her body but her sisters edged protectively closer to Hannah and she stilled.

"Yes, next time, Jonas, I'll do that: leave the three men with guns trained on the window, sneaking up on the house, while I go find a phone and call you. Darn, those cell phones just don't seem to work on the coast most of the time, do they?" Sarah smiled right through her sarcasm. "Next time I'll drive out to the bluff and give you a call before I charge in on my own."

Jonas's gaze didn't leave Hannah's face. "You do that, Sarah." He knotted his fists on his hips. "Did any of you consider Sarah might have been killed? Or how I might feel if I found her dead body? Or if I had to go up to your house and tell you she was dead? Because I thought a lot about that last night."

"I thought about it," Damon said. "At least about Sarah being killed on my account." He reached out to settle his fingers possessively around the nape of her neck. "It scared the hell out of me."

Kate and Abbey exchanged looks with Hannah. "I didn't think of that," Kate admitted. "Not once."

"Thanks a lot, Jonas," Sarah said. "Now they're all going to be making me crazy, wanting me to change my profession. I'm a security expert."

"It may beat being a Barbie doll, but I think you went overboard, Sarah," Jonas replied. "A librarian sounds nice to me."

Hannah clenched her teeth but remained silent. The wind rushed through the street, sweeping the sheriff's hat toward a storm drain. It landed in a dark puddle of water and disappeared from sight.

Harrington swore under his breath and stalked back to his car, his shoulders stiff with outrage.

"Hannah," Kate scolded gently, "that wasn't nice."

"I didn't do it," Hannah protested. "*I* would have had the oak tree come down and drive him underground feet first."

Abbey and Kate looked at Sarah. She merely raised her eyebrow. "I believe Irene and Drew are waiting."

Damon burst out laughing. "I can see I'm going to have to watch you all the time." Why did it seem perfectly normal that the Drake sisters could command the wind? Even Harrington treated it as a normal phenomenon.

They stopped in front of Irene's house. Damon could see all the women squaring their shoulders as if going into battle. "Sarah, what do you think you can do for Drew? Surely you can't cure what's wrong with him."

Sadness crept into her eyes. "No, I wish I had that gift. Libby is the only one with a real gift for healing. I've seen her work miracles. But it drains her and we don't like her doing it. There's always a cost, Damon, when you use a gift."

"So you aren't conjuring up spells with toads and dragon livers?" He was half-serious. He could easily picture them on broomsticks, flying across the night sky.

"Well . . ." Abbey drew the word out, looking mischievously from one sister to the other. "We can and do if the situation calls for it. Drakes have been leaving each other recipes and spells for hundreds of years. We prefer to use the power within us, but conjuring is within the rules."

"You never let me," Hannah groused.

"No, and we're not going to either," Sarah said firmly. "Actually, Damon, to answer your question, we hope to assess the situation and maybe buy Drew a little more time. If the quality of his life is really bad, we prefer not to interfere. What would be the point of his lingering in pain? In that case, we'll ease his suffering as best we can and leave everything to nature."

"Does Irene think you can cure him?" Damon asked, suddenly worried. He realized what a terrible responsibility the Drakes had. The townspeople were used to their eccentricities and believed they were miracle workers.

"She wants to believe it. If Libby and my other sisters were here, all of us together might really be of some help, but the most we can do is slow things down to buy him time. We'll find out from Drew what he wants. You'll have to distract Irene for us. Have her go into the kitchen and make us lemonade and her famous cookies. She'll be anxious, Damon, so you'll really have to work at it. We'll need time with Drew."

His gaze narrowed as he studied Sarah's serious face. "What about you and your sisters? Are you going to be ill like you were last time?"

"Only if we work on him," Sarah said. "Then I don't know how you'll get us all home. You'll have to ask Irene to drive us back."

"We should have thought to bring the car," Kate agreed. "Do you think that's a bad omen? Maybe there's nothing we can do."

"Don't go thinking that way, Kate," Abbey reprimanded. "We all love to walk and it's fun to be together. We can do this. If we're lucky we can buy Drew enough time to allow Libby to come home."

"Is Libby coming back?" Damon asked.

"I don't know, Damon," Hannah said, her eyebrow raising, "that's rather up to you, now, isn't it?"

"Why would it be up to me?"

"I thought you said he was one of the smartest men on the planet," Kate teased. "Didn't you design some top-secret defense system?"

Damon glared at the women, at Sarah. "If I did and it was top secret, no one would know, now would they?"

Hannah laughed. "Don't be angry, Damon, Sarah didn't tell us. We share knowledge, sort of like a collective pool. I can't tell you how it works, only that we all have it. She would never give out that kind of information, even to us. It just happens. None of us would say anything, well," she hedged, "except to tease you."

"So why is it up to me whether or not Libby comes home?"

"She'll come home if there's a wedding," Kate pointed out with a grin.

Chapter 11

DAMON LOOKED AROUND him at the four pale faces.
Each of the Drake sisters was lying on a couch or draped over
a chair, exhaustion written into the lines of her face. For a
moment he felt helpless in the midst of their weariness, not
knowing what to do for them. They had sat in Irene's car, not
speaking, with their white faces and trembling bodies. He had
barely managed to help them into the cliff house.

The phone rang, the sound shrill in the complete stillness
of the house. The women didn't move or turn toward the sound
so Damon picked up the receiver. "Yes?"

There was a long pause. "You must be Damon." The voice
was like a caress of velvet. "What's wrong with them? I can
feel them all the way here." The voice didn't say where "here"
was.

"You're a sister?"

"Of course." Impatience now. "Elle. What's wrong with
them?"

"They went to Irene's to see Drew." Damon could hear the
sheer relief in the small sigh on the other end.

"Make them sweet tea. There's a canister in the cupboard
right above the stove, marked MAGIC." Damon carried the

phone with him into the kitchen. "Drop a couple of teaspoons of the powder into the teapot and let the tea steep. That will help. Is the house warm? If not, get it warm: build a fire and use the furnace, whatever it takes. When's the wedding?"

"How soon can you and your sisters get back home?" Damon asked.

"You know I should be angry with you. Not that burner, use the back burner. That's the right canister."

"I don't see what difference a burner makes, but okay and why should you be upset with me?" He didn't even wonder how she knew what he was doing or what burner he was using. He took it as a matter of course.

"Because I'm concentrating on it, the burner I mean. As for being upset, I think you started something we have no control over. I have no intention of finding a man for a long while. I have things to do with my life and a man doesn't come into it, thank you very much. The infuser is in the very bottom drawer to the left of the sink." She spoke as if she could see him going through the drawers looking for the little infuser to put the tea in.

The house shuddered. Stilled. A ripple of alarm went through Damon.

"What was that?" Elle sounded anxious again.

"An earthquake maybe. A minor one. I've got the kettle on, the teapot is ready with the powder, two teaspoons of this stuff? Have you smelled it lately?" Damon was tempted to taste it. "It isn't a dragon's liver, is it?"

Elle laughed. "We save those for Harrington. When he drops by we put it in his coffee."

"I really feel sorry for that man." To his astonishment the teakettle shrilled loudly almost immediately. He poured the water into the little teapot and tossed a tea towel over it for added warmth. "Are you really going to have seven daughters?" he asked curiously, amazed that anyone would even consider it. Amazed that he was talking comfortably to a virtual stranger.

The house shuddered a second time. A branch scraped along an outside wall with an eerie sound. The wind moaned and rattled the windows.

"So the prophecy says," Elle replied with a small sigh of resignation. "Damon, is something else wrong there?"

"No, they're just very tired." Damon poured the tea into four cups and set the cups on a tray. "And the house keeps shaking."

"Hang up and call the sheriff's office," Elle said urgently. "Do it now."

He caught the sudden alarm in her voice and a chill went down his spine. Damn them all for their psychic nonsense. There wasn't really anything wrong, was there?

The dogs roared a vicious challenge. The animals were in the front yard, inside the fence, yet they were hurling their bodies against the front door so hard the wood threatened to splinter. Damon did as Elle commanded and phoned the sheriff's office for help.

No one screamed. Most women might have screamed under the circumstances but none of them did. When he carried the tray into the living room, all four of the Drake sisters were sitting quietly in their chairs. He ignored the two men standing in the middle of the room with guns drawn. Where before, when confronted with guns and violence, he had panicked, this time he remained quite calm.

He knew they were killers. He knew what to expect. And this time, he knew he wouldn't allow them to hurt the Drake sisters. It was very simple to him. It didn't matter to him if he died, he needed the women to survive and live in the world. They were the ones who mattered, all that mattered. The women *would* remain alive.

Damon set the tray on the coffee table and handed each of the sisters a cup of tea before turning to face the two men. He remembered them in vivid detail. The man with the swollen jaw had taken pleasure in torturing him. Damon was glad he had swung his cane hard enough to fracture the jaw.

Damon straightened slowly. These men had murdered for the knowledge Damon carried in his brain. They had crippled him permanently and changed his entire life. Now they stood in Sarah's home, sheer blasphemy on their part. They had entered through the sliding-glass door and had left it open behind them.

Outside, the sea appeared calm, but he could see, in the distance, small frothy waves gathering and rolling with a building boom on the open water. He felt power moving him, a connection with the women through Sarah. Beloved, mysterious Sarah. He waited while the women sipped their tea. Stalling for time, knowing exactly what he would do.

"You two seem to keep turning up," Damon finally greeted. He took two steps to his right, closer to Sarah, turning slightly sideways so she could see the small gun he had taken from the hidden drawer where Elle had said he would find it. "Do you not have homes and families to go to?"

"Shut up, Wilder. You know what we want. This time we have someone you care about. When I put a gun to her head I think you're going to tell me what I want to know."

Damon looked past the man to the rolling sea. The wind was gusting, chopping the surface into white foam. The waves crested higher. The dogs continued roaring with fury and shaking the foundations of the living room door. Damon calmly raked his fingers through his hair, his gaze on a distant point beyond the men. The sisters drank the hot sweet revitalizing tea. And the power moved through Damon stronger than ever. Around each man a strange shadow flitted back and forth. A black circle that seemed to surround first one, then the other. At times the shadow appeared to have a human form. Most of the time it was insubstantial.

"Would you care for a cup of tea?" Sarah asked politely. "We have plenty."

"Do sit down," Kate invited. She shifted position, a subtle movement hardly noticeable, but it put her body slightly between the guns and Hannah.

"This gun is real," the man with the swollen jaw snapped. "This isn't a party." He grinned evilly at his partner. "Although when it's over we might take one or two of the women with us for the road."

Sarah looked bored. "It's very obvious neither of you is the brains in this venture. I can't imagine that the man in jail is, either. Who in the world would hire such comedians to go looking for national secrets? It's almost ludicrous. Are you in trouble with your boss and he's looking to get rid of you?"

"You have a smart mouth, lady; it won't be so hard to shoot you."

"Do have some tea, at least we can be civil," Abbey said sweetly. There was a strange cadence to her voice, a singsong quality that pulled at the listeners, drew them into her suggestions. "If you're going to be with us for some time, we may as well enjoy ourselves with a fine cup of tea first and get to know one another."

The air in the room was fresh, almost perfumed, yet smelled of the sea, crisp and clean and salty. The two men looked confused, blinking rapidly, and exchanged a long bewildered frown. The man with the swollen jaw actually lowered his gun and took a step toward the tray with the little teapot.

Kate stared intently at the locks on the front door, and the knob itself. Sarah never took her eyes from the two men. Waiting. Watching. The huntress. Damon thought of her that way. Listening, he thought he heard music, far out over the sea. Music in the wind. A soft melodious song calling to the elements. All the while the dark shadow edged around the two intruders.

Hannah lifted her arms to the back of the couch, a graceful, elegant motion. The wind rose to a shriek, burst into the room with the force of a freight train. The men staggered under the assault, the wind ripping at their clothing. The bolt on the door turned and the door burst open under the heavy weight of the dogs. The animals leapt inside, teeth bared. Damon blinked as the crouching shadow leapt onto the back of one of the men and remained there.

Sarah was already in motion, diving at the two men, going in low to catch the first man in a scissor kick, rolling to bring him down. He toppled into his partner, knocking him down so that his head slammed against the base of a chair. Sarah caught the gun Damon threw to her.

The man with the swollen jaw rose up, throwing the chair as he drew a second gun. Damon attempted a kick with his one good leg. Sarah fired off three rounds, the bullets driving the man backward and away from Damon. She calmly pressed the hot barrel against the temple of the intruder on the floor. "I suggest you don't move." But she was looking at the man she shot, watching Hannah and Abbey trying to revive him. Watching the dark shadow steal away, dragging with it something heavy. Knowing her sisters could not undo what she had done. Sarah wiped her forehead with her palm and blinked back tears.

Kate collected the guns. Abbey held back the dogs by simply placing her hand in warning on their heads.

"I'm sorry, Sarah," Damon said.

"It was necessary." She felt sick. It didn't matter that he'd intended to kill them all, or that Death had been satisfied. She had taken a life.

The wind moved through the room again, a soft breeze this time, bringing music with it. Touching Sarah. She looked at her sisters and smiled tiredly. "Hannah, the cavalry is coming up the drive. Do let them in and don't do anything you'll regret later."

Hannah rolled her eyes, stomped across the room, landing a frustrated kick to the shins on the man Sarah was holding. "Thanks a lot, I have to see that giant skunk two times in one day. That's more than any lady should have to deal with."

Abigail leaned down, her face level with Sarah's prisoner. "You'd really like to tell me who you're working for, wouldn't you?" Her tone was sweet, hypnotic, compelling. She looked directly into his eyes, holding him captive there. Waiting for the name. Waiting for the truth.

At the doorway, Hannah called out a greeting to Jonas Harrington. "As usual, you're just a bit on the late side. Still haven't quite gotten over that bad habit of being late you set in school. You always did like to make your entrance at least ten minutes after the bell." She had her hand on her hip and she tossed the silky mass of wavy hair tumbling around her shoulders. "It was juvenile then and it's criminal now."

Deliberately he stepped in close to her, crowding her with his much larger body. "Someone should have turned you over their knee a long time ago." The words were too low for anyone else to hear and he was sweeping past her to enter the room. Just for a moment his glittering eyes slashed at her, burned her.

Every woman in the room reacted, eyes glaring at Jonas. Hannah held up her hand in silent admission she'd provoked him. She allowed the rest of the officers into the room before she took the dogs into the bedroom. Damon noticed she didn't return.

All the women were exhausted. Damon wanted everyone else gone. It seemed more important to push more tea into the Drake sisters' hands, to tuck blankets around them, to shield them from prying eyes when they were obviously so vulnerable. He stayed close to Sarah while she was questioned repeatedly. The medical examiner removed the body and the crime scene team went over the room.

Each of the sisters gave a separate report so it seemed an eternity until Damon had the house back in his control. "Thanks, Abbey, I don't know how you managed to get that name, but hopefully they'll be able to stop anyone else from coming after me."

Abbey closed her eyes and laid her head against the backrest of the chair. "It was my pleasure. Will you answer the phone? Tell Elle we're too tired to talk but have her tell the others we're all right."

"The phone isn't ringing." But he was already walking into the kitchen to answer it. Of course it wasn't ringing. Yet. But it would. And it did. And he reassured Elle he wouldn't leave her sisters and all was well in their world.

It seemed hours before he was alone with Sarah. His Sarah. Before he could frame her face in his hands and lower his head to kiss her with every bit of tenderness he had in him. "There was something I saw, a shadow, dark and grim. I felt it had been on me, with me, and now it's gone. That sounds ridiculous, Sarah, but I feel lighter, as if a great burden is off of me. You know what I'm talking about, don't you?"

"Yes." She said it simply.

His gaze moved possessively over her face. "You look so tired. I'd carry you to bed, but we wouldn't make it if I tried."

She managed a small smile. "It would be okay if you dropped me on the floor. I'd just go to sleep."

He helped her through the hall to the stairs. "Hannah has the turret leading to the battlement, doesn't she?"

Sarah was pleased that he knew. "The sea draws her. The wind and rain. It helps her to be there, up high, where she can see it all. I'm glad you understand."

He went up the stairs behind her, ready to break her fall should there be need. Ready to do whatever it took to protect her. "It surprises me that I feel the power in this house, but I do. I'm a scientist. None of this makes sense, what you and your sisters are. Hell, I don't even know how I'd describe you, but I know it's real."

"Stay with me tonight, Damon," Sarah said. "I feel very weary, like I'm stretched thin. When you're with me, I'm not so lost."

"You'd have to throw me out, Sarah," he replied truthfully. "I know I love you and I want you for my wife. I don't ever want us to be apart."

"I feel the same, Damon." Sarah pushed open the door to her bedroom and collapsed on the large four-poster bed. She looked beautiful to him, lying there, waiting for him to stretch out beside her.

Her window faced the sea. Damon could see the water, a deep blue, waves swelling high, collapsing, rushing the shores and receding as it had for so many years. Peace was in his heart and mind. Soft laughter came from various parts of the house. It swept through the air, and filled the house with joy. Sarah was back. Sarah was home. And Damon had come home with her.

Hot August Moon

KATHERINE SUTCLIFFE

Chapter 1

THE FLIGHT FROM Chicago had been a rough one. Turbulence had caused the Boeing 727 to bounce like a dribbled basketball, adding to the headache that had an excruciating grip on Anna Travelli's head. She needed quiet. She needed darkness. She needed a freaking vacation, for God's sake. She sure as hell didn't need this.

The intense August sun blinded Anna as she stepped from the rental car into the New Orleans blanket of dense humidity, and she regretted immediately that she had not checked in to a hotel and changed into something cooler before coming to the Mother of Grace Cemetery.

Security surrounding the funeral appeared to be intense. Uniformed cops blocked the entrance to the cemetery, keeping the hungry reporters at bay, their sharp gazes zeroing in on Anna as she approached. She wasn't surprised. The triple homicide of the assistant district attorney's wife and two children had made the national news. J. D. Damascus, along with Jerry Costos, had reamed the New Orleans criminal element up the backside. They'd made a great many enemies. The NOPD wouldn't take a chance that one of those creeps would use this opportunity, and vulnerability, to make a statement.

Anna removed her shield from her pocket as a pair of cops approached her; she flipped it open and held it up for their inspection. "FBI," she said. "Special Agent Anna Travelli."

The officers exchanged looks, their raised eyebrows and slight smirks giving away their thoughts on the matter.

"Is there a problem?" She pocketed the shield.

Officer Williams shrugged as he gave her the once-over, admiring her long copper-red hair braided down her back. Williams grinned. "Wondered how long it was going to be before you guys got involved in this case."

"Obviously not soon enough." She looked at the younger cop—Jacobson—his thumbs hooked over his gun belt and his hip shifted in a cocky fashion as he continued to appraise her. She was well acquainted with that look. "You got something to say, Jacobson?" She narrowed her eyes.

He shrugged and grinned. "Sure as hell don't look like FBI. Not with those legs."

She continued to stare at him, saying nothing, not so much as blinking, until color touched his cheeks and he averted his eyes.

As they moved aside, Anna continued on her way, each step exacerbating the pain in her temples, her annoyance at the cops' attitude quickly forgotten as she ducked her head against the unbearable sun and made her way toward the distant mourners. Hundreds of them. Friends. Family. Business associates.

Her gaze shifted from the mourners to the surrounding graves—cement and granite tombs, ancient and new, clustered close enough together one could barely move between them. City of the Dead. Damn creepy.

Although the cops had cordoned off the cemetery for the Damascus funeral, her gaze still shifted along the tombs, searching. It was an established fact that killers would often attend their victims' funerals. The files she had pored over in the last twenty-four hours, since getting the call from headquarters, attested to the fact that the animal who had been slaughtering New Orleans hookers was a power freak. Got his rocks off on domination. Enjoyed inflicting terror in his victims even more than he enjoyed the actual killing. That kind of sicko would take supreme pleasure in watching the tragic aftermath of his heinous murders unfold.

But therein was the perplexity. Laura Damascus and her two children didn't fit the profile of the killer's previous victims.

As Anna eased her way through the crowd, she recalled the conversation she had had with her superior, Dr. Jeff Montgomery. The phone call had come no more than two hours after she had tied up a particularly harrowing and disturbing case—a pair of sexual serial killers who had preyed on thirty-four victims in the Chicago area. Before that there had been a case in Seattle; before that, D.C. She was balancing dangerously on a tightrope of complete exhaustion, if not total burnout, and the *last* thing she needed was to be so quickly reassigned to New Orleans—especially after learning that she was well acquainted with the latest victims.

How the hell could she remain emotionally uninvolved when she had shared pizza and beer with Laura and J. D. Damascus? When she had attended Laura's baby shower and witnessed J.D.'s pleasure on the birth of his son, William?

Not only that. Now she would be forced to come face-to-face with the one and only man with whom she had ever been in love. The son of a bitch who had broken her heart. Jerry Costos, District Attorney. C.B. Chauvinistic Bastard. Had her future been left up to him she would have spent the remainder of her life barefoot and pregnant.

As she stepped to the edge of the mourners, her heart sank and the emotion that she had forced back during the last many hours began to surface. The last six years she had invested in becoming one of the FBI's leading female agents and profilers had honed her ability to shelve personal involvement. Working shoulder to shoulder with the machismo attitude that women were too fragile to handle the gruesome and dangerous circumstances of murder had toughened her into a person she hardly recognized any longer, and too often didn't like. But for such a sacrifice, she had become damn good at her job. One of the best and most respected.

But this. Dear God, this was something else.

Three coffins were placed side by side and draped in blankets of roses and lilies. A mother's coffin. Her son's. Her daughter's. As the priest's voice rose into the humid, flower-fragrant air, the family formed a semicircle around the caskets, faces blanched in shock and despair.

Flanked by his mother and brother, J. D. Damascus wept into his hands, sobs shaking his body. The mourners gasped and cried out as Damascus dropped to his knees, his cries rising to a heartbreaking wail.

Then *he* was there, as Anna knew he would be. Jerry Costos, Damascus's best friend, gently moving Helen Damascus aside and falling to one knee beside J.D., sliding one arm around his shoulders to comfort and support him.

Anna thought she had prepared herself—had erected her infamous steel wall of emotional detachment around her heart in preparation for seeing Costos again. But the moment he raised his tear-streaked face and looked into her eyes, she realized just how wrong she had been.

CALLING ON THE deceased's family so soon after a tragedy was one of the toughest aspects of being an agent. Damn hard to remain composed in the face of someone's grief, yet every minute the investigation was postponed the colder the clues became.

After the funeral many of the mourners congregated at J.D.'s house, a pretty, renovated home in the Garden District. Hundreds of flower arrangements lent a sickly sweet aroma to the rooms. The kitchen and dining room overflowed with food, which the visitors dug into like vultures on carrion. Anna could never figure out what it was about death that made people so damn hungry.

After half an hour of milling through the guests, Anna finally worked up the backbone to approach J.D. She found him secluded in the den with his mother, Helen, and sister-in-law, Beverly Damascus, wife of Eric, Senator Jack Strong's legislative director. It was Beverly who approached her, her eyes swollen and smudged by mascara.

"Agent Travelli, FBI." Anna flipped open her shield. "I'd appreciate a minute of J.D.'s time, if that's okay."

"No, it's not okay. The last thing J.D. needs right now is—"

"Anna?" J.D. left the sofa and moved toward her. "Anna Travelli?"

Anna moved around Beverly to smile at Damascus. "Hey, pal. Long time no see."

"Jesus, it is you." He wrapped his arms around her, holding Anna so fiercely she could hardly breathe. She hugged him as tightly, closing her eyes as she felt the shudders of grief ripple through his chest.

"God, I'm so sorry, J.D. So damn sorry. My heart is breaking for you."

He said nothing, just held her, his fingers twisting into her suit jacket for support. They had once been friends. Very good friends. The only person she could turn to when her relationship with Costos had begun to sour.

At last he pulled away, swiped the tears from his cheeks, and did his best to smile. "To say I'm surprised to see you here is an understatement."

Anna glanced at Helen and Beverly Damascus, both women obviously concerned over her intrusion. "Could I speak with you alone?" she asked J.D.

Only then did his gaze slip down to the shield in her hand. A spasm of pain crossed his features, yet he nodded and glanced at his family, who reluctantly left the room, closing the door behind them.

As J.D. moved to the liquor cabinet, Anna pocketed her shield. "I've been assigned to the case. I know what a difficult time this is for you, J.D.—"

"But you gotta do what you gotta do." He partially filled up the highball glass with vodka—no ice. "I'll make it easy for you. Tyron Johnson killed my family."

She frowned and joined him at the cabinet, watched as he kicked back the vodka like it was water. It didn't take a rocket scientist to figure out that her old friend was accustomed to the drink. A light boozer would have been knocked flat on his ass.

"Who is Tyron Johnson?"

"Local pimp. Pretty boy who controls the hookers in the area. Enjoys beating them up when they cross him." He refilled the glass. "I've dragged his sorry butt into court many times trying to put him away. Always bullied the girls into refusing to testify. The last time he threatened me in front of witnesses."

He turned away and drank again, easily emptying the glass. "Now I'm going to kill the bastard. I'm going to blow off his fucking head."

The door opened, allowing muted conversation to float through the room.

"What the hell are you doing here?"

Anna braced herself. This meeting had been inevitable, of course. But turning to look once again into the eyes of her former fiancé was as difficult as staring into the barrel of a loaded Glock.

Jerry Costos slammed the door. As he moved across the room, Anna drew back her shoulders and turned to face him. Perhaps it was spite that made her withdraw her shield and thrust it toward him.

In the six years since she had left her hometown, and Costos, he had changed little. He'd always had the uncanny ability to cut out a person's heart with his blue eyes, as well as melt a heart. Obviously, he was now more in his slicing and dicing mode.

"Put that damn thing away," he snapped. "I know what the hell you are."

"Then you also know why I'm here."

"When I called the FBI requesting a profiler, I sure as hell didn't think they'd send you."

"Life's a bitch, ain't it?" She pocketed the shield. "The agency felt I'd be an asset since I grew up here. So if you got a problem working with me on this case, take it up with them, Costos."

"Maybe I'll just do that."

"Fine. I could use a vacation. But until they pull me, I'm here whether you like it or not."

J.D. dropped onto the sofa; he stared at the ceiling. "If you two want to open old scars, take it outside."

"Right." Jerry caught her arm. Anna pulled it back, but moved to the patio door while Costos followed on her heels.

The back garden of Damascus's home was lush with blooming flowers, their color somewhat bleached by the intense sunlight. A cobblestone path meandered to an area shadowed by giant oak trees. There, erected beneath the gnarled old limbs, stood a swing set and sandbox wherein sat a little pink pail and shovel and a soccer ball.

Anna leaned against the tree trunk and dug into her purse, extracting her cigarettes. As she looked at the swing set, a sudden breeze moved the swing forward and back, as if the child's spirit remained.

Costos remained silent as she lit her cigarette. She was well acquainted with that silence. The intensity of it could thicken the air.

She glanced at him. "So how is he holding up?"

Costos briefly closed his eyes, ran one hand through his dark hair. "His heart has been ripped out of him. Christ." He sighed. "Frankly I don't know how he's held it together as well as he has."

"So what's your theory on this Tyron Johnson?"

"The guy's a son of a bitch. A two-bit pimp who occasionally beats up his girls if they cross him. He has an alibi for the time of the Damascus murders."

"Reliable?"

"Marcus DiAngelo. Owns the Lucky Lady Casino. Could be mob connected, but so far we've been unable to prove it. J.D. brought him up on charges of racketeering last year, but the bastard beat it."

"Jury tampering?"

"More like judge tampering, I think. His Honor enjoys the tables and is known to lose. I wouldn't be surprised if he was into the Lady for a lot of money."

Jerry reached for her cigarette, took a deep drag from it as he focused on the swing set. Anna turned her face away, the memories of the years they had spent together causing her head to throb harder. She was having second thoughts again about taking on this case. Certainly not too late to back off. Call headquarters and suggest they put another profiler on it.

Jerry crushed the cigarette out against the tree trunk, then tossed the butt into the sand pail. "For the record: I'm not happy that we're going to be working together on this case."

"Ditto."

"I'm not happy to see you at all."

"Live with it, Mr. Prosecutor. Or maybe your problem isn't simply working with me. Maybe it's working with a woman, period. Seems I recall you felt a woman's place was in the kitchen—"

"That's bull, Anna, and you know it."

Anna crossed her arms over her chest and focused on the house. "Doesn't matter any longer. I didn't come back to New Orleans to kick open that old kettle of rotten fish. I'm here to help you find a serial killer who may or may not have murdered Damascus's family. So do we meet with Captain Killroy now, or later?"

He stared at her, the heat of his gaze burning the side of her face. "I'll call Killroy and set up a meeting for the morning."

"I'll want to see the crime scene photographs and the coroner's report first. Then I want an up-close and personal look at the crime scenes themselves. About J.D.—"

"I'll fill you in tomorrow. Just leave him alone for now."

"Fine. I'm staying at the St. Louis."

"Fine. I'll pick you up—"

"Got a car, but thanks anyway."

He stared at her a moment longer, then turned on his heels and walked toward the house.

Releasing her breath, Anna sank back against the tree, and closed her eyes.

HE IS HUNGRY again.

The streets are quiet here. The hookers are scarce. And rightly so.

That pleases him. Very much.

The scent of fear lingers in the air as he moves along the dark wharf and gazes out at the river. Moonlight glitters on the swirls and ripples of the moving brown water and casts halos over the scattered warehouses lining the docks. The fog moves in—gray, hazy fingers creeping up the alleys like specters, little by little obliterating the stars.

A perfect night to feed.

A woman moves out of the shadows and stands in a pool of light from an overhead vapor lamp. She smiles, tosses back her scraggly bleached hair, and licks her overly painted lips.

"Hello, handsome. Looking for a little companionship?"

He pauses, cocks his head to one side, and appraises her face. She isn't pretty. Not anymore. The life has grooved deep creases in her forehead. He would do her a favor by killing her. Put her out of her filthy misery.

"Not interested," he says, and keeps moving. Not his type. He likes them young and more vulnerable.

Onward. Prowling the old sidewalks, in and out of the shadows along St. Peter Street, right on Pauline. Jazz drifts to him from Bourbon Street, the boisterous frivolity of drunks, women's high-pitched shrieks, and laughter.

Ahead. Blond. Petite. Young.

She is nervous. He likes that.

He watches as she shifts from foot to foot, glances over one shoulder, then another. Her hair is long and silky and cascades over her back. She doesn't want to be here. But she has no choice. Perhaps she is fresh to the life. Ah, that would be nice. So much easier to frighten the new ones.

He moves up behind her, so silent she hasn't noticed.

"Hello," he says.

She turns, drawing in a sharp breath. Her eyes are wide and her red lips parted. Blue eyes made green by the yellow lamplight. Blue eyes are his favorite. They turn dark as a deep ocean when they are dying.

She backs away slightly and swallows. "You scared the bejesus outta me, mister."

"Sorry."

He leans against the street sign. One Way. Oh, yeah. One way for her tonight. Isn't she lucky?

"Working?" he asks.

"I ain't out here for my health."

Smiling. "Warm night."

She pushes back a tendril of pale hair stuck to her cheek by sweat.

"Could use a cigarette. Have you got one on you?" he asks.

Looking him up and down. "Sure."

Her hands are shaking slightly as she digs in her purse, extracting a crumpled pack of Virginia Slims. She offers him one, then takes one for herself. Her hands are trembling too badly to handle the lighter, so he takes it from her and lights the cigarette for her.

"Uptight, huh?" He smiles again. "Don't blame you. Young, pretty lady like you isn't safe out here. Not after what's happened recently."

She nods and smokes.

"How many of you has he killed now?"

"Four. Not counting that mother and her kids."

"Nasty business."

"Ah, yeah." She chokes out a tight laugh. "I'd say cutting off our heads is pretty fuckin' nasty."

"He eviscerates them as well."

Frowning. "If that's a pretty way of saying he slices them open, then yeah."

"Did you know them?"

"Sorta. Haven't been around here long."

"Where you from?"

"Dallas."

"What brought you to New Orleans?"

"Needed a clean break."

"Mama and daddy back there?"

Nodding. Smoking. She looks up and down the dark street, then checks her watch.

"Have you spoken with them recently?"

"Last night."

"That's good. That's very good. Pretty young girls from Dallas should keep in close contact with their family."

"My mama's birthday's tomorrow."

Smiling. "Did you buy her something pretty?"

"Said all she wanted was for me to come home."

"Then why don't you?"

She shrugs and tosses down her cigarette. "Don't have the money."

He reaches out and touches her hair. So very soft and pretty. Closer now, he can smell her perfume. Something floral. Like jasmine. "Tell you what, pretty little girl. I've got five hundred dollars in my wallet. If you're real nice to me, I'll give it to you. But on one condition."

She stares at him and he realizes with a heat of pleasure that she is even younger than he first thought. Sixteen, seventeen, maybe.

"One condition," he repeats. "You buy yourself a bus ticket and go home to see your mama on her birthday. Will you do that?"

"You're jokin' me, right?"

"No joke."

"What's the catch?" Her eyes narrow. "You into kinky or what?"

"Let's just say I feel like doing you a favor tonight."

She finally smiles. "Sure. Whatever you want."

"Promise?"

She nods and turns away, moving toward the dark alley.

He follows closely. Her smile is bright and excited as she glances at him over her shoulder.

"What you carryin' around in that backpack anyhow?" she asks.

"Oh, this and that. Tools of my trade, so to speak."

They move into a dark courtyard, then to her apartment door. She fumbles with her keys, and he gently takes them from her and unlocks the door, stepping aside to allow her to enter first.

She giggles. "Now ain't you just the gentleman?"

As he closes the door and locks it, she moves toward the bed, kicking off her shoes, unbuttoning her blouse. "So what's it gonna be? Gotta be good, right? for five hundred bucks."

As the backpack slides from his shoulders, he drops into a chair. "Remove your clothes and dance for me."

"You want music?"

"No." He smiles.

Slowly she peels away her clothes, her hips swaying, her long blond hair feathering over her upthrust nipples. He hums to himself and unzips the side pouch on the backpack. His blood is beginning to thrum, turning warm. Flesh flushing with anticipation. The arousal is there, awakening. Sweet, hot pressure that will only mount as the night progresses. With each delicate prick of his knife. With each whimper and pitiful plea for her life.

"Very nice," he whispers, and her smile grows. "Now get on the bed—on your hands and knees."

"You like it doggie fashion?"

"Um-hm."

As she turns her back to him and moves to the bed, he slips his hand into the pouch and withdraws the ice pick, cups it behind his fingers as he moves toward her.

"Are you ready?" he asks softly.

"Whenever you are," she says.

Chapter 2

ANNA WAS FBI through and through, the highest-ranked female agent to come out of Quantico in the history of the force.

The first three years that she worked in the Criminal Investigation Division, she solved several high-profile cases, including the apprehension of three of the FBI's Most Wanted
serial killers. No doubt, she had a reputation for taking risks
that went above and beyond the call of duty. Her "loose can-
non" techniques too often warranted disciplinary actions from
her superiors, but there wasn't a one of them who didn't be-
grudgingly respect her tactics.

No, Anna didn't always play by the rules.

Anna had known Dr. Jeff Montgomery for three years,
since the afternoon she'd arrived in his office buried in the
bowels of the Behavioral Science Unit at Quantico. Not only,
he informed her, did the agency require her full, patriotic cooperation in joining the Behavioral Science Unit, but she was
to become only the second agent to be recruited into the Classified Parapsychology Investigations Division of the BSU.

They'd knocked heads more times than she could count.
First, over her refusing to acknowledge that her insights into
killers' psyches were due to anything more than her training

and the criminal psychology degree she had attained from Tulane. She hadn't wanted to acknowledge her so-called gift. She didn't care to be looked at like some kind of sideshow freak.

She'd learned soon enough that she had little choice in the matter.

Anna had despised Dr. Jeff Montgomery in the beginning. Resented him for forcing her to embrace her talent, to forge it into something solid, keen, and shining. Ultimately, however, their relationship had become one of grudging respect—at least on her part. He, on the other hand, had fallen in love.

Oh, he hadn't admitted as much to her—not the I'm in love with you kind of admission. Not that overt. Simply the I love ya, kid, kind of thing that passes between good friends. He wouldn't dare admit the depth of his true feelings for her. That sort of thing was frowned upon in the FBI and got in the way of business.

Not that he hadn't put the hits on her early in their work relationship. Not blatantly, of course. He wasn't the type. But he had certainly dropped enough hints that he would be interested in putting in a little overtime with her if she was game. Which, she'd pointed out, she wasn't. Business and love were far too complicated as it was without getting mired in that kind of quicksand. Not that she wasn't attracted to Montgomery. Who the hell wouldn't be? The man could pass as Harrison Ford's twin brother and more than once she had found her mind drifting toward such possibilities. But no way. She had already been down that road—loving a man whose devotion to career had made her a second priority. She wasn't about to relive that sort of heartbreak and disappointment.

However, there was no mistaking the bond that had formed between them. Could hardly avoid it, working together as they did. When he'd called to inform her that she had been assigned to the French Quarter serial case there had been a long moment of tense silence.

Jeff was well aware of her past in New Orleans. Knew she'd never completely gotten over Jerry Costos, and perhaps never would. So she hadn't been at all surprised to find a message waiting for her at the St. Louis when she checked in. CALL ME ASAP, it had read.

She hadn't.

She'd showered and ordered up room service, then fell into

a deep exhausted sleep until the phone had awakened her at just after midnight.

"What's up, Travelli? Fill me in."

There hadn't been much to tell him. Wouldn't be until she met with Costos tomorrow morning.

Lying in the dark, staring at the ceiling with the receiver pressed to her ear, Anna listened to the silence that followed the mention of Costos's name.

Finally, Jeff said, "So tell me this Costos jerk is now a hundred pounds overweight and married with a passel of snot-nosed kids."

She grinned. "Couldn't tell you. Didn't really pay him that much attention."

Right. Sure. Like she was going to admit that Jerry Costos was even better looking today than he was six years ago. Like she was going to admit that she had made a point of looking for a wedding ring on his finger, experiencing a tickle of relief that there wasn't one. Which was absurd and annoyed the heck out of her. If she hadn't vaulted away all her old feelings for Costos she wouldn't have agreed to come to New Orleans. She sure as hell wasn't into masochism.

"You're lying, Anna."

She sighed. "Look, Jeff, we spent all of ten minutes together. He wasn't happy to see me in the least and pulled no punches in telling me so. So if you think working with him is going to be a vacation on Fantasy Island you're wrong. He's as alpha male as he always was. Testosterone shooting out his ears and I DOMINATE branded on his forehead."

"So did you hurt when you saw him?"

Jeff, why are you doing this to yourself? she wanted to ask. "I felt . . . annoyed."

"So you're telling me you felt nothing. No spark?"

"When a red-eyed, fire-breathing bull confronts you, the only spark you're going to feel is the need to castrate him. Which is something someone should have done long ago as a service to all twenty-first-century females."

He laughed. "Okay. Call me tomorrow and fill me in on the case. And remember, I've got your back. Love ya, kid."

"You, too, Montgomery. And thanks."

She hung up the phone. It rang immediately.

"Anna."

Speak of the alpha devil. The unexpected, deep tone of Costos's voice jarred her. Confused her, sending her tumbling back through a time machine of memories she had tried to forget.

"What's up?" she asked.

"There's been another murder. A young prostitute."

She sat up in bed and turned on the lamp. "Same signature?"

Silence.

"Hey, are you okay, Costos?"

"Bad. Real bad. Decapitation and evisceration. Christ, I think I'm gonna puke."

"You're at the scene now?"

"Yeah. Waiting for the crime scene techs and the M.E." He paused. "You'll meet with Captain Killroy and the detectives who're working this case in my office tomorrow morning at ten thirty."

"And the detectives are . . . ? Do I know them?"

"Donovan and Armstrong."

"Michael Donovan? You're joking, right? When did he get transferred to the Eighth Division?"

"Two years ago. After his wife died."

"Donovan and I haven't exactly hit it off in the past, Jerry. You know how he feels about the FBI being brought in on his cases. Is he going to make this difficult for me?"

"I've spoken to him at length. He's cool, Anna. He wants this guy caught, bottom line."

"Right." She sighed.

"Good night, Anna."

"G'night," she said; then, "Jerry?"

"Yes?"

"I don't think it's necessary to have the newspapers in on the fact that I'm here."

"Don't worry," he said. "We'll keep your identity close to my office."

"Thank you." Her eyes drifting closed, Anna listened to the following silence on the phone. Drawing in a deep breath, she replied, "See you in the morning, Jerry."

Anna hung up the phone, stared at it a long moment, as if willing it to ring again . . . as it had years ago, Jerry calling her back immediately saying something sappily romantic like,

"Had to hear your voice again. Love me, Anna? Promise?"

She left the bed, wandered to the bathroom, and splashed her face with cool water. She made herself some chamomile tea from the hot pot the hotel provided. Sitting back on the bed, Anna held the warm cup in her palms.

Where the hell had her head been to have returned to New Orleans? She should have planted her butt in BSU where the agency profilers normally worked on their cases. Then again, she didn't work her cases like most of the agency profilers. Because she wasn't like the other profilers.

She was quite certain she hadn't been born with the gift—if one could be so ignorant as to call it that. It had begun after the tragic accident that had taken her mother's life and left Anna near death—a head-on collision. A semi truck driven by a man who had fallen asleep behind the wheel. She had been twelve at the time, and the sudden flashes that would come at her with no warning throughout her adolescence had been shrugged off by physicians and psychologists as PTS, post-traumatic stress syndrome.

By the time she was eighteen, they had tapered off. Or perhaps she had learned how to block them. They had come winging at her again for a short while after her father had been killed in the line of duty. Carl Travelli, detective for the New Orleans PD Homicide Division, had walked into an ambush that had taken him down in a hail of bullets.

Perhaps she hadn't even realized herself just how the gift had come to affect her life until she been a field agent for the FBI for a year. Her ability to process the crime scene and investigation had brought her to the attention of her superiors. Rising in the ranks had been an easy punt.

She had never spoken of her sight to anyone on the force. Wouldn't dare. Then the call had come from the BSU and she had found herself transferred to the Behavioral Science Unit despite her protests. She wasn't a fact cruncher. No sitting behind a desk for hour upon hour poring over stat printouts and case files. She lived for the streets, the adrenaline punch of the search and confrontation with the perp, just like her father.

But she had learned soon enough that the agency's plans for her were not the norm. Far from it. She had found herself buried into a division that was classified even from the existing BSU.

For six months before joining the Behavioral Science team she had worked with the classified division to better develop her psychic capabilities—but only with the understanding that she would be allowed to work her cases like any other field agent. Up close and personal. She really had no choice. The flashes of images that would come to her were not premonitions of upcoming helter-skelter, but the shocking visions of the crime as it happened—but to accomplish that it was necessary for her to place herself at the crime scene.

She was still pretty damn green. Often questioned the images that would come blazing at her from nowhere—not just images, but energy. Fear. Anger. Confusion. Yet, little by little, she was becoming more confident with each case. Trusting her judgment. Capable of discerning the difference between the gut instincts and training of a top-notch agent and those insights that were born from her special talents.

But what might have become a blessing to the agency had become an increasing burden to her. Too often that meant reliving the victim's horrible death. More emotionally debilitating, and frightening, were the too frequent forays into the killer's psyche. Often she experienced the crime through the killer's eyes while at the crime scene or with the victim . . . if the victim survived, which wasn't often.

Emotional and physical burnout was tapping her on the shoulder. Why else would she continue to lie here in her lumpy hotel bed after getting Jerry's call? The sooner she could get onto the crime scene the more quickly she could utilize her so-called gift to tap into the negative energy that remained following such an act of violence.

God, she was kidding herself. It wasn't exhaustion that kept her sheltered in her hotel room at the St. Louis. It was facing Jerry again. Her confrontation with him that afternoon had been far more unnerving than she had anticipated. Looking into his eyes again had slammed her like a fist.

Six years and he still had a grip on her heart, and it hurt like hell. All the weeks, months, even years of second-guessing her decision to walk away had rushed over her like an avalanche the instant she looked into his eyes.

At twenty-six her dreams—indeed her entire life—had

shone golden as the Holy Grail before her. Children hadn't been part of the scenario. Marriage to a brilliant, kick-ass attorney and a career as an agent for the FBI had been the dream. But Costos hadn't seen it that way. Marriage, a home with a white picket fence, and a yard full of pink-cheeked babies had been his ideal of happily ever after. He simply couldn't handle her career as a field agent for the FBI.

But at thirty-two, she felt her biological clock beginning to tick. No time for romance. Marriage. Or children. At some point in the last year she had begun to question her choices in life. While she felt fulfilled by her accomplishments with the agency, she wasn't fulfilled emotionally. There was an emptiness inside her that grew more hollow with each passing month. While standing in Jerry's presence it had yawned like an abyss beneath her.

Anna put aside the cup of tepid tea and phoned the desk for a wake-up call, then slid under the covers. She wouldn't let herself think about the vulnerability she had heard in his voice. . . . She couldn't.

ANNA HAD ALWAYS been obsessively punctual. Some things just never changed.

Jerry checked his watch. Ten twenty-five. Standing at his office window, he watched Anna leave her car and make her way up the sidewalk. All business. Navy blue suit, skirt short enough to show off her incredible long legs, her mass of red hair slicked back from her face and wound in a knot at her nape as if the severe hairstyle would somehow diminish the fact that she was beautiful enough to stop traffic.

Right. Some things never changed.

He turned from the window and moved toward the coffeepot. His head hurt like hell. What little sleep he had managed after leaving the Bobbie Cox crime scene had left him feeling hungover. His mood was sore and, judging by the muted conversations and the hooded looks of the detectives with their heads together, things were only going to get worse. They weren't particularly happy that he'd called in a profiler. Though Anna's presence here was strictly in an advisory role, the department would see it as a blatant slap from the district attorney's office—as if he didn't trust their abilities to tie up the case.

As he reached for his coffee cup, a spasm of pain flashed through him. Not just pain. Fresh fury. The cup had been given to him last Christmas. A gift from J.D.'s son, Billy. His godson's smiling face decorated the cup with the scrawled words I LOVE YOU, UNCLE JERRY!

"So you wanna fill us in a little on this profiler, Costos?"

The question had come from Detective Second Grade Donovan—fifteen years on the force. Donovan was a no-bullcrap officer with the looks of a movie star and an up-yours attitude that too often made Jerry grind his teeth in frustration. Donovan was the finest detective in New Orleans, bar none, and Jerry fully understood his irritation over the D.A.'s office getting the FBI involved, even if it was only in an advisory role.

Jerry filled his cup with coffee. "What do you want to know, Donovan? A profiler is a profiler is a profiler."

"Like what the hell is this guy doing coming here? Don't they usually tackle this kind of thing at Quantico?"

Jerry glanced at Killroy, captain of the city's Eighth District, who sat nearby, also not happy over the FBI's involvement, but, like the D.A.'s office, his strings were being yanked hard by the political pressure of Governor Damascus. Since the murder of the governor's daughter-in-law and grandchildren, the case had taken on a nationwide focus. His interest wasn't due to any familial heartbreak—the cold son of a bitch didn't give a damn about his family, had disowned J.D. when he married Laura, whom he considered the ruination of J.D.'s future political career. Governor Damascus was more concerned over the impact the serial murders would have on the city's reputation and tourist business. Since all the murders had taken place in the French Quarter, the city's financial heart, tourists would think twice about prowling the streets after dark. Over the last seventy-two hours the D.A.'s office, as well as Killroy, had felt the gnash of the governor's teeth to solve the case pronto, and it hadn't been pretty.

Costos moved to the open office door and glanced down the hall toward the elevator before turning back to Donovan. "I couldn't tell you why they're sending in this particular agent."

Detective Armstrong, sitting beside Donovan, gave an amused grunt and smirked. "Wonder if he'll bring along his tarot cards and crystal ball."

"What's that supposed to mean?" Jerry asked.

"C'mon, Costos. We all know these guys come to the table with little to nothin'. They look at evidence and proffer an opinion which is generally a bunch of bunk. Nothin' more than what we can provide."

He couldn't argue the fact, but with the governor breathing down his neck, he'd had little choice in the matter. But if he'd known the BSU Special Division was going to send Anna, he might have given it a second thought. Just how the hell was he going to work with her, considering their past, and considering the flood of old feelings he'd felt for her the day before?

He heard the elevator door open. Molly, his receptionist, said, "Ms. Travelli? They're waiting for you. Go right in."

Jerry moved behind his desk.

Anna appeared at the door. All business. Her gaze briefly touching his before moving to the others, who stared at her in apparent shock that the profiler was female—not just any female . . . but Anna Travelli. She had butted heads with Killroy and Donovan in the past, during her stint in the New Orleans Field Office.

"Gentlemen," she said in that slightly husky tone that made Jerry's stomach clench. "Hope I haven't kept you waiting."

Jerry cleared his throat. "Not at all. You're right on time. As usual."

Her gaze flashed back to his, and for a brief moment the shared memories of their past collided between them like two freight trains.

Jerry moved around the desk. "Anna, I believe you know Captain Killroy and Detective Donovan. This is Donovan's partner, Detective Armstrong."

The men stood, their shock over seeing Anna more than obvious on their faces. Costos was well aware of their thoughts. Not only were they forced to deal with an FBI profiler butting in on their business, but a woman profiler—and one whose pretty face had been blasted over television screens from one end of the country to the other: *Forensic Files, The New Detectives, Dateline.*

Anna shook their hands in turn, her thin smile an indication of her opinion of their thoughts. Jerry knew that smile. It was enough to make the hair stand up on the back of his neck.

She moved to the conference table at the far side of his

office. "Time to get down to work, gentlemen. I assume you've brought all the necessary files."

The detectives looked at one another, then at Jerry. Donovan grunted and shook his head. Killroy mumbled something foul, and Armstrong smirked and made a crude motion with his hand that made Jerry contemplate putting his fist into the man's teeth.

As the men trailed to the conference table where Anna had taken a chair, Jerry said, "Can I get you some coffee, Anna? A Danish?"

"No Danish, thank you. But the coffee would be nice."

She then turned to Donovan. Their gazes locked and the tension in the room turned thick. Donovan was a damn good cop—one of the best—but he had a hump on as big as New Orleans over the FBI's intrusion into his cases. Not that he treated her with disrespect—he wasn't the type, unlike Armstrong, who apparently had a hard-on for her breasts. Donovan was likable. With the kind of good looks that were enough to stop traffic: dark hair and vibrant blue eyes; six foot two inches with bone structure that made a woman weak at the knees. But he was all cop. Machismo out the ears. He lived and breathed for his job and women were an afterthought.

"I'd like to see the case file on last night's homicide . . . " she prompted him.

He stared at her a moment longer before clearing his throat and responding. "The victim's name: Bobbie Cox." He handed the manila folder into her waiting hand. "Young girl. New to the warehouse district. We're still waiting on the M.E.'s autopsy report. Should be here at any time."

"Did anyone try to reach this girl's family?"

Killroy had placed himself diagonal to her at the opposite end of the table. "We're working on it now."

"Who identified the body?" She flipped open the folder.

"A friend, Susie Lynch, found her and called 911," Donovan responded.

Anna scanned Donovan's report of what he saw when he arrived at the crime scene. "You've indicated that the crime scene boys came up with nothing. The place was clean of fingerprints other than those of the victim." Anna looked to Donovan. "Is it still an isolated crime scene?"

"Of course." His tone indicated his annoyance over her asking about the obvious.

"And you collected the bedding—sheets, pillowcases, blankets, coverlets—not just on the Cox scene, but the other murders as well? They could contain a strand of body hair, dead skin, saliva, or semen from the perpetrator."

"You're not questioning my abilities to do my job, are you, Agent Travelli?" Donovan's resentment at being questioned about his job was obvious by his sharpness of tone.

"C'mon, Donovan. You know we wouldn't question you or your investigation." Jerry placed a foam cup of coffee in front of Anna. As she looked up, into his eyes, he said, "One sugar. No milk, right?"

She looked away. "Gentlemen, the only reason I ask is, without evidence from the other prostitutes' murder scenes, we won't be able to make forensics match to tell if it's the same killer."

As Jerry made himself comfortable at the opposite end of the conference table, Anna asked, "Do we have the other files related to these cases?"

"I've got them all here," Killroy said. "The four prostitutes and . . . the Damascus family." He pushed the four folders in a stack down the table, then, as though not wanting to give it up, passed the Damascus file.

Anna pulled her chair in, began perusing the first file. "I assume you gentlemen have cross-referenced this information through the Violent Criminal Investigation Program at the agency?"

"Right, we've sent all information to VICAP," Donovan replied. "Nothing back yet."

Killroy got on the phone, calling his second whip to find out the status on the Cox family's notification of their daughter's death, and Donovan discussed with Armstrong what their next move would probably be with the case.

Relaxing in the chair and tugging his tie loose at the knot, Jerry watched Anna closely as she perused the crime scene photos of the slaughtered victims. If she experienced any squeamishness over the gory, disturbing mess, she didn't show it. Then again, she'd always had the bullheaded fortitude of a brick wall.

Six years. Still the dedicated Anna. Focused. Uncompromising in her ideals. Had she missed him in the beginning as he had missed her? Had she suffered? Regretted walking away from their relationship?

If they had it to do over, would he give in on those ideals if it meant keeping her? Would she?

Anna stood and removed her jacket, spread it across the back of the chair. She wore a shoulder holster over a crisp white blouse that fit close around her throat. Returning to the chair, she proceeded to read all four of the detectives' observations, the crime scene unit's notes, and the M.E.'s report—aside from the M.E.'s autopsy report on Bobbie Cox, which had not arrived yet—then looked over the pictures again. Rubbed her temple, her brow furrowing in contemplation. Then she reached more hesitantly for the Damascus file. Her hands brushed over the folder, her gaze lifting to his.

"You sure you want to do this?" he asked.

She nodded and looked back at the folder. He knew her thoughts. It was one thing dealing with the murders of strangers. It was another when such a tragedy came at you up close and personal . . . and two of the victims were children.

Anna took a deep breath, then opened the offending file. Her eyes briefly closed. One trembling hand lifted to smooth back an errant strand of copper-colored hair that had fallen over her brow. Her face suddenly looked as pale as the folder under her fingers.

Jerry's first instinct was to reach for her, take her hand, as he once had. But the officers sitting at the table needed no reminders that they were being forced to work on this case with a female who, on the surface, looked as fragile as fine crystal. And neither did she.

Get it together, baby, he thought. *Come on, Anna.*

Anna reached for her hot coffee, took a cautious sip, then set it aside and cleared her throat. "Okay. J.D. seems to believe that we have two killers. That his family's murderer was a copycat. An act of revenge. Opinions?"

"We don't agree," Jerry replied.

She nodded but didn't look at him. "Why? The Damascus murders don't reflect the identical signature of the unknown subject who killed the prostitutes. According to the reports you two wrote"—she indicated Detectives Donovan and Armstrong each with a nod—"all the prostitutes were murdered in

their apartments, bodies found in their beds. Laura—Mrs. Damascus—was found in Woldenburg Park, near the river, and
the children . . . in the backseat of the vehicle belonging to
Mrs. Damascus. And Laura obviously wasn't a prostitute.

"According to the M.E.'s report, Laura died from a punc-
ture wound to her heart—an ice pick, perhaps—while the
hookers died from a prolonged loss of blood before the actual
mutilations. This guy was into torture. However, Laura's was
quick—"

Donovan interrupted. "They were in the fuckin' park, Travelli. He hardly had the time to spare for a drawn-out torture—"

"Why was she in the park at midnight?"

"How the hell are we supposed to know that? Why don't
you look in your crystal ball and ask her?"

Anna shut the file and sank back in her chair, looked from
one detective to the other. Her fingers drummed the chair arm
and the color that had blanched from her face crawled up her
slender throat.

"Our UNSUB," she finally said, referring to the unknown
subject of the investigation, "is what we term a 'domineering
killer,' gentlemen. He gets his thrills from inspiring fear in his
victim. It gives him a feeling of control and power that he
otherwise is lacking in his life. According to the M.E.'s report,
our freak doesn't have sex with his victims. That doesn't mean
he isn't experiencing orgasmic fulfillment. His arousal comes
due to his slavelike control of the hooker. As noted here, he
binds her arms and legs to the bed so she is totally helpless.
No doubt he toys with her. Teases her. Explains in detail to
her exactly what he intends to do to her in order to heighten
her horror. He probably masturbates during the torture. Uses
a condom to avoid leaving semen that could be used to DNA
him.

"He may or may not have had sex with these prostitutes in
the past. He may choose them at random, but I doubt it. There
is something about her that intrigues him. The girls are very
young. Not hardened as badly by the life. Makes sense. This
younger individual will be more intimidated by his threats. The
greater her fear, the greater his pleasure.

"Our UNSUB is highly organized, obviously, as evidenced
by his meticulous care at the crime scene. At the risk of offending you gentlemen"—she glanced around at each of the

somber detectives—"I suggest you send the items you collected from the crime scene to Quantico. Often they're able to pick up evidence that the locals boys don't."

They stared at her, making no comment.

Jerry cleared his throat. "We'll do that immediately, of course."

She flashed him a look, then reached for her purse. "Hope you guys don't mind if I smoke?" She smiled. "If I'm going to be forced to deal with your obvious belligerence over my presence you can deal with my cigarettes."

Again, no comment.

She lit a cigarette and stared at the wall. Jerry could almost hear her mind working, not so much over the case but how she intended to deal with the testosterone swimming in the air and the detectives' increasingly abused egos. Killroy's acne-pocked face was slowly turning purple. Donovan was beginning to simmer, and Armstrong's thoughts appeared to be more focused on Anna's breasts than on what she was saying.

She glanced down at the Damascus file and the confidence on her face appeared to slip. "There's something about this one that isn't sitting right with me. It's all off. Everything. The location of the murder in a public place . . ."

Anna opened the Damascus file again. She nodded. Smoked. Reached for her coffee, but didn't drink it. "According to the M.E.'s report there were apparent signs of struggle. Defensive bruises on her arms, along her rib cage. Cuts on her hands as if she attempted to fend off the knife. This is a total contradiction to the other cases. So what—aside from the decapitation and evisceration, same as the previous victims—would indicate that this was anything except a copycat?" Anna raised one eyebrow and looked from one officer to the other. "Anyone?"

Armstrong sat forward as he withdrew a notebook from his suit pocket. He tossed it on the table. "I've got my opinions, if anybody wants to hear them."

Donovan groaned. "Shit, don't start with that crap again."

"What crap?" Jerry asked.

"You don't want to go there." Donovan glared at his partner.

"Let him talk." Anna sat back in her chair. "What are your thoughts, Armstrong?"

Full of self-importance, the young detective glanced away from Anna and toward Jerry. "I say J.D. killed 'em—his family, I mean."

Silence.

Jerry's face began to burn, as did Anna's. Donovan slumped in his chair and Killroy reached for a piece of gum in his shirt pocket.

Armstrong cleared his throat as he, more reluctantly, flipped open the notebook. "Hey, just because the guy is an A.D.A. doesn't mean he's incapable of losing it. He's as human as the rest of us. Right?"

Jerry turned his gaze on Donovan. "I'm not believing this."

"Sorry," he said.

"It's a well-known fact that J.D.'s marriage was on the rocks. Big time. There were a few very public arguments between them." Armstrong glanced from face to face. "Hey, if Damascus was any Joe Blow off the streets he'd be your number one suspect."

"But he's not Joe Blow. Far from it." Jerry reached for his coffee, the image of J.D.'s son smiling at him from the cup. "Granted, he and Laura had their problems. But no way in hell would he have harmed those kids. They were his world, Armstrong. The only thing that kept him going. Besides . . . sorry to further trash your case hypothesis, but J.D. was in Shreveport."

"Not at the time of the killing." Armstrong swallowed and fingered the notebook. "He arrived back in New Orleans via Delta Airlines at two A.M. The M.E.'s report says Laura was killed sometime between midnight and four A.M."

"I'm not believing this," Jerry repeated.

Armstrong shrugged. "Fine. But he matches your profile. Right?" He glared at Anna. "Right? Besides, who better to copycat the French Quarter Killer than someone who is close enough to the investigation to know the precise particulars regarding the actual murders?"

A knock at the door interrupted them. Molly peered in, holding a file in her hand. "Medical examiner's report is here. The Bobbie Cox file."

Anna extended her hand. "I'll take that."

Molly glanced at Jerry. He nodded, once again feeling the dart of annoyance from the detectives' eyes.

Anna flipped open the file; bypassing the autopsy photos, she read the report, then crushed out her cigarette. "Gentlemen, you may, or may not, have a break here."

Donovan reached for the folder. Killroy jumped from his chair, as did Armstrong. As they hovered over Donovan, he slammed his fist on the table. "Sonofabitch. Evidence of intercourse and a collection of seminal fluid."

Armstrong grinned. "This has gotta help us, right?"

"Not necessarily." Anna crossed her arms over her breasts as she rested back in her chair and waited for their full attention. Slowly, their gazes came back to hers. "She's a hooker. It's realistic to think that she was with another john before the killer got to her."

"And maybe not. Maybe he just liked this particular piece of ass," Killroy said, causing Armstrong to chuckle. Donovan flashed the younger detective a look that shouted his annoyance.

Jerry cleared his throat and checked his first instinct to punch out Killroy's lights. Then he told himself that if Anna expected anything else from these men she was in the wrong business. Besides, Anna Travelli could give as good as she got, and then some.

"There are obvious differences between the Bobbie Cox and Damascus cases," she said. "Aside from the evidence of intercourse as reported in Bobbie's M.E.'s exam, the signature of our killer is identical to the previous killings. He bound her wrists and ankles to the bed with thin wire, tortured and mutilated, decapitated, and left her body as is."

She turned to Jerry, one eyebrow raised and her lips curved in a smile that raised every cautionary instinct in him. "If we're to discount the idea that the Damascus murders were perpetrated by a copycat, then I must assume you haven't allowed the media in on all the particulars of these cases."

Jerry looked away, drummed one knuckle on the table as he glanced at the detectives.

"Wonderful." Anna shook her head. "So you've got a snitch leaking information to reporters. So we may very well be looking at a copycat."

He reached for his coffee, his gaze still locked with hers as he drank, inwardly cringing over the cold, bitter brew and the sharp assessment in her green eyes.

Her smile flattened. "Right. 'Nuff said. So who was the idiot who leaked classified information to the press?" She turned her attention to Armstrong.

He frowned. "Why the hell are you lookin' at me?"

"Because you look like the kind of idiot who would do such a thing."

His mouth dropped open and his face flushed.

"So what, exactly, did your snitch leak to the press about the killings?"

Donovan's mouth flattened and his face became hard as stone. "Obviously the decapitation, evisceration, and the binding of the hands and feet—which were obvious to the witnesses who discovered the victims. The UNSUB cut out their hearts and placed it in the cavity of what was left of their uteruses. Among less gruesome tactics, this information was not made public knowledge . . . until Carla Simpson, the hooker who was killed before Laura. At that time, somehow, this information was leaked to the press."

"For a price, I assume." Anna shook her head and looked Donovan straight in his blue eyes. "Find out who's recently bought himself a BMW and you'll find your snitch."

She flipped through the reports again. "You're going to continue to grill Tyron Johnson, right? As well as this Marcus DiAngelo character. What else have you got on Johnson?"

Jerry leaned back in his chair. "High school dropout. Dumb as a box of rocks. He's mean as a snake, but his girls stand by their belief that he's not a killer."

"Could be they're scared of him—of retaliation."

"I suspect those girls would spill their guts if they thought he was butchering his own," Killroy said.

"Maybe." Anna shoved back her chair and stood. "I need time to go over these files. Alone. Do you gentlemen have a problem with that?"

Jerry stood and moved around the table. "I have an office you can use."

She collected the files and tucked them under her arm, didn't so much as give the glaring detectives a second glance as she moved to the door. Jerry caught up to her in the hallway, took hold of her arm, and turned her to face him.

"Attitude isn't going to win you any friends around here, Anna."

"I'm not here to make friends, Jerry. I'm here to do a job. But as long as you want to bring up attitude, I can certainly do without yours."

"What's that supposed to mean?"

"The hump you've got on for me, that's what. Get over it, Jerry. I have."

She turned away. He grabbed her arm again.

"Hey, I had no intention of digging up our past—no point—not here—but since you have, let's get something straight, Anna. You got over it damn easy because you were the one who walked away. Not me. I think my so-called hump is pretty damn justified."

Anna looked down at the grip he had on her arm, then back into his eyes. "It's history," she said, her voice tight with emotion. "We've both got on with our lives—"

"Maybe you have. You weren't the one who was practically abandoned at the altar."

"If my future had been left up to you I'd have six kids hanging off my arms and legs and another one in the oven."

His mouth flattened. "People change, Anna."

"Do they? Then why did I get a gut feeling that you were getting some kind of perverse pleasure over those guys' behavior toward me?"

"What did you expect, that they would appreciate the fact that you questioned their abilities to rightly judge this case and the evidence?"

"If you didn't question it yourself you would never have contacted the agency for help. Right or wrong? Or maybe it goes beyond that. Maybe you didn't want the agency involved at all. Maybe you're getting pressure from above. Governor Damascus breathing down your neck, Jerry?" She glared at him, then nodded. "Figured as much. No doubt he's playing the grieving grandfather, right? Might win him a few sympathy votes in the next election. From my understanding, he's going to need them. The bastard is going down in Louisiana's record books as one of the most unpopular governors in the state's history . . . and that's saying a lot.

"I know exactly where Charles Damascus is coming from. He can't have this sordid publicity hurting the tourist business so he's leaning on you to clean it up, and fast. So you go through the motions. Call Quantico, but not for anything more than an advisory. If you really gave a damn about solving this case in an expedient manner, you would have handed it over to the agency completely. But that wouldn't get you and the force the accolades you want when—if—you catch this creep. And Charles Damascus couldn't use that success in his reelection campaign."

Jerry stared down into her eyes. "If you were a man, I'd belt you."

"If I were a man, Costos, those detectives in that room might have actually listened to me."

She slapped the files against his chest. "I've seen everything I need to see here for the moment. Now I want to go to the Bobbie Cox crime scene."

"Fine," he said through his teeth. "I'll speak to Donovan and the captain. They'll need to come along."

"You do that," Anna said more softly.

Chapter 3

~~~~~~~

JERRY INSISTED THAT he ride to the crime scene with Anna. She didn't like it. Aside from the fact that she needed time alone to prepare herself for what was to come, his close proximity rattled her. She suspected he had more on his mind than her handling of the investigation.

He had removed his suit coat and tie, rolled his shirtsleeves up his forearms, and slumped comfortably into the car seat. For the first five minutes of their bumper-to-bumper crawl through the French Quarter, he'd said nothing, just stared out the passenger window, fingers drumming on his thigh—a certain indication that he was formulating exactly what he intended to say to her.

"Hot summer," he finally said.

Anna hit the blinkers and made a right on Pauline.

"The hottest summer in fifty years." He searched the sidewalks of perspiring tourists.

Anna's fingers tightened on the steering wheel.

Finally, he looked at her—silent for a long moment. "So how are you, Anna?"

She nodded. "Great. And you?"

"I'll be better once we solve this case."

"Have you spoken with J.D. today?"

"I talked to Beverly. He had a rough night. Spent most of it at the cemetery." He raked one hand through his dark hair. "Christ, those kids were his world, Anna. He's blaming himself for this."

She frowned. "Why?"

"He was supposed to have come home the day before the murders, but didn't. She wanted a divorce. He was into avoidance."

"The marriage was never good, Jerry. We both know that. I'm surprised it lasted as long as it did."

"He loved his kids. I loved his kids. You know how I feel about kids."

She glanced at him, into his eyes that were blue and searching. "I know." She smiled. "I expected you to be married by now with kids of your own. What happened?"

"I keep looking for another Anna Travelli, I guess." He grinned. "Only one who wants kids."

"I never said I didn't want kids. I just didn't want them so soon. I had a right to my own dreams. It was your own problem with those dreams that screwed it all up."

He looked away again, out the car window, his hand clenching into a fist. "I had no problem with that. I simply didn't want my wife wearing a shield and possibly staring down the barrel of some nut's .357. So hang me, why don't you? What the hell kind of husband wouldn't worry over burying his wife?"

There it was. The same old problem. Funny, however, that hearing it now from his lips, she had a hard time dredging up all the old arguments. How could she? Over the last six years she'd attended five funerals for agents killed in the line of duty. Good husbands and fathers who had left grieving wives and children behind.

Laying his head back against the seat, Jerry closed his eyes. "Maybe I was wrong. I probably was. Maybe if I had it all to do over, I'd do it differently. All I can say, Anna, is I've missed you like hell. Once I got over my desperate need to choke you for walking out on me." He grinned. "So, have you missed me? Have you pined away for me these last years? Are you in love with someone? If you are, I don't want to know about it. I think it would break my heart."

The gentle confession roused the old, recognizable heat in Anna's heart. A flame that had never burned more hotly for any man since Jerry Costos. And probably never would.

"There isn't anyone," she heard herself admit, knowing even as she did so that she was opening the door to something she wasn't certain she could handle, or wanted to.

Ahead, the crime scene had been taped off and barricades erected, blocking the street from pass-through traffic. Reporters and curious bystanders hovered along the verges like vultures drawn to the scent of death. Uniformed cops kept a sharp eye out for anyone whose ghoulish curiosity might impel them to slip under the tape and intrude on the scene.

Anna parked the car next to the curb, glanced into the rearview mirror to see Detectives Donovan and Armstrong park behind her.

Jerry reached for her hand, his own closing warmly around hers. "Are you saying that I have a chance with you, Anna?"

Her gaze went back to his as she tugged her hand away. "I came here to do a job, Jerry."

"Is that a nice way of saying go to hell, Costos?"

She opened the car door.

"Fine," he said. "I get the picture."

As she stepped out on the street, the unbearable heat and humidity bore down on her, and the sun's reflection from the old brick pavement momentarily blinded her. Donovan and Armstrong joined her, the younger detective popping gum between his teeth and Donovan mopping the sweat from his brow with a handkerchief.

"So what exactly is this BSU Special Division?" Armstrong asked, his gaze slowly moving down her, then up again to her breasts.

"Specialized agents capable of dealing with machismo assholes," she said. "And if you continue to stare at my breasts, Armstrong, you're going to find out exactly how we deal with the situation."

She gave him a flat smile, then turned and walked away, dipped under the crime tape, and moved onto the sidewalk while Jerry joined Donovan and Armstrong and followed.

"I don't get her," Donovan said. "This isn't normal profiler stuff. They usually do their thing at Quantico. What the hell is she doing coming to New Orleans anyway?"

"What difference does it make," Jerry snapped, "whether you talk to her on the phone or face-to-face?"

"I don't know what the hell she expects to find on-site. She acts like my CSI don't know their asses from a hole in the ground. They got their photographs and evidence, and then some. What more does she need?"

"Suck it up and shut up, why don't you? Let the lady do her job."

Anna moved along the sidewalk, her gaze sweeping the area. A stretch of warehouses formed a barrier to the south, the river beyond a wide brown stretch where flatbed barges crept. She paused by the One Way street sign near the curb.

The visions always began with a flash. This one came at her so unexpectedly she felt as if someone had blindsided her.

"Anna?" Jerry touched her arm. "Are you okay?"

Anna briefly closed her eyes. Come and gone. Too fast to grasp. She gave Jerry a reassuring smile and nodded. "Okay. Just the heat, I think."

"You're white as a sheet."

She rubbed her temple and squinted as the sun bore down on her. The traffic noise pounded at her head, as did the conversations of the cops surrounding her. Whatever insight had winged at her had been obliterated. No doubt about it, however. The crime that had taken place the night before had begun here. ONE WAY spotted before her eyes like the afterburn of a camera flash.

Followed by Jerry, Donovan, and Armstrong, Anna moved down the alleyway, into the shadows, high weathered brick walls towering on either side of her, carefully sidestepping the overflow of trash from a Dumpster, ignoring the cops who paused to watch her, their conversations a distant murmur as she did her best to focus. Jerry had his hand on her arm. Distracting. Too distracting. She pulled away.

Bobbie Cox's apartment was little more than a hole in the wall. An efficiency. One room and small bath to one side. Blood stained the tattered mattress, the walls, and much of the floor. Evidence of the CSI's search showed in the print powder they had used on the furniture and walls.

The stench of blood took her breath away. She fought back her gut reaction to gag as she moved to the middle of the room and turned slowly, focusing her attention on the bed.

"Just what the hell is she doing?" came Donovan's voice.

"She's FBI, man." Armstrong laughed. "What difference does it make?"

"Knock it off," Jerry said.

"Ooo, touchy." Armstrong elbowed Donovan. "Kinda tender over Ms. Travelli, isn't he?"

Jerry moved up beside her, regarded her sternly. "What the hell are you doing?"

She flashed him a look. "My job."

He cleared his throat. "You looked at the files. I hardly think that you're going to find anything more here than you did in the reports."

"I work better up close and personal, Jerry."

"The smell of blood must trigger her bloodhound instincts." Armstrong grinned at Donovan. "Maybe if I dab a bit behind my cars she'll come sniffing at me."

Anna narrowed her eyes at Armstrong. "Not in this or a hundred lifetimes, pal."

Nothing. Absolutely nothing. Too many distractions. She was drawing a blank and the longer she stood there in the unbearable heat the queasier she became as the foul odor of blood crawled up her nostrils.

"This is futile. I can't concentrate." She pulled Jerry aside. "We come back later. Tonight. Just the two of us. No interference. Okay?"

"What difference is it going to make?"

"Trust me on this one, Jerry. I need my space."

He frowned and shoved his hands into his trouser pockets. "Killroy won't be happy."

"Killroy answers to you—right or wrong?"

"Damn it, Anna. I've got the entire department pissed at me for bringing you in on this. Now you're trying to strong-arm the case detectives out of the process?"

"Hardly. Hey, if you want me to walk away, I'll walk away. Otherwise, I have the freedom to do what I've got to do the way that I do it."

He sighed. "Fine."

ANNA SPENT THE next long hours at the police department memorizing the Cox reports and photographs, comparing them to the Damascus murders. Donovan brought Tyron Johnson in for questioning—grilled him out the ying-yang but the sleazy pimp never backed off his story about being with Marcus DiAngelo on the night of the Damascus murders. He had alibis as well for the times of the other murders and went so far as to demand a lie detector test. But when pushed for the names of the girls' regular johns, he shut up tight as a clam, declaring his clients were above reproach. He didn't hand over his girls to just anyone and pointed out that most of his girls' clients were pickups anyway. Tourists out to experience the heights of good old New Orleans debauchery along with the bars on Bourbon Street. Then, of course, there were the Tulane students with a pocketful of Daddy's money to burn. Nameless johns came and went.

Right. That very fact was what made this kind of case the most difficult. And why the perp was harvesting the heads of the lost women walking the streets at night. They were easy prey. Most had broken ties with their family. Friends were scarce. Few, if any, would miss them when they were gone.

Anna arrived back at her hotel room at just before ten P.M. Jerry would pick her up at eleven thirty. She showered. The hot water did little to wash away the stink of blood that had permeated her skin and hair.

As Anna pulled on her jeans and T-shirt, tied the laces on her Nikes, then pulled her hair back in a ponytail, she thought about her upcoming meeting with Costos. He'd been more than vocal about his resistance to this midnight jaunt to the crime scene. Drilled her repeatedly about the necessity of it.

She couldn't tell him about the Parapsychology Division, of course. It was as hush-hush in the FBI as the CIA's Grill Flame, the most secretive operation of the Stargate program. Even during their four-year relationship, she had never mentioned her occasional flashes of insight. Perhaps because she hadn't understood them herself. Or wanted to.

What now?

Jerry knew her better than anyone had in her life. He hadn't become the most successful D.A. in New Orleans in the last fifty years for nothing. He had a way of mentally processing a crime, and the criminal mind, that made defense attorneys and their clients quake in their shoes. Within his first four years as district attorney he had become a legend. Any criminal with a fiber of intelligence knew if he was arrested in Orleans Parish he was going down for the maximum count Jerry could wring out of the judge and jury.

He already suspected that her assignment to the French Quarter Killer was not the norm. He'd noted immediately her mind and body's response to the flash that had assaulted her that afternoon on the Pauline Street sidewalk.

Anna reached for her shoulder holster and gun, checked the Glock—loaded and ready—secured it in the holster, then reached for the jacket she had tossed over the back of a chair.

She needed time—just a few minutes on her own—to prepare herself. Not just for the physical and emotional blows that would come from the crime scene, but from Jerry. She couldn't allow what they had once shared—still shared—to get in the way of the investigation. It would, of course. She was certain of it.

Reaching for the phone, she called the desk. The operator responded with a bored, sleepy, "How can I help you, Ms. Travelli?"

"I'd like to leave a message at the desk for Jerry Costos: Meet me at Pauline."

HE REMEMBERS HER, of course. Anna Travelli. Hard to forget her kind. Their paths had crossed many times during her tumultuous love affair with Costos.

He has followed her career with interest, catching her interviews on Forensic Files, The New Detectives, *and, most recently, on* Dateline. *Profilers are big news these days. Especially one of her caliber. Doesn't hurt that she has a nice ass and spectacular tits.*

If he had the time, he might hang around awhile, toy with her a bit. Might be fun to bring her down a peg. Add to the pleasure of humiliating the NOPD and Jerry Costos. What sport. Had he known slaughtering women would make him feel so gloriously wonderful—indeed powerful—he might have done it long ago.

Too bad about the children, of course. Killing them had been an unpleasant necessity, and a very sad occurrence, considering everything. Actually felt a pang of conscience over it. But what the hell. He'd get over it.

Besides, the killing of Laura and her children has succeeded in stimulating the sense of panic in the city. He can feel it, the fear, dancing upon the tips of his nerve endings. It tingles through him in tiny bursts of electricity. Makes him feel buoyant. Enthused. Confident. Oh, yeah. Confident is good. Control is the key. Power the ultimate aphrodisiac.

He watches as Anna drives from the St. Louis. Alone. No Costos. Her plans have obviously changed. Perhaps Costos is meeting her at the crime scene instead of her hotel. Good. Very good. This will give him some time alone with the lady— at least in his thoughts. Time to imagine what he could do to her, should he so desire. What a shame to bury her head in the bayou. Much too beautiful to waste. Might even change up his M.O. again—as he did with Laura and the kids—and leave her head as a souvenir for Costos. Position it on the D.A.'s car, a bug-eyed, mouth-frozen-in-a-soundless-scream hood ornament for his Silver Mercedes SL.

He chuckles and cruises, keeping a safe distance from the rental car. Not that she would notice, of course. She is too preoccupied with her speculations about the crimes, and about her old lover, reminiscing with thoughts of how he fucked her and licked her and made her beautiful body writhe beneath his. She has no doubt creamed her panties already.

Wouldn't it be fun to watch them go at it? More fun to slaughter them during the act. Imagine what the headlines across the country would do with that one.

She pulls the rental car to the curb, parks it beneath a streetlight, bumper to bumper with the cruiser wherein a cop is smoking and drinking coffee to keep him awake. The cop exits the cruiser and meets Travelli on the street, nodding as she flashes him her FBI shield; then she moves to the sidewalk and stands next to the One Way street sign as the cop returns to the car and continues to smoke.

Might be fun to creep up behind the cop and slide the ice pick into the prick's throat.

Ah, yes. He is hungry again.

Chapter 4

THE HOT AUGUST night bore down on her, the humidity
and heat causing sweat to bead on her body and run down her
sides beneath her clothes. The dread looming greater in her
mind didn't help.

Moving close to the One Way sign, Anna glanced over her
shoulder, toward the cruiser where the cop continued to smoke
and look out at her. The overhead flickering vapor light made
his face appear oddly blurred.

The silence and emptiness, and the yellow crime scene tape,
gave the area a surreal feel, as did the advancing rumble of
the freight train crawling its way along the tracks next to the
river.

Turning, slowly, she allowed her gaze to move toward the
north intersection of Royal and Pauline as she stepped back
against the street sign and prepared herself.

She closed her eyes. Took a deep breath. Told herself to
relax. Empty her mind. Breathe, breathe. Focus.

She sank harder against the signpost, felt its hard form press
along her spine, cool even through her jacket and T-shirt.

It began then, the heat. Spread at first like warm sparks of
electricity along her spine.

Breathe evenly. Relax. Her instructors at Quantico had
drilled into her head that she must not fight the flashes. Must
not brace herself in preparation for their onslaught. Easier said
than done when the flashes were not only too often horrifying,
but painful as well.

"Hello," he says.

*She turns, drawing in a sharp breath. Her eyes are wide
and her red lips parted.*

A groan worked up Anna's throat. She pressed her fingertips to her temple, the heat at her back growing more intense,
uncomfortably so.

*Blue eyes made green by the yellow lamplight. Blue eyes
are his favorite. They turn dark as a deep ocean when they
are dying. He leans against the street sign. One Way. Oh,
yeah. One way for her tonight. Isn't she lucky?*

Too hot. Too hot. The flesh of her back was burning. The
flashes of sound and images came and went so fast she
couldn't hold them.

Concentrate on Bobbie Cox. Get in her head. Into her eyes.
What is she seeing?

*She nods and turns away, moving toward the dark alley.
He follows closely. Her smile is bright and excited as she
glances at him over her shoulder.*

Anna moved through the dark, down the narrow alleyway
between two buildings. The heat pulsated around her. She
reached out, feeling the jagged ridges of the old bricks scrape
her fingertips. The stench of garbage and damp mildew was
overwhelming, yet there was something else—

*Closer now, he can smell her perfume. Something floral.
Like jasmine. One Way. Oh, yeah. One way for her tonight.
Isn't she lucky?*

A pressure on her. Biting into her shoulders. Weight. Something on his back.

A sound.

The image in her head suddenly gone, Anna blinked as her
eyes adjusted to the night shadows. The sweet aroma of Bobbie's perfume vanished, replaced by the stink of the alley, rank
of old age and neglect. Something had intruded. A sound.
What was it?

She turned and looked toward the street—a rectangular
tunnel-like image where the cruiser sat beneath the vapor light.

The cop was no longer smoking. His head rested back against the seat, as if sleeping.

Deep breath. Easier now. The flashes were coming easier. So damn close. What had disturbed her?

Focus on Bobbie. Get in her head. Imperative. Best to see through the victim's eyes. Tough. Always tough until the end when the victim's energy exploded to the forefront with horror.

She stands at the apartment door. Keys in her hand. She feels elated as she hums to herself, Happy Birthday to you ... Surprise, Mama, I'm home! Maybe she won't come back to New Orleans. Maybe this time she'll get her act together—go to business school like Mama wants. Hate the life. What had she been thinking? Nuts and perverts. But this guy isn't so bad. Good looking, clean, compassionate. Five hundred bucks! Happy Birthday to you ...

Hands reach for the keys—nice hands, well manicured. She tips back her head and looks into his eyes—

The image blurred. Hold on hold on—

Focus!

The vision pulsed, bright and dim, melting like some macabre watercolor picture left out in the rain. Bobbie's voice in her head crackled like radio static, one station bleeding over into another, the intrusion shattering the sound and vision so the killer's eyes disappeared into a pinpoint of light that was obliterated by darkness.

Suddenly there were hands on her—hard hands—gripping her shoulders from behind.

Anna's heart thundered as her body tensed. In one motion, she slid her hand under her jacket and withdrew the gun, angled one way with a swift shift that drove one elbow back into the body near hers with enough impact that there came a grunt as she was released.

Spinning, throwing herself back against the apartment door, Anna lifted the gun and leveled it between Jerry's eyes.

"Shit." He stumbled back, gripping his ribs, his dark eyes wide. "It's me. Jesus, don't shoot. It's me, Anna."

Anna released her breath and sank against the door, slowly lowered the gun. "For God's sake, what are you doing coming up behind me like that?"

"What are you, deaf? I called your name three times." He

straightened. Winced. "What the hell are you doing here?"

Anna replaced the gun in its holster, her hands trembling. "What do you expect coming up like that in the dark?"

"I told you. I called you. Christ, it was as if you were on another planet. What the hell were you humming 'Happy Birthday' for?"

"Was I?" She took a deep breath and released it. "Are you okay?"

"I'll live." He moved up beside her. "Since when did the FBI encourage stupidity?"

She frowned. "Meaning?"

"You know as well as I do that agents never go out on their own—at least not in this kind of situation. That's asking for trouble."

He was right, of course, so she wasn't about to argue.

"I needed some time, Jerry. On my own, okay? Besides, I've got backup."

"I had to wake up your backup. Lotta good he was going to do you."

Jerry scratched his head as he regarded her. "So you wanna tell me why you found it necessary to come out here alone?"

"No."

"Same old Anna. As immovable as a brick wall." He fingered aside a stray hair on her cheek, tucked it behind her ear. "Brings back memories. The two of us standing in the dark outside your apartment door and me wondering what would happen if I kissed you."

"The tough-ass D.A. Jerry Costos afraid to kiss a woman?" She grinned. "Hard to believe."

"I wasn't a D.A. then."

"You are now."

"So how about it? Just a kiss for old times' sake?"

Lowering her gaze, Anna did her best to ignore the fluttering of emotion around her heart. "Hardly seems like the time or place."

He slid one hand around her nape, thumbed up her chin so she was forced to look into his eyes. "There never was a good time for us, was there, Anna? Both too damn caught up in our own careers and too narrowly focused on our own ideals to give an inch."

He pressed his lips to her temple—a warm sigh escaping

him. "Okay, I was unfair. I screwed up. Maybe I didn't realize just how much until now."

Anna backed away. Odd that she didn't want to. Time and space should have eradicated the effect his touch had on her, and her need to give in to them. She tried her best to fight the familiar feelings of attraction . . . and desire . . . for Jerry. They had been good together—sexually. And, for a while, emotionally. Even now, in this horrible place that inspired fear and disgust—even with the lingering images of a victim and her killer still burning like acid behind her eyelids—she experienced a rush of old and unwanted emotions that turned her body warm, closing off her throat.

How easy it would be to give in to them. Open her mouth under his. Relish the feel of his hands on her body—so pleasuring, gentle, and hungry.

"Anna." Jerry reached for her, fingers tenderly closing around her arm and pulling her close. "You haven't a clue how I felt when I arrived at the hotel to discover you were out here alone. Jesus. I might be a D.A., but I'm a man first. Don't judge or crucify me because I give a damn that you could be out here in trouble. Christ, I've lived the last years kicking myself up the ass that I drove you away. Every time word came down that an agent had been wounded or killed in the line of duty, I felt gut-punched with fear that it had been you."

Anna turned her face away, refusing to allow Jerry to see the emotions in her eyes.

He tucked his finger under her chin and lifted her face. "I wanted like hell to get over you. I thought I had until I came face-to-face with you at J.D.'s place. I'd tried damn hard the last years to hate you for breaking my heart. And one look into your eyes blew that all to hell."

"Don't," she pleaded. "Jerry, it's over."

"I don't think so. I know you too well, Anna." He pulled her against him, hard, those eyes that could cut through a perp's heart and soul like a cleaver now centered on hers—smoldering and yearning, making her knees weak despite the war of refusal that was going on in her heart.

"Don't," she repeated throatily, to no avail. His mouth slanted over hers with a purpose that drove her head back, kindling that hot rush of desire that had haunted her memory the last six years—awake, asleep, even in the arms of the few men with whom she had become briefly involved.

His tongue raked the inside of her mouth, flirted with her tongue, drawing a groan from her that made the heat of the night intensify until sweat beaded on her body—hot pinpricks of pain that slid across her skin, making her shiver, making her tremble until, despite her denial, she lifted her arms around his neck and kissed him back. Body pressed against body, her heart pounding against his chest, the erection in his pants like hard burning lead against her loins. Another time, another place they would have fallen to the ground and made shameless love under the watching hot August moon.

Oh, God, she was tempted. So tempted. His hand cupping her breast under her T-shirt, fingers sliding over her aroused nipples until they ached and strained so badly the pleasurable pain made her yearn to cry out.

No. No. She had a job to do. Already his closeness was playing havoc with that. She'd worked too damn hard, for too long, to allow these impossibilities to screw up her priorities, not to mention her life.

Turning her face away from his kiss, her lips still moist and swollen, she shoved him away, backed against the old wrought-iron railing flanking the steps up to Bobbie Cox's apartment, and covered her mouth with the back of one hand.

"If you ever really gave a damn about my feelings," she said, "you won't do this. You won't make me feel this way. You won't mess with my priorities, number one of which right now is to help you find a killer. Please, Jerry. I've worked too damn hard all these years to become what I am. Don't fuck it up for me."

A look of frustration and anger flashed across his face—a familiar look that slammed her back to those years ago. He simply wasn't capable of seeing her as anything other than a female whose priorities should be sex, marriage, and children first, and to hell with a career.

Jerry glared at her a moment longer, his face lit by moonlight and grooved by shadows. His breathing sounded hard as he clenched his teeth and removed the apartment key from his pocket.

Hands reach for the keys—nice hands, well manicured.

Anna blinked, the unexpected stab of light and image sharp

and blinding. She stumbled back, her hand flying to her eyes that, suddenly, felt as hot as burning coals.

"Hey." Jerry reached for her. "You okay?"

She took a deep breath and forced herself to relax, and nodded as she looked into Jerry's eyes. Yet, it was there still. Flashes of shadowy images—tickles of nervousness and anticipation.

Nuts and perverts. But this guy isn't so bad. Good looking, clean, compassionate.

"Anna?" Jerry reached for her, his hands gripping her arms as he searched her face. Only, for a moment, it wasn't *his* hands that were gripping her—and for a moment she felt that she was no longer Anna Travelli, but Bobbie Cox—the grip on her arms crushing and painful, the eyes staring into hers like black holes leading straight to hell.

The whoop of the cruiser's siren shattered the silence and wrenched Anna out of the momentary horrifying hell. The sound of running footsteps echoed down the alley.

"Mr. Costos!" The cop who had been sleeping in the cruiser appeared through the darkness. "We got a signal thirty-four and possible forty-two. Aggravated battery with a weapon. Hooker assaulted!"

RED AND BLUE lights flashed from the cruisers positioned on the narrow side street. By the time Anna and Jerry arrived, a crowd had begun to form and the wail of the advancing EMT unit reverberated throughout the area.

The victim lay behind a Dumpster amid a scattering of broken glass and garbage. A uniformed cop, his hands already protected by latex gloves, squatted beside her while four others proceeded to cordon off the area, securing the crime scene.

A young woman stood in the shadows, flanked by two officers. Hooker, by the looks of her. Bleached hair and short skirt, skimpy top, stiletto heels. The flashing red and blue cruiser lights reflected from her tear-streaked face as she hugged herself and sobbed uncontrollably.

"I heard her screaming. She was screaming, like, horribly. 'Help me!' I was there—down there—" She pointed to the distant street corner. "I ran down here and saw him—on her. You know what I'm saying? Raping her, right there in that garbage."

"Did you get a good look at him?" an officer asked. "Can you describe him?"

"I screamed at him. You know? Screamed at him to stop it."

"Can you describe him, ma'am?"

Anna stepped around the sobbing woman, struggling to put on her latex gloves, and moved up beside the victim, easing down to one knee beside the cop who continued to hold her wrist between his fingers, checking her pulse. He glanced at Anna.

"FBI," she said, appraising the young woman's badly beaten face and the bleeding wound on her throat. "Is she going to make it?"

"I think so."

The woman groaned. Her eyes opened slightly, focusing on Anna.

The instantaneous assault of image and sound flashing before Anna's eyes rocked her back. Fear rose up inside her, her heart swelling to the bursting point and pain exploding through her face. She couldn't breathe; the pressure on her throat was crushing.

She jumped to her feet, stumbled against the wall, her hands flying up to clutch at the nonexistent fingers around her throat.

Then they were gone as fast as they had come, leaving her slumped against the hard bricks, gasping for air while reality rushed back on her with a force that bludgeoned as hard as the visions had.

The squawk of radios and the siren of the arriving EMT filled up the night.

"D929 to 951. Suspect last seen at Desire and Chartres Street, fleeing southeast along the Pauline Street Wharf," an officer said into his radio. "Hispanic. Wearing jeans and baggy white T-shirt. Suspect is armed with a knife."

"K," Dispatch responded. "All cars in Sector D respond to 929."

ANNA STOOD AT Rosalyn Barker's side as the ER doctors and nurses spoke softly and comfortingly to the dazed young woman. They had ministered her wounds easily enough. Lacerations on her face from the beating. The knife injury to her throat had done little more than draw blood.

Collecting evidence from a rape victim's body was tedious and time consuming, and too often added to the woman's sense of violation. Her feet in stirrups and her knees forced open, Rosalyn did her best to check her anger and keep her gaze fixed on the ceiling the entire time.

Outside the curtained-off cubicle, the buzz of conversation droned on. Occasionally, Anna caught Detective Armstrong's voice fending off reporters' questions with, "No comment at this time." Donovan sat in a corner chair in the cubicle, scrawling out notes dictated by the attending doctor, sealing each vial container, and writing his initials on them.

"Who are you?" Rosalyn finally asked in a weak voice.

Anna moved closer to the bed and smiled. "My name is Anna. I'm with the FBI."

"You don't look like a fed."

"Is that a compliment?"

Her swollen lips turned up. "Yeah."

"Bitch of a way to spend your evening, huh? Are you up to answering a few questions, Rosalyn?"

Her battered eyelids drifted closed, then she nodded.

"Will you describe this man to me again?"

"I already done that."

"Once more. For me this time."

She swallowed. "Mexican. Just as tall as me."

"And you are . . . ?"

"Five six."

Anna scribbled the information down on paper as Rosalyn continued.

"Stocky. Really strong. Long shaggy black hair."

"Any distinguishing marks on his body?"

Nodding. "Tattoos. Everywhere. On his neck, his arms, covering his hands. He was . . . creepy. Really creepy." She winced and lifted her head, glared at the doctor who was swabbing her vagina for evidence. "Dickhead, that hurts."

He glanced up at her. "Sorry."

Her head dropped back to the pillow. "The dude stank bad. Like rotten fish. Said he wanted a blow job. I told him no way. To fuck off. Looked and smelled like he hadn't bathed in a year. I ain't that hungry, know what I mean?"

"Did he attack you at that point?"

"He left." She touched her neck. "Then he come up behind

me. From the alley, I guess. Put his hand over my mouth and stuck the knife to my throat. Dragged me into the alley and started beating me. Kept saying he was going to cut off my head."

"Think carefully. The knife. What did it look like? Was it a big knife? A small one?"

She frowned and remained silent a moment. "Sorta big."

"Like a butcher knife?"

"Not that big."

"Maybe like a steak knife?"

"Maybe."

"A switchblade? Pocketknife?"

"No. Bigger."

"Did you notice if he was carrying anything on his back?"

"Nothin' on his back."

"Okay." Anna nodded. "Had you seen this man before, Rosalyn?"

"No. Would have remembered him."

Anna closed the notebook and slid it into her jeans pocket. Having completed his task, the doctor left the cubicle, and Donovan stood to follow him out. Anna grabbed Donovan's arm. "I'd like a couple minutes alone with Ms. Barker."

He nodded and left.

Anna moved to the bed. "Ms. Barker, I know it's difficult, but I want you to try to relax for me. I want you to look straight into my eyes and say nothing. Just look at me. Will you do that?"

She nodded.

Anna took a deep breath, and wrapped her fingers around Rosalyn's hand.

ANNA LOOKED OVER Donovan's shoulder as computer images of possible suspects flashed one after another across the monitor screen. She'd said very little since leaving the victim. As usual, the flashes of insight that Anna had experienced through Rosalyn's touch had left her exhausted and more than a little shaken.

Around her, the anticipation of the NOPD's Eighth District vibrated the air. At last, they had gotten a break, a detailed description of the perp they were certain was their French

Quarter Killer, as well as hard-core evidence that could help nail him in court.

Anna had more than a hunch that they were wrong. She'd suspected as much when hearing Barker's description of her attacker. She became certain of it when experiencing the crime through the victim's eyes and touch. The images that had so painfully assaulted Anna were not the same as those she'd experienced those few moments at the Bobbie Cox crime scene.

Several mug shots flashed up on the screen, side by side like a lineup—potential perps, all resembling Barker's description. Hispanic. Black shaggy hair. Tattoos. Her gaze zeroed in on one.

"That's him," she said, fighting against the sudden onslaught of hot energy that rushed through her.

Jerry moved up behind her, placed one hand on her shoulder as he looked at the screen.

Donovan turned in his chair, his expression bemused and skeptical, his eyes bloodshot from lack of sleep. "Yeah? How the hell do you know that?"

She gave him a flat smile. "He fits the description."

Armstrong joined them, sipping hot coffee from a foam cup. "They all fit Barker's description."

"Bring up his sheet," Jerry told Donovan.

Donovan punched a button and the details of Angel Gonzales's previous crimes flashed across the screen. Convictions for assault, child molestation, larceny, and parole violations. Outstanding warrants in Texas and Mississippi for Assault with a Deadly Weapon. Hookers attacked with a knife. Perpetrator considered Dangerous.

"Run off copies of those five suspects," Jerry said. "Take a drive over to Charity and show them to Ms. Barker. If she identifies Gonzales, we've got our man."

Anna walked from Donovan's office, down the long corridor past offices and groups of conversing cops. She needed a cigarette. Badly. And a drink. A stiff one. Not to mention sleep.

She exited the building. The miserably hot night settled over her like a damp wool blanket as she sat on the steps and stretched her long legs out, dug into her purse for a cigarette. The doors opened behind her.

Jerry sat down beside her. He regarded her in silence for a moment. "What's the problem?"

She watched traffic move along the street. "Gonzales is your man, all right. Barker's assailant. But he's not your serial killer, Jerry." She looked at him and shook her head. "It's all wrong. Nothing about this M.O. matches the profile of the killer."

He reached for her cigarette and took a deep drag. "Go on."

"Your killer never raped his victims."

"Bobbie Cox—"

"Bobbie Cox—hooker—may well have serviced one or more men before the killer got to her. The collection of semen from that victim is circumstantial at this point and you know it. Even if the DNA matches the perp who assaulted Barker, that doesn't mean Bobbie didn't have sex with Barker's assailant before the killer got to her.

"His pattern is definable. He performs his gruesome ritual in the victim's apartment. He binds and gags them, tortures, then kills."

"So this time the woman refused to service him. He attacked her. He told her he would cut off her head."

"Come on, Jerry. You know as well as I that the news has been all over this. You even admitted you've got a snitch in the department who leaked information to the press. Every lunatic in this city knows the details of this creep's signature— including the fact that he cuts out his victim's heart and tucks it into what's left of her uterus—thanks to your snitch."

She took her cigarette from him and smoked. "Your killer gets his jollies by domination and from inspiring fear in his victim."

"I venture to say that threatening to cut off Barker's head inspired her with tremendous fear."

"Your killer is smart, Jerry. Organized. He's rational enough to choose his victim, not at random, but in a calculated manner. The techs so far have been unable to pick up any evidence whatsoever at the crime scenes."

"So he got sloppy once. Maybe he was pissed that she refused to service him."

"A killer like this doesn't get sloppy."

"They all get sloppy, Anna, or we would never nail them."

"I can name a few who didn't. The Green River Killer,

Zodiac, Twin Cities, the Colonial Parkway Killer."

They remained silent for a moment, each watching the cars crawl along the street, then Jerry looked at her in that way he had of staring right into her psyche. He reached out and took her hand.

"What the hell is going on with you, Anna?"

Feeling his fingers close around her hand, tightly, so tightly she almost flinched, she looked up at the moon before responding. "I don't know what you mean. I'm here to do a job, and I'm attempting to do it. I simply don't have the desire, or the time, to get emotionally involved—"

"That's not what I mean." He tucked her hand in his lap, then reached for her face, forcing her to look into his eyes, his own staring hard, narrowed like two hard cold blue stones.

"When I picked up your message for me at the St. Louis, you had another message. A Dr. Jeff Montgomery. I know the name, Anna."

Heat rushed to her face and she attempted to tug her hand away. He wouldn't allow it.

"Montgomery once worked for the CIA's Stargate unit. Parapsychology stuff. ESP and psychic investigations. I want the truth out of you. All of it. You owe me that. This is my goddamn case and my neck is on the line and I want to know what the hell I'm dealing with."

"Then speak to Dr. Montgomery," she said, annoyed. "I have my orders to keep my mouth shut."

"I already did."

She blinked, felt her heartbeat accelerate and her body begin to sweat again. "You're lying."

"PID, Special Division. Classified. You've been trained—or brainwashed into believing—that what you do is some psychic bullcrap."

"And you don't believe in psychic bullcrap. Not Jerry Costos. Just the facts, ma'am."

His grip on her hand turned more gentle, but his gaze continued to hold hers. "Maybe. Maybe not. Even during our relationship, there were times when I recognized there was more going on in your head than you were willing to admit. There was buzz about you from the field agents after the California Interstate Killer case. Billy Cowan, a San Jacinto, California, truck driver who liked to pick up teenage hitchhikers to rape and mutilate, leaving their bodies along the freeways of Southern California. You rescued his next victim—the daughter of the Los Angeles mayor, Ralph Lasley. Sheila Lasley and her friend Michelle had hitched a ride with the infamous killer. Michelle had escaped. You reached the young woman as she clung to life, too near death to pass on information to the authorities. But somehow, without her muttering a word, you got the description of the killer, the interior of the truck, and the cubbyhole in which he hid his victims until he found the time to kill them. Thanks to you, Sheila Lasley was located— tied and gagged, but alive—in the truck parked at a truck stop on the California-Mexico border.

"Shortly after that, you disappeared from the field. I assume that's when you went underground into the PID. It doesn't take a rocket scientist to determine that this Dr. Montgomery, formerly of Stargate, had something to do with it."

Raising one dark eyebrow, he continued. "When I came up behind you at the Cox crime scene, you were humming 'Happy Birthday.' It just so happens that Bobbie's mother's birthday was the day after she was killed. Now I want the truth out of you. All of it. Anything you tell me will continue to be classified information. You know me well enough to know that I've got your back, Anna."

Anna remained silent, focused now on the hazy moon overhead that was fast becoming diluted by the fog that was crawling over the city, diffusing the light of the street lamps. She had lived the last years in total secrecy—alone in a world where the slightest slip of the tongue could jeopardize the PID Division. If she must confide, she knew Jerry Costos would keep the information at the cost of his job . . . and his life.

She took a deep breath, and her confession trembled. "Leave it to you to dig up the dirt even on the FBI. You realize that if you breathe a word of this to anyone, the government will come down on you like a jackhammer."

"I understand. Anna, I just want to help."

Anna nodded. "Okay. I'm a PID special agent. I don't work the BSU Profiler Division by sitting on my ass in a cramped office punching computers and paralleling previous serial cases, victims, and perps. I leave that to others, VICAP, et cetera. To do my thing—whatever that is . . ." She gave a throaty laugh. "I have to work the actual crime scenes. I experience the crime through whatever negative energy remains at the scene. We got lucky with Barker. I was able to witness her attacker precisely through her eyes. Which is why I know beyond a shadow of a doubt that Angel Gonzales attacked her. I recognized him immediately."

She swallowed. "FYI. It's hell, Jerry. The fear, the pain . . . it's all there. Here." She pointed to her head. "The focus I must call upon is depleting and horrifying. I'm green yet. Very green. It doesn't come easy. I'm not a seer who reads minds. I don't look into crystal balls and predict the future. It's the evil I tap in to. And each time I do, I feel as if I'm being murdered myself . . . or, more horrifying, perpetrating the murder, if I'm lucky enough to grab on to the assailant's thoughts."

She briefly covered her eyes with one hand. "I become the assailant. I feel his thrill, his fury, his sickness. The focus it takes to go there . . . it's not easy. If it were, I'd go mad. Every human being I meet on the streets—can you imagine the infiltration of wickedness that would bombard me? Look around us—the sickos who are walking our streets. Our next-door neighbors whose closets are full of skeletons. It's gotten to where I'm afraid to look into people's eyes—afraid of what I'll see there. That's where Montgomery comes in—the training of focus. Tempering this so-called gift so I can lead some form of a normal existence. I choose whose minds I wish to crawl into. This is a job. I refuse to allow it to annihilate my existence. Were I suddenly unable to control that focus . . . my life would become a constant terrifying nightmare. Hell. Total hell surrounded by impending doom and evil."

His arm slid around her shoulders, and he pulled her close. "Christ. I had no idea." Jerry kissed her brow, which was damp with sweat. The fog embraced them, chilling despite the heat of the night.

As they remained silent for a long while, the lights from the passing cars became little more than dim strips of vaporous illumination, and radio music and the distant wails of police sirens were muted by the heavy damp gray blanket of mist.

Anna felt her body go limp against his—her confession leaving her weak with relief. Tears stung her eyes at the knowledge that, at long last, she had a shoulder for support—someone who gave a damn about the circumstances which had become a burden that weighed more heavily upon her with each passing case. Once, she had obsessively embraced the FBI like a lover. Now she feared it—not the agency—but what had become, or was becoming, of her.

A car parked at the curve and a man got out. Anna recognized him immediately as he moved toward them through the fog. Eric Damascus, J.D.'s brother, Senator Strong's legislative director. She didn't like him. Never had.

Jerry released her, and she pulled away and dug into her purse for another cigarette as Damascus moved up the sidewalk.

"Shit," Jerry said. "Here comes trouble."

"Costos, how's it going?" Eric glanced at Anna. "Agent Anna. Long time no see. What brings you back to New Orleans?"

She gave him a flat smile but didn't return his look. Damascus was a Grade A number one jerk. Always had been. As Senator Jack Strong's newly appointed legislative director, he would sell his own mother's soul to the devil if he thought it would win him points with the senator and pave the way for Eric's own rise through the political ranks.

As Anna refused to acknowledge him with so much as a glance, Eric turned his attention back on Jerry. "I understand you've finally got a break on the killer."

"Who told you that? Senator Strong?"

"My dad, as a matter of fact."

"Word travels fast."

"Why not, when it involves catching the man who murdered the governor's grandchildren." He moved to the door. "Donovan in his office?"

"Donovan's not telling you shit. If he does, I'll have his shield. And by the way, how is J.D. holding up?"

"How the hell would I know?"

"Because he's your brother?"

Eric smirked and entered the building. Jerry shook his head. "That guy's a fucking snake."

"So is Jack Strong."

"I'll have a word with Killroy. I suspect he called Charles Damascus the minute we put an APB on Barker's suspect."

"Killroy your snitch?"

Jerry raised one eyebrow, then shrugged. "Killroy is one of the good guys."

"Come on, Jerry. Are you going soft on me? We both know when it comes to murder there are no good guys. Everyone is a potential suspect. Guilty until proven innocent." She shook her head. "The perp who attacked Barker might be trash and one brick short of a load, but he's not your serial killer. I'd wager my shield on the fact that the French Quarter serial killer is good looking, clean, and an overall charmer."

"Is that the profiler talking or the PID?"

She shook her head. "Barker herself said the guy was a creep. Filthy. Stank to high heaven—like fish. Probably works the docks."

She rubbed her temple, the images she had received at Bobbie Cox's apartment distinct in her mind.

This guy isn't so bad. Good looking, clean, compassionate. Hands reach for the keys—nice hands, well manicured.

"The M.E. reports all described the victims as between five six and five eight. Your killer is taller. Six feet. Your height. Maybe." She smiled and looked into his eyes. "The perp who attacked Barker was five six. Same height as she is."

He stared at her. "So what the hell makes you think the killer is six feet tall?"

She tips back her head and looks into his eyes.

Jerry looked into her eyes and nodded. "Okay. Understood."

Chapter 5

⁓

AT FOUR-TEN A.M. Rosalyn Barker identified Angel Gonzales as the man who assaulted her. An APB for Gonzales was immediately dispatched.

At seven, Anna sat on her hotel bed, watching the morning news and images of Jerry and Captain Killroy sharing their mutual enthusiasm over at long last identifying the man whom they believed to be the French Quarter Killer.

Anna smiled up at Jerry as he handed her a cup of coffee and sat down on the bed beside her.

"I wish you looked more excited." He sipped his hot coffee as Anna looked back at the television screen.

"You've identified the man who assaulted Rosalyn. I'm very happy about that."

"But you aren't convinced he's a serial killer."

"No." She shook her head. "I'm sorry. Gonzales might have killed her if he had the opportunity. Probably not. I think his threat to cut off her head was an attempt to scare her. The knife he used to assault Rosalyn doesn't even match the M.E.'s description of the weapon used to eviscerate the previous victims."

Jerry stood up and began to pace. Anna watched him,

knowing only too well what thoughts were going through his mind. Jerry was damn good at his job—prided himself at being the best D.A. in the state.

"I understand how you're feeling—"

"Do you?" He raked one hand through his hair. "My neck is on the line here, Anna."

"I understand."

"I've got the senator and governor breathing down my neck, not to mention this city—the safety of this city—and the media—"

"You've never let them manipulate you before, Jerry."

"I've never had a situation like this, Anna. Not on my watch."

"Is Senator Jack Strong or Governor Damascus going to stand beside you if you bungle this, Jerry?" She set her coffee cup down and left the bed, caught his arm so he was forced to stop pacing. "Hey." Touching his cheek, she smiled. "We both know they won't. If you're wrong about Gonzales, it'll be you the people of this state will fry."

He took her in his arms and held her. "I want this son of a bitch, Anna. The freak killed my godson and goddaughter. He destroyed my best friend's life."

"Don't let it get personal, Jerry. You can't. You know that. When the heart gets involved . . ." She closed her eyes and swallowed. "The mind gets confused."

He held her tighter, and although she knew she should pull away, she couldn't find the strength to do it. She was ignoring her own advice—but it'd been so damn long, she'd missed him so much. Men had come and gone in her life the last six years and still no one had managed to touch her in the ways that Jerry Costos could.

Not emotionally, or physically.

They lapsed into silence as they held one another, Anna's ear pressed against his warm chest, the noise from the morning traffic outside the window dwindling with the sound of her heart beating in her ears.

"Anna," he whispered, the words spoken so softly they were almost lost amid the hum of the air-conditioning unit fluttering the curtains over the window. "I want to make love to you."

Her mouth partially opened to deny him, once again—too

afraid to go there—too afraid of getting hurt, of hurting him, but his mouth moved across her lips, silencing her protests.

He groaned as the heat of his body magnified against her own. She moved her hands over him slowly, fingertips exploring the back of his neck, the moist skin behind his ear, the abrasiveness of his unshaven cheek.

Anna's hands slid around his neck, pulling him harder into the kiss, flirting her tongue with his, skin shivering as she felt his fingertips trail under her T-shirt and up her back, closing around her rib cage, which felt vulnerable beneath the strength of his hands. He kissed her cheek, her chin, her throat, and nuzzled the tender skin over her collarbone. Her fingers twisted in his hair and clutched at his shirt—she gasped as he brushed her nipple with his thumb.

The phone rang.

Anna groaned.

Jerry groaned. He held her fiercely and said in her ear, "For God's sake, don't answer it. Not now."

It rang again, and again, refusing to be denied.

With a silent curse, Jerry turned away, leaving Anna standing alone while the phone shrieked its insistence. She fought to steady her voice as she answered, "Travelli."

Silence, then, "It's Jeff. Have I caught you at a bad time?"

Anna heard the hotel door slam, and she sank onto the bed, her lips curling in a tight smile. "No, as a matter of fact." She sighed. "Your timing is perfect."

ONE WEEK AND no sign of Gonzales, despite the NOPD's investigation. Since no further killings transpired, Killroy felt certain that Gonzales was the serial killer and had hauled butt out of New Orleans the first time his photo was splashed across the newspapers and television screens. Anna didn't buy it, still. No way did she believe Angel Gonzales was the French Quarter serial killer—not after the visions she had picked up at the Bobbie Cox crime scene—but she had talked herself blue in the face to Killroy, Costos, and Donovan, and none of them were ready to back off their suspicions regarding Gonzales, especially since life, and business in the French Quarter, had resumed its normal raucousness.

She paced her hotel room, phone to her ear. "You've totally tied my hands, Jeff. I'm useless here. Why don't you pull me in? Put me on a case where I might actually accomplish something."

"I can't do that, Anna. Not if you're certain about the images you picked up on the Cox case. Simply bedazzle them with your brilliance as you have in the past."

Anna flopped on the bed, fell to her back, and stared at the ceiling. "I want out, Jeff. I want a normal life again. I want to work cases just like any other regular agent."

Silence.

"I'm tired of keeping men at arm's length," she said, her voice weary. "Tired that I may do or say something to give the division, or myself, away."

"Costos is wearing you down, I take it."

"Negative."

"Anna, you must realize that there is no going back. You are what you are."

"A freak."

"This gift was there even before you joined the FBI. We simply helped you hone it, control it, and better understand it. You can walk away from the division, but the gift won't go away. It's what you are, Anna."

"Special Agent Anna Travelli is *what* I am, Jeff. But it's not *who* I am . . . and it never will be."

A TROPICAL STORM moved in two days later. The rain fell in bursts that ran along the street, swirling with dust and litter. It did little to hamper the heat. If anything, the occasional downpour exacerbated the unbearable humidity that clung to their skin and clothes. The turbulence also brought out the wickedness in men whose main source of entertainment was the back-alley whores. Fewer witnesses. Fewer squads and cruisers. Rain to wash evidence into oblivion.

Anna stood at the window and looked down the street, at the boozed-up browsers from the Quarter gyrating to jazz bands like Rockin' Dopsie, Jr. and the Zydeco Twisters, Counting Crows, and Ladysmith Black Mambazo, none of whom could care less if lightning were to streak from the sky and incinerate the cymbals on their washtub drums. Anything to make a buck. Anything to survive one more day in the Vieux Carré.

Scarlett Brown and Jenny Decker smirked as Detective

Armstrong completed the task of wiring them, not an easy chore since their clothes consisted of crotch-length spandex skirts and halter tops. Their expressions were concerned, their laughter tight with emotion they wouldn't dare show to the cops who were taking great care in hiding the transformers the best they could under the hookers' meager clothing.

Anna didn't care much for Detective Donovan's plan. The French Quarter Killer was smarter than to take this kind of bait. Since word had been blasted across the city, indeed the entire country, the French Quarter Killer hadn't made so much as a move. Anna suspected he was simply relaxing, if not in New Orleans, then someplace else, watching the circus of panicking tourists and mountingly frustrated cops who were focused on finding Angel Gonzales—still believing him to be the serial killer.

Although Detective Mike Donovan agreed to go along with Killroy and Costos's plan to put decoys on the streets, he kept his mouth closed as much as possible about his hesitancy. Not only was he putting Tyron Johnson's girls in a sticky situation, not to mention a number of undercover female cops, he was well aware that his own reputation was on the line. The media, both the television and the papers, were coming down hard on them. Just the night before, MSNBC had done an hour-long special on the French Quarter Killer—interviews with distraught parents of the murdered women, and even with Anna, Donovan, and Killroy. By now the entire country believed that Gonzales was the serial killer and since his face had been blasted from one coast to the other, the citizens were frothing over the fact that he had not yet been found.

Throughout the reporter's overeager grilling, Anna had kept her opinions to herself. It simply wasn't good form to publicly argue the police department's stand on the investigation. Remaining closemouthed through the interrogation was not her style, but as Dr. Jeff Montgomery had pointed out, better to let the real killer stew in his self-satisfaction. With the department focusing on Gonzales, the real French Quarter Killer would do one of two things. His annoyance that someone else was taking the credit for his killings would drive him out to make a statement, or another killing. After all, it was simply a game to him. A power and control issue. He was a man who needed the attention to bolster his importance in the world.

Gonzales, on the other hand, was a thrill seeker. Such assaults were sporadic sprees—strike out at anyone—man, woman, child.

The FBI's VICAP Division had processed this case in record time. The only case files that had come close to matching the French Quarter Killer involved four prostitutes murdered in Maryland the year before. Evisceration, decapitation, and total dismemberment—heads missing—but no removing of the heart. Just like the New Orleans killings, their apartments had been clean of evidence even though the crimes had been committed there.

Anna tailed after Costos and Donovan on the evening they intended to plant the wired hookers throughout the Quarter.

"Just listen to me," she said. "Think about what I'm saying. If this guy was going to hit again, he would have already done it. He might be crazy, but he's smart. You've got squad cars and cruisers crawling along these streets like a damn funeral procession. Your so-called hookers have UNDERCOVER COP stamped on their foreheads. Anyone who frequents these girls on a nightly basis is going to know them. They stand out like a freaking neon sign."

Donovan entered his office, tossed his files onto his cluttered desk, and dropped into his chair, glancing at Costos. "Does she ever shut up?"

Jerry glanced at Anna, his eyebrows lowered. "Not if she can help it."

Anna planted her hands on Donovan's desk and leaned toward him. "You listen to me and you'll make First Grade Detective and get all the pats on the back you can take from the governor and senator. The citizens in this town will put a statue in your honor on Jackson Square."

He sighed and leaned back in his chair. "So talk. But make it fast. We've got eight undercovers wired and ready to walk."

Anna sat in a chair and crossed her legs. "Okay. Listen. Don't so much as breathe until I'm finished." She glanced at Jerry. "That goes for you, too."

Jerry propped one shoulder against the bulletin board on the wall where photos of the slain women were thumb-tacked to it.

Anna never took her gaze from Donovan's blue eyes. He looked haggard and sleepless. But for the shoulder holster and gun he wore over his shirt, he could have passed for a hungover Tulane student.

"Look, Mike. We haven't exactly seen eye to eye during this and previous investigations. You don't like the FBI shouldering its way into your job. You specifically don't like me—a profiler. I understand. You feel we come with crystal balls and tarot cards."

"Hey, I never made that comment. That was Armstrong."

"Profiling is a . . . science. Statistics that rarely fail."

"Get to the point, Travelli."

"You call this creep's bluff. Call in the media. Inform them that you've made an arrest of the man you feel is your French Quarter Killer. Refuse to release his identity. You might even say your supposed perp has already confessed, not just to the serial killings but to the assault on Barker. Pull in your cruisers and squads."

He stared at her. "You're nuts."

"These creeps know they can't take any risks at this point. Wouldn't dare. So you accomplish two things. One: Gonzales is going to feel safe and go on the hunt again—beat up and rape a hooker or two. Two: Your serial killer is going to be mighty pissed that someone is stealing his thunder. Both men will hunt again. Your serial killer is going to make one hell of a statement. He's going to try his best to make the NOPD and the FBI look like idiots. Remember, it's the power and control he's after. Notoriety. He's got something to prove, Mike. Right now he's feeling untouchable and arrogant enough to believe he can continue to get away with murder."

Donovan slumped in his chair, looking as if he hadn't slept in a week. The normally pristine, starched white shirt he wore was sweat-stained in the armpits, and his tie lay curled on his desk like a sleeping navy blue snake. He hadn't shaved in days. He needed a haircut. A lock hung down his brow, accenting his dark blue eyes bloodshot from sleeplessness.

"Seems to me, Travelli, that you're still assuming that Gonzales is not our serial killer."

"He's not," she snapped, then glanced at Jerry, who raised one eyebrow and shrugged.

Donovan narrowed his eyes. "Why don't you just go back to Quantico and do whatever it is you do. I believe my department has this case well in hand without your help."

Anna slowly left her chair and leaned her weight on his desk, hands propped upon the stack of files open before him. "I would like nothing better. Right now we've got a child killer in Baton Rouge. Cult stuff. Sacrifices. I've got a killer in East Texas that the populace is convinced is an alien from outer space who's kidnapping women and cutting out their uteruses, leaving their bodies as calling cards in crop circles. Nasty business. But my superior is convinced that the French Quarter Killer is going to strike again given the first opportunity and you guys are fighting us tooth and nail. Stop being such a damned macho, bullheaded cop and cooperate."

Donovan fingered his lower lip and glanced at Costos. "So you're saying not to put the girls out tonight."

"Not in the least. Put 'em out. Just, for a few days, feed the press and public what they want to hear. I'll guarantee Angel Gonzales and your serial killer will hit again the moment they think they're off the hook."

Donovan lowered his dark eyebrows and chewed on a toothpick, glanced up at Jerry.

Less aggressively, Anna rewarded Donovan with a smile. "I know your reputation, Detective. You haven't made Second Grade by sitting back on your laurels and watching the uniforms catch the bad guys. Gonzales is going to strike again. And so is your killer. Maybe next time it won't be hookers. Next time it might be little girls."

ANOTHER WEEK PASSED. No one booked but the usual drunken tourists with pockets full of cheap Vieux Carré souvenirs. It was midnight when the phone rang, jarring Anna from sleep.

"Donovan. Okay, Travelli. You win. We do it your way. Are you happy?"

"You've let the media know?"

"By the book, Agent Travelli. Just like you said. Name withheld. Do you realize what's going to happen to me if this ploy of yours doesn't work? I'll be writing fucking parking tickets on Bourbon Street."

"Trust me on this one, Detective. If we take a fall on this case, you can blame it totally on the FBI."

There came a deep laugh, throaty—sleepy. "You can count

on that, Travelli. I'll see it written on every station bathroom wall in this district and seven others."

BY NOON OF the next day the media swarmed like locusts around the Eighth Precinct, demanding information—name and photograph—of the suspect the NOPD had supposedly apprehended. Killroy offered his normal plastic smile and waved their questions away with hands that were sweating with nervousness and the intense humidity of the midday sun. Diane Sawyer and Geraldo Rivera had done their best to book Killroy and Costos on their shows.

To Anna, it seemed as if the entire city had let out one great sigh of relief. She felt guilty over it. Guilty that she allowed tens of thousands of innocent women to let their guards down when she knew deep in her gut that the French Quarter monster as well as Barker's assailant were still out there—lurking—laughing to himself because the NOPD had arrested the wrong man.

The next few nights saw only the normal incarceration of drunks and pickpockets and domestic disturbances. Wires in place, Armstrong gave Janet Beech, an undercover cop passing as a hooker, a fleeting smile. "You know exactly what to say if a suspicious perp propositions you, right?"

"I'm done for the night," she said, lowering her mouth closer to her halter collar.

Armstrong shook his head. "Why don't you just wave a red flag over your head and let him know we're about to bust his sorry ass?"

Janet tossed her dreadlocks and cocked her hip. "You can kiss my ass. I'm out there risking my neck and you're sitting in some squad car eating a beltbuster and drinking root beer."

Anna sat in a chair near the door, legs crossed. There was that quivery little feeling in her stomach. Something was going to happen tonight. Gonzales would make a move, thinking he was safe. And so would the killer. The night was hot and still, the full August moon glowing like white neon over the city. Her dad had always called such a night "Hunter's Moon." Something about a full moon brought the lunatics out to prowl.

Finally, Armstrong stepped back. "Okay, ladies. Go strut your stuff. And I do mean strut. I want you on the street corners swiveling those hips like there's no tomorrow."

Sherry Ritchy, with a yellow sheet as long as Anna's leg, gave Donovan the once-over. "Clean sheet after this, right?"

"Cross my heart . . . just as long as you stay out of trouble. Haul your little butt back to Hallsville and work at Wal-Mart."

Donovan looked back at Anna. "Costos called. He's hung up on a case. You might as well go back to the hotel and wait."

"You'd like that, wouldn't you, Mike?"

"I got enough on my hands right now without worrying whether or not some FBI *special agent* gets her head cut off."

THERE WAS SOMETHING about New Orleans at night that brought out the dark psyche in a person. Every street and alley. Every building, old or new. Streetlights and old coach lamps. Laughter in the darkness. Jazz drifting out over the murky river and the crowded city of ancient tombs in the cemetery. It all had a certain rhythm to it that Anna had never experienced anyplace else.

Yeah, it was home. As a student at Tulane she'd smoked her sweet Mary Jane and obliterated herself in New Orleans's famous Hurricane drinks. She knew the old warehouses where voodoo priestesses gyrated over bloodied goat heads and stabbed needles into straw dolls and burned black candles.

At two A.M. Anna parked her rental car at the corner of Royal and Pauline Streets. She noted immediately that the old street lamp had been broken. The moonlight overhead painted the brick street with what looked like a thin coat of milk wash.

That feeling she had experienced in Donovan's office gnawed more strongly at her. Not just a tickling in her belly any longer. But a hard grip of dread and anticipation that made beads of sweat crawl down her scalp.

It was the eyes that had continued to bother her. That brief glimpse of the killer's eyes she had viewed through Bobbie Cox as they paused on her doorstep with keys in hand. Those eyes had been familiar. Very familiar. There had been no trepidation in Bobbie's soul before she was slaughtered. Only an odd exuberance.

Surprise, Mama, I'm home! Happy Birthday!

Dr. Montgomery had drilled into her head the first day of training in the PID that everyone is born with the gift. Call it hunches. Coincidence. Serendipity. Instinct. Guardian angels whispering in one's ear.

At times, when she least expected it, those feelings had shimmied up her spine like icy fingers, stopping her in her tracks, breath held in her lungs, heart banging in her ears.

She hadn't honed her talent well enough to predict catastrophe before it happened. But she had been disabused of the idea that destiny was an entity that shouldn't be fucked around with. It wasn't destiny that chose some poor schmuck to have his head blown away in a drive-by shooting. Destiny was not being at the wrong place at the wrong time. Such destiny was death by evil. God simply blinked, and in that infinitesimal moment Satan himself snapped his fingers and obliterated a soul.

However, she had, over the last years, learned to recognize the foul stench of impending evil—but only when she focused on it. Not easy. A little like a one-hundred-pound weight lifter attempting to heave a five-hundred-pound barbell.

But tonight, the stench drifted to her as vaporous as the fog slithering through the streets. As filthy as the dark brown river slapping against the piers.

Donovan and Armstrong, Costos and Killroy might well entrap Angel Gonzales with their decoy whores. But the French Quarter monster was on the hunt again. She could feel his presence. It crawled over her skin like the fine point of his weapon.

She moved silently along Pauline to the alley that led to Bobbie Cox's apartment. With any luck, and no disturbances, she just might be able to grasp enough of the dreadful event to help the case. The police tape had long ago been removed. There remained no evidence whatsoever that a brutal murder had transpired here days ago. Life goes on . . . and on . . . and on. . . .

But not for Bobbie or J.D. Damascus's family.

She instinctively reached for her gun—reassuring to know it was there as she breathed in the tainted scent of sour beer and urine and *him* as she moved down the dark alley toward Bobbie's apartment. She already dreaded the coming experience. Feared the horror. The pain. The spiraling of the soul leaving the twitching mutilated body of a human being.

Pausing.

Anna narrowed her eyes, the rise of heat through her body causing sweat to pool in her armpits and run down her ribs.

SHE IS QUITE beautiful, he thinks. Always thought so. Hard not to appraise Anna Travelli and not get a hard-on. Therein is the problem. The others had not interested him in that way. He would never fuck a whore. Cut off their heads, yes. But fuck them, no.

He stays close to the shuttered buildings, where the moonlight cannot reach. The light of the moon stirs his blood, and his hunger. He can smell her perfume. Nothing floral for this one. It is the feel of feminine masculinity about her that intrigues him. She would not scream and beg for her life. She would fight him as powerfully as a man. She might even kill him.

A tantalizing thought. Someone really should kill him. His soul is more than worthy of Hell.

And so he follows, creeps around the edge of what once had been an old mill house and presses his body hard against the aged, sharp bricks. Watches as she pauses, reaching for the gun in the shoulder holster beneath her lightweight jacket. She senses him. He can tell.

Her head turns slowly and she looks back down the alley. He stands very still, not breathing, simply admiring the reflection of moonlight on her face and hair that shimmers like fiery gold.

Again she moves, nearing the whore's apartment. He wonders why she has come here, alone. In the dark. What does she expect to find here that the police have been unable to locate?

She steps around a corner, disappearing from his sight. Taking a deep breath, he slowly releases it, and follows.

IT WAS THE sudden overwhelming sense of menace that made Anna grab again for her gun. Foolish of her to have ignored her own perceptions. They had screamed at her like a thousand sirens the moment she'd stepped from the car.

As he moved up behind her, she drove her elbow hard into the pit of his stomach, slammed her heel down as hard as she could on his foot. The animal-like howl erupted in her ear, but his hands continued to claw into the flesh of her throat, cutting off her breath as she struggled to shift her body enough to aim the gun—impossible.

She fired the Glock anyway, heard the bullet ricochet off the metal roof of a building, a ping and whine that echoed up the alleyway. The shock of the gunfire momentarily startled her assailant enough that she was able to throw her head back, ramming it into his chin with such impact she heard his teeth smash together.

Her knees buckled. Her weight dragged him down, his feet entangled with hers as they hit the ground, rolling. She dug her fingernails into the backs of his hands and swung the butt of her gun as hard as she could into his cheekbone.

She heard shouting, the blaring of sirens, the banging of running feet on the brick alleyway. The dark suddenly became a collision of red and blue lights, streaks of flashlights, and shadows of uniformed officers surrounding her, all with their weapons aimed at her and the man beneath her.

"Drop it!" an officer shouted. "Drop the gun!"

Anna rolled to her back, clutching her throat, which was slick with blood. "FBI," she cried as she lifted her shield in one trembling hand.

Then Donovan was suddenly there, backlit by flashlights as he dropped to one knee beside her, his expression concerned.

"Okay," she managed, closing her eyes. "I'm okay."

She rolled to her side, then rocked to her knees, the gun still in one hand as she looked down into Angel Gonzales's face.

Mike gently helped her to stand as the accompanying officers rolled Gonzales to his belly and handcuffed his wrists behind his back.

Anna dropped onto the steps outside Bobbie Cox's apartment, her legs bent at the knees and one hand still clutching her gun. Mike sat beside her and they watched as Armstrong dragged Gonzales to his feet and began to recite him his rights.

Mike looked at her finally, his disapproval apparent. "I'd ask you what the hell you were doing out here alone, but I don't expect it would make much difference."

"We all have our stupid moments, Donovan. Now isn't the time or place to rub it in my face."

"Nice collar. Chalk up another one for the infamous Special

Agent Travelli." He released a relieved sigh. "Damn glad this is over with."

Anna slid the gun into the holster, then slowly turned her gaze up to Mike's. He tossed her a bottle of Purell to wash the blood from her hands and throat.

Detective Michael Donovan stared at her . . . saying nothing.

JERRY STOOD AT Anna's side as the doctor at Charity Emergency finished his delicate task of stitching closed the claw marks on Anna's neck. There were bruises as well. Her throat had swollen so badly she could hardly swallow. The physician suggested they should keep her overnight to be on the safe side, but Anna refused.

Silent, slightly drowsy from the painkillers the doctor had provided, Anna left the hospital at Jerry's side, his arm wrapped protectively around her, his face still white with fear and concern.

She knew his thoughts. Thank God that he was keeping them to himself . . . at least for the moment. She was in no need of an argument. Too many thoughts still raging in her brain.

He did not return her to the St. Louis Hotel, but took her straight to his apartment a few blocks down from the courthouse. Typical bachelor pad. Slightly unkempt; Mardi Gras photographs on the walls; unwashed dishes in the sink.

He walked her directly into his bedroom, sat her on the bed, and proceeded to remove her gun holster, then her bloodied shirt. She was too damn tired, and hurt too damn bad, to stop him.

He removed her Nikes then wriggled her tight jeans down her legs, tossed them into a pile of his own unwashed clothes near the bathroom.

She attempted a smile. "You always were a lousy housekeeper. With your money, you could afford a maid."

"I wouldn't trust my own mother alone in this apartment. I'm not in the habit of allowing strangers into my place to happen upon some kind of information that could blow one of my cases."

He returned from the bathroom with a damp cloth, pressed her back on the bed so her head rested on a down pillow. He mopped her face, still streaked by blood, sweat, and tears, and he tried to smile.

"I don't think I've ever seen an FBI agent cry."

"Don't rub it in, Costos."

Jerry gently sat on the bed beside her, his fingers lightly touching the deep, crusting gouges on her neck. "Christ Almighty. He almost killed you."

Anna reached for his hand, curling her fingers around his own, and tried to smile. "Please. Let's not go there. Right now I don't need to hear how a woman has no place in the agency. I don't want to hear how you would suffer if I were killed. I do understand how you feel, Jerry. Completely. But like I've said to you a thousand times: I'm no different than any other cop. We have a job to do. Every time we strap on a gun and take on a suspect, we put our lives on the line. It doesn't matter if I'm a woman. Men die, too. Good men. In the line of duty. They leave wives and children and parents behind . . . because they want to make the world a safer place for their families. Where would the civilized world be without us?"

She blinked sleepily. The searing pain on her neck and the ache between her shoulders were duller now. Soon the memories of the attack would be quieted. Soon the realities of the case would return.

Focus. She didn't want to think about those realities now. Focus. On here. Now. On the man who looked at her with such craving and love in his eyes she felt her heart melt.

Struggling to sit up, she slipped her hands around her back and unclasped her bra. She lay back down and lifted her arms to him. "For old time's sake," she whispered.

Jerry unsnapped his jeans and slid them down his hips. He tossed his shirt aside, lowered his body gently down on hers, and buried his head in the crook of her neck, his breath warm and moist against her ear.

"I love you. I'll never stop loving you," he murmured.

She slid her fingers through his thick, dark hair. It slightly curled around her fingers. And she realized, in that moment, that the thoughts that had fractured through her mind in those terrifying moments at Gonzales's hands, that it had been Jerry's face that had flashed before her eyes. Images of his smile. His tenderness. His teasing. And his heartbreak.

As he lifted his head, her lids fluttered open, looking

through the dark into his eyes that regarded her with so much desire her heart felt, for an instant, as if it had stopped beating entirely. An ecstasy of emotion flooded through her as he brushed her mouth in a tenuous kiss.

"I love you, Anna," he told her again, the pain resonating so in his voice that tears rose to her eyes.

He moved. Peeled her panties down her legs, which she opened freely, sighing as his fingers stroked her, sliding into her, until she was wet and slick and aching.

"For old time's sake." He smiled, sinking his body deeply into hers, fingers twisting into her hair. He moved against her, tenderly at first, until the strain of passion overcame them both. Until their bodies writhed with remembered fervor, and fever. Seeking. Sliding. Insistent. The tip of his penis teasing her entrance, but barely, until their groans quickened and her body moved as abandonedly as his. Until the end came much too swiftly for them both and the fall back to earth was like snow drifting from heaven.

Quiet, motionless, they lay together. Arms and legs entangled. She closed her eyes—so easily she could give in to the painkilling drug the doctor had pumped into her veins. So easy to glide away into oblivion, forget the last hours. Forget the last years. Forget Jerry Costos . . . just for a little while.

But she wouldn't. She couldn't.

Jerry rolled to his back, pulled her against his side, and cradled her as he stared at the ceiling, releasing a sigh of relief.

"We got him, Anna, thanks to you. You deserve one hell of a commendation."

"No," she whispered, lifting her head to look into his eyes. "You got Gonzales, Jerry. *He's* still out there, the French Quarter Killer."

His gaze hardened and he looked away. "You're wrong."

Laying her head on his chest, she listened to his heart thud. "I hope you're right," she said, and nothing more, just lay unmoving until his breathing became deep and his arms around her relaxed.

As easily as possible, she slid from the bed, slipped on her clothes, and checked her watch. Just enough time to get back to the hotel, collect her belongings, and catch the five A.M. flight back to Quantico.

She paused at the bedroom door—told herself not to look

back. But she did anyway. Jerry appeared to be sleeping—but she doubted it. He would watch her walk out of his life once again, knowing that it had been inevitable.

Anna blew him a kiss and whispered, "For old time's sake." Then she silently left the apartment.

Too damn bad they could never make a go of it.

HE WHISTLES TO himself as he folds the newspaper in half and tucks it under his arm. The stewardess for Delta Airlines requests that all first-class passengers board. She flashes him a smile and says, "Good to see you again. Have a great flight."

He gives her a wink and a smile, shifts his fine leather briefcase to the other hand before moving down the long boarding tunnel to the waiting 727. There really isn't a reason to read about the Gonzales bullshit. Jerry Costos and Mike Donovan will pat themselves on the back and New Orleans will breathe easier for a while . . . but only for a while. Of course he'll be back. When the time is right.

Once again, FBI Special Agent Anna Travelli will be awarded a commendation of which she, in her heart of hearts, knows she is unworthy. She's well aware that Gonzales is not the French Quarter Killer. Smart lady, that one. Soon, very soon, they will no doubt meet again.

Smiling, he tosses the newspaper into a garbage bin and enters the plane.

Don't miss
BAD MOON RISING
by Katherine Sutcliffe
to find out what happens next with the
French Quarter Killer!

After Midnight

FIONA BRAND

Chapter 1

A SHADOW SLID through the open double doors of the barn, flowed over hay bales that glowed in the late morning sunlight, and dissolved into the dense shade at the rear of the large corrugated iron building.

Jane O'Reilly's head jerked up. She blinked and frowned, her fingers tightening on the paintbrush she'd been cleaning, aware that something had flickered at the edge of her vision, but not sure what it could have been. She hadn't heard a vehicle labouring up her dusty drive, which meant that if anyone was around, they were on foot—and that wasn't likely because she lived so far out of town. The only time she'd ever gotten foot traffic in the seven years she'd lived in Tayler's Creek had been when a tourist had broken down and had wanted to use her phone. Even then, the tourist had been a rarity—without a cell phone, and way off the beaten track—because as Down Under towns went, Tayler's Creek lived up to the cliché of the one-horse, one-pub town; the shopping centre itself so small that if you blinked while driving through, you missed it.

Gaze warily glued to the bright shaft of sunlight and the spiraling drift of dust motes floating in the beam—as if something, or *somebody*, had just stirred up the small whirlwind—

she slipped the paintbrush into a jar of cleaning solution and straightened from her crouched position.

Logically, the movement that had startled her could have been caused by a bird, a rat, or even Jess, her dog, but she had a sense that whatever had moved had been large rather than small, and there had been no accompanying sound effects—just the flickering shadow, as if someone had walked silently past the barn door.

Stripping off her rubber gloves, she shoved them in the pocket of her overalls, automatically rolling her shoulders to ease the ache that had crept up on her while she'd been painting the shaded side of the barn. The movement sent a bead of perspiration sliding down her spine, the cold trickle making her feel even hotter and stickier as she skirted the towering aromatic bales of hay. An unfamiliar and faintly annoying apprehension gripped her as she kept to the concealment of the shadows. Unconsciously, she'd made no noise, and now she stopped to listen as she examined every inch of the scuffed, graveled area in front of the barn. She wasn't paranoid, but ever since Patrick had died four months ago, leaving her widowed and alone on the one-hundred-acre block, she'd been conscious of her vulnerability.

Underscoring that vulnerability was the fact that, the previous day, for the first time in living history, Tayler's Creek had made the front page of the national daily for all the wrong reasons.

According to the report, a couple who had recently moved to Tayler's Creek, the Dillons, had become the latest victims of a slew of brutal home invasion crimes that had been perpetrated in the top half of New Zealand's North Island. Aubrey Dillon had been shot at close range, and killed. His wife, Carol, had been raped and beaten and left for dead while the criminals had made off with over forty thousand dollars' worth of appliances.

A small shudder ran through Jane. She loved the peace and quiet of the country, the slow pace and the sense of order and permanence that went with a life that was immutably tied to the land and the seasons. Farming had its setbacks, but there were none that would ever tempt her to go back to the frantic pace of city life with the constant worry about crime and security. Before she'd married Patrick and they'd both moved to the farm, she'd been a city girl, an account executive in a high-profile bank, with career prospects, long nails, strappy high heels, and a burgeoning ulcer. Country life, to put it mildly, had been a revelation, but after the initial shock—and that first broken nail—she'd taken to it like a duck to water. She'd found her peaceful oasis, even if at the moment the illusion of safety was evaporating as fast as the water that flowed through her property.

She hadn't known the Dillons, but whether she'd known them or not didn't matter, the crime had been ugly—doubly shocking for a small town where the main topics of conversation tended to be the price of beef and wool, and how badly they needed rain to lift the dropping water table. Like everyone else in Tayler's Creek, she was edgy and alarmed, and ready to jump at any shadow.

Jess barked, breaking the tension that still held Jane rigid. Letting out a breath and feeling faintly ridiculous for over-reacting, she stepped outside, bracing herself against the hammer blow of heat and blinking at the hot glare as she skimmed the drive and the semicircle of farm buildings. She hadn't expected to see a vehicle, and there wasn't one.

Berating herself as, if not paranoid, then definitely neurotic, she did a circuit of the buildings, studying the ground, as if she could somehow discern the shape of a footprint in dirt that was packed as hard as iron, or spy a broken stem in the bleached, matlike covering of Kikuyu grass that sprang back, tough and resilient, beneath her sneaker-clad feet.

As she checked the stockyards and the slatted dimness of the shearing shed, it occurred to her that if there had been anyone at all on her property, there was a simple explanation as to who it could have been—her nearest neighbour.

Her heart stuttered in her chest, and her stomach did a nervy little somersault at the prospect of coming face-to-face with Michael Rider, an instant freeze-frame forming in her mind: dark eyes, taut cheekbones, tanned olive skin, black hair that flowed to broad shoulders.

Michael Rider existed in the category that any sane woman would label as dark and dangerous. The fact that he was her neighbour didn't make him any more reassuring. In any city he would stand out; in the small town of Tayler's Creek, he was as exotic and barbaric as a jungle cat in suburbia.

She'd been avoiding him for the past three days, ever since she'd seen the lights on at his house and realized that he was back after yet another six-month absence. Although, if Rider *had* called, she was certain he would have made his presence known. She couldn't imagine him doing anything as underhanded as sneaking, despite the fact that he was a special forces soldier and probably trained to sneak.

When she was satisfied no one was hiding, crouched ready to spring, in any of the outbuildings, she shook her head in amused exasperation and strolled through the line of shrubs that screened the barn from the house, riffling slim, tanned fingers through her dark bangs and lifting the thick plait that lay against the back of her neck, allowing air to cool the overheated skin at her nape.

Checking her watch, she noted it was an hour short of lunchtime, but already the sky was hazy, the heat intense; the heavy, somnolent silence broken only by the sawing of crickets, as if every living creature, aside from the legions of glossy black insects, had gone into temporary hibernation. Even the breeze had died, so that the sun blazed down unchecked, sucking up moisture and leaching all the rich colour from the landscape; the distant, wavering heat shimmer lending the hills a sere, arid cast, when just weeks ago they'd been green and lush with early summer growth and an overabundance of rain.

Jess barked again, and Jane postponed the idea of a glass of lemonade, frosted with condensation and tinkling with ice cubes, and walked around the side of the house. She saw Jess in the far paddock—where she'd been, no doubt, hunting rabbits—standing stock-still, staring into the dark rim of the bush that flowed over a good deal of Jane's land.

The cold unease she'd felt in the barn returned, amplified. Just because there hadn't been a vehicle, didn't mean that someone hadn't walked through her place—unlikely as that event might be.

She called Jess, and the small black and tan huntaway trotted toward her, hackles up. Jane dropped her hand to the dog's head, soothing the rough fur.

She hooked her fingers through Jess's collar. "What is it, girl? What did you see?"

Jess whined and turned her head. A long pink tongue streaked out and licked Jane's wrist. Jane released her hold on the little dog and stood beneath the white blue arc of the sky, a hand shielding her gaze as she watched Jess disappear into the edge of the bush.

Minutes later Jess scooted free of the trees and trotted toward Jane with a stick in her mouth.

The saliva-coated offering plopped on the ground beside Jane's foot, and the tension holding her rigid dissipated. For the first time since Patrick had died, her home hadn't felt safe—*she* hadn't felt safe—and the feeling had rocked her. Maybe there had been no cause for alarm and she had overreacted, but she still felt unnerved and a little shaky.

But then nothing had felt normal or right since Patrick had died. She was still unsettled, still adjusting. Still on edge with her new status as a widow, and with being alone on an isolated property.

When Patrick had been alive, he'd filled her every waking moment with his schedule of medication and bathing, the hours she'd spent trying to coax him to eat—the regular visits to the hospital for chemotherapy and radiation treatments. Later on, when the treatments had stopped, there had been hours spent with the pastor and the steady stream of relatives coming to say good-bye.

When Patrick had finally lost his battle with the cancer that had struck out of the blue, stunning them both, and all of the rituals and formalities that accompanied death had been completed, she'd found herself abruptly alone—wrung out and empty, as if Patrick's death had sucked away all her emotions, and she was simply running on automatic. It was as if, when Patrick had died, a part of her had shut down, too. She went through the motions. She ate her meals, and she slept eight hours a night; she cleaned her house and weeded her garden and tended to the animals. She'd even started doing the extra jobs, like painting the barn. The physical exertion helped fill the void, but the numbing repetitive work didn't solve the curious sense of blankness, as if, like a pupa, she was isolated and enclosed, caught in a curious stasis, waiting for change.

According to her doctor, there was nothing physically wrong with her, other than the natural cycle of grief. The way she was feeling was perfectly understandable given the strain she'd been under. He'd prescribed antidepressants if she wanted them, but so far Jane had resisted medication.

The years of taking prescription medication for an ulcer that hadn't disappeared until she'd walked away from nervy stocks and volatile futures, which shifted like wet sand with every ebb and flow of the markets, had been enough, and besides, she was stubborn. She was thirty-two, and she'd finally grown into a quiet acceptance of the slow rhythm and flow of country life and her own body. If what was happening to her was a natural cycle, then she would let it run its course.

A shiver struck through her despite the heat and the hard-earned comfort of logic and reason, and wrapped her arms around her middle in automatic reflex. Sometimes she felt so blank and hollow that the emptiness would roll up from deep inside in cold, aching waves, the chill so intense that her skin would roughen, and no matter what she did she couldn't get warm.

Objectively she could feel the warmth, see the intensity of the light, but it was as if the sun, as powerful as it was, couldn't warm her, as if some essential part of her—the hot flicker of life—had been extinguished.

She'd been married to Patrick for ten years. In that time they should have had children. Before they'd found out about the cancer they'd tried, because they had both wanted a family, but nothing had happened. It had been the fertility tests that had shown up the cancer. Once Patrick knew the reason he hadn't been able to make her pregnant, and that he was going to die, he'd begun to make plans. He'd worked for as long as he could at his teaching job. He'd painted the house and finished building the barn. He'd leased out the orchard so that Jane didn't have to cope with managing the fruit trees at the front of the property. He'd even tried to convince her to sell the sheep, but Jane had put her foot down at the thought of letting the southdowns go. There weren't that many—she was down to thirty now—and the sheep kept her in a steady supply of wool for her weaving business. Besides, she was strong and healthy and more than capable of looking after the sheep and the few hens she kept.

Now that Patrick was gone, sometimes it felt like her marriage had been a mirage, or a chimera, a magical creature of illusion, that had dissolved almost before it began, leaving her stranded, all the bright promise gone.

She'd spent the past seven years marking time, preparing for emptiness, and now it was finally here.

THE NOONDAY SUN poured down on Michael Rider's back, burning his already tanned skin to copper and sending a trickle of sweat down the deep groove of his spine as his calloused, long-fingered hands closed around the Glock 19. A magpie squawked, striking a discordant note and causing a ruckus in the large, gnarled branches of the towering, ancient magnolia that occupied one corner of his backyard, as he slotted an empty clip into the handgun.

As weapons went, there was nothing pretty about the Glock; it was matte black and made of composite materials that seemed to actively absorb light. Without its fully loaded magazine, the weapon weighed in at a lean one pound seven ounces. In plain English, that meant it was light enough to make carrying concealed a breeze.

Not that he'd be carrying concealed anymore, or going anywhere he was *likely* to need a weapon. He was finished with war, and the way he saw it, war was finished with him. He was thirty-three, and he'd spent more than a third of his life either training for battle or actively participating. In the last thirteen years, he'd pushed his luck to the limit and he had the scars to prove it. He'd picked up a knife wound in Afghanistan that had netted him seventeen stitches and a stint in a military hospital in Germany because the infection that had gone with the cut had come close to killing him. He'd collected a bullet wound from a shady situation in Timor that had never made the news, and just to round things off, he'd broken his leg when a jeep he'd been a passenger in had rolled during a training exercise. That time he'd been laid up for four months, with further downtime while he'd rehabilitated the wasted muscles and regained his fitness. The limp had faded, and he'd made it back into active service again, but his leg still ached on him occasionally—especially when it was going to rain. A sign of old age creeping up on him fast.

A wry smile curved his mouth, as he adjusted his comfortable sprawl on the verandah steps and tilted his head back, enjoying the sun on his face and the smell of freshly cut grass. He replaced the weapon with the others he'd pulled out to clean and inventory for a buyer who ran a gun shop in Winslow. A month ago he'd viewed these weapons as necessary tools—now he kept seeing them as finance for fencing wire and fertilizer, or maybe even a start on the prime beef herd he aimed on breeding.

His dark gaze absently inventoried the down-at-heel corner of his farm he could see as he savoured the vision. His paddocks lush with blue-green grass; a herd of big, fat, lazy cows; some prime quarter horses just to make the place look pretty; and not a noxious weed in sight.

He grinned as he ran a soft cloth over the oiled parts of a Ruger. These days the only battles he intended to fight would be with the aforementioned weeds and a mortgage company.

With deft movements, he reassembled the weapon. The Ruger was—had been—his weapon of choice, and he'd carried it with him for more years than he cared to remember. He could break the rifle down and reassemble it blindfolded if he had to, and in the field he'd had to operate in pitch-blackness on more than one occasion.

Rising to his feet, he eased the stiffness from muscles unused to digging postholes and chopping firewood as he stepped off the verandah onto the lawn. With the ease of long practice, he lifted the Ruger to his shoulder, automatically bracing himself as he looked through the crosshairs of the telescopic sight. The twisted limbs of a distant puriri tree sprang into stark, ice-pure prominence; the magnification was disorienting, so that for a moment the gnarled bark and dark, glossy green foliage looked close enough to touch.

He drew in a breath and let it sift from between his teeth, then abruptly lowered the rifle.

Like the sidearms, the Ruger had to go. He'd rotated off a peacekeeping mission in Timor two weeks ago, and as soon as he'd hit New Zealand soil and read the letter that Marg Tayler—an old friend of his mother's—had sent, and which contained the one piece of information he'd been waiting on, he'd handed the SAS his resignation. He'd been in years longer than he'd ever wanted to be. He was a civilian now, and a horse and cattle breeder had no use for a sniper's weapon.

The sound of vehicles coming up his drive registered. Two police cruisers were partially visible through the thick border of overgrown shrubs that edged the drive as they pulled to a halt on the gravel just metres away.

A car door slammed as the bulky, sweating figure of Sergeant Tucker climbed out of the first car. Tucker was in his late fifties, balding and solidly built. He had run the small police station the entire time Michael had lived here and was as local as anyone could get, having been born in Tayler's Creek. Tucker was followed by three other uniforms, one of whom Michael recognized as the only other local cop, a young rookie called Zane Parker.

The rusted hinges of his white picket gate creaked as Tucker pushed it wide.

Zane followed behind, pushing the trailing branch of a climbing rose away from his face. "Shit, he's armed."

Michael heard the unmistakable sound of rounds being chambered in automatics, then the two unfamiliar cops appeared.

Michael eyed the four cops fanning out around him, and cursed beneath his breath. Tucker and Parker weren't armed, but the other two were. He remained completely still, the Ruger held loosely in one hand. "It's not loaded."

"Put the weapon down. Now." Tucker's voice was hollow, as if he was having trouble breathing, but Michael wasn't about to argue; he knew the drill, and respected it. The rules of engagement that he'd played to for the past thirteen years had been greyer and more savage than those ever confronted by civilian policing, but they shared rules in common. Number one was that anyone with a gun, loaded or not, was a threat.

Slowly, he went down on his haunches and laid the Ruger on the ground. Damned if he'd drop it and damage any part of it. The weapon was a Rolls Royce model, and worth upwards of five thousand dollars on the collectors' circuit. The fact that the gun had seen active service in the SAS would make it worth even more, and right now every cent he could squeeze out of these weapons would count. He needed all the money he could put together to get his farm operational.

Parker eased forward, crabbing sideways as if Michael were a wild animal, before darting in to snatch up the gun.

Tucker swore. "That's *evidence*, Parker."

Parker dropped the gun, and Michael winced. Seconds later

Parker pulled on thin latex gloves, picked up the gun, and retreated in the direction of the cruisers.

Parker's fumbling aside, the two officers keeping him pinned with their guns were colder, more controlled. Michael didn't recognize either of them, which meant they were probably backup from Winslow, the closest city to Tayler's Creek.

The two city cops were rock steady, and there was nothing sloppy about the way they maintained their weapons in the ready-to-fire position, so that if they needed to pull the trigger, a fractional movement of the finger was all that was required. To keep up that level of battle readiness required intense concentration and hours of weapons training, because after only a few seconds it was easy to let your focus slip, and the gun waver.

Michael eyed Tucker coldly, already knowing what Tucker must be hauling him in for, but asking anyway. "What am I wanted for?"

Tucker's face was red and sheened with sweat. A pulse pumped at the side of his jaw. "Murder. And rape."

Chapter 2

JANE LET OUT a breath, bent down, and eyeballed Jess. "You're supposed to be a guard dog."

Jess panted happily and dropped on her back, signaling it was time for a rub.

"Oh, great. And before that, you were supposed to be a sheepdog."

Obligingly, Jane rubbed Jess's belly, then threw the stick until Jess lost interest and flopped down beneath a shady tree.

On the way back to the barn, Jane checked the level of the water troughs. It had been so dry lately that she'd had to pump water from the bore just behind the barn every day just to keep the sheep in water. She hesitated as her hand settled on the latch of the pump shed door, apprehension pooling in the pit of her stomach at the prospect of walking into the small, dark building. Irritably, she shook off the jumpy, spooked feeling, gripped the door handle, and wrenched. The door held stubbornly, jarring the muscles of her upper arm, then came open with a rending creak, sending her staggering back a half step.

Hot air blasted out at her. The tiny shed was like an oven, dark and stifling, the corrugated iron crackling and pinging in the noonday heat. Too hot for birds and mice. Definitely too hot for an intruder.

"There, nothing," she muttered as her eyes adjusted to the dimness. "There's no one on this farm but me—and enough animals to start a zoo."

Crouching down, Jane rotated the valve that controlled the flow to the troughs, and primed the pump. By the time she'd started the motor and waited for it to settle into a steady rhythm, she was wet with perspiration and all she wanted was a cold drink and a shower. As she strolled around the side of the barn and headed for the house, she decided that she was too hot, too thirsty, and too tired to care if anyone tried to sneak up on her.

And if anyone got between her and a cold glass of lemonade, *she* would be the one behind bars for murder.

She paused before entering the kitchen to toe off her sneakers and ease out of the old bib overalls she was wearing over her tank top and cut-offs. Breathing a sigh of relief to be free of the heavy drill cotton, she bundled up the paint-stained garment and carried it through to the laundry, before pouring herself a glass of lemonade from the fridge.

As she slowly sipped the lemonade, enjoying the feel of the sweet, icy liquid sliding down her throat, her gaze was caught by the blinking light of her answering machine.

Her stomach contracted. Someone had left her a message.

In contrast to the wary apprehension she'd felt in the barn, this time her alarm was close to panic, which was crazy considering that half an hour ago she was coping with the fact that she could possibly have a killer stalking her. Setting the half-empty glass down on the bench, she approached the answering machine and pressed the playback on the single message that was recorded.

Abruptly, the room filled with low, dark, masculine tones. "It's Michael. I know you're there, Jane. You've got my number. Call me."

The terse statement was laced with impatience that she hadn't bothered to return his previous calls, and followed by a pause, as if he was debating saying something more, then the faint hum of static terminated with a click.

Jane drew a deep breath and let it out slowly. She felt hot and cold, wary and electrified. For a pulse-pounding moment,

Rider's presence had been so palpable she'd had the unnerving sense that he was in the room with her. After weeks of numbness, the intensity of her reaction, simply to the sound of his voice, was as intrusive and unsettling as the man was himself lately, as hard as she'd tried, she couldn't stop thinking about him, couldn't stop prodding at the past.

She'd been running away like a frightened rabbit ever since she'd realized he was back. Too afraid to face him, too afraid to touch on what she felt, because her feelings for Michael Rider were, and had always been, raw and confused.

He turned her on—it was that plain, that simple. She didn't have a clue how it had happened, or why. She had been *happy* with Patrick—she should have been immune—but when they'd bought the farm and moved to Tayler's Creek shortly after Patrick was diagnosed, she'd looked into Rider's dark gaze for the first time and felt like the ground had been cut away from beneath her. The tension had been instant and acute, and they'd been warily circling each other ever since.

Michael's wife, Clare, had left him within months of that first meeting, and Jane had been sharply aware of Michael living alone in the house. She'd made a practice of never walking in the direction of his place, never bumping into him if she could avoid it. She was married, and her husband was dying, and she was appalled that she'd been weak enough to fall in instant lust with her neighbour.

What had happened was out of character, and way out of line. For Jane her wedding vows were sacrosanct. She had married for love, and she had married for life. All the statistics might be against lifelong marriages, but she had wanted that with Patrick, and she'd been careful to never allow him to suspect that she was even remotely affected by their neighbour.

Rider's dark face drifted into her mind again, and she stiffened. Ever since he'd come back, she'd been on edge, waiting to run into him, and dreading it. It was cowardly, but she'd spent more time away from the farm in the past three days than she had in the past three months.

When Patrick had been alive, the protection of her married state had been absolute and she hadn't had to address the problem of how she felt, but now the buffer of her marriage was gone. Like it or not, she was alone and single, and, her confused emotions aside, the stubborn fact remained that even with Patrick gone, Michael Rider still felt forbidden.

She pressed the rewind button on the answering machine, then on impulse let the message play again, steeling herself against the effect of that dark voice.

A shiver skimmed her spine at the low demand to call him. It was ridiculous to feel . . . hunted. The odds that Rider was still interested in her as a woman were so remote as to be practically nonexistent. Years had passed since the initial shock of attraction. In that time he had been away more than he'd been home, and he'd probably had a string of gorgeous girlfriends.

If she'd had any sense she should have replied to the first message instead of panicking. Rider had probably just wanted to give her his condolences and offer his help if she needed it. He'd helped Patrick out a number of times with the heavier jobs on the farm. Apart from one occasion when he'd caught Jane alone, he'd never betrayed by a word, or a look, that he felt anything beyond friendship and compassion.

She rewound the tape, and this time, erased it with a stab of her finger—consigning the message to the ether along with all the others. The finality of the action sent a pang of cold through her that felt suspiciously close to loss. Irritated that she should feel anything that profound, or that *wimpy*, in conjunction with Rider, she spun away from the machine, finished her drink, and headed for the shower.

If she was honest, the problem wasn't that Rider might still want her, but that *she* still wanted him.

She had to get a grip, get a life.

She had to go into town to get groceries, and she also intended to drive to Winslow and get a security alarm. When Patrick had been alive, she'd felt safe and secure in her home, which only went to prove how people could fool themselves, because, as ill as he was, for the last few years Patrick had been physically incapable of defending himself, let alone her.

Whether she wanted to believe it or not, Tayler's Creek was no longer a safe haven. Somebody had broken into the Dillons' home and committed both murder and rape. Her imagination may have got out of hand this morning, but imagination or not, those moments in the barn had convinced Jane that getting an alarm was more than a good idea, it was a necessity.

* * *

TUCKER PULLED A warrant from his shirt pocket and handed it to Michael. "We'll also be searching your house and property."

"On what grounds?"

"Your truck was parked on Linford Road just four doors down from the Dillons' place two nights ago. One of the neighbours took your license plate.

Michael briefly closed his eyes. Linford Road was long and windy, a country lane lined with the latest craze in subdividing—small "lifestyle retreats" ranging from five to ten acres for the well-heeled who wanted to live in a farmlike setting and commute to work in Winslow. A lot of city people from Winslow had bought into the deal. Initially, there had been a lot of excitement about the subdivision, because it brought an injection of funds into an area that wasn't so much depressed as slow and sleepy. But it looked like the Linford Road subdivision had attracted something else that wasn't so positive for the small town. "That would put me at least half a kilometre from the scene of the crime. I went to see Jake Robertson about doing some fencing for me."

"At eight o'clock at night?"

Michael's gaze was steady. "He's at work during the day."

Tucker flushed. "We're trying to get hold of Jake," he admitted. "He's working over toward Winslow at the moment."

"That's right. On a government block. His cell phone cuts out over there. Just out of interest, have you got any other suspects, or am I it?"

"I'm not at liberty to reveal—"

"I *am* all you've got." Michael eyed Tucker in disbelief. He could feel the fury building. It generally took a while to get him well and truly riled, but Tucker and the Keystone brigade were getting him there.

Parker approached with a set of cuffs.

Michael's expression grew colder. "You won't need those."

"Winslow Central advises differently."

"Because I'm SAS?" Michael swore beneath his breath and allowed himself to be cuffed. "Didn't anyone tell them we're supposed to be the good guys?"

Tucker retrieved his warrant and took a half step back, as if, even cuffed, he was afraid Michael might harm him. Michael decided that was the first sensible thing Tucker had done in the last half hour.

"I know you're SAS, Rider. And I don't like this any more than you do, but there's a man dead, and a woman hurt in hospital. I have to play it as it comes."

"And in this case I guess I'm the easy option because I'm military and not local. Hell, I've only lived here for fifteen years."

Tucker snapped his notebook closed. "It's not that."

"What then? Motive? I've been back three days. I haven't had time to buy groceries yet, let alone go out and murder anyone."

"Opportunity."

"Every male in Tayler's Creek and Winslow had *opportunity*."

Tucker's gaze shifted to the weaponry that was laid out on the tarpaulin. "Not many of them are armed like you are."

"You won't find a weapon there that isn't registered. Those guns were part of my kit."

Tucker's gaze sharpened. "You've left the SAS?"

"I resigned two weeks ago."

Tucker pulled out his notebook again, flipped the cover, and scribbled a note. "That's something we can check on."

"If you're looking for a dishonourable discharge, don't hold your breath. And when you test the guns and ammunition you'll find the ballistics won't fit. The perp used a twenty-two, and I don't own one. But a twenty-two is a pretty standard kind of gun around here. Most farmers use them for rabbit and opossum control."

Tucker's eyes sharpened. "How do you know a twenty-two was used?"

Michael wondered idly if Tucker was aware that in Special Forces one of their offensive training units concentrated specifically on how to use cuffs to disable and kill. "The same way everyone else in this town knows it. I read it in the local paper."

Michael watched as the guns were bagged and loaded, then climbed into the rear of one of the police cruisers and allowed Parker to belt him in. "Guess you'll be busy checking all the guns that belong to the locals. I'm betting there must be at least a hundred of them."

He heard Tucker swear beneath his breath, then the door thunked closed, cutting off the sound and enclosing him in the stifling interior. One of the cold-eyed Winslow cops climbed in beside him, and the other took the wheel.

As the police cruiser maneuvered down his long shady drive in Tucker's dusty wake, Michael clenched his jaw and settled in to wait out the process.

Minutes later, he was hauled out of the backseat and a flash exploded in his eyes. The local press. A couple of shopkeepers walked out of their businesses to see what all the commotion was, along with a small stream of customers. A woman pushing a supermarket trolley paused at the boot of her car, long, shiny dark hair swinging forward as she rummaged for keys. Michael's belly clenched, his heart slammed hard in his chest. Jane.

Hunger ate at him, sharp and deep. He'd been back in Tayler's Creek just three days, and in that time he'd spent a lot of time sleeping, and the rest of the time trying to contact Jane O'Reilly. Every time he'd knocked on her door, mysteriously, she hadn't been at home, despite the fact that the whole place was wide open. Every time he'd rung, he'd gotten her answering machine, and she hadn't bothered to return his calls.

She was his next-door neighbour, but damned if he'd been able to catch her at it.

A hand landed in the centre of his back. Grimly, he resisted the shove. His gaze locked on Jane as he willed her to look at him, cold fury welling at the steel manacling his wrists.

If it hadn't been for Jane's dog hanging around his place, he'd have begun to wonder if she hadn't packed up and left town. Or worse, buried herself with her husband.

Chapter 3

THE AFTERNOON SUN poured down, radiating off asphalt with all the heat of a blast furnace as Jane slid her key into the boot lock. Automatically, she moved back a half step as the lock disengaged. Her disinterested gaze lifted with the motion of the boot and snagged on a pair of cold, dark eyes. For a frozen second her heart stopped in her chest.

Michael.

She blinked, barely registering the fact that for once she'd used his first name rather than the more impersonal address of "Rider." He was dressed in a pair of tight, faded jeans, his torso bare, and for a dizzying moment she wondered if she'd imagined him. His hair hung loose to his shoulders, and his skin was deeply tanned, as if he'd recently spent a lot of time in a tropical climate. His face was altogether leaner, sterner, than she remembered, his exotic looks hammered into a tough maturity that made her stomach clench.

His gaze flashed over her and she almost flinched at the cursory appraisal, then the uniformed police constable pushed him toward the station doors, and he was forced to look away.

Numbly, she watched the broad shape of his back as he disappeared into the station, and registered that the shiny glint she'd noticed around his wrists was a pair of handcuffs.

For a moment she went blank, then the reality of what was happening sank in. Rider was under arrest. If he were just being brought in for questioning, the police wouldn't have cuffed him, which must mean they had enough evidence to carry out the arrest.

There was no question in her mind about why he was being taken in. After spending just fifteen minutes in town she'd soon discovered there was no other topic of conversation than the home invasion, but everything in her rejected the thought that Rider could have had anything to do with the Dillon murder. In all the time she'd known him, they had barely spoken, let alone touched on subjects like values and ethics, but at an instinctive level she *knew* Michael Rider to his bones. The sexual attraction aside, she would trust him before she trusted Sergeant Tucker.

The doors of the police station swung closed, and Jane lifted a bag of groceries out of her trolley and dumped it in the chilly bin in the rear of her station wagon, automatically placing ice packs in with the groceries so nothing would spoil in the heat. She noticed her hands were shaking, and remembered she hadn't stopped to eat lunch, she'd simply finished her lemonade, showered and changed, and left for town. But that wasn't the only reason she was shaking. She was furious—quietly, deeply furious. She wanted to march into the police station and demand to know what Tucker thought he was doing—

"Do you reckon he did it?"

Jane glanced at the red-haired woman who'd paused beside her, a toddler clasped on one hip. Yolanda Perkins was a plump, happily married mother of four. She and her husband, John, owned a small farm, and John also operated a lucrative earthmoving business. Yolanda had often been heard to say that, given John's indifferent skills with anything that had hooves or ate grass, the D-eight bulldozer was the only thing that kept them solvent.

Jane lifted her final bag of groceries into the rear of the station wagon and transferred her attention to the small crowd that had gathered on the sidewalk, which included a TV news crew, who had materialized out of a brightly painted van. "No," she said flatly. "He didn't do it."

Macie Hume, the barmaid at the local pub, stepped out of

the shade of the supermarket overhang, a shocking pink hand-bag, which clashed wildly with her lime green microskirt, in one hand, and a polystyrene cup of coffee from Stevie's take-out bar in the other. She eyed the police station and grinned. "I don't care whether he did it or not, I can think of a better use for those cuffs."

Marg Tayler, who had managed the local drapery since time immemorial, and whose family Tayler's Creek had been named after, emerged from the narrow frontage of her shop, crossed her arms over her thin chest, and eyed Macie. "He's taken," she remarked gruffly.

Macie set her coffee down on the car parked next to Jane's, rummaged for sunglasses, and slid them onto the bridge of her nose. "Do tell. Who's the lucky girl, then?"

"That's nobody's business but his own."

Macie settled her hip against the car bonnet and sipped her coffee. "I might decide to make Rider *my* business. I'd hate to see all that man go to waste."

"Like you haven't tried already," someone called from beneath the shady overhang. "What are you gonna do, Macie, write to him in prison?"

Macie sipped her coffee and flipped her middle finger in the general direction of the comment.

Marg frowned at the gathering crowd, her eyes glittering with the light of battle. "Why don't you people just go home and leave the boy alone. When he's been here at all, he's never done anything but help." She fixed an older man with a sharp glare. "*You* can attest to that, Mason. Didn't he help dig that cow of yours out of the river last spring?"

Mason Wheeler, another local identity whose family had been one of the original settlers of Tayler's Creek, looked uncomfortable. "That he did."

"And did he try to shoot you while he was about it?"

A crease formed between Mason's bushy eyebrows. "Don't be ridiculous—"

"I'm not being ridiculous." She tapped her forehead. "I'm using this. Wish Tucker was capable of doing the same; maybe then we'd get some crimes solved. For my money, Tucker needs to retire. I'd put Rider in the job."

Mason looked outraged. "He can't take Tucker's job. He has to be trained."

"He's trained," Marg retorted flatly. "Afghanistan, Bosnia, Bougainville, Timor . . . You want me to go on?"

Mason crossed his arms over his chest. "That doesn't mean he can do a policing job."

Marg rolled her eyes. "What it means is he's been *doing* a policing job, and he's got the medals to prove it. Ever heard of peacekeeping, Mason? It's in the papers a lot these days, on account that some people can't settle their problems with common sense and discussion, they have to use a gun to finish their arguments. That's the job Rider's been doing, and he picked up a bullet a couple of years back for his trouble. If Tucker ever comes near a live round, aside from a misfire because he's dropped his gun, I'll eat every hat in my store. And that," she muttered beneath her breath, "would probably kill me."

Someone muttered that it would take a hell of a lot more than that to kill the old bird.

Marg didn't bother to turn her head. "I heard that, Owen," she said calmly. "I was talking to your mother this morning. Shouldn't you be in Winslow today, picking up your benefit? Or have you finally got a job?"

There was a muttered imprecation, as Owen Mullens, a lanky blond youth who had more of an affinity for surfboards than anything that might have a paycheck attached to it, slunk back into the shadows.

There was a small silence as Marg marched pointedly back to her shop, which was wedged between the supermarket and the police station.

Ely Murdoch, the head of the community council, and Tayler's Creek's self-appointed mayor, cleared his throat and adjusted the bill cap shading his craggy face. "Well, *whoever* did do the crime stole the Dillons' home theatre that was worth upwards of twenty thousand dollars. *And* all the videos." He shook his head. "Apparently the screen was one of those fancy new ones you hang on the wall."

There was another small silence, then someone murmured, "Wonder what was on the videos?"

Jane snapped her boot closed, abruptly sickened by the prurient interest in the petty details of the crime, when Rider was probably at this very minute being read his rights and questioned. She was more certain than ever that he could never have committed such a crime. Marg had hit the nail on the head when she'd stated that Michael wasn't a criminal, he was one of the good guys.

She glanced at Mason, who seemed set and determined that Michael was guilty. "In this country people are innocent until proven guilty. Michael hasn't been proven guilty yet."

Mason's expression was cold. "The police don't cuff people for no reason. An arrest's been made, which means they must have evidence."

Cold skimmed the length of Jane's spine. Her mind replayed the image of Michael being pushed down the path to the entrance of the police station, and it registered that her own inner certainty aside, she knew less about her neighbour than she'd thought. She knew he was a special forces soldier; she knew he was trained to kill, and neither fact was reassuring.

Nothing about Michael Rider was designed to make people feel comfortable. He was too overtly male, too mysterious, a double handful of everything that was wild and dangerous. She was beginning to think she was crazy, fixating on him for so many years.

He was an unknown quantity. Even more so than she'd imagined, because according to Marg, he wasn't single as Jane had thought; he was involved with someone.

The fact that he had a girlfriend should have filled her with relief, given that she'd spent the last three days hyperventilating about the possibility that he might want *her*. But she didn't feel relieved. After months of living in an emotionless limbo, something had finally broken through her numbness. Against all odds, against all common sense, imagining Michael Rider sprawled in bed, naked, with another woman *hurt*.

Yolanda shifted her toddler to her other hip and stabbed a finger at Mason. "You've changed your tune. I heard you say just the other day that Michael Rider was a hero."

"That was before Aubrey Dillon got shot, and his wife got raped."

"There are plenty of men in this town who had their eye on Carol Dillon; I don't think Rider was in the running. Carol must be in her forties, a little old for Rider."

"Rape is rape. Age don't come into it."

Macie made a sound of disgust. "God give me strength, we have an expert." She viewed Mason over the rim of her coffee cup. "Why would a guy who looks like Michael Rider bother with rape?"

Mason looked triumphant. "Everyone knows rape is a power crime."

Macie rolled her eyes. "Take one look at Rider, buddy. I don't think he has any issues with power. He's been beating women off ever since his wife left seven years ago. I know," she said wryly. "I'm one of them."

"Way to go, Macie."

Macie flipped another finger in the direction of the supermarket overhang. "And if Rider didn't do the deed, that means the murderer is still out there, maybe lining up his next target."

"Maybe the murderer's a woman."

Yolanda snorted and gave Mason an incredulous look. "Get a grip, Mason. There was a rape. The police took *samples,* which means there was semen. I could be wrong, but I don't think women have managed to produce semen yet. If they had, we'd be able to cut men out of the reproduction process. Now, *that* would be world news."

Mason's neck flushed bright red. "I'm going to tell your husband you said that."

Yolanda rolled her eyes. "Oh yeah, four kids down the track and one vasectomy later—like he's going to be threatened. He knows that if he so much as comes near me with sperm, I shoot to kill. Look, maybe they've got the right guy, and maybe they haven't, but I'm not going to take it for granted. If I were you I'd get an alarm system installed and lock up tight, because until I hear that Rider did do the crime, I'm going to assume that the murderer is still out there."

"I heard Rider's got guns, including a twenty-two."

Jane jerked her keys from the boot lock. "Practically everyone in the district has a gun, and Rider's got more reason than most to own guns. He's a professional soldier."

"He's used to killing."

"Yeah, right, so he's bright enough to leave the SAS and open fire on his hometown? I don't think so."

"John Tucker brought him in cuffed," Mason said stubbornly. "There's no smoke without fire."

Jane eyed Mason coldly. There hadn't been any logic in

this conversation from the get-go, she didn't know why she expected any now. "In five years, Tucker's biggest arrest was that crew from Winslow who were stealing farm bikes and rustling cattle. Apart from that he rousts drunks and prosecutes shoplifters. Homicide is not exactly his strong suit."

"I don't care what Tucker's expertise is. He's got a suspect, and that's good enough for me."

"Then you're easy to please. I hope you sleep well tonight, Mason, because I won't be."

There was a general murmur of assent, punctuated by a sharp cracking sound as Macie crumpled her coffee cup.

"I don't care if he did do it." Macie glanced in the direction of the police station as she straightened with a graceful movement and slung the strap of her purse over one shoulder. "Speaking for every female on the planet, it would be criminal to lock *that* up for any length of time."

Chapter 4

GRIMLY, MICHAEL STEPPED out of the police cruiser onto the gravel drive that formed a circular area in front of his house. In contrast to the dry heat of the day, the evening was hot and brassy, laden with the pressurized steam-bath heat that presaged cyclone weather. The humidity was already climbing out of his comfort zone so that his skin was sheened with sweat, and his leg was aching, which meant it was going to rain. His head was aching, too, but that was because he'd been battering it against Tucker's entrenched police procedure all day long.

He'd had no alibi, since apart from the hour he'd spent at Jake Robertson's house, he'd spent that evening home, alone, so they'd had to wait on the sketch that the police artist had put together that morning with Carol Dillon, along with the fingerprint records, which hadn't yet been entered into their data system and had to be faxed along with the sketch.

While they'd waited for the paperwork to feed through the machine, he'd gone through the rigmarole of having his prints taken. Tucker had wanted a DNA sample as well, but Michael had held his ground on that one. The hell he was going to have a needle stuck in his arm on Tucker's say-so, when he didn't have to. It was bloody-minded—he wouldn't miss the few cc's of blood they required to get their DNA, and basically he didn't begrudge it, because he had no intention of committing any crimes—but by that time he'd been seriously pissed.

When the fax had come through, the print had been so dark, no one had been able to make out any conclusive detail, so an officer had been dispatched from Winslow with a copy of the evidence file.

When the records had finally arrived, the sketch had shown a male Caucasian with long, dark hair, which had, apparently, been another deciding factor in the decision to take him into custody, but the hairstyle had been wildly different from his. For some reason no one had seen fit to tell Tucker that while the murderer did have long hair, it was distinctively styled: cropped short on top, with rat tails hanging around his shoulders.

On the evidence of the sketch alone, Tucker's case was shaky, because there was no way Michael could have grown his hair back to full length in the two and a half days that had passed since the murder and rape had taken place. When they'd finally confirmed that his prints didn't match any of those found either at the Dillons' residence or any of the other sites of the recent wave of home invasion crimes, Tucker had had no choice but to let him go.

Michael watched while his guns were unloaded and deposited on the lawn beside the drive, his cold gaze on Parker as the nervous officer nearly dropped the Ruger again.

When the cruiser accelerated down his driveway, leaving behind a cloud of dust, Michael took a deep breath, and let it out slowly. "Welcome to Tayler's Creek."

Sonovabitch.

Sometimes he wondered why he bothered to come back.

Although, he'd seen the reason today, and her expression had been so blank, he had to wonder if she even knew he existed.

Broodingly, he surveyed the house, and what land he could see. The paddocks weren't in great shape, because he'd leased them for grazing for years, but that was nothing he couldn't fix up with hard work, sweat, and herbicide. In contrast, the rambling old colonial farmhouse was in good condition because he'd systematically renovated and repaired it every time he'd had leave to burn. He'd scraped paint, replaced weatherboards, repainted, and replaced the roof. He'd built a deck off the family room and, when he'd finished on the house, he'd put in a lot of time renovating the stables and the implement shed. He'd kept his hands and his mind busy; otherwise he would have gone crazy wondering what was happening over at the O'Reilly place.

The house had originally belonged to his parents, who had bought the property fifteen years ago, but when his father had died, his mother had decided to move to a tidy little two-bedroom town house in Winslow, rather than cope with the large, sprawling homestead. Michael and his ex-wife had bought the place because at the time it had suited their needs—the farm was large enough that it would provide enough income that he could quit the SAS and they could start a family. The second he'd laid eyes on their new neighbour, Jane O'Reilly, that plan had crashed and burned.

He'd toyed with the idea of selling up and moving elsewhere with Clare, but he'd known instantly that that wouldn't work. Normally, he was disciplined and focused—a real pain in the ass to most people. He was used to controlling every area of his life, including his libido, but no matter how hard he'd tried he'd found he couldn't make himself want Clare. He'd wanted Jane, it had been that simple.

He hadn't wanted to hurt Clare, but as hard as he'd tried not to, he had hurt her, although from all accounts, she hadn't taken too long to get over him, and was now happily married to a barrister in Auckland.

Eyes narrowed, Michael surveyed the sky, which had turned leaden; the clouds churned and clotted, and were struck through with molten shafts of light as the sun dipped into the west. The air was thick with moisture and tasted like brimstone. After weeks of drought, there was going to be an unholy bitch of a storm, and the bad weather suited his mood.

Michael went down on his haunches beside the guns, picked up the Ruger and examined the walnut stock. There was no evidence of a scratch, which meant Zane could live, although he wasn't making any promises about Tucker. If he ever turned up on his property again in an official capacity,

Michael was likely to put a hot round in his butt and the jail term be damned.

Jaw tight, he began carting the guns and ammunition into the house and securing them in his gun safe. When he was finished, he took a shower, changed into fresh jeans and a T-shirt, and grabbed the keys to his truck. Jane's driveway was situated a kilometre north on the main road, although as the crow flies her house was a lot closer, the walking distance from his house to hers, less than half that.

He could walk over there now, but it was ingrained in him not to take that casual an approach. He'd always taken pains to keep his distance and preserve a certain formality in his dealings with both Jane and Patrick, unwilling to hurt a dying man, because he couldn't keep his hands off Patrick O'Reilly's wife, but right now he was too steamed to walk anywhere.

When he drew up next to the O'Reilly cottage, the long extended twilight had condensed into early dusk, helped along by the thick mantle of cloud. All the lights were off in the house, and Jess was barking.

Michael knocked on the front door. When there was no reply, he walked around the side of the house, his gaze brooding as he knocked on the kitchen door, then scanned the smoothly mown lawns, the neatly weeded vegetable garden, and the lush shrubbery. Jess was tied up, which meant Jane was out.

He strolled over to the kennel and went down on his haunches beside the little dog. She whined and shoved her muzzle at his hand. He rubbed behind her ears. "At least you're not afraid of me."

He had a strong suspicion that Jane was frightened out of her skin of him, and the way he felt right now, she should be.

He did a quick circuit of the outbuildings, automatically testing the locks, the urge to check the security of the buildings ingrained. The O'Reilly place was, in stark contrast to his, as neat and tidy as a new pin. A small herd of southdown sheep grazed in the paddock adjacent to the house, their wool recently clipped. The fences and the stockyard were in good repair, and the barn had just had a fresh coat of paint. He checked her garage and saw that it was empty.

Cursing beneath his breath, he thumped the side of the small weatherboard building. Damned if he'd leave without letting her know he'd been here. Jane had been avoiding him for days. The blank stare she'd given him in the car park outside the police station was the sum total of their interaction since he'd come back.

He strode back to his truck, reached into the glove box, pulled out a pen, and ripped a sheet from his diary. Scribbling a note, he anchored the piece of paper on the doormat of the front door with a rock he found in the garden.

It was hardly satisfactory, but it conveyed his message. He was finished with playing games. He'd waited seven years.

As far as he was concerned that was seven years too long.

JANE EDGED THE car into her garage. It was dark, the night moonless and overcast as she slung the strap of her handbag over her shoulder and hauled her bags of groceries out of the boot. Juggling the bags, she locked the car and the garage door, then trudged the short distance to the house and set the groceries down on the path while she went to let Jess off the leash.

Jess strained at the collar, tail wagging as Jane struggled to unclip the leash. A wet tongue swiped across her face, then the clip came free, and Jess bounded off into the night, doing her customary tour of the grounds as Jane collected the groceries and mounted the steps to the verandah. As she set the groceries down, the pale luminescence of a piece of white paper caught her eye. She retrieved the note, and set the rock that had anchored it to the doormat to one side, unlocked the door, and flicked on the hall and porch lights.

The note was brief and to the point.

"Call me, Michael."

Raw heat flushed through her, making her belly clench and her knees turn to jelly. The moment Michael's gaze had locked on hers outside the police station replayed itself in her mind, and abruptly she was spun back almost seven years when she'd opened the door, and found him on her doorstep dressed in jeans and a T-shirt, his hair damp as if he'd not long stepped from the shower. His wife had left just days before, and she had also been on her own because Patrick had been in hospital for an operation.

He hadn't asked to come in, and she hadn't offered any hospitality. The lack of manners on her part had been unspeakably rude for a small country community, but erecting some kind of barrier had been necessary, because the moment she looked into his dark gaze the reason he affected her so badly was suddenly clear, and the revelation shook her to the core.

His dark gaze pinned her. "The reason Clare left is that she knows I'm in love with you."

The words dropped into a pool of silence and for a moment she wondered if she'd misheard, or even worse, if her guilty mind had somehow supplied the words she wanted to hear.

She'd felt dazed, at once present and peculiarly removed from the scene taking place, as if there were two Janes—one who dealt in the solid currency of reality, and one who floated in a fantasy world.

He was in love with her.

Her heart slammed in her chest, and not for the first time, she wondered what it would be like to stretch out in bed with him, to have that sensual male mouth on hers: to have him naked on top of her.

It should have shocked her that she was even considering what it might be like to make love with her next-door neighbour, but instead, all she could think of was that on top of everything else that was going wrong in her life, she shouldn't have to want Rider.

Rider must have read something in her expression, because instead of backing off, he stepped into her, his hands curved around her waist—the contact electrifying. "Damn," he murmured. "I didn't mean to upset you, and I wasn't going to do this."

His head dipped and his mouth captured hers. Jane's heart slammed in her chest and for a moment she was frozen, then, somewhere in the murky depths of her mind, sharp need welled out of the confusion that always gripped her whenever she thought about Michael Rider and the hazy notion of pushing free dissolved. If the kiss had been practiced or slick, maybe she could have resisted, but it was so hungry it made her toes curl.

His tongue stroked along hers and a low moan welled up from deep in her belly, and she closed off the guilt, wound her arms around his neck, and kissed him back.

His hands closed on her bottom and she found herself lifted, until the hard ridge of his sex settled against the sensitive flesh between her legs. He pressed more firmly against her, and the tension coiled almost unbearably tight.

She broke the kiss. "If you keep doing that—"

"You'll come." His gaze locked with hers, dark and fierce. "God, don't say it—"

One hand closed on her hair, pulling her head back, the movement fierce as his mouth sank on hers. His tongue was hot and wet and salty in her mouth, and her whole being tensed as he walked her back a half step until she was pinned against the doorjamb, his muscled body tight against hers. Her breasts felt swollen and constricted, her skin so sensitive that every touch made her shiver and jerk, the hot ache between her legs so acute it bordered on pain.

She felt the hard, male shape of him straining for entrance despite the constricted layers of clothing, felt the shudder that swept him as he moved against her, and the gloomy afternoon dissolved in a raw flash of heat.

The buzz of the phone, the click of her answering machine engaging, registered, and abruptly, she recoiled.

Patrick. She'd forgotten about Patrick.

She'd forgotten she was married.

All Rider had had to do was kiss her and she'd practically forgotten her own name.

She shook her head, her throat tight. She still felt drawn, magnetized. She wanted to bury her face against the warm skin of his throat, breathe in his scent, open her mouth against his skin and taste him, and for a moment she teetered on the brink, shoved off balance by needs that were so alien and powerful she could barely breathe, let alone think.

She wanted Rider. It wasn't rational, and it wasn't right.

His dark gaze caught hers. His mouth dipped again, barely touching hers, and her body reacted, her hips sliding against his, and for a split second, she didn't care, she just wanted.

He lifted his head and pressed her face into his shoulder, and for endless seconds she clung to him, memorizing his scent, soaking in his warmth.

His breath stirred in her hair. "I've got to go."

"I know."

He eased back. "It's okay. Like I said, I didn't mean to"— his thumb swept across her lips—"do this, but I'm glad I did, because I'm going away and I don't know when I'll be back."

"Or if I'll be back" hung in the air, and as it turned out, that time he almost hadn't come back.

Jane didn't see him for more than eighteen months. Eventually, she'd heard secondhand in town that he'd been wounded on some overseas operation. The next time she'd been in Winslow, she'd gone to the library and searched back in the newspaper files, and finally found a small mention of the incident, where "a soldier" had been knifed and evacuated to a military hospital in Germany, his condition serious.

Worry had eaten at her, and her weight had plummeted, until she'd taken herself in hand and forced herself to eat. One day, months later, she'd turned around in the supermarket and seen him, larger than life and drop-dead gorgeous, loading groceries into a trolley. She couldn't remember what she'd gone to the supermarket to buy, she'd simply turned on her heel, walked back to her car, and driven home. She'd gotten through the rest of the day, she'd managed to function, but that moment in the supermarket had stunned her.

She'd had visions of him in intensive care, close to death. She'd even worried that he *had* died, and she simply hadn't heard. In the supermarket, he hadn't looked as if he'd suffered anything as traumatic as a life-threatening wound. If anything, he'd seemed even bigger, more muscular—more of everything.

Jane stared at the note in her hand, brought back to the soft scent of the night air, the whine of mosquitoes on the prowl. "What did you want to tell him?" she muttered to herself. "That you were head over heels in love with a man you barely knew?"

Because the fact was, falling in lust with a man had never happened to her before. She wasn't promiscuous, and she hadn't had that many relationships. Sexually, she'd always been as dead as a doornail unless she was emotionally involved. Crazy as it seemed, somehow she *had* become emotionally involved with Michael Rider; she had fallen in love.

Jess lolloped inside, her claws clicking on the hall floor. Automatically, Jane picked up her groceries, readjusted the strap of her purse on her shoulder, closed the door, and locked it. She was tired and she was hungry, and her feet were aching. She'd spent hours driving around Winslow, tramping the streets trying to buy a security alarm—without any luck. Apparently, they'd sold out within a day of the news breaking about the home invasion in Tayler's Creek. Security firms and appliance stores had more alarm systems on order, but it would take a couple of days for them to be shipped, and then there was a waiting list. If Jane wanted an alarm, she would have to stand in line like everyone else.

After stowing the groceries, she walked slowly upstairs, flicking light switches as she went, the note crumpled in her hand. When she got to her room, she stowed her bag and dropped the note on her dressing table, and walked over to the dormer window and looked in the direction of the Rider place. The faint glimmer of lights shone through the trees.

Her gaze shifted, caught by her own reflection in the glass, and for the first time in months she took the time to examine herself. She was medium height and slim, her breasts a respectable size and shape, her hips narrow enough that she had difficulty buying pants that fit and often had to shop for teenagers' sizes. She'd lost weight—enough that most of her clothes were loose on her now—but with Patrick dwindling away, her appetite had faded and she hadn't wanted to eat.

Her hair was long, and dark enough to be mistaken for black, her eyes a light amber and faintly slanted, and her skin was tanned a honey colour from spending so much time outside.

She lifted a hand to her lips. She hadn't worn lipstick in— She tried to think, and couldn't remember the last time she'd worn so much as a clear gloss, let alone makeup.

She was still attractive, despite the passage of years, and now she was fiercely glad she was pretty, glad that even if she felt old inside, the outer packaging looked young.

Her waist was small, her hip bones jutting faintly, her stomach flat. Her hand came to rest on the strip of tanned skin left bare where her tank top had separated from the waistband of her shorts, and the heat of her palm against her skin sent a small shiver through her. The weight loss had made her more sensitive, as if the gradual paring away of her normal subcutaneous layer had left all of her nerve endings exposed and unprotected.

Abruptly, she wondered what it would be like for her belly to swell with a child.

A part of her longed fiercely for the physical changes that pregnancy forced on the female body. For more years than she cared to count, she'd *wanted* her belly to balloon and her breasts to grow heavy with milk. She'd wanted a baby to hold in her arms, to suckle at her breasts, and she wanted to be tired because her life was filled with kids, and not just emptiness.

She'd ached with wanting a baby, and still did, but as the years had passed and all of her energy had been focused on Patrick, the sharp, panicked feeling that her childbearing years were slipping away had dulled into acceptance.

Maybe Patrick's death had sharpened her need to have a baby, or maybe it was simply that her biological clock was ticking loudly because she was over thirty—but she didn't just want children in the misty, uncertain future, she wanted to be pregnant *now*. Too much time had slid by while her body had simply marked time. She wanted to know there was a baby growing inside her.

She was young enough to remarry, young enough to start a family if she wanted, but her mind flinched from the process of getting pregnant. After years of having a separate room from Patrick, the thought of sleeping with a man, the shattering vulnerability of making love, quite frankly scared the living daylights out of her.

She picked up the crumpled note, smoothed it out, and looked at the firm, slanted writing.

Call me.

Just like that.

If she called Rider, within five minutes she would be flat on her back and penetrated.

A raw flash of heat went through her, starting a dull throbbing between her thighs.

Michael was big, taller than Patrick had been—six foot two, at least—heavier and more muscular, and intensely male. Sex with him would be hot and vital, and there was no question in her mind that he would make her pregnant. The thought of having him on top of her, sliding inside her and climaxing, sent another raw shudder through her and her breasts tightened, the nipples erect and almost painfully sensitive.

When she was ready for that—if she was *ever* ready—she

would call him, and it registered that, regardless of Rider's availability, and frightened out of her skin of the process or not, she was mentally preparing herself to have sex with Michael Rider.

Chapter 5

AT FIVE IN the morning, Jane woke from a fitful sleep, drenched with perspiration, the tank top and panties she'd worn to bed clinging uncomfortably to her skin. Untangling the single sheet that was wound around her legs, she pushed the damp cotton aside, paced to her window, and pushed it wide. Sometime in the night a fitful wind had got up, but the heavy mantle of cloud remained, blanking out the moon and stars, so that darkness pressed in—thick and absolute. The faint tang of ozone filled her nostrils, along with the rich scent of rain and the pervasive sweetness of the jasmine and honeysuckle that persisted in her garden despite her attempts to weed them out.

Smothering a yawn, she showered, washed her hair, and changed into fresh clothes, then walked out to the sheds and began battening down for the storm.

Despite the canopy of cloud and the steady breeze, the heat was oppressive, and by lunchtime, coated in dust and grime from wrestling farm equipment into sheds, and jittery from expecting at any moment to hear Michael's truck coming up her drive, she was ready for a break. Changing into her swimsuit, she called Jess and walked along the worn track to the creek that flowed through the wild reverted country at the rear of her property. Here, the land was twisted and strange, filled with a jumble of large boulders and creepy caves, but the river was deep enough to swim in, and surrounded by ferns and nikau palms, with the added bonus of a small waterfall plunging off a limestone shelf.

As she swam, she gradually became aware that aside from the deliciously cool sound of water flowing, the bush had grown silent, as if the approaching storm had cloaked everything in a blanket of humidity, muffling sound. Tension skimmed the length of her spine as she climbed a small sloping rock face, retrieved her towel, and knotted it around her waist. Just minutes ago, Jess had been lying in the shade, happily panting; now she was nowhere to be seen.

Jane swiveled around, searching the thick bush edge, which was choked with trailing vines of supplejack and thick, spiky coprosmas. Her instinct was to call out to Jess. The little dog was more than likely exploring, but Jane didn't like the thought that she might have gotten stuck down a hole, or lost in one of the limestone caves. Here, the country was as unpredictable as it was strange, and every now and then, when a piece of limestone eroded enough, a hole simply opened up in the ground.

Oddly loath to break the silence, Jane held her hands to her mouth and called. A rustling on the other side of the bank drew her gaze. She called again. When there was no response, she reluctantly dropped the towel and climbed back down the rock face and slid into the water. A few strokes took her across to the other side of the river. Grasping moss-covered rock, she hauled herself up the bank to the spot she'd seen the thick clump of ferns move. She parted the coarse leaves, half expecting to find an opening to one of the limestone caves. There was an opening, but it was little more than a shallow concavity in the rock.

There was no sign of Jess, but the ground was trampled as if someone had hunkered down there, the vantage point high enough that whoever it was had been able to watch her swim.

Her gaze probed the bush edge, all the fine hairs at her nape lifting as she backed away from the trampled ground, clambered down to the river, and swam across to the other side. The little hidey-hole could have been made by kids coming here to swim and build huts, but the property was isolated. Apart from the Jackson family, who lived a couple of miles away, there were no children who were likely to come and spend time here.

Snagging her towel, she cinched it around her waist and headed back to the house, calling Jess as she went.

It wasn't inconceivable that a feral goat or pig had taken up residence on her land, although that scenario wasn't likely, because with the threat of tuberculosis from wild animals, most of the surrounding farmers were hot on animal control.

Maybe she was overreacting, but, whatever—or whoever— had been hunkered down there in the ferns above the swimming hole, she wasn't taking any chances.

TUCKER'S OFFICE WAS small, cluttered, and smotheringly hot, despite the fact that he had a window open to catch the breeze.

Jane sat down in the chair adjacent to his desk and set her purse on the floor. "There was someone watching me swim."

Tucker's face was weary. "Join the club. Martha Holbrook said someone was watching her take a bath last night, and Anna Wheeler claims she saw a face at her window while she got undressed, but her husband said it was probably the next-door neighbour's cat trying to get in the window. You sure it wasn't kids?"

"I don't know who, or what, it was. It could have been kids, I just . . ."

"Have a feeling. I know." He rubbed a hand over his balding head. "The whole town's having 'feelings.' I'll send Zane out to look around. Is your house secure and alarmed?"

"It's secure, but not alarmed. I tried to buy an alarm in Winslow yesterday. They were sold out."

Tucker grunted. "Figures. I'll get Zane to do a check on your locks. Have you considered going to stay with someone until we catch this guy?"

Jane picked up her purse and got to her feet. She hadn't expected Tucker to jump through any hoops for her, but all the same, it didn't make her happy that he was treating the matter so casually. "I've got Jess and the hens to feed, and the sheep to keep an eye on. Leaving's a great idea, but it's not practical."

"What about getting someone to come and stay with you?"

"I'll see."

The problem was she didn't really have anyone who was close enough for her to ask that kind of favour. One of the results of Patrick's illness was that she'd concentrated so much on him that she'd neglected the girlfriend thing. They'd both lost touch with the friends they'd had when they'd lived in Auckland, and since moving to Tayler's Creek, she somehow hadn't ever moved past the acquaintanceship stage into friendship with anyone. She had plenty of people she could pass the time of day with in the street, but no actual friends.

Zane followed her back to her house, and walked with her out to the river. She pointed out the spot where the ferns were flattened. He found a place along the river that had stepping stones, then walked upstream to examine the trampled area, taking notes. When they returned to her house, he walked through her house and checked her doors and windows. "Your doors are good, but you need bolts for the windows. And make sure you get that alarm installed."

He scribbled the name of a couple of reputable security firms on her telephone pad, both of which she had already tried to buy alarms from when she was in Winslow. As he set the pen down, his pager beeped.

He checked the message, and blushed. "My girlfriend," he mumbled, as he clipped the pager back on his belt and pulled his cell phone from his pocket.

Jess thumped her tail on the verandah decking as Jane watched Zane drive away, still talking to his girlfriend. Jane absently stroked her head. "Well, that was the cavalry. So much for security."

As the dust cloud from Zane's vehicle dissipated, she decided that she couldn't wait the week it would take for a security system to be installed.

She didn't feel safe. In fact, she felt distinctly *unsafe*. There wasn't a lot she could do to increase her security, but she had to try. Jess was her main alarm, but it was always possible that Jess could be harmed by an intruder—maybe even poisoned or shot.

She had a gun. It wasn't much of a gun, and it was possibly more of a hazard than a help because it could be taken away from her in a confrontation—but she wasn't intending on using the weapon for anything other than warning off possible intruders.

Collecting the key to the reinforced cupboard that Patrick had built in the mudroom, she unlocked first the padlock bolt that secured the door, then the steel bar that locked the gun against the back of the cupboard wall. The gun felt heavy and unwieldy as she set it down on the floor, then collected the bolt, a box of ammunition, and the two magazines that went with the rifle. On impulse, she grabbed a bottle of gun oil and a cloth—she supposed since the gun hadn't been used for so long it would need a clean. She hadn't touched the thing in years, not since Patrick had given her lessons on how to load and shoot it, and made her practice until she could hit a target with reasonable accuracy.

She carried all the pieces out to the kitchen table and laid them down. The gun looked dark and lethal in her bright, sunny kitchen, and the smell of gun oil was pungent and faintly acrid, already overlaying the gentler scents of the garden floating in the open door. Lifting the weapon, she examined it, then began systematically dismantling and cleaning the ancient twenty-two, using the ritual to refamiliarize herself. When she was finished, she reassembled the weapon and fed shells into the two five-shot magazines.

Minutes later, she walked out into the empty paddock nearest the bush line, with Jess at her heels, and placed a row of empty cans on fence posts. When she was satisfied she had enough targets, she fetched the gun, positioned herself twenty paces back from the tins, and took aim. She decided she didn't have to be too far away from the target, because if anyone attacked her, it was going to be a close-quarters thing; she wouldn't have time to do anything but bring the gun up and shoot, anyway. Apart from that eventuality, she wouldn't be doing anything but firing into the air as a warning.

The gun bucked gently against her shoulder, and the shot went wide. She altered her stance a little, to allow more flexibility when the recoil hit, and this time she managed to wing the tin. The third shot, she blew it off the post. Methodically, she hit two more tins, then changed the magazine. As she lined up the next target, she had a disorienting flash of the way she'd been ten years ago, before she'd hit Tayler's Creek—with a wardrobe of pretty clothes, long nails, high heels, and enough makeup to fill a suitcase. Now she was barefoot, her shorts and halter-neck top stuck to her skin with sweat, her hair tangling around her face where it had blown loose from her plait, and her skin tanned and bare of makeup.

She wasn't the city girl she'd been before, and she wasn't the quiet, empty person she'd been just days ago. She had changed, but she liked the changes in herself.

She didn't know if she could actually walk in high heels anymore, or where on earth in Tayler's Creek she could even wear high heels, but she decided then and there that she was going to try. Wearing high heels would mean more clothes, because unless she put on weight, she wouldn't fit any of the old ones, and that meant shopping.

Blankly, she considered what it would be like to once again take part in the utterly female ritual of shopping—to stroll through malls and browse through boutiques, choosing clothes and shoes not because they were practical, but simply because they made her look and feel good.

She felt dazed at the prospect, and somehow lighter, as if a weight had just slipped from her shoulders. But then the past few days had been filled with change, ever since Michael Rider had intruded back into her world and forced her out of the rut she'd sunk into. The process had been painful, and she'd resisted like crazy, but for the first time in years, she felt free, and despite her tiredness and the grimness of what she was doing, she felt . . . strong.

A wry smile curved her mouth. It was scary to think that the moment of empowerment had happened while she was holding one of the most potent symbols of male power—a gun—in her hands.

A MISTY HAZE, the peculiar characteristic of cyclones in New Zealand, built up as the day passed. The cloud cover remained heavy, and the breeze began to gust.

Jane moved from trimming branches near windows, to working on the home alarm system she'd devised. She hauled water up the stepladder and filled the bucket that she'd set on the roof just above the entrance to the kitchen. When it was half full, she climbed back down the ladder, and pulled on the rope attached to the bucket to test it. Water cascaded down, partway soaking her despite the fact that she took care to step back.

She replaced the bucket, balancing it carefully on the edge of the guttering, and refilled it with water. It was a kid's trick, but it was effective.

She repeated the same booby trap over the front door, and to finish off, she gathered up empty paint tins from the barn and empty cans that were stored in a rubbish bin liner ready to be taken to the recycling station. She punched holes in each can, using a hammer and a nail, then strung them together in two bunches with baling twine, and tied a cluster to each bucket of water. Now when either of the buckets came down, they would not only soak the attacker and, hopefully, hit him on the head or the chest, but the attached cans would tumble down around him, making plenty of noise.

There wasn't a lot else she could do. If an intruder decided to smash glass and come in one of her windows, then she was sunk. She had Jess for protection, and if she had to, she would use the gun.

Chapter 6

AT FIVE MINUTES past midnight, the power failed.

Jane sat up in bed and set down the book she'd been trying to read. The wind was howling, and thin drizzle spattered her windows. Jess's tail thumped on the floor. Jane patted her head as she reached for the phone on her bedside table and discovered that that was dead, too. Either the storm had knocked the lines out, or someone had wrapped their car around a power pole, bringing the lines down.

Jackknifing out of bed, she dragged on her shorts, pulled a shirt over the soft cotton singlet she'd worn to bed, and padded downstairs, holding the torch she'd left beside the bed. Jess had followed her, and now she flopped down on the kitchen floor, set her head down, and let out a gusty sigh. Reassured by Jess's relaxed mood, Jane rummaged in the hall cupboard and extracted the battery lantern that was stored there, carried it through to the kitchen, and adjusted the knob until the room was filled with a soft glow.

She tried the phone again. The line was still dead. She paced the kitchen, stared out at the wild night, and was abruptly gripped by a sense of isolation.

Although she'd spent a lot of time on her own over the

past few years, she hadn't often been alone. Barring the time he'd spent in hospital, she'd always had Patrick for company. Now the house seemed to echo with emptiness, the sense of being cut off from everyone and everything intensified by the loss of the phone.

A sweep of headlights briefly illuminated the kitchen, throwing the potted plants that lined the window into stark relief and giving a ghostly cast to the room. Above the whine of the wind, she thought she heard tyres crunching on gravel.

Grabbing the torch, she flicked off the beam, took a hold of Jess's collar, and slipped out the door, bracing herself against the full brunt of the wind where it slammed into the east side of the house, and shivering as she was instantly soaked by the thin drizzle that was being driven in horizontal gusts. Outside, the sound of the wind was eerily amplified, rising to a high-pitched animalistic howl that tightened the skin all along the length of her spine. She wasn't normally this nervy, but then she wasn't in the habit of receiving midnight visitors either.

As she edged around the corner of the house to see who it was, Jess lunged free of her hold and shot straight down the steps and out to the drive, which meant that whoever the intruder was, he would probably be licked to death before he could get to the house. At the same time, it occurred to Jane that a murderer wouldn't be likely to have his lights on, but with the power and the phone out, she wasn't taking any chances.

And as isolated as she was, a convoy of murderers could turn up and it wouldn't matter how many lights were blazing; she couldn't expect any help from anyone but Rider who, from all accounts, was too busy with his new girlfriend to notice what was happening to his neighbour.

Wiping moisture and wet strands of hair from her face, she peered in the direction of the drive. Movement registered out of the corner of her eye, as if someone was walking toward the kitchen rather than the front door. The flicker of movement was followed by a gravelly curse, then the rattle and clang of tins as the bucket came down. She heard something that sounded suspiciously like a groan, but the sound was muffled and indistinct.

Gripping the torch, she peered around the corner of the

house. The faint wash of the light from the kitchen windows flowed over a familiar male form.

Switching the torch on, she hurried forward, knelt on the wet grass, and began dragging the tangle of cans and rope off Rider, her hands feverish. The bucket must have caught him on the head, knocking him out.

In the dim light his eyes flickered, and his gaze locked on hers, narrowed and glittering. "Since coming back I've been arrested, cuffed, and fingerprinted, tortured by spending four hours solid with Tucker and Zane Parker." He lifted a hand to his head and winced. "Now, I've been attacked by a bucket. Whoever said Tayler's Creek is Sleepy Hollow lied. It's a war zone."

The bite to his words barely registered beyond the fact that his irritation told her that he was obviously okay. She swatted his hand aside. "Let me see."

The lump was situated in the centre of his forehead. Unexpected amusement quivered through her. When she was a kid the bucket trap had never netted much success. Obviously her targets had all been too short. Rider, at around six-feet-two, was the perfect height. The bucket had caught him clean—right between the eyes.

He pushed himself into a sitting position and fingered the lump. "Oh yeah, you got me good. I saw stars." His gaze swept her, still glittering, and not a little irritable. "You're getting wet."

Understatement of the universe. Already her shirt was clinging to her skin, and her hair was sopping. Retrieving the torch, she got to her feet. "In case you hadn't noticed, Rider, there's a storm; everything's wet."

His teeth flashed white in the dim light as he eased to his feet, stumbling slightly as he straightened, as if he was having trouble orienting himself. "Some things look better wet than others."

Her amusement was replaced by a spurt of anger, and she was glad she'd resisted the urge to grab his arm and steady him. Rider had obviously come to check on her because the power and telephone were out, which was nice. Very neighbourly. She was sorry he'd gotten hurt, but obviously the bucket hadn't hit hard enough to anaesthetize his libido. "I saw Marg Tayler in town yesterday," she said pointedly. "She said you were involved with someone."

"Did she, now?"

Fury flickered at the expressionless mask of his face, the stony male reserve that was one of Rider's defining qualities—and did she detect a hint of male smugness in that low, gravelly voice?

Her jaw clamped, and in that moment everything changed. For years she'd been on the defensive—running—and she *hated* that. One thing she had never been was a coward.

She shouldn't feel one iota of emotion for Rider, but unfortunately she felt considerably more than that. Against her better judgment, against her *will* she'd been tied to Rider for the past seven years as if she'd been married to *him* instead of Patrick. To say she was ticked was putting it mildly.

Rider's head came up, as if he'd somehow latched on to her thoughts. Light glistened off the sharp cut of his cheekbones, the strong shape of his jaw. "What did you expect?" he said coldly. "That I'd live years on about two minutes of lip contact?"

Her chest contracted on a sharp pang that she refused to label as hurt. "It wasn't just lips."

And it may have been two minutes, but it had felt like an hour of teeth and tongue, hot, steamy breath, and full, pulse-pounding body contact. To say he'd kissed her didn't cover it. His intentions and arousal had been explicit, and so had hers. Fully clothed as they'd both been, within the two minutes they'd been "lip-locked," they'd practically had sex on her front porch. The only thing that had prevented actual penetration had been the sound of the answer phone engaging and a crippling surge of guilt.

She had climaxed.

Heat washed through her at the memory of just how far they'd gone, fully clothed, and despite the fury that burned like a hot coal in her chest, her breasts rose, tight and aroused against the wet drag of her shirt.

Rider's gaze slitted. "So, who have the local gossips put me in bed with this time? Macie Hume? Or are they having another stab at firing up a scandal with the Irwin twins?"

The Irwin twins? Jane stared at Rider in disbelief, ignoring the moisture trickling down her face and running in small riv-

ulets down her spine and between her breasts. Rider in bed
with twins?

Her jaw clamped. She was getting crazier by the minute.
She had no idea there were so many single women in Tayler's
Creek—let alone twins—and no idea what she was doing outside in the dead of night, in the middle of a cyclone, having
this conversation with Rider. "If you don't mind," she said
stiffly, "I'm going inside. Thanks for coming over, but as you
can see, I'm fine. I don't need your help."

His hand curled around her arm, jerking her to a halt. "I
thought you understood how I felt."

His voice was rough, his palm hot, burning through the wet
cotton of her shirt.

She resisted the urge to pull free. Damned if she'd fight
with him. "What do you mean?"

His gaze burned into hers. "I don't cheat."

Her cheeks warmed at the memory of her own guilt. He
had kissed her, but she had been the one who had climaxed—
and she'd wanted to do a lot more. She didn't know what their
little interlude could be classified as; but whether it was labeled
an affair or not, it had felt like one. "You could have fooled
me."

"You're angry." There was a wealth of satisfaction in his
voice. "Well, hallelujah for that. It beats the hell out of indif-
ference."

He released her. "I don't cheat, and I'm here. Figure it out."

She blinked, feeling abruptly unsteady, as if the ground
beneath her feet had just shifted. She'd felt like this once before, and she didn't trust the feeling. The last time, Rider had
kissed her and almost wrecked her life.

"You're finally getting it," he muttered, turning away, "but
don't expect me to go down on my knees begging—"

"Wait!" She touched his back, then snatched her fingers
back as he spun, his gaze as cold as obsidian. "Look, I'm
sorry—" She drew in a breath and let it out slowly. "Um—
don't go."

His expression was wary. "What do you mean, 'Don't
go'?"

Her stomach clenched at the risk she had to take. She would
rather walk over hot coals than admit to Rider that she'd been

obsessed with him for years. "If you don't cheat, and you're here," she said carefully, "that must mean . . ."

"Christ," he snapped, "I can't stand it. Just come here."

Jane's heart slammed in her chest. The invitation, couched as an order—as if she was one of the soldiers under his command—the way his gaze zeroed in on her mouth, was about as subtle as a hammer blow. "Anyone ever tell you you've got a problem with anger?"

He stepped toward Jane, crowding her space. "I've been pissed for seven years. Most people *know* I've got a problem with anger. Some of them were even interested enough to find out why."

It was Jane's turn to be wary, although the wariness was almost instantly overridden by a heady dose of excitement as his hands fastened on her arms. In the nerve-racking, swampy sea of her relationship with Rider, she finally knew what came next, because they'd played this part before.

His hands slid up her arms, making her shiver, glided over her shoulders, slipped under her hair, and cupped her face, and she had to resist the urge to give in without any fight at all and melt into his arms.

"I know you, O'Reilly," he murmured. "I've had a lot of time to think, to analyse. While you pretended I didn't exist, I researched you. Before you buried yourself in Tayler's Creek and started dressing like Huckleberry Finn you used to buy and sell stocks and consult on mergers. You're gorgeous and you've got a brain. Well, figure out this merger."

She swallowed, unnerved as his head lowered. She wanted him to kiss her so much that her mouth was actually watering, but her mind couldn't shake loose of one compelling fact. She'd agonized over Michael Rider for seven years, and now she was finally free, and so was he. But, forbidden or not, Rider was still high-octane danger. She knew how to play the percentages, and whichever way she added this "relationship," she was going to get burned.

His mouth grazed her forehead, the contact fleeting and unexpected, and totally unfair. Her eyes closed, and her palms flattened on his chest. She could feel the hard points of his nipples, the rapid slam of his heart, and the faint panicked urge to push him away dissolved as every bone in her body turned to jelly. He felt hot and muscular and wet, and God help her, she wanted him. *"There's nothing wrong with my clothes."*

She caught the flash of his grin. "Just that you're wearing too many."

His lips brushed hers again, unexpectedly soft and gentle, when everything else about him seemed hard as nails—tough and uncompromising. She drew in a shivering breath, tasted Rider, then his tongue filled her mouth, hot and unutterably male and every nerve ending in her body melted.

After the emptiness of the past years, the antiseptic smells of medication and hospitals—the curious stillness of waiting for death—he tasted like fire and heat and rain, as earthy and powerful as the rugged hill country that enfolded Tayler's Creek.

His hand settled in the small of her back, urging her closer, until her breasts were pressed against his chest, the contact hot, electrifying. He was wet, his T-shirt soaked, his skin burning through the dampness.

He broke off the kiss as he peeled off his soaked shirt, then his hands clasped her waist and shifted upward, sliding her shirt and the cotton singlet up in one smooth, slick sweep. When he didn't find a bra, his hands curved around and gripped her breasts, holding them firmly, his thumbs stroking over her erect nipples, making her shudder as he leaned forward and captured her mouth again.

Heat rolled through Jane as she wound her fingers in his wet hair and held on, drinking in his taste and scent, the heady feel of his skin against hers. Her breasts were swollen and tight, her lower belly throbbing, and rain and moisture filled the air, making even the simple act of breathing difficult.

He bent and took one breast in his mouth. One hand cupped and gripped her bottom, his fingers digging into the soft flesh, and abruptly liquid heat spasmed through her so that she shuddered and arched, her mind blanked out by the exquisite rill of pleasure.

Vaguely, she logged the short, sharp word he said, but her mind was still swimming, caught up in a curious stasis where light and sound faded. She had the dizzying sense of movement, felt the cool sharp shock of wet grass against her back. She registered the rough slide of her shorts and panties being drawn down her legs, the abrasion of denim as he slid down his jeans and between her thighs, and vulnerability assailed her even as she tilted her hips in automatic reflex, the slight movement opening her fully to him.

She felt the stroke of his fingers, the bolt of pleasure from even that simple touch, then he shifted upward, making a low sound of satisfaction as he completed the job of stripping her shirt and singlet from her torso. The blunt shape of his naked sex lodging between her tender folds tipped her over some invisible edge, and she arched, straining against the pressure, the hot, ridged muscles of his belly. Her fingers sank into the heavy muscles of his back. He jerked beneath her touch, then his mouth came down on hers and he shoved deep. For an endless moment she clung to him, her body quivering at the hot shock of penetration.

He said something low and indistinct, then withdrew and slid home again, forging deeper, the pressure relentless as delicate inner muscles stretched taut.

He groaned low in his throat, his gaze locked on hers. "How long?"

She didn't pretend to misunderstand. The second she'd realized that she was attracted to Rider, she'd been incapable of making love with her husband. Whenever Patrick had touched her, she had frozen. Patrick's cancer had been both a hell and a saving grace in that respect. It had kept her tied to him when honour demanded she give him the honesty and respect of the truth—and a divorce—but it had also meant separate rooms. She briefly closed her eyes. "Seven years."

He went still and suddenly the unreality of lying naked and entwined with Rider on the wet ground in the middle of a cyclone hit her. He was large enough that he took the brunt of the wind, and protected her from most of the rain, but they were both soaked. Rider's shoulders glistened in the faint glow from the kitchen, water trailed from his hair and dripped from his nose, but wet or not, where his skin touched hers, she burned.

He framed her face, his palms warm and calloused against her skin. "I nearly went crazy thinking about the two of you in bed."

The confession was startling, even though she'd known he'd left his wife for her. Abruptly, a feminine confidence she thought she'd never feel again warmed her, along with knowledge, as solid and real as Rider. Despite the passage of time, despite the doubts that had eaten at her, in all the ways that counted he was *hers*. "It didn't happen," she said flatly. "I couldn't."

Some of the tension left his body. His breath stirred against her cheek. "Thank God for that. I wouldn't wish what happened to Patrick on my worst enemy, but . . ."

He had wanted Patrick out of the picture. The unspoken words hung between them, as raw and uncomplicated as Rider's weight pressing her into the wet ground, the heat pouring off his skin, the hot, stirring pleasure as he moved inside her.

The pitch of the wind altered, adding a keening edge to the building savagery of storm. He dipped and his mouth closed over one nipple, and her body shimmered out of control again as hot, dissolving pleasure gripped her.

He lifted his head, his face slick with rain, his gaze fastened on hers as he shoved deep, and she felt the hot liquid pulse as he held himself deep inside her. The moment was primal and extreme, and she was fiercely glad he hadn't worn a condom. She *wanted* his penis naked inside her. In an utterly female way, she quite simply wanted *him*, and had done so from the first time she'd laid eyes on him.

At a primitive animal level, the coupling was preordained and logical. She was a female who had been cordoned off and alone for years, and he was a strong, dominant male in his prime. The fact that he could impregnate her, and probably already had, didn't terrify her. She *wanted* his semen. Planning didn't come into it. She'd been locked in deep freeze for years, the chill mired deep in her bones. Getting involved with Rider was the equivalent of stepping into the heat of a blast furnace. He was wild and risky and unexpectedly vulnerable, and she was certain of only one thing: She wanted more.

Her arms wound around his neck and she stretched and arched beneath him, glorying in his weight pressing her into the ground, the continued penetration as he kept her beneath him, and the delicious throbbing wetness deep inside.

Experimentally, she gripped him more tightly and felt him twitch and thicken.

"More?"

She lifted her face to his, studied the taut line of his jaw, the sharp cut of his cheekbones. "Much more," and then the liquid glide started again, and she couldn't think, could barely breathe. The thrusting seemed to go on for a long time, although time was hard to measure; it slipped away in the darkness and the roar of the wind, the rain slicking their skin, the heat that built in waves, stretching the tension tight until it was close to unbearable.

His teeth fastened on the tender flesh at the join of her neck and shoulder, and the small erotic nip sent her spinning over the edge, heat and darkness lapping at her as she clung to his shoulders.

She caught the edge of a short, harsh word, then his mouth locked on hers and he shoved deep and she felt him come inside her again, the pulsing shiveringly deep and prolonged.

They lay in an exhausted tangle, until finally, Rider moved, pulling her up with him. They made it to the kitchen with its lamp still glowing softly on the table. Rider slammed the door, framed her face, and lowered his mouth to hers, the kiss long and drugging.

Before she was able to feel the vulnerability of being naked while Rider still had his jeans on, he walked her back three steps, lifted her onto the table, parted her legs, and stepped between them. She looped her arms around his neck as his mouth moved over hers again, the kiss intense and oddly sweet as the rain pounded on the windows, violent and tropically heavy.

He lifted his head, and when he spoke his voice was dark, and faintly hoarse. "This time I want you to watch, I want you to know who's making love to you."

Her gaze snagged on his, and she wondered that she'd ever thought his eyes cold. "I know who you are."

His hands tangled in her hair, his forehead dropped to hers. "Sometimes I wondered if you even knew I was alive."

She cupped his face, and suppressed a smile, feeling as giddy as a teenager. "I don't know if anyone's ever told you this, Rider, but you're hard to miss."

Incredibly, his smile bordered on embarrassed, then her breath caught as he began to enter her by slow, deliberate increments. Outside in the dark, she'd been aware of shape and proportion, but it had been too dark to make out any detail. In the soft lantern light, every part of him was visible, and like the rest of him, his genitals were sleek and beautifully formed, his shaft long and muscular, his testicles heavy and pulled up tight against the shaft.

She wrapped her legs around his waist, the movement tilting her hips and deepening the penetration. His thumb eased up from the place they were joined, and slid over the tight bud of her clitoris, once, twice, and heat spasmed through her again and she began to climax. His arms came around her and she felt him thicken inside her, the long, hard pulsing of his release.

Eventually, he lifted his head from the curve of her shoulder, his expression soft and faintly wry. "You see why I spent so much time away? If I'd stayed in Tayler's Creek, Tucker would have resurrected some old law about adultery, locked me up, and thrown away the key."

His arms tightened around her, and he lifted her from the bench, collected the lantern from the table, and carried her upstairs.

She indicated which room was hers, and he set her down on the bed, pulled a fistful of foil packets from his jeans, and placed them on her bedside table alongside the lantern. "I can use these if you want, but it's too late for them now."

The breath stalled in her throat as he peeled out of his jeans. Way too late. And he'd come over with more than just a handful, he had a *supply*.

She caught the edge of a male grin. "I've been carrying them since I got home. You had to know I was going to try and get you into bed."

He pushed the covers back, climbed into bed with her, and pulled her close. "But the hell I wanted to use them."

Fully naked, he was beautiful; his shoulders wide, his chest broad, his belly flat and ridged, his legs long and muscled. She touched a scar that curved over his stomach, another that made a puckered shape just above one hip. When she questioned him about the injuries, he answered with typical male brevity, then switched to questioning her, seemingly more interested in the small day-to-day details of her life, and the complicated dynamics of her large, extended family—who were mostly resident in Auckland—than the fact that he had nearly died, twice. As the conversation ebbed and flowed, the tension that had gripped her when she saw the injuries dissipated, and she was happy to simply wallow in the totally unexpected contentment of just being with Rider.

A series of heavier than normal gusts of wind buffeted the house hard enough that the entire structure shook, and for long minutes they were silent, their attention riveted to the sounds of the storm and the creaking protests of the old house. When the wind dropped to a more normal velocity, Rider propped himself on one elbow and stroked hair back from her face. "What will you do if you get pregnant?"

"Probably jump for joy."

Some of the wariness left his face. "You don't mind?"

A baby . . . Her stomach tightened on a kick of excitement. If she was pregnant, there was no question in her mind; she wanted her baby. "What about you?"

"You might regret asking that question." His gaze was direct, and without a shred of humour. "Ever since I first saw you I've fantasized about getting you pregnant."

Emotion swelled in her chest. Marg Tayler's terse statement that Rider was "taken" popped into her mind, and a tension she'd barely been aware of dissipated.

Rider wanted her—enough that he'd waited for her for years. At the first opportunity, he had bound her to him in the most primitive of ways by stripping and penetrating her on her front lawn. He hadn't taken the time to remove his jeans, and he hadn't sheathed himself when it would have taken him only seconds to do so. He'd *wanted* to be naked inside her, and he had wanted to make her pregnant.

What Rider had done had been ruthless and dominant, and she'd gloried in it. She hadn't cared that they'd both gotten soaked, or that he could make her pregnant. After years of closing him out—of repressing the most feminine, vulnerable parts of herself—she'd needed him to be wild for her, she'd needed the raw, earthy shock of lovemaking.

Urgency rose up inside her, fierce and sharp. She didn't regret all of the years they'd put this relationship on hold, because Patrick had been important to her; he had needed her. But it was their time *now*. She touched Rider's jaw, and felt the tension there. "Then let's do it."

Possessive heat flared in his eyes, but this time, it was going to be her way. Placing her hands on his chest, she pushed him flat and took a moment to admire the body that had been driving all of the women of Tayler's Creek—single or married—crazy for years.

His dark gaze flashed over her as she straddled him, and

his hands cupped her waist. "When you get pregnant," he said flatly, "we get married."

As Jane wrapped her fingers around his shaft, she thought he muttered, "If not before," and a peculiarly female satisfaction curled through her. Three days ago, she'd thought of herself as civilized to the nth degree, and driven by logic rather than emotion, but in the space of those few days her world, and her view of herself, had been turned upside down. In any other circumstances Rider's hard-ass male demand that she marry him would be considered outrageous in the extreme and ignored. As proposals went, it was a disgrace, but in this case, what mattered to Jane was that Rider was vulnerable enough that he wanted to make certain of her.

Fitting the broad head of his penis to her opening, she slowly lowered herself, hovering at the brink of penetration until the exquisite pressure was almost beyond bearing. They'd already made love three times, but this time her awareness and sensitivity were heightened to an almost painful degree.

Taking a deep breath, she increased the downward pressure until the first tight constriction was breached and she took him inside her in a slow, hot glide, heat pouring through her at the massive sense of impalement.

She settled herself more firmly over him, shimmying slightly to ease the tight fit, her eyes briefly closing at the exquisite sensation of fullness. "You're supposed to have a ring, Rider."

His hands slid to her hips, locking her tight against him. His gaze fastened on hers, dark and hot, and lit with humour. "Michael. The name's Michael. And don't worry, I've got the ring."

WHEN SHE WOKE it was still dark, but greying, as if morning was close.

She wasn't sure what had pulled her from sleep, and she was surprised she'd woken at all, because she felt heavy and exhausted. Vaguely, she noticed that the wind was no longer buffeting the house, although it was always possible that an extra strong gust, or even a flash of lightning, had woken her. Yawning, she allowed her lids to drift closed, then a rending creak jerked her back to full awareness.

Rider's arm tightened around her, telling her that he was awake.

The creak came again, out of sync with the steady whine of the wind, as if someone were peeling corrugated iron from the roof.

A chill ran the length of her spine. She could feel the coiled tension in Rider's body. Another short, sharp creak practically made her jump out of her skin, and suddenly she was sure.

"There's someone on the roof."

"He's in the ceiling."

A finger pressed on her lips, signaling quiet, then Rider slid from the bed and pulled on his jeans. Jane climbed out of bed and slid drawers open as quietly as she could, extracting underwear and a fresh shirt and shorts by feel. When she was dressed, Rider's hand locked around hers.

He bent his head and spoke close to her ear. "Stay here, so I know where you are." He pressed a cold, smooth object into her hand, which she realized was his cell phone, which he must have had in his jeans pocket. "Call emergency services, and don't let up until they dispatch a police cruiser. Get Tucker if you can. Tell him we've got his boy—if he's interested."

Rider disappeared into the hallway, then just as quickly reappeared, flattening himself against the wall and motioning for her to get down. Jane ducked down beside the bed and began dialing, keeping an eye on the inky opening of the doorway as she strained to see in the darkness.

A large shape coalesced out of the thicker shadows, and a weird elongated shape slid into the room. Cold welled in her stomach when she realized the strange shape was the barrel of a gun, and the reason it was so high was because the stock was resting against a man's shoulder.

There was a flurry of movement. A grunt erupted, followed by a vicious curse, then Michael's figure merged with the intruder's as he gripped the gun and wrenched it down. The detonation of the gun firing split the air with a flat crack, and a voice sounded in her ear, distant and disorientingly normal, so that it was long seconds before she registered that emergency services had picked up her call. Sweeping the panic from her mind, she answered the voice, holding a hand over her free ear to block the sound of the two men locked in combat.

The fighting surged toward the bed as she gave her details to the operator. She shuffled back, crouching in the corner, keeping a wary eye on the struggle as the intruder fell back against her dressing table. Glass shattered, and he reeled to his feet and lunged at Rider. The edge of the bed caught Rider in the back of the knees, and he tumbled back, off balance, and rolled to the side, evading the charge by inches, and almost landing on Jane as she scrambled to the other side of the room. Rider gained his feet and the attacker came at him again, frighteningly fast, but instead of stepping in close, Rider took a step back and jerked the shadowy figure with him. This time the attacker landed on her dressing table chair and the dainty antique snapped like kindling as the two men went down on the floor.

She heard the soggy thud of a fist connecting, a heavy grunt, then Jane darted forward and retrieved the gun, which had been dropped on the floor.

Backing into the hallway, she slid the cell phone, which was still connected to emergency services, into her shorts pocket, and ran her hands over the weapon. She was almost certain it was a twenty-two, the same as her gun, which was under the bed. She didn't want to use the weapon. She didn't want to *touch* it, but the alternative was trying to get across the bedroom to retrieve hers without getting caught up in the fighting.

Suppressing a shudder, she felt beneath the gun for the magazine. From the short length, she discerned that it probably held three shots, which meant, if it was fully loaded, that there were two left. She pulled the bolt into the firing position and heard a round slick into the chamber, then fitted the stock to her shoulder and aimed, but her target was a blurred whirl of muscle and shadows and the sheer savagery of the fight rendered the threat of the gun close to useless. The two men were so absorbed in the battle that they hadn't noticed she had a gun trained on them, and the odds were that even if she *did* pull the trigger, she would hit Rider.

Lowering the gun, Jane searched the room, which was gradually lightening, and spotted the battery lantern, which was now lying on its side by the wall, miraculously still intact. Setting the gun on the floor, she retrieved the lantern, turned the knob, and light spread through the room.

The assailant was almost as tall as Rider, and brawny across the shoulders. Something about the small shape of his head compared to the width of his shoulders, his hair cut close around his skull, was familiar. Jane was sure she knew who he was, although she'd only seen him a handful of times. Earl Sooner, one of a small number of beneficiaries who were resident in and around Tayler's Creek. He owned a small acreage on the other side of town, although most of his block was covered in gorse and bush. According to local gossip, the only productive use Earl had ever put his piece of land to was reputed to be an illegal one, although he had never actually been busted for growing cannabis.

The fighting surged toward her again, and she scrambled back until the wall stopped her. Locked together, the two men hit the doorframe, making the whole house shudder, then reeled back into the bedroom. With a quick twist, Rider flipped Sooner onto his stomach on the floor, then went down on top of him, his knee wedged in the small of Sooner's back, forearm pressed up tight under Sooner's neck, arching his head back at an acute angle. Sooner's face went red, then purple, his eyes bulging. Spittle frothed from his mouth as he fought the hold, then abruptly his eyelids drooped and he went slack in Rider's grip.

Rider's gaze found hers. Blood was trickling from a cut on his cheekbone, and he had a swelling over one eye, but otherwise he appeared to be unharmed. "Have you got rope?"

"I've got plenty, but it's in the barn."

"Get it. I'll make sure he doesn't wake up anytime soon."

Jane didn't hang around to ask just what Rider had done to knock Sooner out, or what measures he'd take if Sooner came back around. Jess was crouched at the bottom of the stairs, and shadowed Jane to the kitchen, whining for assurance, keeping so close, Jane kept tripping over her.

Jane dropped a consoling pat on her head. "Me, too, girl."

She collected a second torch from the pantry, because the last one was outside on the lawn somewhere, and she was almost certain she'd left it turned on, so the batteries would be flat.

The trip to the barn was unnerving. The dawn was gray and murky, the wind still strong enough that it sounded like surf pounding through the trees, and the rain drove in ghostly sheets across the yard, instantly soaking her as she crossed the open area of lawn in front of the house.

It wasn't until she stepped onto the graveled area in front of the barn that she remembered that her feet were bare, but the sharp stones hardly registered as she picked her way across to the barn, set the torch down, and heaved at the crossbar that anchored the door closed. When she finally got the bar clear and wrenched one of the doors wide, the barn yawned, cavernously dark and creepy. Inside, the sound of the wind and rain was amplified, because acoustically, the barn resembled nothing so much as a steel drum.

Jess stuck to her like glue as she navigated the piles of hay, rubbing at her legs and shivering as Jane uncoiled a length of light rope from a nail on the wall. For good measure, she grabbed a coil of baling twine as well. This much rope was overkill, but what the heck? Sooner was dangerous. It was better that he was half suffocated by rope than that he got free.

By the time she made it back to the kitchen, her clothes were plastered to her skin and her hair trailed wetly over her cheeks and dripped down her spine. She slammed the kitchen door against the wind, the cessation of noise almost eerily abrupt. Jess shook herself, sending a flurry of droplets across the floor, while Jane selected a sharp knife from the knife block for slicing the rope. Gripping the torch more firmly, she climbed the stairs. Her pace slowed as she approached her bedroom door, apprehension knotting her belly, because it occurred to her that while she was in the barn, Sooner might have come around. Her heart thumped hard in her chest at the thought of Rider hurt or incapacitated. As a precautionary measure, she held the knife at her side so that it wouldn't be immediately obvious, although the knife would be close to useless when stacked up against a gun.

When she paused at the open door, for a moment the tableau of Rider holding the unconscious Sooner in a neck lock on the floor was abruptly disorienting. She hadn't known what to expect, but the whole time she'd been out, searching for the rope, Rider hadn't moved. He'd kept his hold on Sooner with a tenacious, rocklike patience that sent relief pouring through her.

In stark contrast to the still tableau of Rider and Sooner, her room looked like it had been the centre of a bomb blast, and the sheer, numbing violence of what had happened hit her all over again. Her bedroom was wrecked. Her dressing table listed to one side, the chair smashed. Broken glass, shards of porcelain, and bedclothes were strewn over the floor. One of her matching bedside lamps was on the floor—the base was whole, but the shade was crumpled beyond repair. The drapes at one window had been torn down, and the metal curtain rod was bent at a drunken angle. It was odd, but she had no memory of anything happening to the drapes.

Rider took the rope and began cinching Sooner's wrists and ankles up tight.

Jane studied the unconscious man's face. He was in his forties, not unhandsome, his shoulders bulky, as if he worked out. One eye was swollen, and his lip was cut. Other than that, he simply appeared to be unconscious. "Is he all right?"

Rider rose to his feet, and she noticed the reddened patches on his torso where he'd been hit. "I pressed on his carotid and restricted the flow of blood to his brain. He's not hurt, just unconscious."

His gaze slid over her as if he had to reassure himself that she was okay, then he pulled her into his arms. "You're wet. What are you trying to do to me?"

She touched the split on his cheekbone, then used the wet sleeve of her shirt to dab at the blood. "In case you haven't noticed, we're still in the middle of a storm."

"I had my mind on other things."

"Uh-huh, and now the bedroom's wrecked."

"There's a bed at my place. Once we get rid of this turkey, will you come home with me?"

Warmth welled inside her and she couldn't stop the smile that spread across her face. She was wet, her hair tangled— she must look like she'd been dragged backward through a hedge, but Rider made her feel gorgeous and wanted and so gloriously female she could weep. "Yes."

Something like relief flared in his eyes. "Good. And you'll marry me."

Her smile turned into a grin. Yep, he was male. Give him an inch, and he took a mile. "I don't remember being asked."

"It was in the small print. You should read the contract before you fall in love."

She wound her arms around his neck. "Who said I was in love?"

"You did. Every time I looked at you." His grin was faintly wicked. "And you did look."

A faint voice came from her pocket. She retrieved the phone and spoke to the agitated operator. "Tucker's on his way."

Rider groaned. "Am I supposed to be relieved?"

She handed him the phone. "You'd better talk to them. I think the Armed Offenders Squad is also on its way, which means we could be under siege at any minute."

Rider swore beneath his breath, and took the phone, his voice curt as he explained the situation.

Minutes later, he put the phone down and opened a window. "Tucker's here, along with the AOS. Hang on, while I call them off."

He leaned out the window and had a brief conversation, then pulled it closed against the wind and rain. It was almost fully light now, the day grey and cool.

Jane looked at the gun, which was lying on the floor in the hallway, where she'd left it. "Yuk. I think I handled the murder weapon."

His arm came around her, tucking her in close against his side. "Don't worry about it. If Tucker can't figure this one out without eliminating your prints, I'll personally feed him that weapon. Then forensics will have a hell of a job getting their evidence."

Epilogue

⌒

BY MIDMORNING, MICHAEL and Jane were finished with
statements and interviews. Sooner had been charged on a number of counts including murder, attempted murder, and rape,
and had been taken into custody. In a panic, Sooner had tried
to lay assault charges against Rider, alleging that Rider had
attempted to murder *him*.

The crime squad detective from Auckland, who was heading up the case, had looked at the faint red marks around Earl's
neck and commented that if those marks were his sole evidence he was going to have problems, because from where he
was sitting it looked like Sooner had been the victim of a
heavy date, not a near-death experience.

Sooner had sputtered and argued, but they had him cold on
the Dillon case. He had nowhere to go but down. His fingerprints matched the ones taken from the Dillons' house, although they couldn't tie him in to any of the other home
invasion cases, and in any case the M.O. was different. All of
the other home invasions had been carried out by a team of
three people, including one woman, not a lone male.

As it turned out, Earl's crime had been a copycat one, designed to cover up a crime that had been not so much carried

out as botched in a drunken fit. And the investigation hadn't been helped along by the fact that their primary witness, Carol Dillon, who had been having what could only politely be called a sexual liaison with Sooner, had lied.

Early in the afternoon, Earl's hidey-hole at the back of Jane's farm was located by a specialist sniffer dog, and Rider and Jane went to look at the haul.

Tucker and Zane were in their element, cordoning off the area with police tape and helping the crime squad boys catalogue the evidence.

They found two televisions and a DVD player, plus a forty-inch, state-of-the-art flat screen. To go with the viewing screens there were video cameras and sound equipment and some seriously good stereo gear, although most of the stuff was ruined, since the limestone cave Sooner had chosen wasn't waterproof, and had partially filled with water during the storm.

Sooner hadn't limited himself to stealing the expensive chattels, he'd also taken a number of kitchen appliances, including a toaster and a sandwich maker, and what looked like a part of Carol Dillon's blender—minus the motor.

Zane bagged up the sandwich maker, which was stacked near piles of videos. "Looks like he was planning on snacking while he watched whatever."

The "whatever" turned out to be homegrown Tayler's Creek porn, starring mostly Carol Dillon and Earl Sooner, and occasionally, just to break the tedium, Aubrey Dillon.

Once the videos were discovered, all the facts of the case became clear. Mrs. Dillon had been raped, but it had been by a man she had regularly had sex with—on video—which was the reason she had denied knowing her attacker. She hadn't wanted the police to find out that she and her husband were involved in producing homegrown porn movies for a small, but lucrative, mail-order business at their rural retreat on Linford Road. She'd given the police artist an incorrect description of Sooner, adding long hair, specifically so they wouldn't find him, because she'd been frightened that Earl would come back and kill her if she reported what had really happened.

Apparently Sooner had gotten a little too rough during one session for Aubrey's liking and he'd been fired. Later on that night, Sooner had come back with a twenty-two, shot Aubrey, raped Carol Dillon, and loaded his truck with every appliance he could get his hands on. He'd removed all the videos, so he couldn't be linked with the Dillons, and had trashed the house to make it look like a home invasion.

He then drove onto the back of Jane's property, using a reserve that bordered her land as access, and hid the gear in one of the caves. When Jane became suspicious and started snooping around the caves, he decided he needed to do one more copycat crime.

BY THE TIME the police were finished gathering evidence, it was near dark. After feeding the hens and checking the sheep, Jane put Jess in the backseat of her station wagon and followed Rider back to his place.

When she reached the front door, Rider unlocked it, swung Jane into his arms, and carried her across the threshold. "You'll have to humour me, I've got a romantic streak."

He set her down in the middle of a large, roomy lounge with glossy wood floors, rich, patterned rugs, and bifold doors that opened out onto decks bordered by large areas of lawn. The sun was sinking fast, but shafts of sunlight found their way through the clouds and filled the room with a warm glow.

The first, and only, time she'd been in this house, at a party the Riders had thrown to welcome her and Patrick to Tayler's Creek, her world had literally been turned upside down.

Without warning, tears filled her eyes. Rider's hands framed her face, not allowing her to hide. "I know," he murmured. "The last seven years have been a bitch. You loved Patrick. If I'd ever thought differently, I would have taken you away from him in a second."

The flat assertion sent a small shiver skimming down her spine, and if she'd had any further doubts, they were abruptly gone. From the first, she'd been overwhelmed. She'd feared the loss of control, but in stark contrast to her fears, she had never felt more female, more empowered, and she had never felt so much.

She rubbed her palms up over Rider's jaw, threaded her fingers through his hair, and surrendered the last threads that tied her to Patrick. "Did I ever tell you that I fell in love with you seven years ago, and I've been in love with you ever since?"

He went still, his expression controlled, remote, reminding her of the way he'd been with her for so long—still and silent. She'd thought he was cold; now she knew that he'd just been wary—and she realized how out of character that was for him.

His gaze searched hers, a glimmer of humour surfacing. "That calls for a celebration."

Without warning, he swept her into his arms and started toward a hallway. He was moving fast enough to make her head spin, and she was feeling giddy anyway.

She clung to his shoulders, catching glimpses of rooms. "Where are you taking me?"

He grinned, suddenly looking like nothing so much as a pirate. "Where do you think?"

Only Human

EILEEN WILKS

Chapter 1

HE DIDN'T HAVE much face left. Lily stood back far enough to keep the tips of her new black heels out of the pool of blood that was dry at the edges, still gummy near the body. Mist hung in the warm air, spinning halos around the street lamps and police spotlights, turning her skin clammy. The smell of blood was thick in her nostrils.

The first victim, the one whose body she'd seen four days ago, hadn't had his face ripped off the way this one had. Just his throat.

Flashes went off nearby in a crisp one-two as the police photographer recorded the scene. "Hey, Yu," the man behind the camera lens called.

She grimaced. O'Brien was good at his work, but he never tired of a joke, no matter how stale. If they both lived to be a hundred and ran into each other in the nursing home, the first thing he'd say to her would be, "Hey, Yu!"

That is, assuming she kept her maiden name for the next seventy-two years. Considering the giddy whirl she laughingly called a social life, that seemed possible. "Yeah, Irish?"

"Looks like you had a hot date tonight."

"No, me and my dog always dress for dinner. He looks great in a tux."

O'Brien snorted and moved to get another angle. Lily tuned him out along with the rest of the crowd—the curious behind the chain-link fence, the uniforms, the lab boys and girls waiting with their tweezers and baggies and fingerprint gear.

They'd arrived almost as fast as she had, which said something about how nervous the brass was. That a crowd had assembled in this neighborhood said something about everyone else's nerves. Spilled blood often drew people the way spilled sugar draws flies, but not in this area. Here, people assumed that curiosity came with a price tag. They knew what a drive-by sounded like, and the look of a drug deal going down.

The victim lay on his back on the dirty pavement. There was a Big Gulp cup, smashed flat, by his feet, a section of newspaper under his butt, and a broken beer bottle by his foot. Defensive wounds on the right arm, she noted. Something had torn right through his jacket. There was blood on that hand, but she didn't see any wounds.

His other hand lay about ten feet from the body, up against the pole to the swing set.

A playground. Someone had ripped this guy's throat out in a playground, for God's sake. There was a hard ache in Lily's own throat, a tightness across her shoulders. She'd seen death often enough since she was promoted to Homicide. Her stomach no longer turned over, but the regret, the sorrow over the waste, never went away.

She crouched, careful of the way her dress rode up on her thighs, and studied the focus of all the activity.

He'd been young. Not young enough to have enjoyed those swings anytime recently, though. Twenty or less, she guessed, maybe five-foot-ten, weight around one-eighty. Weight-lifter's shoulders and arms, powerful thighs. He'd been strong, perhaps cocky in his strength—used to fighting, probably used to winning.

Strength hadn't done him much good tonight.

Whatever had torn out his throat and made a mess of his face had left the eye and cheekbone on the right side intact. One startled brown eye stared up at nothing from smooth young skin the color of the wicker chair in her living room.

He was wearing a red T-shirt, black hightops, black cargo pants, and a black jacket.

Gang colors. Not that she thought this was a gang killing. The bloody paw prints leading away from the body were a pretty good clue about that.

A pair of size eleven shoes, black and dusty, moved up beside her. They were connected to long, skinny legs encased in uniform trousers. "Careful, Detective. Don't want to get your pretty dress dirty."

Lily sighed. Officer Larry Phillips was half of the patrol unit that had been first on the scene. She hadn't run across him before—the San Diego PD was too big for her to know many beat cops. A few minutes spent taking his report had given her a pretty clear picture, though. He was pushing fifty, still on the streets and sour about it. She was female, twenty-eight, and already a detective.

In other words, he didn't like her. "This is your turf, Officer. You know him?"

"He's one of the Devils."

"Yeah, I got that much." She stood and glanced up at him. Way up—he was a long, stringy man, well over six feet. Of course, Lily had to look up to meet almost anyone's eyes. She'd persuaded herself that didn't irritate her anymore. "You think you could look at his face instead of his clothes and see if you can ID him?"

"Why? This wasn't a gang killing." He had a toothpick in his mouth. She found herself staring at it, waiting for it to drop, wondering if it was glued to his lip. "Not even murder, really."

Three years ago a case like this would have been handled by the X-Squad. Now it went to Homicide. "The courts say otherwise."

He snorted. The toothpick didn't budge. "Yeah, and we know how smart those bleeding heart judges are. According to them, we're supposed to treat the beasts like they were human. That mess at your feet proves what a great idea that is."

"I've seen uglier things done by men to other men. And to women. And I still need an ID."

Another cop joined them, this one young, short, with shiny black hair and a greenish cast to his complexion—Phillips's partner, the other half of the responding unit. "I, uh, I think it's Carlos Fuentes."

Phillips raised one scornful eyebrow. "You basing that ID on his shoes? Not much else to go on."

"It looks like him around the eyes. I mean the eye. And the build is right. Fuentes is supposed to be good with his knife," he added. "Fast."

"Was he left-handed?" Lily asked.

"No. No, I'm sure he was right-handed. That fits—it's his right arm with the defensive wounds. If he were attacked by a dog—"

"Dog?" Phillips was incredulous. "You think a dog did this?"

"It could have been," Rodriguez insisted. "You always tell me not to jump to conclusions. Well, until they run the tests we won't know that this was done by a—by—"

"A lupus," Phillips drawled. "That's what we're supposed to call them now, right?"

"It could have been a rabid dog. Or one trained to attack. Maybe Fuentes was meeting someone, making some kind of deal. When it went sour the other guy sicced the dog on him."

Phillips made a disgusted sound.

She flicked a glance his way. Phillips wasn't much of a partner if he wouldn't take the time to educate the kid. Lily looked back at the younger officer. "Where's Fuentes's knife?"

"I don't . . ." His voice trailed off as he looked around. "He must not have had time to draw it."

"Right. Now look at the body, and think. You said he was good with a blade, and fast. He's right-handed, so when some animal comes at him out of the darkness, he uses his left arm for defense. Like this." She flung up her own arm. "He reaches for his knife at the same time. And the beast didn't pay any attention to the defensive arm. It knew he was reaching for a weapon. Went for his right hand, bit it off, and spat it out. Dogs don't do that."

His throat worked as he stared at the corpse. "If—if it had been trained to go for the right arm . . ."

"It bit the hand off," she repeated patiently. "And flung it away. You can't train an animal to do that. What's more, Fuentes looks like he could have bench-pressed three-fifty or better, but he couldn't even slow the beast down."

"Where do you get that?"

"Observation. Aside from the blood and the body, you can't tell there's been any kind of fight here. The beast hit him quick and hard. He might not even have had time to know his hand was gone. He had good instincts, though. He tried to pull his head down, protect his neck. That's when he lost some of his face. Then it ripped out his throat."

The rookie was looking sick. Maybe she'd pushed reality on him a little too firmly.

"Now, now. You're not supposed to say 'it,' " Phillips said with heavy sarcasm. "We have to say 'he' now, treat 'em like people. Full rights under the law."

"I know the law." She turned away and frowned. A van from one of the TV stations had pulled up. Dammit. "I need you two to join the uniforms at the entrance. I don't want any media ghouls messing up my crime scene."

"Sure thing, Detective." Phillips gave her a mocking grin, turned, then paused and took the toothpick out of his mouth. When he met her eyes the mockery and anger had faded from his, leaving them dead serious. "A word of advice from someone who put in some time on the X-Squad. Call them whatever you like, but don't mistake the lupi for human. They don't think like we do, and they're damned hard to hurt. They're faster and they're stronger, and they like the way we taste."

"This one doesn't seem to have done much tasting."

He shrugged. "Something interrupted him, maybe. Don't forget that they're only legally human when they're on two legs. You run into one when it's four-footed, don't arrest it. Shoot it." He flicked the toothpick to the ground. "And aim for the brain."

Chapter 2

LILY'S EYES WERE gritty and hot the next morning when she made her way through the mass of desks in the bullpen. It had been two in the morning when she'd returned to her little apartment on Flower Street.

The lab crew had put in an even longer night, though. The preliminary report was waiting on her desk. She settled into the battered chair that was just beginning to adapt its lumps to her own bottom, took a sip of her coffee, and skimmed it quickly.

It held one surprise. For some reason they were holding off on the complete autopsy "pending official notice." Her eyebrows went up. What did that mean? Otherwise it was pretty much what she'd expected. No blood other than the victim's, no tissue. A few hairs. At least they'd been able to establish that the attacker had been one of the Blood, though.

Science depended on things happening a certain way without fail. Water boiled at 100°C at sea level, no matter who did the boiling. Mix potassium nitrate, sulfur, and charcoal together in the right proportions and you ended up with gunpowder every time, no random batches of gold dust or baking soda to confuse matters.

But magic was capricious. Individual. The cells and body fluids of those of the Blood—inherently magical beings—didn't perform the same way every time they were tested. Which made it possible sometimes to identify the traces magic left in its wake, but played hell with lab results.

Still, the lab tech had been able to determine that the blood in the wounds had been contaminated by magic, probably by some body fluid from one of the Blood. Saliva, obviously, but the tests couldn't confirm that.

The report did list some negatives. Lily snorted when she read them. No one with a functioning brain would have suspected a brownie anyway, and gnomes were timid and extremely rare. Gremlins could be nasty, but there hadn't been a gremlin outbreak in southern California in years. Besides, they were way too small. The damage she'd seen last night hadn't been inflicted by a gremlin pack.

What the lab work couldn't tell them, the other physical evidence did. Lily knew very well which species they were dealing with—one of the lupi.

Werewolf.

She sat back with a sigh, turning back to the first page to give the report a more thorough reading. The man at the desk next to hers tilted his head back and howled.

"Cute, Brunswick," she said without looking up from the report. "Very lifelike. You been tested?"

The woman at the desk behind Brunswick snorted. "Him? You've got to be kidding. Lupi are supposed to be virile, charismatic, sexy as hell—"

"Hey, I'm sexy! Just ask my wife."

"They're also tomcats."

"Can't call a wolf a cat."

"Don't nitpick. You know what I mean—they'll stick it anywhere, anytime, to anyone who'll let 'em. You want me to ask your wife if that's true, too, studmuffin?"

Two of the nearest men laughed. Brunswick was protesting his innocence when Lily's phone rang. "Homicide. Detective Yu speaking."

"You're wanted in the chief's office."

It was Captain Foster. She knew it was him—yet her first reaction was that this was a prank. It had to be. A lowly detective with only two years on Homicide was not summoned to the office of the chief of police. "Chief Delgado, sir?"

"How many chiefs do we have?" he snapped. Which was a bit unfair—there was only one chief of police, but there were several deputy chiefs. "He wants you there right away."

The line went dead. Lily gave the phone in her hand one incredulous glance, then set it down and stood.

The chief's office was, naturally, on the top floor. There was no point in speculating about why he wanted her, she thought as she punched the button for the elevator. And proceeded to do it anyway.

For once the elevator arrived immediately. She stepped on, brooding over what the summons might mean. It had to be something to do with last night's homicide.

Maybe Delgado wanted her for a press conference. The media were in a feeding frenzy. But Delgado usually handled that sort of thing himself when it was a major case. He might ask her captain to participate, but it was unlikely he'd want her.

The line between her brows deepened as the elevator let people on and off. Finally they reached the top floor.

Could the captain have told Delgado why he'd given the investigation to one of his newer detectives? No, she couldn't believe that. Foster was too careful. He hadn't even spoken of it to her in so many words.

Lily had only been to the top floor once before. The carpet was thicker here, the lighting more subtle. The hallway had doors with brass nameplates and ended at an office with living plants and framed pictures on the walls.

The pale oak desk was ruthlessly neat. The woman behind the desk was a sixtyish civilian named Adele Crimmings, a.k.a. the chief's enforcer. Lily had heard dozens of stories about her. She had sharp eyes, a crisply tailored blue dress, and white hair cut so short it looked as if she'd recently completed basic training.

"He's expecting you," Ms. Crimmings said when Lily identified herself. She touched a button on her desk, announced Lily's arrival, then nodded at her. "Go on in."

Delgado had a big corner office with wooden blinds at the tall windows. His own desk was larger than his secretary's, and nowhere near as tidy. He was seated there, a small, trim man with coppery skin stretched tight and shiny across flat cheekbones. His tie was a very dark brown with narrow gold stripes. His suit jacket was on the back of his chair, and the sleeves of his white dress shirt were rolled up. He had very little hair on his forearms.

Delgado wasn't alone. Another man stood in front of one of the big windows, his back to the room—an Anglo, judging by the color of the skin on the long-fingered hands. A rather pale Anglo, for California.

He was at least six feet, slim, and standing utterly motionless. His arms hung loose at his sides, his feet didn't shift, his head didn't turn as she entered the room. Shaggy brown hair waved past his collar. The sunlight glanced off that ordinary brown hair, igniting it, drawing a burnished halo around his head. The casual elegance of his black slacks and loose black jacket fairly screamed money. The cuffs of his shirt were black, too.

The man in black, she thought with a mental sniff at the dramatics of it. She wondered if he was an actor or a director. And was annoyed to notice that her pulse had picked up.

"Detective Yu," Delgado said. "Thank you for coming."

"Sir."

"I have someone here you need to meet. You'll be working with him," he said as the other man, at last, turned to face her.

Lily's breath caught in her throat as she saw the narrow face, the tilted slashes of the eyebrows, the slightly sallow skin, and the cool gray eyes that met hers with no trace of a smile. It was a striking face, stark and clean, the lines of it swept back the way stone is smoothed by wind. Not handsome, but not a face one would ever forget, either.

She knew him. Knew who he was, at least. She'd seen his photograph often enough, though he was certainly no movie star or director. Most recently, she'd seen it in the file she'd started four days ago. The one on the first killing.

Her heart pounded and her eyes widened in disbelief. "You want me to work with a *werewolf?*"

BY THE TIME Rule turned around, he was fairly sure he had his reaction to her scent under control. Or at least concealed. His heart was thudding against the wall of his chest like Thumper introducing himself to Bambi.

I can't possibly know. Not for sure. Yet her scent . . . Fear and exaltation filled him. He studied the face of the woman he'd never believed he would meet.

Something in the smoothness of her face, the sleek roundness of her body, appealed to him. Her eyes were as black as the braid that hung down her back. And greatly irritated at the moment. She would move well, he thought, and wanted to see her move.

There wasn't a great deal of Lily Yu physically, but he had the sense that quite a lot of person had been packed into that trim, tidy form. She wore plain black slacks and a jacket the color of the poppies that dotted the hills in the spring. He smelled the metal-and-gunpowder odor of the gun concealed by that jacket.

No fear scent, though. That intrigued him. Even Delgado gave out a whiff of fear in his presence, though he controlled it admirably. That, and the fact that she'd risen to detective at such a young age, told him the dainty packaging was misleading. A man who didn't look beyond that packaging might mistake her for doll-like. He wondered if any had been foolish enough to say so—and if they'd drawn back a stub.

Metaphorically speaking, of course. Humans didn't respond so vigorously to insult. "Obviously you recognize me," he said.

"Detective," Delgado snapped. "Your captain assured me you didn't suffer from racial prejudices."

"Sorry, sir." Those pretty black eyes slid from her chief to Rule. "My apologies, Mr. Turner. The old-fashioned term slipped out. Or should I say 'Your Highness'?"

"My title is used only among the clans and by journalists. Strictly speaking, it doesn't translate as prince. That is merely the closest approximation." Her skin was ivory—not the bland pallor of one who avoids the sun, but a dense, saturated color. She smelled wonderful, very female, the muskiness of her skin faintly overlaid with soap. No perfume.

He smiled slowly. He hated perfume. "You may call me Rule. I would like it if you did."

Delgado cleared his throat. He looked irritated, which Rule understood. This was his territory, and they were ignoring that. "Detective Yu," he said firmly, "this is Rule Turner, prince of Clan Nokolai. Mr. Turner, Detective Lily Yu."

"Mr. Turner," she said with a curt nod.

That put him in his place, didn't it? His smile widened.

Delgado was speaking. "Mr. Turner spoke with the mayor last night. He offered his expertise. Obviously he has an intimate knowledge of lupus culture and, ah, habits. He will cooperate fully with you."

"Pardon me, sir, but I'm unsure exactly what that means."

Delgado's eyes flickered to Rule. Knowing the man's discomfort, Rule took the burden of explanation from him. "Initially, at least, it means we must visit the morgue. I need to smell the corpse."

Chapter 3

LILY LEFT THE chief's office fifteen minutes later, confused and irritated. Now she knew why the autopsy had been held up, though.

Maybe Rule Turner could identify the killer from the scent he'd left on his victim's body. Maybe not. She couldn't take his word at face value. People lied. They did it all the time, to protect small hurts or embarrassments as well as for more serious reasons. But if he claimed to identify the killer, that would be information, whether it was true or a lie.

She had to figure out his goal, what he had to gain by helping them investigate. Lupi weren't exactly civic-minded about cooperating with the police. Of course, Rule Turner was politically active on behalf of his people, something of a spokesman. Not to mention a favorite of the gossip mags.

He was also a civilian. Lily did not like working with civilians, but she could concede the necessity at times. Her confusion had little to do with her professional irritation.

Those eyes . . . she'd never heard that it was dangerous to look into a werewolf's eyes. But there was a great deal she didn't know about them, wasn't there?

The man beside her kept pace silently. At least, she supposed that was the right word for him. Could you be a man without being human? Never mind, she told herself, moving briskly. The courts had ruled that lupi had the same rights and obligations as other citizens . . . when they were in human form.

His human form was pretty devastating, she admitted silently. Or maybe that was an aspect of his magic, whatever it was that enabled him to turn into a wolf. Or gave him no choice. Legend said that werewolves couldn't avoid the Change at the full moon.

"You move quickly, Detective," Turner said as they reached the elevator.

She jabbed the down button. "Habit. People with short legs learn to move fast, or we get left behind."

"Is that what it is?" He sounded thoughtful. "I thought you were trying to leave me behind. You're not happy with Chief Delgado's instructions. I'm afraid I disturb you."

"You annoy me," she corrected. "Cocky, arrogant men usually do."

"Arrogant, perhaps. Cocky is for puppies."

"You said it, not me. Where were you last night between ten o'clock and eleven twenty-five?"

"At a party with about twenty other people. A party at the mayor's house."

So much for wiping the amusement out of his eyes. "Were you there when the mayor was called? Is that how you heard about the second killing so quickly?"

"Yes. The mayor asked for my assistance."

The stupid elevator was taking forever today. She punched the button again. "If you're ready to start acting as an expert consultant, I have some questions."

"Of course. I hope they're personal." He stroked his hand down her braid. "Lovely. It feels as soft as it looks."

The shiver that ran up her spine was as distressing as it was instinctive. She stepped away. "None of this is personal, and you need to keep your hands to yourself."

"I'll try."

"You'll have to do better than try."

"We are a profoundly physical people, Detective. It's difficult for us to remember that others don't have the same need to touch and be touched that we do."

She lifted a scornful eyebrow. The Nokolai prince had been mixing and mingling with normal humans quite regularly at events from San Diego to Hollywood to Washington, D.C., for the last few years. He knew perfectly well how to behave—when he wanted to. "And here I thought you were hitting on me."

"That, too, of course. Will you go out with me tonight?"

Her lips twitched before she could stop them. Maybe his existence wasn't illegal anymore, but that smile ought to be. The way it spread over his face was a crime—so slow and intimate, as if smiling were a sensual indulgence to be savored, not rushed. . . .

The elevator finally arrived. Three people got off. She stepped in quickly.

He followed. "What impersonal questions did you want to ask?"

"I know lupi have a toxic reaction to silver, because the X-Squads used to use rounds made from a silver alloy." A very expensive alloy. She had a round in her clip right now, having requisitioned it and two more after the first killing. "What about garlic or crosses?"

"No and no. Old wives' tales." He pushed the button for the basement level, which held the parking garage. The elevator doors shut.

"I thought it might be. I'm afraid a lot of what I know is the sort of garbage spread by movies like *Witch Hunt*."

"At least you know it's garbage."

He was tense. She wasn't sure why she was convinced of that—he stood easily, spoke smoothly, and that remarkable face was still, unrevealing. "I've also heard that lupi are claustrophobic."

"It's hardly a phobia. We simply prefer open places."

Not small, enclosed spaces. Like an elevator. Abruptly she pushed the button for the next floor down, and the elevator slowed.

"Why did you do that?" he snapped.

"There's no reason for you to be uncomfortable. We can take the stairs."

The elevator halted smoothly and the doors opened. Two people were waiting to get on. The woman was a civilian, fortyish and plump—a clerk or secretary, from the look of her.

Lily knew the man slightly, a Vice officer named Burns. She nodded at him.

He didn't notice. He was staring at Turner. If he'd been a dog, his hackles would have been raised. The woman was staring, too. But the expression on her face was entirely different.

The tableau lasted only a second before she and Turner got off, the other two got on, and the elevator doors closed. She glanced at him as they started down the hall, wondering if he'd noticed the woman's reaction. She had to look up, of course. He was too blasted tall.

He was looking straight at her, those rainy-sky eyes amused and knowing.

"You tend to evoke a reaction from people, don't you?"

"Usually. Why don't we start my expert consultation with listening? You can tell me what you think you know about lupi and I'll correct any misinformation."

"Good enough." The door to the stairwell was metal with the usual red Exit sign over it. She reached for it.

Somehow he was there before her, opening the door and holding it for her. He hadn't seemed to rush, yet he'd moved very quickly. Lily stopped, studying him. He looked elegant and not at all civilized in spite of his trendy black clothing. "Legend says lupi are fast. Really fast."

He just smiled.

Something shivered down her spine. She got her feet moving and didn't speak again until they both were on the stairs, headed down. "I know the legal history best. Until 1930, the only federal law related to lupi was the one making it a crime not to report someone, ah, afflicted with lycanthropy. State laws varied widely. Most of them treated lupi as humans who had a dangerous disease. Some called for them to be killed outright. Then Dr. Abraham Geddes proved that lycanthropy could not be transmitted, as had previously been believed."

"The Change isn't catching," he agreed mildly.

"Right. It's an inherited condition. Folklore and experts alike agree that the trait is sex-linked. There are no female lupi."

"True."

"I guess the experts can't be wrong about everything. Anyway, soon after that came *Carr* v. *the State of Texas*. The

Supreme Court's ruling effectively made lupi legally human, but with a congenital disease, one that, well . . ."

"Makes us mad. Incurably insane. We were locked up, if discovered. Usually in chains."

"Yes. Well, that was some time ago. There continued to be a good deal of debate about whether lupi were human. Some of those of the Blood are obviously nonhuman, of course."

"Gremlins, brownies, the odd pooka or banshee."

"Pookas? I thought they were—never mind." She shook her head. Later she could ask if pookas were really extinct or not.

They'd reached the fourth-floor landing. He was still moving easily. She was, too, though her heart rate was up slightly. She wondered if he could hear it. Lupi were said to have extremely acute hearing. "In 1964 Dr. Beatrice Pargenter discovered a serum that inhibited the Change, and everyone who considered lycanthropy a disease applauded. It was considered an enormous, and humane, breakthrough. Congress passed the registration laws, which remained in effect until five years ago."

"You do have your legal history down."

"I've boned up."

Rule Turner's forehead was smooth. No tattoo, nor any sign that one had been removed. The authorities had used a special, silver-infused dye to tattoo the registration number, since the body of a were would otherwise have healed the tiny wounds inflicted by a needle within minutes. "You never registered, did you?"

"Why, Detective, I do believe that's a personal question."

"And I do believe you're obnoxious. That's a personal comment, by the way. I understand the drug was very unpopular with the lupi."

"Since the side effects ranged from vertigo to nausea to impotence—yes, it was unpopular. But even if they'd been able to refine their damned drug, no one wanted it."

His voice had lost its subtle balance between seduction and mockery. The emotion she heard was real, and personal.

They'd reached the subbasement. He pushed open the door and held it for her, as he had before. She went through it, uncomfortably aware that he was inviting her to expose her back to him.

The parking garage looked like others everywhere—gray

and ugly. The air was hot and smelled of exhaust fumes. The light was flat, fluorescent, and grimly bright. "You didn't want to give up the Change."

"We no more wish to give it up than you would want to be chemically lobotomized. Still, I suppose it was an improvement over being killed or castrated."

She paused, startled. "Castrated?"

"Ah. A gap in your legal history, Detective." His eyes were oddly pale in the artificial light. "Yes, for a few years some states dealt with 'the lupi problem' the way scientists have dealt with fruit flies—by rendering us unable to breed. It was considered more humane than shooting us on sight, like rabid dogs."

He radiated anger, far more than the glimpse she'd had before. His face was taut with it. An old anger, she thought, but one that hadn't lost any of its power over time. Over the castration? Yes, she decided. His people had been killed, imprisoned, chained, drugged, tattooed, but it was the castration that made him vibrate with suppressed rage.

Had he been . . .

No, that was stupid. According to the file on her desk, Rule Turner had two sons, by two different mothers. Neither of whom he'd bothered to marry.

Even if he hadn't been a lycanthrope, he would so not be her type. She nodded to the left. "My car is this way."

"Mine isn't. I prefer to drive myself."

"Life is full of these little disappointments." She started walking without waiting to see if he followed.

After a bare second's pause, he did. "Are you used to having your way, Detective, or simply testing my willingness to cooperate?"

"I'm used to driving myself. California hasn't allowed the kind of vigilantism you described for over three decades, you know." And never castration.

"Which is one reason my clan chose to settle here."

Lily knew about the Nokolai enclave in the mountains outside the city, of course. She'd gone there shortly after the first murder—and been turned away at the gate, politely but firmly. It was outside the city limits, so she lacked the authority to insist she be allowed inside. The lupi were a secretive people. Not without reason, given the persecutions of the past. But those persecutions hadn't been entirely without reason, either.

Before the change in the laws, the enclave had masqueraded as a religious commune. Most people knew differently now, but they didn't realize that the land that made up the enclave was owned by the Nokolai chief personally. So was the other property Lily had found—a ranch in northern California, some choice L.A. real estate, and several condos here in San Diego.

The Nokolai chief was a rich man. His son seemed to do pretty well for himself, too.

She stopped at a plain white sedan that looked like a dozen others lined up beneath the low ceiling. He stood on the other side of the car, waiting for her to unlock it. Their eyes met. Her spine tingled. "There's a bill due to come before the House this fall," she said. "The Species Citizenship Bill. According to what I've read, you're strongly in favor of it."

"Interested in politics, are you?"

"The Supreme Court ruling already gives you citizenship. The Species Citizenship Bill won't change that, but it will declare lupi and others of the Blood nonhuman."

"But entitled to the rights and responsibilities of citizenship whether we're on two feet or four." He studied her face a moment, then nodded as if he'd confirmed something. "You don't approve of a law that would treat a beast as a person."

"I don't understand why you'd want to be declared non-human!"

He lifted those tilted eyebrows. "I am a lupus of Clan Nokolai. What else matters?"

Arrogant bastard. Lily swung her door open and slid inside. She could well believe he was royal. She could also, all too easily, believe he was a predator.

She let him in and started the engine. He slid in beside her and, after a second's hesitation, reached for the seat belt.

It occurred to her that a car was another small, enclosed space. She punched the buttons to let down the windows. "Hope you don't mind," she said casually. "I like fresh air."

"Not at all. I'm sure the air will grow fresher soon."

At the moment it smelled of oil, exhaust fumes, and hot concrete. Heat rose in her cheeks, but she didn't think he'd notice. She was, quite literally, thick-skinned. Neither bruises nor blushes showed much. "Do you really think you'll be able to sniff out the identity of the attacker?"

"I don't know. My senses aren't as acute in this form. It's worth trying."

"A less acute sense of smell would be a blessing at the morgue." With sudden alarm, she added, "Unless you plan to, ah—"

"I won't Change. Aside from the discomfort, and the danger of doing so in these surroundings, it is not allowed. Not within the city."

"The Change is uncomfortable?"

"It can be. We are tied to nature. Changing while surrounded by buildings, concrete, and steel instead of earth and sky, is . . . possible. But it exacts a price."

She thought about that as she pulled out into traffic. Had whoever Changed in order to kill done it in a park, or some other pocket of nature? "You say you're forbidden to Change within the city limits. You're not talking about the law."

"My Lupois forbade this many years ago."

"Lupois?"

"You would say 'king' or 'high prince.' Though perhaps 'clan chief' is closer." He was sitting with his forearm propped on the window opening. Air streamed through, pouring itself around that narrow, sculpted face, whipping his hair around it.

She spotted a gap in the other lane between a panel truck and an SUV, accelerated smoothly, and whipped into it. The panel truck honked. Turner's hand clenched tightly on the door. Charitably, she chose to overlook that. "The Lupois is your father."

"Yes."

The Change was intensely important to him, to all lupi, from what he'd said. If the Lupois had the authority to forbid or restrict it, that was considerable power. "And do all members of your clan obey the Lupois in this?"

"I would have said yes, until I heard of the first killing. Now I don't know."

"You think it's someone from your clan."

"I don't know," he repeated, and she heard a thread of anger or frustration in his voice. "We are the only clan near San Diego, but we aren't the only lupi."

He would want it to be someone outside his clan, she thought, signaling for the turn. "I know about big, close-knit families. I come from one myself. A brother, two sisters, three uncles, four aunts, lots of cousins. Both of my father's parents are still living. Then there's Grandmother."

If he thought it was ridiculous for her to compare her extended family to a lupus clan, he didn't say so. "You say 'grandmother' as if she were the only one to bear that title."

"She's one of a kind, all right. My sister and I call her Tiger Lady—though not to her face. I'm named after her. That is, I bear the English version of her name."

"My name is Anglicized, too."

She glanced at him quickly. "Turner?"

"No, Rule. It was originally Reule. French."

"So what does it mean?" The light was about to change. She accelerated through it without quite running up the bumper of the car ahead of her.

"Little wolf." He exhaled. "Get a lot of tickets, do you?"

"No." She hadn't seen him tense this time, but out of the corner of her eye she did catch him relaxing again. She grinned. "I'm a good driver, actually. Good reflexes. Not as fast as yours, I suppose. I guess it might be nerve-wracking to have someone whose reflexes are half the speed of yours in the driver's seat."

"Only if they think they're invulnerable," he said dryly.

"You're the one who ought to feel invulnerable. It takes a lot to hurt a lupus, doesn't it?"

"Because we heal so quickly, we can take a lot of damage. But we have the same nerve endings humans do. We hurt every bit as much."

He thought of himself as a lupus. Not as a human. For the next few blocks she couldn't think of anything more to say.

Chapter 4

LILY HATED THE morgue. It was an unprofessional reaction, one she'd tried to overcome, but she had yet to set foot inside the cold, white walls without feeling repelled.

It wasn't the bodies that got to her. Nor the smell. It was what happened to those bodies here that made her skin feel two sizes too small. Autopsies were necessary. They were also the final, most complete invasion of privacy possible.

The attendant was new—at least, Lily hadn't run across her before. She was young, African American, her hair cropped very short to show off an elegant head and neck. And she was staring at Rule Turner.

Did the man have that effect on every woman whose path he crossed? "Detective Yu," she said, holding out her shield in the soft leather case her brother had given her for her birthday last year. "I understand you've got Carlos Fuentes chilled down. We need to have a look."

She blinked, then stood. "Sure. This way, Detective."

Lily's shoulders and spine were tight as she and Turner followed the attendant down a short hall.

"You don't like this place, either," he said abruptly.

She looked at him. There was strain around his eyes, and

his lips were thinned. "I guess it smells pretty bad here to you."

"It's not the smell that bothers me."

The attendant spoke cheerily as she pulled on one of the handles and slid the long drawer out. "Here you go."

What blood was left in the body had settled, of course. The back and buttocks would be livid, but the undamaged part of his face, his shoulders, and his upper chest were waxy and pale. He looked cold beneath the thin sheet. And very dead.

Lily's lips tightened. She glanced at Rule. "The sheet—?"

"I'll need it off."

The attendant looked surprised, then upset as she removed the sheet. That puzzled Lily. Why would a morgue attendant be upset at being asked to remove a sheet from a body? The obvious assumption was that Rule was here to identify the victim and, given the condition of the dead man's face, looking at the body made sense.

Oh. Lily's lips twitched. The young woman didn't like the idea that Rule might be intimately familiar with another man's body. Well, no one enjoyed having their dreams snuffed out. Even the brief, silly ones.

Rule bent close to the ravaged throat and sniffed.

"Hey!" The attendant grabbed his shoulder and tried to pull him back. She might have been tugging on a Buick, for all the effect she had. "Just what do you think you're doing?"

"Exactly what he's been asked to do." Lily took the woman's arm and firmly urged her back. "By Chief Delgado."

"He was asked to sniff a corpse?" she exclaimed, outraged.

Lily lifted both eyebrows as if the question were absurd, rather than the action. "Yes."

The attendant looked as if she would have bolted from the room if regulations hadn't called for her to remain. Lily didn't much want to watch him, either, but perversity or pride kept her from looking away.

He made a thorough job of it, smelling all up and down the body, paying close attention to the wounds and the cold, flaccid hands. He was intent, focused, and somehow still impossibly elegant. Not like a beast at all—more like a wine connoisseur about to deliver a verdict on the bouquets of various vintages.

And that thought was both absurd and macabre. Lily bit her lip to keep from giggling like an idiot.

At last he straightened, met her eyes, and shook his head slightly.

"You couldn't tell."

"He was killed by a lupus," he said flatly. "Beyond that . . ." He shrugged. "Very little scent remains."

"We already knew the killer was a lupus."

"Perhaps you did. I didn't until now. There are some who might want to fake the slaying of men by lupi."

Lily remembered their audience, a wide-eyed attendant who might talk to the wrong person, like a reporter. She jerked her head, indicating she wanted him to follow, and headed for the door.

He thanked the attendant politely. She should have done that, she thought, upset and not knowing why. Had she counted so much on his sense of smell to give her a lead? That was foolish.

He caught up with her at the door and took her elbow. "I want coffee. Something to get the taste of this place out of my mouth."

Before she stopped to think, she'd agreed. Together they left that cold, bright room with its neatly filed bodies.

INSTINCT TOOK HER to Bennie's Bar & Grill. Bennie's was large, dark, and noisy, known for its cheeseburgers. As soon as she stepped inside, Lily sighed. Usually her instincts weren't this lousy.

Bennie's was a cop hangout.

It wasn't crowded at this hour. She only spotted two faces she knew as they headed for the back, but everyone seemed to recognize the man with her. The looks she and Rule drew varied from startled to snarly. Cops were good with faces, and his was memorable.

By the time they sat in a booth near the rest rooms, she was feeling self-conscious and prickly. "I wonder if this is how a white woman felt in Selma in 1960 if she went into a restaurant with a black man."

He shook his head slowly. "Our fellow customers aren't going to take either of us out in the alley and beat us up for having dared to be seen in public together. The waitress won't even refuse to serve me."

She grimaced. "I'm overreacting, you mean."

"There are parallels. If people hadn't started refusing to sit at the back of the bus back then, measures like the Species Citizenship Bill wouldn't be possible now. Have you given any thought to going out with me?"

She blinked. "For a supposedly sophisticated man, you have lousy timing. I just watched you sniffing a corpse."

"It's a subject that will keep coming up, good timing or not."

A waitress drifted up—young, blond, and pierced. There was a ring in her eyebrow, three studs on one ear, and another ring in the belly button her midriff-hugging top exposed. She set Lily's water in front of her without glancing in her direction. Her eyes were wholly on Turner, huge with fascination . . . and fear.

And he knew. Awareness of the girl's fear was there in the flicker of his eyes, the softness of his voice as he ordered coffee.

"I'll have a cup, too," Lily said, peeling the paper from her straw. "Make it blond."

The waitress nodded and left.

Lily crossed her arms on the table and leaned forward. "Is it because you're a lupus? Or do you get all this attention because you're a celebrity?"

He didn't pretend to misunderstand. "I'm probably the only lupus she'll ever meet—knowingly, at least."

Lily nodded as a piece fell into place. "That's the reason for all the black, isn't it? I've never seen a photograph of you where you're wearing colors. Just black. You want people to recognize you. You want them to know they're meeting a lupus."

Amazingly, a touch of color sharpened those hard cheekbones. "Black is good theater."

"And your face is unforgettable. When people see you, they remember. You do the mystery bit well—a hint of glamour, the allure of the forbidden or the dangerous. That's the image you want people to associate with lupi. You're sort of a poster boy for your people."

"Thank you."

He was insulted. She grinned. "You don't like being called a boy or cocky, which is for puppies. I think you've started to believe your image."

All at once he grinned back. "Maybe I have."

The grin transformed his face, turning it from dark and disturbing to someone outrageously appealing-—but someone who wore ragged jeans on weekends, played baseball with the guys, and changed the oil in his car. Lily didn't even think about trying to reply. She was too caught up in that grin, what it did to his eyes and the way it lifted her heart.

"Here you go." The waitress deposited their coffee, dumping a couple of containers of creamer beside Lily's cup.

Lily hadn't so much as glimpsed her approach. Shaken, she tore one of the creamers open and dumped half the contents into her coffee.

Had he used some kind of magic on her? Or did it just spill out from him naturally, without his willing it? If it wasn't magic . . . she didn't want to think about what it would mean if she could react like that to him without any magic involved. "Does magic have a smell?"

His eyebrows lifted. "It can. Why?"

"You knew the attacker was lupus. Our lab did, too—at least, they could tell it was someone of the Blood, because magic leaves traces. I wondered if you were smelling the same kind of traces they found."

"I don't think so. Magic does have a distinctive scent, but only when it's active. When a spell is being performed, for example. What I identified was the smell of lupus, not magic itself."

"Is there anything else you can tell me about the killer?"

He frowned and sipped his coffee. She was not surprised to see that he drank it black. "He wasn't a juvenile."

"You can tell that from the scent?"

"No. The body wasn't eaten."

Coffee sloshed in her cup. She set it down carefully. "Explain."

"It's pure superstition that an adult lupus will be overcome by bloodlust and attack whatever moves. Young lupi lose themselves in the beast, but we learn control. If we didn't, we really would be the ravening beasts depicted in movies like *Witch Hunt*."

"So a child or adolescent wouldn't have acquired control yet."

"Not a child. The Change arrives with puberty."

She thought of a particularly improbable photograph she'd seen while waiting in the checkout line at the grocery store recently. A woman had been sitting up in a hospital bed with several blanket-wrapped bundles tucked into her arms. Bundles with puppy faces. "The *National Tattler* would be disappointed to hear that."

"I doubt the *Tattler* allows facts to interfere with its editorial focus."

"I guess not. Talk about raging hormones." Lily gave herself a moment to think by sipping her coffee. This was completely new information. She hadn't heard it, read it, anywhere. Why would he trust her with this knowledge? Was it true? "You're saying that a young lupus kills. And eats what he kills."

"If he is allowed to, yes. But we are careful with our children. None go through the Change unsupervised."

Her lips twitched. Embarrassed, she took a quick sip of coffee.

"Something amuses you?"

"I have an odd sense of humor," she said apologetically. "I thought of those ads—you know, the public service ones?— where parents of teenagers are told to nag them about where they're going, who they'll be with, all that. And I pictured one aimed for the parents of teenage lupi: 'Where are you going? Who else will be there? Have you eaten? I expect you back before the moon rises, young man!' "

He burst into laughter. "You're not that far off."

A bubble of happiness lodged beneath her breastbone. She liked the sound of his laughter, the way his head went back to open his throat to it, the smooth line of his throat . . . *uh-oh*, she thought, the bubble popping. *What's happening here?*

She poured more creamer into her coffee so she could stir it around. A light touch on her cheek made her look up, startled.

"Hey. The light suddenly turned off in your face. What happened?"

She could have told him again to keep his hands to himself, but it would have been dishonest. Somehow, between one grin and a moment of shared laughter, they'd stepped outside their proper roles and entered undefined territory.

But the very lack of definition made complete honesty impossible. She couldn't refer to a relationship that hovered over them only in potential, a heavy cloud that might hold storm and lightning—or might pass on without shedding a single drop. She certainly couldn't tell him that his promiscuity repelled her.

Lily chose her words carefully. "You have two sons yourself, I understand."

"It seems you do read the *Tattler*."

"Like I said earlier, after the first killing I did some research."

"On me?" His mouth twisted. "What exactly is it you suspect me of?"

She shrugged, uncomfortable but unwilling to apologize for doing her job. "You're very well known. You live in the enclave—"

"Clanhome. We don't call it an enclave."

"All right, then, you live at Clanhome, but you have a condo here in the city and you travel all over the place, partying with the Hollywood crowd, meeting with policy makers in Sacramento and Washington. You've made yourself into a public figure, and I have to think that's intentional—you're trying to replace the old stereotypes with an image you've consciously created. Of course I found out what I could about you."

One corner of his mouth tipped up, more in irony than humor. "You're perceptive. Has it occurred to you that if I've been creating an image, whatever information is available about me would be part of that image?"

"And not necessarily true, you mean? But the image tells me things, too. Like what you want people to believe about lupi. Why does your father so seldom appear in public?"

He studied her for a moment, his mouth drawn into a thin line, as grimly expressive as those remarkable eyebrows. "You should ask him that. He prefers not to come into the city, however. You'll have to go to Clanhome."

"I tried that. They wouldn't let me inside the gates. I've called. A very polite young woman told me she'd pass on my message. You can get me in, though."

"I could get you in, yes, but just getting inside the gates won't do you any good. No one would answer your questions.

You need the backing of the Lupois. Give me a few days to arrange things."

Or to hide whatever needed to be hidden. "What needs arranging?"

"My father is away right now. Wait until he returns."

The muscles along her cheeks and jaws tightened. He was concealing something, and doing a clumsy job of it. "Why can't you arrange for me to speak with people at Clanhome yourself? Aren't you in charge with your father gone?"

"It doesn't work that way." His fingers stroked up and down the mug absently.

"How does it work, then?"

"I'm not like a vice-president, able to step in if the real leader is unavailable. I'm the prince and the heir, and . . ." His smile flickered. "A poster boy for my people. I have no authority of my own. I simply uphold the Lupois's authority."

"Okay." He seemed to think he was telling her something significant, but nothing he'd said so far was startling. "How do you get to be prince, anyway? Is it strictly hereditary?"

"To be named prince, I had to prove three things. That I was of royal blood, yes, though we do not follow primogeniture. My father has two other sons, both older than I am."

"I didn't know that."

"Very few do. My brothers, unfortunately, did not succeed at the second test. Since a king must be able to pass on his power, the prince must be able to sire children. As you know, I have two sons."

Had he gotten those sons on their mothers in order to become prince? The possibility left a foul taste in her mouth. "And the third thing?"

"That I could tear out the throat of any who issued a formal challenge."

That left her with nothing whatsoever to say.

His mouth crooked up on one side, but there was no smile in his eyes. "Think about it. The Lupois rules for life. If anyone disagrees with his decisions, they have two alternatives. They can try to change his mind. Or they can kill him."

Slowly the ramifications sank in. "When you say you support his authority, does that mean you're a sort of bodyguard? Or are you more like his muscle?"

"Both, perhaps, in the sense that the army is the 'muscle'

of the president. We are not a passive people, but we have great respect for honor and custom. Any member of the clan may challenge the Lupois."

"What does this challenge consist of?"

"Battle. In wolf form."

A sick certainty grew in the pit of her stomach. "A trial by combat, you mean. Your father is over sixty. He couldn't defend himself against a young opponent. You do that for him. You answer any formal challenges to his authority."

He didn't answer, just looked at her gravely the way an adult might watch a child struggling to understand some complicated matter.

She did not like being patronized. She didn't much care for the implications, either. "How is the winner determined in one of these battles?"

"It varies, depending on the nature of the challenge and the will of the Lupois. In a serious challenge to the Lupois's authority, the winner is the one still alive at the end. Don't look so shocked, Detective. It's only illegal to kill one of us when we're on two feet, after all."

Chapter 5

THE SUN HAD set, but the sky still flew crimson and purple flags in the west. A boy who should have been inside at this hour whizzed by on his skateboard. Lily's breath heaved in her chest as she neared the outdoor stairs to her apartment. Sweat trickled down her temples and stung her eyes. Worf's claws clicked dully on the concrete beside her. His big head drooped, but he was panting happily.

Lily's dog was undoubtedly a good deal more satisfied with their run than she was.

It had been four days since the last killing. She knew little more now than she had when she had looked down at the ripped throat of the first victim, a young man whose only crime seemed to be that he'd been in the wrong place at the wrong time.

There was nothing to link the two victims other than the manner of their deaths. She'd found no hard evidence, and only two possible witnesses. An old man and a teenage girl both spoke of seeing a tall, well-dressed man—an Anglo—near the park where Fuentes was killed. The timing fit, and the man's clothes, bearing, and race had made him stand out in an area mostly Hispanic. Neither witness had gotten a clear look at his face, but they thought he was smooth-shaven, neither especially old nor very young.

When they reached the iron stairs Worf stopped, whimpered, and looked up at her with pathetic eyes. "Forget it," she told him. "I'm not lugging seventy pounds of lazy up those stairs."

His tail waved twice hopefully. Her lips twitched. Worf was a peculiar-looking fellow. His body looked like a barrel set on stubby legs, his ears drooped along with his jowls, and his kinky fur was the color of mud. Lily's vet thought the dog might be a mixture of Labrador, basset, and poodle. She'd found him huddled in the alley, looking pathetic and half-starved, about six months ago. He was scared of cats and he hated stairs.

"Forget it," she said again, and started up the stairs. Worf heaved a huge canine sigh and followed. They were near the top when she heard the phone ringing inside her apartment.

It might be Rule.

She cursed herself even as she scrambled up the last steps, nearly tripping over Worf, who decided they were racing and tried to get to the door first. She wasn't supposed to want the man to call again, dammit. But whoever was calling, it wasn't police business—Dispatch would use her beeper.

And so far Rule had called every day, discussing the case and then asking her out.

Every day, she'd turned him down. So he just might be getting tired of calling. Which was a good thing, she told herself firmly as she grabbed the phone, cutting off her answering machine's spiel. "Hello?"

"You've been out running again, haven't you? At *night*, Lily. You know how unsafe that is."

Lily sighed. "Hello, Mother. I'm a big girl now, and a cop, and I keep to well-lit areas where there are people."

"None of which makes you invulnerable."

Her lips quirked up as she thought of Rule's opinion of her driving. "I had Worf with me."

"As if that lazy creature was any kind of protection! I don't know why you kept that animal. You aren't home enough to take proper care of him, and he's too large for an apartment. Besides, you know how Grandmother feels about dogs."

"Grandmother isn't living with Worf. I am." She picked up

his water dish and carried it to the sink. "What's up? You
didn't call to lecture me about pet ownership."

"I don't need a reason to call my daughter. But I did think
it was time to finalize some of the details for Grandmother's
party. It's this Friday."

Lily managed not to groan. "I know that, Mother. The
cake's ordered, the invitations went out weeks ago, and it's
being held at Uncle Chan's restaurant. He won't let anyone
mess with his menu, so there's no point in discussing the food.
I've bought a dress, and yes, I've bought a present, wrapped
and ready. What's left to discuss?"

Stupid question. Her mother had plenty to say. Lily's older
sister was attending with her husband, of course. And her
brother was bringing his fiancée, a young woman whose vir-
tues included the possession of a good Chinese family, a position at an accounting firm, and respect for her elders. While
Worf slurped up his water and Lily grabbed a bottle from the
refrigerator, she learned that her younger sister was bringing
a doctor from the hospital where her older sister worked.

She also learned who each of her cousins was bringing, and
their financial and family histories. By the time her mother
reached the real point of her call, Lily was sprawled in her
favorite chair, one leg dangling over the padded arm, prepared
for what came next.

Her mother didn't disappoint her. "So who will you be
bringing, dear?"

"I haven't asked anyone." Lily slumped farther down in the
overstuffed chair. "I don't see that it's necessary."

"Of course it's necessary. This is a formal party, Lily. You
will look foolish if you attend without an escort. You will
cause your father and me to lose face, and Grandmother, too."

She closed her eyes. The "face" argument was one she
couldn't counter. "I'm not seeing anyone right now. Do you
want me to ask someone from Homicide? Or there's a very
nice Vice officer—his name is Lawrence, but we all call him
Curly. I think he'd agree, and he might even shave, since it's
formal. He works undercover a lot," she explained. "The three-
day beard helps him blend in."

Stony silence greeted that bit of flippancy.

She sighed. "I'm sorry, Mother. But there really isn't anyone I want to ask."

"I'm well aware that your job exposes you to the wrong sort of men. This is only one of the reasons your father and I had hoped you would choose a more appropriate career. Who do you ever meet, other than police officers and criminals?"

The words came out before she could stop herself. "I did meet a very good-looking man a few days ago. His family owns quite a bit of land—a vineyard, a cattle ranch, some other properties. He manages some of their investments and, ah, has contacts in the government. He's asked me out several times."

"And you haven't accepted? He *is* single, isn't he?"

Extremely single. From what she'd heard, lupi didn't believe in marriage. "I would hardly have mentioned him if he weren't."

"I don't know what you are looking for, but you must be realistic. You aren't getting any younger, and while you're a very pretty girl you don't always take the care you might with your appearance. And your job—well, we've covered that subject many times, so I won't go into it now. You must learn to make some accommodations, dear. I suppose this man isn't Chinese, but surely you don't think that would make him unacceptable?"

"Ah . . . no, he isn't Chinese. Actually, he—"

"Asking him to accompany you to the party is not a lifetime commitment. You make too much of a simple thing. Of course, I can arrange an escort for you, if you prefer. Su Lin Chen's nephew is doing very well. He will inherit the restaurant, you know—"

"Freddie Chen?" She sat up, alarmed. "Mother, if you ask Freddie Chen to escort me to Grandmother's party I'll never speak to you again. He's an octopus. A sweaty octopus. With bad breath."

"Then ask this other man. What is his name?"

"Rule—" Lilly's beeper went off. "Just a minute. I've got a call." She unclipped the beeper from her belt and checked the number quickly. "Got to go, Mother. I'll call you later."

"Ask him," her mother said. "Or I will speak to Su Lin." She hung up.

The number on Lily's beeper was one she knew all too well. She had it on speed dial on both her land line and her cell phone. Lily punched it, listened, asked two questions, then headed for the door, grabbing her holster on the way out.

*   *   *

THIS TIME THE victim was a woman. Charlene Hall had been forty-eight, African American, probably single. No wedding ring, and her credit cards were in her name. She had a California driver's license, an unpaid traffic ticket, and a whole slew of those wallet-sized school photos millions of parents buy every year.

A dozen pictures, Lily thought, her gut clenched tight with pity. All of the same two boys, taken over many years. The two pictures on top were the most recent. One showed a young man in a sailor's dress uniform, his dark face solemn, his eyes gleaming with pride. The other was a family shot minus the husband-father element. The boy who in one photo had been missing three teeth was a young man now, his smile still wide and happy. He wore a suit in this photograph, and stood behind a young woman holding a baby dressed in blue ruffles and lace.

Charlene Hall had taken these photographs with her everywhere. Even when she went for a run by the lake at Mission Trails Park.

Lily glanced at the body, almost ignored at the moment. Charlene had worn the same brand of running shoe Lily favored. Lily sighed. It was too much to hope that her mother wouldn't read about this.

There was no crowd this time, and so far no press. Just the police, a couple of park rangers, the victim, and the poor guy who'd found her. They were only twenty yards from the start of the trail near the sturdy adobe building where tourists bought sodas, postcards, and film. Charlene had nearly made it back when the killer struck.

Lily was talking with the man who'd found Charlene when Rule arrived.

"Detective?" called one of the patrol officers from farther up the trail. "This the guy you're waiting for?"

She turned. Rule stood beside the officer at the edge of the lights cast by the police spots. His face was shadowed, his expression shuttered. He was wearing black.

Rule waited for Lily to come to him. He was a patient man, he reminded himself. Which was just as well. He would need to be. If she felt what he did, she was fighting it. Maybe she felt nothing more than a sexual buzz. He rubbed his chest, but the ache wasn't one he could touch.

The scents were rich here, away from the nose-clogging odors of the city. The green smells of growing things mingled in a pattern too complex to easily yield its separate notes, but he was aware of creosote, cypress and sumac, wild mustard and cholla. The lake, invisible from where he stood, was a rich, damp presence blending water, fish, a whiff of decay. He smelled dust and people, one or more of whom gave off the faint, sour tang of fear.

The ground was hard and dry beneath his feet. A lumpy three-quarter moon squatted near the horizon, peering at them through the dark lace of leaves in the trees to his right. He felt its pull in his blood, a song without words or notes: one long, slow pulse timed to a rhythm those around him would never hear.

He couldn't see the body. Too many people were in the way. But he smelled blood, sweet and sharp. And waste, the body's involuntary surrender to the insult of sudden death.

Lily stopped in front of him, her pretty black eyes flat and official, but the pulse in her throat throbbing. "Thank you for coming right away."

"I want the killing stopped, too."

She nodded and turned. "This way."

The smell of blood grew heavier as he followed. A couple of the people standing near the body shifted, and he saw. Shock stopped him in his tracks.

"What is it?"

His voice came out hoarse. "You didn't tell me it was a woman."

Lily's frown mixed concern with puzzlement. "Does it matter so much?"

"It matters." He wasn't over the shock yet, but the rage gathering inside would clear it away soon enough. His hands clenched.

"Why?" she asked sharply. "I know lupi are patriarchal, but use your head. Carlos Fuentes didn't have any more of a chance than this woman did. Not against a lupus."

"Forget the PC talk. You don't understand. Women . . . women conceive. They carry babies—our babies, human babies. We don't hurt women. Ever." The rage was rising, threatening his control. He clenched his hands tightly, throttling back the need to howl, to seek and find the one who had done this. The need to Change.

Slowly his fists relaxed, and with the release of clenched muscles some of the need drained away. Not now. This wasn't the time or the place, but that time would come. He would make sure of it. "Whoever did this is a rogue," he said, cold and certain. "And subject to our laws as well as yours."

She closed her hand around his arm as if to hold him back. "The law he'll answer to is the one I'm sworn to uphold. Not some weird trial by combat."

He shook her off and moved to kneel by the body.

It had been a clean kill, at least. The dead eyes stared up, sightless and shocked, but the woman's face itself was intact, if blood-spattered. Rule picked up one of the cold hands and cradled it gently in his, silently apologizing for what one of his kind had done, promising retribution and asking permission for what he must do. Then he bent and sniffed the gaping wound where her throat had been.

This was why Lily had asked him to come, after all. The scent would be fresh.

The first whiff told the tale, but he took his time, wanting to leave no doubt. Then, gently, he laid the dead hand back on the ground and stood.

Lily was watching. "You know. This time you could tell who it was."

He jerked his head to the left. "Walk apart with me so I can tell you."

Her eyebrows went up. After a moment, she nodded. Together they moved farther up the trail the dead woman had taken—fleeing, at the last, from one she couldn't escape.

He stopped by a scrappy little oak, its leaves whispering to each other in the breeze. They'd left the pool of light from the police spots behind. Here it was dark, and closer to the lake. That strong, clean scent cleared some of the other smells from his senses.

Lily stood close enough for her scent to fill him, too. Not close enough to touch. "What did you learn? Who was it?"

"Leidolf."

"Is that a first name or a surname?"

"It's a clan." The rage was still there, simmering beneath

the surface. Waiting. "It wasn't one of the Nokolai who did this."

"You can tell by the scent?"

"Just as you could tell an Englishman from a Hawaiian by the way he looks."

She exhaled once, sharply. "So what does this mean? I don't know how to sort one lupus from another by clan. I didn't know there *were* any other clans around here."

"There aren't, not officially. But lupi travel on business or for pleasure the same as everyone else. It's customary for clans to offer hospitality when asked. My clan may be hosting the one who did this right now." He took a deep breath, letting it out slowly. "We aren't that far from Clanhome, as the crow flies—or the wolf runs. He could easily have cut across the hills after he killed."

"That occurred to me. Rule." She gripped his arm. "You are not going to punish him yourself. If you want your people to be treated the same as everyone else, you have to be subject to the same laws. Justice from the courts, not private vengeance."

"Your courts have never given us justice. And this . . ." He turned away, thrusting his hand through his hair. "I thought this was political, and so subject to your laws. Now . . . it may be a clan matter."

"What do you mean?"

"Leidolf may be moving against Nokolai." There was so much he couldn't tell her. "It happens. Clans have warred in the past."

"Killing random humans is a mighty roundabout way for one lupus clan to declare war on another."

"My father supports the Species Citizenship Bill." His smile was grim. "Do you think only humans oppose full citizenship for lupi? There are those among my people, too, who hate the idea. Citizenship means Social Security numbers and all those computers keeping track of us. It means limits, changes to some of our customs. They don't want to be that visible—or that subject to human law."

"Whoever did this is going to end up very visible. I'll see to that." Anger boiled up suddenly and she paced in front of him, taking short, jerky steps. "She had two sons. I don't know their names yet, but one is in the Navy. The other has a wife and child. Once I've learned who they are, where they live, I'll have to tell them their mother is dead because someone had a political point to make."

He put a hand on her shoulder. She was all but vibrating with anger. "Killing has always been a political tactic for some. Why do you work homicide when it hurts you this much?"

She shrugged him off. "I don't know what you mean. I'm a cop. It's what I always wanted to do."

"It hurts you to see life wasted." Again he asked, speaking softly, "Why homicide?"

"Because murder is the worst! It doesn't kill just once. It throws out waves of destruction that poison so many lives."

"This happened to you. Someone you loved was murdered."

"My friend. My best friend. Sara Chen."

He ached. It took all his control to keep from reaching for her, holding her. But she wouldn't want that, not here and now. "How old were you?"

"Seven. A man grabbed her on the way home from school one day. I saw him snatch her. They found her body a week later. They arrested him a week after that." She swallowed. "I followed it in the papers. My parents didn't like that—they thought I was hurting myself, that I was obsessed and should let it go. I couldn't."

"No. I can see that. What happened?"

"He never went to trial. The police were sloppy. They didn't secure the evidence properly. Seven months later, he killed again. That time, the cops did it right. He didn't get away with it."

She'd given him a piece of herself, something important wrenched up from deep inside where it still hurt. He lifted a hand and rubbed his knuckles along her cheek slowly, thanking her. "This woman isn't dead because you were sloppy, Lily. You know that."

She blinked. "I didn't mean . . . I don't think it's my fault."

Yes, she did. But she was pulling back now, embarrassed that she'd revealed so much. "That's good. I admire your passion. And your courage."

Oh, definitely she was embarrassed now. She turned away, trying to get her cop face back. "The point is, the law has to be the same for everyone. Fuentes has to matter as much as Charlene Hall. And whoever killed them, for whatever reason, has to be stopped."

"Of course. Aside from the personal injustice of murder, if there's sufficient outrage it will affect the vote next fall. Especially if there are killings elsewhere."

She stopped moving. "You're talking about a conspiracy."

"I'm speculating. I have no evidence. But with this latest death . . ." He drove his fingers through his hair. "Killing a woman will garner a great deal more outrage than killing a gang member did, won't it?"

"This is going to make trouble for you. She was killed much closer to the Nokolai Clanhome than the others. Rule, I have to talk to your father. I have to talk to a number of your people, but your father first."

"He'll be back tomorrow. I'll speak to him." He took her hand, closing his fingers around it firmly. "When are you going to go out with me?"

Her laugh was uncertain. "I mentioned something before about your odd sense of timing. We're at a murder scene, for God's sake."

He stroked his thumb along the pulse point in her wrist. "So let's agree that we have to stop meeting this way, and meet some other way. Over dinner, perhaps. I'm growing impatient."

"That's not my problem."

"I want to discuss something other than death and politics with you. I want to see your face when you're not being a cop."

"I'm always a cop."

Perhaps. But she was a woman, too. And her heart was beating fast and hard right now, like his. It took all his control to keep from bending to taste that pretty, unsmiling mouth, but he knew how little she'd appreciate that. Her people might see. His mouth crooked up. "I guess tonight is out."

"Good guess," she said dryly. But she didn't snatch her hand away.

"Tomorrow won't work, either. As I said, my father returns then, and we'll have a good deal to discuss. How about the next night? I can get tickets to a play, reservations for dinner."

She eased her hand away from his. "That's Friday night,

and I'm booked. A family party—Grandmother's eightieth birthday." She started back down the path, but had taken only a couple of steps when she paused, looking back at him. The tilt of her lips held challenge. "Ah . . . it's formal, a big bash at my uncle Chan's restaurant. Would you care to go with me?"

Chapter 6

LILY WASN'T SURE at what point she'd lost her mind. At six-oh-seven that Friday she slicked color over her lips and tried to figure that out.

What had prompted her impulsive invitation to Rule? Hormones run amok? Her conversation with her mother earlier had put the idea in her head, but she hadn't been serious. She certainly hadn't intended to ask him. All of a sudden the idea had burst open in her mind like a flower gone from bud to bloom instantly, and she'd done it.

Maybe it had been that brief, startling gentleness he'd shown. The way he'd stroked her cheek, the softness in his voice. For a moment, understanding had shimmered between them, fragile and precious.

Or she'd thought it had.

Lily shook her head, turned to open her closet, which was off the bathroom, and almost tripped over Worf. "No shedding or drooling allowed," she told him firmly. "Sit."

Obediently he lowered his rear end, but continued to pant at her happily. She kept an eye on his lolling tongue as she reached for her dress.

Never mind the reason. The fact was that she'd succumbed

to impulse. A flash of lunacy, she supposed. And winced. *Lunacy* was not a comfortable word, considering the effect a full moon had on the man she would be with tonight.

The moon would be full in three days. She'd checked.

All in all, this hadn't been a good day. She'd spent too much of it in court, for one thing, testifying against a scumbag with a lawyer bright enough to know his client's only hope was to make Lily look crooked, incompetent, or both. He hadn't succeeded, but it hadn't made for a fun morning. That afternoon she'd argued with enough bureaucrats to drive a saint to violence. Finally the Department of Health had condescended to let her copy its list of lupi living in San Diego, complied back when the government was registering them.

Rule's name hadn't been on the list. No surprise there. Neither was his father's. But eighty-seven others were. She'd barely started checking the names and addresses against the phone book to see who was still around.

Not everything had gone wrong today, she reminded herself. Neither her mother nor her grandmother had answered when, smitten by conscience, she'd called to let them know the name of her escort tonight. There was no point in hoping her family wouldn't realize who Rule was. Shoot, her grandmother read *People* regularly, and the magazine had done a spread on the Nokolai prince only last March.

Her mother was not going to appreciate the joke.

So why was she humming? Lily froze with the dress draped over her arm. This was nuts. Anyone would think she was looking forward to the evening.

Her dress. That was what had her humming, of course. She slid it from the hanger. Worf stood up, wagging his tail. "Sit," she told him again.

Her dress was ankle-length silk in a color that made her think of sapphires drenched in darkness, the color of the sky when dawn is barely a promise in the east. Lily had found it on sale a month ago and fallen in love. Even the sight of the price tag hadn't deterred her.

It was magnificent, she thought with sudden uncertainty as she surveyed herself in the mirror. A dream of a dress—sexy, feminine, sophisticated. Too sophisticated, maybe. She sure didn't look like a cop. Rule was going to think she'd dressed for him. He would think tonight was . . . personal.

He'd be right. Nerves snapped in her middle like a string of firecrackers.

Maybe if she took her hair down she'd look more like herself.

Lily had her hands in her hair, the first pin unpinned, when the phone rang. She stepped into her shoes on the way to the living room, the bobby pin still in her hand. She spared a glance at the clock as she picked up the phone.

Six twenty-two. Rule would be here any minute. "Hello?"

"You left a message on that infernal machine," a light, high voice said in Chinese.

"I am sorry, Grandmother, but when I couldn't reach you I felt it better to use the machine than to say nothing." Her grandmother did not approve of answering machines. She wasn't too fond of telephones, television, or microwaves, either.

"Your message said that you have invited Rule Turner to accompany you to my birthday celebration."

"Yes, Grandmother," Lily replied, careful of both her courtesy and her accent. Her command of the tongue seldom pleased her grandmother.

"He is lupus. A prince of one of their clans."

"Yes. I didn't want you to be taken by surprise."

"I have not been surprised since the Mets won the pennant. Did you tell your mother about this man?"

"I left her a message, the same as yours. I don't know if—"

"Good. Say nothing more to her." She hung up.

Lily shook her head. Phone conversations with her grandmother tended to end abruptly. Not that conversations in person were much different. She glanced at the clock. There might still be time to finish taking her hair down if she—

The doorbell rang. Worf let out a deep *woof* and surged to his feet. Lily took a steadying breath, jabbed the bobby pin back in her hair, and turned to face the door.

Battle stations.

HE DROVE AN Explorer. That surprised her. It seemed so— well, so middle-class normal. Half the people in California drove some kind of SUV.

"I ought to sell tickets," Lily muttered as he slid into the driver's seat beside her. Rule Turner was eye candy no matter what he wore, but in a tux the impact could wreck a woman's breathing.

"Pardon?" The knowing glint in his eyes suggested he'd heard her very well.

"Never mind." She found herself watching his hands as he started the engine and took them out into traffic. His fingers were long and slim. No scars, of course, nor any little nicks or scabs. Lupi healed such things. What was more surprising was how little hair there was on the backs of his hands. She'd always thought lupi were hairy. "Listen, I'm sorry about the way Worf acted. He's usually friendly."

"He didn't like my scent. The two of us will work things out," he said as he guided the vehicle smoothly through traffic. "Once he accepts me as dominant, he won't need to challenge me."

Nor did his beard seem especially heavy, though naturally he would have shaved . . . wouldn't he? Did lupi need to shave? "You're assuming you're going to see my dog often enough to work on a relationship with him."

"That's right. I am."

Her lips twitched. A sensible woman wouldn't find his arrogance so appealing. And maybe it wouldn't be, if she didn't suspect he was amused by himself, too. "So, what did your father say? Am I cleared to go talk to your people tomorrow?"

"He agreed to put it before the Council."

"What Council? I thought the Lupois's word was law."

"You might think of the Council as an advisory body, the elders of the tribe. Or maybe they're more like church deacons. The Lupois doesn't answer to the Council, but it pays to have their backing, particularly if he is considering breaking with tradition."

"I can't wait much longer, Rule."

"I know. I have a suggestion. Why don't we talk about something other than the investigation tonight?"

"Such as?"

"What do you usually talk about on a date?"

"The usual—his work, his hobbies, his ex-wives."

He clucked his tongue. "Sexism rears its ugly head. Surely there are a few men who don't just discuss themselves?"

"Well, they mostly don't want to talk about my work, unless I date a cop. And I don't date cops."

"I'm glad to hear that. Of course, I'd rather you didn't date anyone except me."

Her mouth went dry. "You don't have any right to say that. You're moving too fast."

"I'm being honest. Why don't you date cops?"

"They're lousy bets for anything long-term. Besides, it would be icky."

He grinned. "Icky?"

"You know—the way it would feel to work with someone you've . . . someone who . . . never mind."

"Do you 'never mind' with every man you date?" He slowed for the turn. "I ask not to condemn, you understand, but in hope."

She shook her head. "There you go, jumping to conclusions. I was talking about kissing, not grappling under the covers. And how uncomfortable it would be to work with someone I've had carnal thoughts about, or who I know has had those thoughts about me."

"If you think that only the men you've dated have carnal thoughts about you, you're far more naive than I would have believed."

The husky note in his voice turned the banter personal. Intimate. She licked her lips and tried to keep things light. "Of course not. According to studies, men have carnal thoughts every ten seconds or so. Women know this. We just prefer to ignore it."

"I wasn't talking about the occasional random hard-on. I was talking about the way men react to you. You're an intensely desirable woman, Lily."

Suddenly the air burned in her lungs, thick and sweet, and she was overwhelmingly conscious of her hands. Of the need to touch him—and the need to keep herself from doing any such thing. Lily looked down at her lap, smoothed the silk of her dress, and listened to her heartbeat pounding and pounding in her throat. She couldn't think of a thing to say.

After a moment he sighed. "And now I've made you uncomfortable. Too much honesty too soon. What do you do when you aren't arresting lawbreakers?"

"I like to run, hike, paddle around in the ocean. I've done some rock climbing. What do you do when you aren't jet-setting around or turning hairy?"

He chuckled. "Hairy or smooth, I like to run, hike, and paddle around in the ocean, too. Climbing, though, is better done with hands."

"That makes sense. Um . . . I should probably warn you about my family. My grandmother knows who you are. I'm not sure my mother does—I left a message with your name—but she'll figure it out pretty quickly."

"Will that be a problem?"

"Probably," she said gloomily. "You're certainly not Chinese. If you were a surgeon, that might not matter. Or a lawyer, as long as you worked for a prestigious firm. She's very big on personal achievement. About my grandmother, though . . ." Her voice trailed off.

"The one you call Tiger Lady?"

"For heaven's sake, don't call her that tonight. The closest Chinese translation is, uh, not respectful." She sighed. There was no way to explain Grandmother. One had to experience her. "Just treat her as if she were royalty."

HE WAS MAKING mistakes with her. Rule knew that, but he couldn't seem to stop. He wanted to claim her, and he didn't want to wait. But whenever he let his urgency slip out, she retreated.

Lily wasn't sure about him. That was only natural. Even if he hadn't been what he was, she would have wanted time to know him, to know her own mind. He understood. He even agreed. But his blood was up, and the discipline of years was stretched taut just by being with her.

It didn't help to know she was as attracted as he, however she tried to hide it.

Tonight's date was about as safe as a first date could be, he thought wryly as they entered the restaurant. They were on her turf, surrounded by her family. He would rather have taken her someplace quiet and private, someplace where he could look at her as much as he liked. Touching would have been nice, too. But it eased something inside him to look at the curve of her throat or the slightly crooked incisor that only showed when she grinned. "You have a lot of relatives," he murmured.

The restaurant itself was less obviously oriental than he'd expected. The tables were round, white-draped, with western place settings. A few people sat at those tables, but most milled around—easily fifty in this room, he estimated, and there was at least one more section to the restaurant. All wore evening dress, with many of the men in tuxedos. He'd wondered about that. A tux had seemed excessive for a family birthday party. He'd worn it anyway; Lily had said the party was formal, and he admitted to possessing his share of vanity. He looked good in a tux.

"I'm not related to everyone. Just most of them." She slanted him an amused glance. "Grandmother is probably holding court on the terrace. We'd better find her and deliver this." She lifted the small, elegantly wrapped box in her left hand. "It may take awhile. You do draw attention."

It took awhile. Rule was tense, hyperalert in the way typical of this time of the month, his balance a delicate thing. Scents and sounds assaulted him with every new person to meet and charm. Outside, unseen, the moon was yet unrisen, but he felt it sliding nearer the horizon with every pulse. The sensation was pleasant, but distracting.

The discipline of years helped him stay focused on the room and the need to mask his feelings. He was helped by his curiosity about these people—Lily's people—and by his awareness of the woman at his side. That, too, was a sweet distraction pulsing through him, making even the moon's call less compelling.

It didn't take long for him to note a common theme in the comments of her relatives. The unspoken text emerged in jokes that weren't quite funny, in sympathetic comments or the blanks left by avoiding one particular subject.

Lily's family didn't approve of her job. They didn't want her to be a cop.

On their way to the terrace he met cousins, uncles, aunts, one of Lily's sisters and her date, along with miscellaneous offspring, spouses, or significant others. And he met Lily's mother.

Julia Yu was a slim, elegant woman who towered over her daughter by nearly a foot. She had beautiful hands, very little chin, several pounds of hair piled in elaborate twists on top of her head, and Lily's eyes. They opened wide when she saw his face.

She recovered quickly, greeting Rule with a polite smile.

She smelled faintly of herbal soap and hair spray. "I didn't place your name at first, Mr. Turner, but your face is instantly recognizable. I'm so glad you could join us tonight."

"I'm delighted she asked me," he said with perfect candor. Sharing Lily with all these people wasn't his first choice, but he could learn a great deal about her from her family. Especially her mother, he thought, and smiled. "Please call me Rule. Your daughter has your eyes, doesn't she? Lovely and full of mysteries. Her voice is rather like yours, too—lower than one would expect, and with the random music of a waterfall."

She blinked in surprise. "What a lovely compliment. Thank you. Lily also has something of her father's stubbornness, I'm afraid, and an unfortunate sense of humor. I'm not sure where that comes from." Something in the look she gave her daughter freighted her next words with hidden significance. "Have you introduced Mr. Turner to Grandmother yet, Lily?"

"We're making our way there now. I told her to expect him, of course."

"Ah." A subtle change in her posture told Rule some tension or worry had eased. "I won't hold you up, then. I believe your father is on the terrace with Grandmother."

Rule wasn't ready to abandon the conversation that quickly. Between Julia Yu's courtesy and her curiosity about a man her daughter might be interested in, he was able to hold her in conversation for several minutes. By the time he and Lily moved away, he'd had the satisfaction of coaxing a smile of genuine pleasure from her.

"You flirted with my mother," Lily said.

He wasn't sure if she was upset or amused. "I said nothing that wasn't true."

"You also flirted with two of my cousins, my sister, my great-aunt, and the wife of one of my brother's business partners. With every woman you've met tonight, I think. Is this a lupus thing, or is it just you?"

"It would be rude not to acknowledge a woman's beauty."

Her eyes were puzzled. "I expected you to say it didn't mean anything."

"That wouldn't be true. I . . ." He struggled to explain what was too basic to be fitted comfortably into words. "When I compliment a woman, it always means something. Not that I intend to take her to bed, but that I appreciate her. That I know she's a woman, and lovely."

"You meant everything you said, didn't you? You told Mrs. Masters—who must be seventy—that her pearls made her skin glow. You looked at her as if you enjoyed looking at her, and you meant it."

"Of course."

She didn't say anything more, but she took his hand. He felt absurdly pleased, as if he'd been awarded a great honor.

The rear of the restaurant overlooked the beach. The sun was slipping down the western sky when they stepped onto the terrace, an incandescent ball flipping its light scattershot across the waves it would kiss in another thirty minutes. He couldn't see the moon, but felt it hovering near the horizon to the east, a silvery song in his blood. The air was twenty degrees warmer than inside, and smelled wonderful. He breathed deeply of salt, sand, and ocean.

Rule was suddenly reluctant to proceed to the people knotted up at the other end of the terrace. "I wish we could walk on the beach together." Or run. He yearned to feel the sand beneath the pads of his paws while air screamed through his lungs as his muscles flexed and flung him along.

"Another time," she said softly, and when he looked at her he thought he glimpsed a shadow of his own longing... which, of course, was ridiculous. She had only the one form. "We may as well get this over with," she added more dryly, and nodded at the crowd at the end of the terrace.

They were halfway there when Rule stopped,

"What is it?"

Frankincense. His nostrils pinched in a useless effort to close out the toxin. Already he could feel his sense of smell closing down. "Do you truly not know?" he snapped.

"I wouldn't have asked if I did."

The smoky stench came from the knot of people directly in front of them. He shook his head, wanting to leave. "Never mind. As you said, let's get this over with."

He might as well. The damage had been done.

Chapter 7

LILY TAPPED ONE man on the shoulder and some of the others moved aside, revealing a tall chair with a carved wooden back. A velvet throw was draped across the seat and arms of the chair. A very small woman sat on that throw. She wore a long gown in Chinese red buttoned to the base of her skinny throat. A padded stool supported feet no larger than a child's, and a small brazier rested beside the footstool. It reeked of frankincense.

The woman taking up so little space in the thronelike chair didn't look eighty. Her black hair was liberally streaked with white and pulled into an unforgiving knot on top of her head. Her skin was very pale, her eyes very dark.

Had Rule been in wolf form, his hackles would have lifted.

Power. It radiated from that tiny, erect figure. Rule couldn't smell the magic on her, but he sure as hell sensed it.

"Grandmother." Lily dropped his hand to move forward. She bent to brush a kiss on one thin cheek. "Happy birthday."

"You are late. How could I enjoy my celebration without my favorite granddaughter?"

Lily smiled. "Last week Liu was your favorite granddaughter."

"Ah! You are right. Liu is never impertinent. She must be my favorite."

Two pairs of eyes met—both black, one wrapped in wrinkles, one surrounded by smooth young skin—in complete and affectionate understanding. The old woman patted her granddaughter's cheek. "I like you anyway," she announced. "What have you brought me?"

Lily handed her the prettily wrapped box. She opened it with hands that showed her age more than her face did, though the nails were long and painted screaming red. "Ah!" Her smile was as delighted as a child's. "A graceful piece, and the jade is good quality. It will go in my collection." She handed the little statue of a cat to a middle-aged woman who sat beside her, addressing her in Chinese, then turned back to Lily. "I am pleased. You may introduce your escort now."

Lily rose and moved to one side. "*Zhu Mu*, this is Rule Turner, prince of the Nokolai. Rule, I am honored to present to you my grandmother, Madame Bai He Tsang."

Rule knew an audience when he was granted one. He stepped forward, clamping down on the anger. "Madame Tsang, I am honored."

Keen black eyes took a head-to-toe journey over him. "So you're the lupus my granddaughter chose to bring to my party. You're terribly pretty."

"Thank you."

"It wasn't a compliment."

"I know," he said gently, as one might to a child who flaunted her poor manners.

Unexpectedly she chuckled, and he glimpsed Lily in the amusement in her eyes. "You have style, I'll give you that. Much more durable than mere prettiness. More entertaining, too. That doesn't mean I approve of my granddaughter allying herself with you."

"Respectfully, *Zhu Mu*," Lily said, "one date is a very temporary alliance. And entirely my own choice."

"I wasn't speaking to you." The old woman glanced back at Rule. "I don't like the way you treat your women."

"You know nothing about how I treat my women." He couldn't smell a damned thing. Anger curled in him, stretching, trying to reach past his control.

"You are lupus. This means you treat them in the plural, I

know that much. You wish to keep them . . . what is the saying? Barefoot and pregnant." Her thin lips curved in a feline smile. "I hope the smoke from the incense isn't bothering you. Some people don't care for the scent."

"I can't say I notice the smell." Not anymore.

Lily glanced from the brazier to her grandmother. Her eyebrows lifted as if she'd figured out what was happening.

"Ah, do you not? I find it a trifle strong. Hong," Tiger Lady said, turning her head toward the fiftyish man to her left. "Take the brazier away. I am tired of it." Then, without another word to Rule, she began conversing with the woman on her right in Chinese.

He was dismissed. Rule wondered if he was supposed to salute or retreat backward so as not to turn his back on Her Highness. He ought to be amused, but felt more like snarling than laughing.

Lily spoke quietly. "The incense had some effect on you, didn't it?"

"Nothing permanent." He sounded more grim than he wanted to. "I won't smell anything for a few hours."

"I am sorry. Grandmother . . . well, she is a law unto herself. I suppose losing your sense of smell is as disturbing as it would be if I were suddenly deafened or blinded."

"It doesn't truly incapacitate me." It just made him feel vulnerable. Bereft. And angry with himself for not having obeyed his instinct to retreat to the beach. "And it is only temporary."

"Can you stand meeting one more of my relatives? My father's here. He's much nicer than Grandmother, I promise."

Of course he had to meet her father. Walter Yu turned out to be a pleasant man not much taller than his daughter, with clever eyes, a wispy mustache, and gold-framed glasses. He was a stockbroker, and soon engaged Rule in talk of the market, which had yet to recover from its recent tumble. Rule had no trouble responding appropriately, but a good portion of his attention was elsewhere.

Why hadn't Lily warned him that her esteemed grandmother was a witch?

That was an assumption, of course, but the old woman had power. That much was certain. And the use of frankincense to baffle a were's senses was common lore in several branches of magic, as he knew from a delightful association a few years back with a green witch. Obviously Lily's grandmother had been afraid a lupus would be able to sniff out which brand of magic she practiced, which raised some interesting questions. Many spells and some branches of magic were illegal.

Did that explain the attitude of Lily's family about her being a police detective? It might be another reason Lily had chosen homicide—so she wouldn't risk being faced with investigating the old woman someday.

But dammit, she needn't have tricked his sense of smell away from him. Rule couldn't have sniffed out what type of magic the old woman practiced. That was a myth. Unless she were actually casting a spell, all he would be able to sense was her power, and he didn't need his nose for that.

Very few people realized that, though, he admitted grudgingly. It suited his people to keep their secrets.

No doubt it was unreasonable to complain if others preferred to keep secrets, too. And in truth, although the Gifted hadn't been persecuted as severely as his people, the old woman would have grown up hearing tales of burnings, brandings, purges. To be Gifted remained a stigma.

But it was difficult to be reasonable when he couldn't *smell.*

The buffet was lavish, but the plate he filled held no appeal. He pushed a bite of swordfish around on his plate and pretended to listen to Walter Yu discussing the euro.

Lily leaned closer and said quietly, "So, how long are you going to pout?"

"Pout?" Rule lifted his brows slightly. "If I'm not eating, it's because food lacks flavor when I can't smell it." Even humans knew that to be true.

A smile tugged at her lips. "Not eating, not speaking— sounds like pouting to me. Or a snit. You did say the effects were temporary?"

His sense of humor nudged at him. "Nonsense. Princes don't pout. We may sulk occasionally, but we don't pout."

"I see." She nodded gravely. "I suppose the difference between sulking and pouting is obvious to a prince."

"It's obvious to a man. All men sulk on certain occasions." He leaned closer. "You see, if I were to kiss the place where your neck curves into your shoulder, I wouldn't be able to smell your skin. I've been thinking about that. Also the backs of your knees, and other places you would probably prefer I didn't mention. When I take you home tonight and kiss you, I want to be able to inhale your fragrance while I'm tasting you. It makes me quite sulky that I won't be able to."

He saw the small shiver that left goose bumps in its wake, but she lowered her eyes, hiding from him. "Does this mean it would be safe to take that walk on the beach you mentioned earlier?"

"Of course not. I'm sulking, not stupid. I have other senses."

Her husky laugh might as well have been teasing fingers. "Trust me, you weren't going to make it to the backs of my knees tonight."

"But the kiss . . . ?"

"You did say you had other senses."

Hunger rose, strong enough to choke out the moon's song. Yet her words relaxed him, too. Or maybe it was the look in her eyes, honest as the kiss she admitted she wanted. "Tell me. Will your grandmother feel compelled to burn frankincense every time I see her?"

"I never try to predict Grandmother. Do you expect to see her again?"

"Oh, yes." He reached for her hand and closed his fingers around it. "That is, unfortunately, inevitable. You are very close to your family."

LONG BEFORE DESSERT, Lily accepted that she'd lost her mind. She was going to have an affair with Rule. The decision hummed in her blood and made her thoughts hop around like popcorn in a hot skillet.

This risk was huge. Lupi had a closed, wholly masculine society, for heaven's sake. They were more chauvinistic than her father. They didn't even believe in monogamy. Well, she would make it clear to Rule that while they were involved, he would have to bow to her beliefs on this one issue. No other women. For however long it lasted. Oh, God. She rubbed her stomach, where nerves were jumping. No matter how sensible she tried to be, she wouldn't walk away from this unscorched.

And she didn't care. Not really.

Rule would be honest with her, she thought as she spoke

with her aunt Caroline, who was a grandmother twice over now and smug about it. He would tell her if he couldn't promise even a temporary fidelity.

It wasn't as if she were going into this blind, she assured herself as her cousin Lynn complained about the man she'd been dating, her mother, and her job. Her father had taken Rule to meet someone—Larry Hong, she thought. The only one of her cousins with a career even less respectable than her own. He was a mostly unemployed actor.

Lots of women had affairs with men they didn't intend to marry. Lots of women had affairs with Rule Turner, to be specific. She was making too big a deal of this.

Then she saw Rule making his way to her and her throat went slick with need. The lights were suddenly brighter, the edges crisper, and the colors brighter. She wanted to skip or sing. Or maybe hide in a closet.

No, she wasn't making too big a deal out of this. It was big—huge, scary big.

"Would you mind if we left now?" he said when he joined her. "I've an early appointment in the morning."

"No," she said through a too-tight throat. "I wouldn't mind."

They took their leave of Grandmother, who was still out on the terrace. The old woman was thoroughly enjoying her party and pleased with herself over something—maybe the way she'd tricked Rule. It was hard to say with Grandmother. Lily intended to have a talk with her soon.

"Is she really eighty?" Rule asked as they waited in the small vestibule for his car to be brought around.

"As far as I know. With Grandmother, very little is certain. I really am sorry about what she did. Have the effects worn off at all?"

"Not yet. What she did wasn't necessary, but I understand why she did it."

She doubted that. "I really need to talk to her. You may have guessed that some of the information I have about lupi came from her. Obviously she didn't tell me everything she knew. She didn't mention frankincense."

The valet returned and handed Rule his keys in exchange for a few bills. "Frankincense does affect lupi," he said, opening the heavy door. "But I couldn't have sniffed out what type of magic she uses."

"You said something about that before—that magic doesn't have a smell, except when it's active. Is that true for innate magic, too?"

"What do you mean?" He held the door for her.

"Well, the sort of thing you do isn't a spell. It's innate. Does—"

Flashes—blinding, leaving purple ghosts swimming in her vision. A swarming, shoving crowd of people. Questions shouted. A microphone jammed near her face.

"How long have you been dating?"

"Does Shannon Snow know about your new—"

"Prince, what do you think about the killings?"

"—lupi really superior lovers?"

"When the chief told you to work with the werewolf prince, did he know you two were—"

"Detective Yu, how do you explain your relationship with a suspect?"

Rule recovered faster than she did. He slid an arm around her waist and started forward, smiling easily. "You've taken us by surprise, I'm afraid. I don't have a statement at this time."

Maybe it was the way Rule moved, the assurance that others would remove themselves from his path. Or maybe even reporters were wary of crowding a lupus too closely. For whatever reason, he was able to clear a path, though the reporters still swarmed close, questions popping like sniper fire.

"No comment," Lily said. And, "Mr. Turner isn't a suspect." Then, finally, they were in Rule's car, the doors closed on the avid faces, the engine started.

"I hope this was the last little surprise your grandmother had planned for me tonight," Rule said grimly as he pulled away from the restaurant.

"Grandmother? Oh, no." Lily's fingers clutched her purse tightly. She wanted to hit something. "She's going to be furious."

"I sure as hell didn't tip the reporters."

Lily didn't say anything for a long time, turning over the facts, trying to make them fit some way other than the obvious. The valet must have been bribed to let the reporters know when Rule's car was brought up. She hoped they'd been generous—the young man would be out of work by morning. But that didn't explain how the reporters knew he was there, with her. Finally, reluctantly, she spoke. "One of them knew the chief had told me to work with you. My family doesn't know that. Yours?"

"Aside from my father, no. And there is no possibility that he phoned the press about my relationship with you."

She sighed and pulled her cell phone out of her evening bag. "Then I'd better make some calls, because someone well up the food chain at the department did."

Chapter 8

BEING AMBUSHED BY reporters had blown Lily's mood and her confidence. She'd been ready to turn Rule down when he walked her to her door, but he'd forestalled her, damn him. He hadn't even tried to kiss her, leaving her with a mouthful of arguments and no one to use them on but herself.

She'd done that, all right, tossing and turning until nearly three in the morning. Finally she'd snarled, flung back the covers, and grabbed her running shoes, a pair of shorts, and Worf's leash.

Pounding the pavement had pounded a little sense into her head. The best she could hope for with Rule was a hot affair that didn't leave her too singed when it ended. Having a fling with him could do real damage to her career now that the newshounds were watching. It might even rebound on the department. Some reporters equated investigative journalism with slinging mud at the police.

The plain, cold truth was that the price of an affair was too high.

Either reaching a decision or exhaustion had done the trick, and she'd dozed off at last. When she blinked her eyes open again, the clock read nine-thirteen.

It was Saturday. All over the city, people were mowing lawns, packing the kids to the beach, hitting garage sales, or sleeping in. Lily considered anything past nine o'clock sleeping in, so she'd observed one of the weekend traditions. She intended to be at headquarters by ten o'clock.

Her first clue about what kind of day it would be came at nine thirty-five when she raced, dripping, from out of the shower to snatch the ringing phone. Her mother told her to look at the morning paper, then hung up.

It could have been worse, Lily thought when she saw the headline. Her mother might have stayed on the phone.

The article itself couldn't have been much worse. The reporter didn't quite accuse Lily of covering up for a killer because she was sleeping with the Nokolai prince. She just made a lot of insinuations. She also hinted at graft in the police department and possibly the mayor's office.

Then Lily saw the article below the fold. A man had been badly beaten near the scene of the second murder. In front of witnesses. Turned out he was especially hairy, and someone thought he was a lupus.

The second page had a story about the infamous lupus rampage back in '98, heavily salted with some of the more sensational lore about werewolves. Lily shoved her chair back and stood. "Dammit, don't they see what they're doing? People are scared enough without this crap."

She paced, trying to think of anything she could do that she hadn't done. Three people dead at the hands—or teeth—of this killer. One man in the hospital because the killer was still loose. And what did she have? A list of lupi registered in the city five years ago. Two witnesses who'd seen a man near the scene of one murder. And a date she couldn't repeat.

Lily scowled. It was a good thing she hadn't gone to bed with Rule. If she had, the hotheads slamming her and the department would have live ammo. Right now they were firing blanks.

She grabbed her keys and tried to be relieved about that, but the phone rang before she reached the door. She almost didn't pick it up, thinking it might be a reporter. But the caller ID told her it was her downstairs neighbor. Mrs. Hodgkin took Worf out most days around lunch so he could relieve his bladder, and sometimes at supper, too, if Lily was working late.

Mrs. Hodgkin claimed that her arthritis was acting up and she wouldn't be able to manage the stairs anymore to take Worf out.

Since the older woman tied herself into yoga pretzels regularly, Lily doubted that inflamed joints were the problem. No doubt Mrs. Hodgkin read the paper, too.

Why were people so quick to judge? They knew nothing about Rule except that he was a lupus. And they believed the myths—that lupi were indiscriminate killers. Or crazy. Or both.

The myths were based on fact, she reminded herself as she slammed out of her apartment. Some lupi did kill. Not as often as the more sensational press liked to claim, but the rampage the paper had dragged up had happened. For reasons no one had ever known, a lupus in Connecticut had gone berserk. Sixteen people dead, thirteen injured. And Rule himself had said that adolescent lupi couldn't control the beast.

Lily scowled and clicked the "unlock" a dozen feet from her Nissan.

"Ms. Yu?"

Lily turned. A pretty young teenager with a spiky haircut was running across the parking lot toward her. Lily identified her automatically: Cili Yosamoff, apartment 614A. Two younger sisters, and a father who worked nights. She had a fondness for black—clothes, lipstick, and eye makeup.

Cili stopped in front of her, breathless and smiling. "I wondered—would you mind—I mean—oh, here!" She thrust out a pen and pad of paper. "Could I have your autograph?"

Lily blinked. "My what?"

"And maybe you could ask the prince for his, too? I mean, he's so rad, isn't he? I was just maxed out when I read that you're, like, dating him!"

"Oh. Sure." *Why not?* Lily thought, taking the pen and scrawling her name across the paper. Maybe the girl would decide that cops were cool, too, if one of them could date a rad guy like Rule. "I'll ask the prince to sign something for you next time I see him," she said, handing back the pad.

"Jenny is just going to *die* when I show her the prince's autograph." Her friend's imminent demise gave her great satisfaction. "Is it true that lupi, like, don't do drugs or alcohol or anything?"

Lily had no idea. "Absolutely," she assured the girl gravely. "They have too much respect for their bodies, in whatever form." Her name might be dirt with some people—like her mother, her downstairs neighbor, any number of reporters and fellow citizens. But it looked like she could count on support from the fifteen-and-under set. "Would you be interested in earning a little running-around money?"

"Well . . . yeah. Probably." Heavily mascaraed eyes blinked at her dubiously. "I guess it would depend on, you know, what you want me to do."

"I need someone to walk my dog."

AT HEADQUARTERS LILY noticed a distinct chill in the air. A sergeant who usually greeted her looked away. A patrol cop made a crack to his partner about people who would do anything for their five minutes of fame. And it was quiet— much too quiet—when she walked into the Homicide bullpen. Only three officers were there, and all were terribly busy. Too busy to look up, much less greet her.

Until Brunswick started howling.

She could have kissed him. It was so obnoxiously normal. The other man laughed and the female detective told him to put a sock in it.

"You really need to do something about that sore throat," Lily said as she sat at her desk, fighting back a grin. "You're sounding hoarse."

"I want details," he said, spinning his chair to grin at her. "Times, places . . . especially times. As in, how many. Scuttlebutt has it that lupi are real gifted in the stamina department, but I—"

"You can tell us about your sex life another time, Brunswick," Vivian Shuman said, and grimaced at Lily. "Ah . . . the captain said he wanted to see you in his office when you showed up."

Great. Lily sighed and shoved her chair back. "Do I get a blindfold?"

CAPTAIN FOSTER WAS a short, squat man with a round head, no neck, and all his features crowded together in the bottom half of his face. He chewed gum constantly, had a lousy temper, and was one of the best cops Lily knew.

From the expression on his face when she walked in, she could have used the blindfold.

"You're off the lupus case. Pass everything you've got to Simmons."

Her head jerked slightly and her whole body went stiff, as if someone had yanked her straight up by the hair on her head. "What?"

"You heard me. You've compromised the investigation." His mouth twisted. "Of all the dumbass stunts to pull! You couldn't find a human to date? Or just put your hormones on hold?"

"I wasn't aware my private life was subject to your approval. Sir."

"It is when I spend an hour in the chief's office trying to explain why the detective I insisted on has made more progress with her *private life* than her investigation. A man was beaten last night because he's got hair on his back, for Chrissake. People are scared. The mayor is scared. And you get your picture plastered all over the front page, cuddled up to a lupus closely tied to your investigation."

"Captain . . ." Her jaw clamped hard on all the things she wanted to say. She started again. "Turner is not a suspect. He's solidly alibied for two of the three killings—one of those alibis being the mayor. Working with him was the mayor's *suggestion,* as relayed to me by the chief."

"You weren't working with him last night. Dammit, Yu, just because the man has an alibi doesn't clear him! He could have arranged the killings."

"I see. You consider him a suspect because he's a lupus."

"Use your head." His jaw flexed. He was chomping down hard on his gum. "We know the murders were committed by one of his people. Even if he isn't personally involved, you can't trust him. Lupi don't exactly have a history of cooperation with the police, yet he's apparently eager to help you track down one of his people. Dammit, I shouldn't have to tell you all this."

"No. You shouldn't." Lily's anger was cold now. Icy. He was questioning her competence, her integrity. "I assume, then, that if I were dating the head of the NAACP you would remove me from any cases where we knew the perp was African American."

Foster's mouth opened—and closed. His jaw worked. He wanted badly to tell her that was altogether different. And couldn't.

She leaned forward. "Sir, I'm aware that Turner's agenda may not be as altruistic as he'd have us think. Maybe he means to misdirect me, if he can. Or even warn the killer. But I consider that a very low probability. His first priority is the welfare of his clan, with that of lupi in general a close second. He's been doing everything possible to promote the Species Citizenship Bill that's in subcommittee now, and these killings damage its chances."

"You think he agreed to help us for political reasons?"

Lily took a deep breath, letting it out slowly. "I think he wants to find the killer every bit as badly as we do—only he wants to find him first. And turn him over to his clan for punishment."

Foster studied her in silence, for once not chomping on his gum. Maybe he was wondering the same thing she did: had Rule involved himself with her for the same reason he'd become involved with the investigation?

Finally he spoke. "Lupi in wolf form aren't protected by law, so he might be able to carry out some kind of vigilante justice if he gets to the perp first. But it would reflect badly on him and his people, damage his cause."

"Not necessarily." She'd thought all this out last night. "He's good at PR. Reporters love him—he's great copy. If he spins it right, the Citizenship Bill might gain backing. See, right now the Justice Department and most law enforcement associations oppose the bill. But if he makes headlines for taking justice into his own hands—legally—that could change. Can't have the reporters saying we approve of lupi circumventing the law, can we?"

She'd reached him. He started chewing again, more thoughtfully. "You think that's what he's after? Making political hay out of these murders by committing legal murder himself?"

"I don't know," she added, careful with her voice and her face, sick in the pit of her stomach. "But it seems possible."

He told her to brief him on where she was now, what she planned to do next. And before she left he told her to divide the list of registered lupi with the others who were in today and start checking them out.

The case was still hers. Lily stood. Her knees felt spongy. "One more thing. No one was supposed to know Turner was working with me. And the only people who knew he would be at the party last night were my mother and grandmother. And they didn't tell anyone."

"Trying to teach me how to suck eggs? I'm aware of the obvious. Someone leaked the story to the press. I want to know who and why. Leave that to me."

So Lily went back to the bullpen and told the other detectives they'd been conscripted. There were groans and teasing—she'd gone in to get her ass chewed out and come out with the captain's backing to pull them off their current cases. She told them clean living gave her an edge, got a couple of snickers, and waited to feel better.

She ought to be relieved. The captain had been ready to yank her off the case, but she was still in charge. Yet she felt was sick. As if she'd betrayed Rule by telling Foster what he might be planning.

And that was just stupid. She'd known Rule only a handful of days. She would ignore her stupid, cartwheeling emotions and get on with the job.

Being a cop came first. Always.

WITHIN AN HOUR Lily had the paperwork for a search warrant ready to submit. She called Rule, but his machine picked up. She left a message. Around noon she hit the streets with six names of lupi confirmed to be still living in San Diego.

By three she'd spoken to three of the lupi on her list and eliminated one conclusively. He worked nights as a bouncer and was solidly alibied for all three nights in question. The other two were less certain. Each claimed an alibi for one of the murders, but it was possible that more than one lupus was involved. The physical evidence was inconclusive. They'd retrieved hair from two of the three crime scenes that looked alike—mottled silver and charcoal—but the lab couldn't prove that it had come from the same lupus without DNA testing. And the stuff wouldn't behave under testing.

Lily really, really didn't like Rule's conspiracy idea, but she couldn't ignore it.

At five-fifteen she left another message on Rule's machine. It was nearly eight when he returned her call. "I'm sorry I didn't get back to you sooner." His voice was rough, but she couldn't tell what emotion moved him. "It's been a difficult day."

"Tell me about it. I called because I wanted to give you notice. I've put in for a search warrant to get me into Clanhome. I expect to have it by Monday at the latest." He was silent so long she wondered if her phone was working. "I told you I couldn't wait much longer."

"I have to talk to you. It will take me thirty minutes to get to your apartment."

"I'm not there. I'm working."

"At this hour? What—never mind. Just tell me where I can meet you."

She knew what she heard in his voice now—urgency. Against her will, it convinced her to see him. She gave him the name and address of a bar down the street and disconnected, frowning.

There was no way of knowing what he meant to say until she saw him, so she shoved it into a corner of her mind, climbed out of her car, and went to talk to Amos Whitburn, the fifth name on her list.

Amos Whitburn turned out to be ninety-two, and even lupi weren't proof against age. He moved well—arthritis didn't seem to afflict weres—but he was nearly blind. Cataracts. Crossing him off her list didn't take long, which meant that she arrived at the bar well before Rule did. This gave her plenty of time to wish she'd picked another spot.

The area should have warned her. It wasn't a slum, but it was on the far lower end of working class. The bar itself was what she'd expected—dark, dingy, and smelling of beer. She'd been in plenty of places like this since she joined the force. But usually she'd either been in uniform or flashing a badge. Tonight she was in wrinkled linen—baggy walking shorts, sleeveless shell, and a loose, lightweight jacket that covered her weapon. Not exactly come-hither clothes, but it didn't seem to matter.

Lily took her Diet Coke to a corner where she could keep an eye on the room. Her stony stare worked on the first two men who started toward her—they veered away, pretending they'd been heading to the men's room all along.

The next guy was more persistent. Probably trying to win a bet, Lily thought, disgusted, as he approached. He'd been sitting with the other two.

"Hey, there, honey. My name's Biff."

Oh, surely not. Would any woman do such a thing to her child? Lily looked up. Way up.

He was huge. Six-four, maybe two-thirty. He wore a red ball cap and jeans tight enough to endanger his future offspring. His head was too small for his body, but his features were regular enough that he probably thought he was good-looking. He carried two beers in one hand, and smelled as if he'd already drunk several. His hands were the size of catcher's gloves.

"I don't want a beer, and I don't want company."

"My treat," he said genially, setting both amber bottles on the table and reaching for the other chair.

She kicked the chair away. "My mama told me never to talk to clichés."

"C'mon, honey, don't be that way. I'll treat you real nice. Ask anyone here. Matthew!" he bellowed. "Tell the lady what a nice guy I am."

The bartender looked over, bored. "Real nice."

"There, you see? I'm not gonna hurt a sweet little thing like you. Would you rather have somethin' else to drink? Maybe a Tom Collins. Hey, Matthew, get this—"

"No. Go away. I'm waiting for someone."

"Hey, I'll do just as well! Probably better." He beamed at her, dragged the chair back, and sat down. "I'm a fun guy."

Lily put her arms on the table and leaned forward. "Let me explain. I don't want company while I wait, I don't want a drink, I don't want to dance or talk to you or look at you. You'll have to trust me on this. You won't do at all. You will get up now and go away."

He leaned back, still smiling. But his eyes lost their amiable gloss, and underneath they were pure mean. "Well, now, I don't quite see how a little bitty thing like you is gonna make me do that, if I don't want to." He rested his forearm on the table, closed his hand into a fist, and made his biceps clench.

His friends—the two men Lily had sent off with the Stare— sat at a table about ten feet away. The bar wasn't crowded.

They had a great view, and were nudging each other and chuckling.

Real funny, hassling a woman because they thought they could get away with it. Briefly Lily toyed with the idea of stating her price, letting him agree to buy an hour of her time, and then arresting him. She sighed. It was a pleasant fantasy, but impractical. Instead, she reached inside the flap of her purse—and saw Rule near the door, headed for her.

He was not happy.

Time to move mean-and-stupid along. She pulled out the leather case with her shield and showed it to him. "You want to leave now."

He looked at it, his heavy eyebrows pulling down.

"You heard the lady." Rule's left hand clamped down hard on Big Biff's shoulder. His fingers dug in. His face wore a curiously intent, inward expression. "But you weren't listening, were you?"

Biff's eyes bulged in sudden pain. He went stiff and made a choked sound.

"Rule!" She spoke sharply. How had he crossed the room so fast? "Don't break anything."

"Hmm?" He glanced up, his eyes meeting hers. His eyes. Dear God. The color had bled into the whites until they were wholly dark, gleaming. "Oh, yes," he said mildly. "Sorry about that. Here, let me help you up."

He didn't give Biff much choice, hoisting him bodily from the chair. The big man swayed for a second, blinking fast to get rid of tears of pain.

Just how strong *was* Rule?

"What the hell—?" Biff's protest was weak. He was trying to regain his swagger as he turned. "I don't know who the hell you think you are, grabbing me that—holy shit."

He'd seen Rule's eyes.

Lily shoved her shield back in her purse and stood. "I don't like it here. Too many friendly people. Let's go somewhere else."

"Hey!" Biff's voice rose. "Hey, I know who you are. You're that werewolf!"

Silence scattered like sparks around the room, striking those closest first and spreading fast. Biff's buddies shoved to their feet.

"You're right," Rule said, but he was looking at her, not Biff. His eyes still looked weird, but the whites showed at the corners again. "We need to leave."

The crowd was decidedly unfriendly now. There were mutters from a couple of men at the bar. Biff's two buddies started toward him. Lily and Rule headed for the door.

"Hey, you!" the bartender shouted. "You didn't pay for your drink!"

Lily barely slowed. "I gave you a five."

"No, you didn't. You come back and pay or I'm calling the cops."

"I *am*—"

"Here." Rule tossed a bill in the general direction of the bar, grabbed Lily's arm, and pulled her toward the door. He let go as they stepped outside.

It was dark and drizzling, a drab wash of grays and blacks. Parked cars lined the street on both sides, but there wasn't much traffic. Hardly any pedestrians, either. The traffic light on the corner was barely visible through the haze, a dim red glow.

"My Explorer is this way." He set off to the left.

She thought of pointing out that her car was the other direction, decided it wasn't worth arguing over. "Don't grab my arm again."

"What?" His head swiveled. "Oh. Your gun. You want your right hand free. Sorry—I didn't think of that."

"What's the thing with your eyes?"

His voice was clipped. "I needed to Change."

"Ah . . . are you okay now?"

He didn't answer. That worried her.

They'd reached the corner. The light was red and a car was coming, so she stopped. So did he. The drizzle was heavier now. Lily's clothes were damp, her face and hands wet, but the rain was warm and made her feel clean and private, alone with him on the street.

As soon as the car passed they stepped together into a shiny-wet street—without a word, both of them moving at the same instant.

Weird. Lily asked, "Is it because the moon is nearly full?"

"He was threatening you."

"Biff is a bully and an asshole, but I had things under control. Until you played macho man and your eyes went spooky."

"It excited him to force himself on you. You couldn't smell his reaction the way I could, but you must have known he enjoyed making you uncomfortable. A man who gets off on intimidating a woman in public is likely to do worse in private."

Lily wanted to understand. She wanted that with an urgency that strummed along her nerves like adrenaline, turning her skin sensitive, as if she could feel each tiny, separate drop of mist that fell on her. But there were so many pieces to him. Pieces that didn't fit any pattern she knew.

Inhuman pieces. "So," she said, trying to sound casual, "this need to Change—that's part of those protective instincts of yours? When you feel that a woman is in danger, you—"

He stopped dead, grabbed her shoulders, and said fiercely, "It was *you* he threatened, Lily. Not some woman. You." And he crushed his mouth down on hers.

Chapter 9

LILY'S MIND WENT blank. Unwilled, her hand lifted to his cheek and found it smooth, damp, and warm. Her head tipped back. Her mouth opened to his.

His taste was like nothing she'd ever imagined—subtle, layered, clean as the wind. And necessary. She burrowed into him, the feel of his body a shock of pleasure against hers. Baffled by pleasure, buffeted by quick slaps of need, she lost her grip on herself. The sound she made held both protest and discovery.

He tore his mouth away. "Sweet Mother." He wrapped his arms around her, tight, and leaned his head atop hers. "Give me a minute. I need a minute."

So did she. Her heart galloped madly in her chest. If she let him go—if she couldn't touch him, feel his skin, smell his breath—something inside her would rip open. "What have you done?" she gasped. "What did you just do to me?"

His body was hard with need, but his hand on her hair was infinitely gentle. She lifted her head. He was smiling with such sweetness her breath caught.

He started to speak—then his body, already taut, quivered.

His smile evaporated. "They're coming. Half a block behind us."

She'd heard nothing and, in the rain-muffled night, saw no one. But instantly she knew what he meant. Biff and his buddies had followed them. "Your car?"

"The end of the block."

They ran, splashing in shallow puddles. But he jerked to a stop fifteen feet short of an alley and pushed her against the wet brick of the nearest wall, putting himself in front.

Two men emerged from the alley.

"No!" She shoved her way out from behind him, reaching for her weapon. "Let me handle this," she said quickly, her voice low. "We don't need a massacre here."

There was no more time to argue, to reason. Fear coated her mouth as she sighted on the chest of the nearest man, a blond guy with a droopy mustache. He held a knife in his right hand, point up like he knew how to use it.

"Police!" she shouted. "Stop right there!"

He did. The man beside him—tall, skinny, with dirty black hair to his shoulders—didn't stop until she swung the gun barrel toward him.

"Dammit, Biff, you didn't say she had a gun!"

"She's a cop, asshole!"

That was Biff's voice, from her right. He and two more men emerged at a run from the veils of rain. Biff had a metal baseball bat. One of the others held the ragged top of a beer bottle. Lily swung her gun that way. They stopped—and the two on the left surged forward.

Rule made a sound low in his throat. "Stay back."

His voice sounded funny—soft and growly. Lily wanted to look, to see what was happening with him. She didn't dare take her eyes off the men. Very low, she said, "You watch the ones on your side, let me know if they budge."

His whisper barely reached her. "They aren't moving. Yet."

She recognized the ones with Biff. They'd been at the bar. The other two hadn't. Where had they come from so fast? "Any of you idiots done time before? Assaulting an officer, that will get you three to five years' hard time. That's if I don't shoot you," she added casually.

It almost worked. One of them muttered, another took a step back.

Then two more men came running up from the right—a
Hispanic man with a knife, and a second Biff. Same little head,
bland features, and outsized body. Except this one's cap was
blue, and he was holding a tire iron instead of a baseball bat.

Twin Biffs? Sometimes, Lily thought, God had a lousy
sense of humor.

The first Biff grinned a mean, gloating grin. "Hey, bro.
Knew you wouldn't want to miss the fun."

"Sent Pete and Baker to flank them, didn't I? Needed to
get my iron." The second Biff slapped it against his palm.
"Gonna see if a were's brains look all pink and gray like a
real person's."

"Were bitch," one of them spat.

Lily was intensely aware of Rule beside her, fairly vibrating
with needs she didn't understand but could feel shimmering
out from him the way heat radiates from hot concrete. He was
very, very angry.

She reached out without looking and touched him lightly,
hoping he could hold on a little longer. Wondering just how
stupid you had to be to push a lupus prince to the edge of
control. "If all of you scatter real quick, I won't charge you
with assaulting an officer. Or shoot you. Lots of paperwork
for me either way."

"Hell, we aren't going to mess with you," Biff said, that
mean grin fixed tight to his face. He swung the bat back and
forth. "All you have to do is walk away."

Oh, yeah, they'd like it fine if she and Rule separated. She
shook her head. "You don't understand about the paperwork.
If you make a move, Turner here is going to smear pieces of
the lot of you all over the street. You would not believe how
many reports I have to fill out about that sort of thing."

The second Biff gave an ugly laugh. "Seven of us, two of
you. The odds work for me." Some of the others yelled agree-
ment or insults involving weres, were-lovers, and how they
ought to all be exterminated.

They were working themselves up. They were almost ready
to move. She could see it in the way they stood, the restless
movements of their feet and hands. If they attacked, there
would be a bloodbath. "Well, now, I guess you don't read the
papers? Or maybe you don't have a good picture of what a
lupus can do. Me, I've seen what's left afterwards. This one

guy had a knife. The lupus bit his hand off, knife and all, and spat it out. Then he took off the guy's face. Then he killed him."

"We've read about the killings!" one of the men on Rule's side shouted. "Lousy, filthy weres. We take this one out, we ought to get a medal."

"That's right," her second admirer from the bar said loudly. "And taking out a were's whore, that ought to be worth a couple of beers."

"I'm a cop," she said patiently over the jeering laughter while her stomach tied itself in queasy knots. "You really think you can beat me up, maybe kill me, and the other cops are going to say, 'Oh, well, I guess she had it coming'? You can't be that dumb. They'll take this neighborhood apart to find you, not because they give a shit about me personally. Because no one is allowed to make war on cops."

That worried them, but it didn't convince them. She sighed. "Rule, I think they need to see to believe. Maybe you could show them how fast you can move."

"If I move, I'm going to kill someone." His voice was really rough now and hoarse, close to a beast's growl. "I want to kill them."

"Jesus," someone whispered. Then the Hispanic one said, "This is stupid. This is just stupid. No one said anything about killing or getting killed."

Biff sneered. "You chickening out, Bobby? Fine, you go on home, let the little woman tuck you up safe in bed."

Bobby muttered something under his breath and turned to walk away. Another man hesitated, then hurried after him.

"Hey! The rest of you gonna turn chickenshit, too?" Biff Number Two cried out. "I came to kick some butt, clean this city of at least one were-slime. You with me, Pete? Baker? Let's get with the program!" He smacked the tire iron against his palm again and started forward. Two others followed.

Lily took aim. Her head was clear, but her heartbeat was going crazy.

Across the street, a woman shrieked once. Twice. Lily didn't take her attention away from the men for a second, but they looked.

"She went back inside," Rule growled. "She'll call the cops. Some of your colleagues will be here soon, Lily."

Lily held her pistol out with both arms, one hand steadying the other. Aiming ostentatiously straight at Biff Two. "But we've still got a few minutes before they show up. You guys want me to fill out all those lousy forms, come on. Take another step."

"Hell." The one with the beer bottle threw it into the street, where it smashed. "I'm out of here."

Two more of them left, tossing out insults to make themselves feel less as if they'd lost the battle. Only Biff One and Biff Two remained, but Biff Two was furious. His brother grabbed his arm, said something low and angry to him. Biff Two shrugged free and spat at them. The spittle landed well short of her feet.

A siren sounded in the distance. That was all it took. The twins ran off.

Lily needed to holster her gun, but her hands were shaking and her arms felt like noodles. It took her two tries. Then at last she was free to turn to Rule. His eyes held darkness, corner to corner. Tension drew grooves along his face. "You all right?" she asked.

"No. Do you think that really is your colleagues on the way?"

"We try for fast response time, but I doubt it. I'd just as soon not wait around and find out, though. I wasn't entirely joking about the paperwork."

"Weren't you?" A small smile ghosted across his face. "Let's go."

They made it the last half-block to his Explorer without anything happening, and in complete silence. He unlocked both doors, locking them again as soon as they were in, and started the engine. Then he crossed his arms on the steering wheel, leaned his head on them, and shook.

Lily didn't mistake his reaction for fear. Whatever had been happening to him, he'd fought it and fought hard. There was a price to be paid for that. She unclicked her seat belt and slid over and put her arms around him.

The shakes stopped. He went very still. Then, in one of those too-fast-to-see movements, he had his arms around her, pressing her up against him as if he needed to soak her up. He ran his hands over her sides, her back. His breath was harsh against her hair. "One heck of a meeting spot you picked for us."

"Sorry about that." Sensation chased itself over her skin like thousands of tiny shivers. Everywhere he touched came alive, and there was a tugging down low in her stomach, a pulsing beneath. "God." She clamped her hand on his arm as if gripping an anchor in a high wind. "I was so scared."

"You didn't sound it. You sounded tough. And bored, as if you did that sort of thing twice a day." He rubbed his face against her hair "But I could smell your fear. I wouldn't have let them hurt you, Lily. They would never have touched you."

"I know. I was scared you were going to kill people. And that I'd have to." Her voice hitched. She turned her face into the living cubbyhole formed by his neck and shoulder and breathed him in. Her insides seemed to be vibrating. She needed more. More touch, more skin, more connection. "I've never killed anyone. I've drawn my weapon, fired warning shots, but I've never had to aim to kill."

"Warning shots weren't going to work with them. But you handled it. You talked them down. Lily. I'm coming apart." He nuzzled the side of her neck, then licked it.

A delicious tremor shimmered through her. The air was suddenly hot. Her fingers dug into hard muscle covered by cloth, and she wanted the cloth gone. He could smell her reaction, she realized. He knew how desperate she was for him. "What is this? I feel like I'm rattling at top speed over bumpy ground. Like everything's about to shake loose. Is it you? Are you doing this, or is it me?"

"It's us." He gathered her face in his two hands and tipped it toward him. His eyes shone in the dim light. Normal eyes once more, or so close to it she couldn't tell the difference. "Us, Lily. This is what we bring to each other. I need you."

She stared at him in a vast, humming silence, her skin and bones and need a thin bridge stretching between one moment and the next, when everything would change.

"There's a hotel." His hand trembled as he brushed her hair back. "Six or seven blocks from here. It isn't what I want for you, for our first time together, but I don't know if I could make it to my apartment, or yours."

He needed her. "Yes," she said. And her voice came out clear and strong, just as if she knew what she was doing.

*   *   *

LILY WOULD HAVE insisted on driving if she'd been sure
she was in better shape than Rule. They were lucky the traffic
was so light.

They rode in silence. She kept waiting for doubts to surface,
for common sense to point out all the reasons this was a bad
idea. What did sex really mean to Rule? She didn't know,
couldn't guess. She wasn't sure what this meant to her, either.
Though she tried to persuade herself her hunger was fueled
by reaction, the aftereffects of adrenaline and danger, her decision felt vast. Like she was taking a leap off a crumbling
edge, straight out into darkness.

Yet for all those seven blocks, and the minutes she waited
in the hotel lobby while Rule procured a key, the urgency
thrummed in her and the doubts never spoke. She wanted this,
wanted Rule with a ruthless clarity that didn't shut down
thought. Just dismissed it.

The hotel was about ten bucks a night above seedy, but the
elevator worked, their room seemed clean, and the door
locked. Other than that, Lily only gathered a quick impression
of orange—a tangerine bedspread, faded peach wallpaper, a
bad print of a New England autumn scene hanging above the
bed. Then she was in Rule's arms.

"I want to make this right," he said, nuzzling her hair. "Ah,
you smell so good. I wish you could know . . ." He put his
hands on her shoulders, slipped her jacket off, letting it fall to
the floor, and kissed her.

The urgency remained, the pleasure and the sense of having
opened a door on a vast unknown. But something new lapped
over her. From his mouth she absorbed the knowledge of his
delight, a wordless rejoicing. His hands stroked with slow in-
timacy over her back, her hips, telling her they were alone
now, and they had time. All the time they needed.

Still her fingers trembled as she found the buttons of his shirt
and, one by one, undid them. She ran her hands up his chest to
his neck, leaning back slightly so she could see his face—the
heavy-lidded eyes, the smile on his beautiful mouth. And she
touched his hair, ran her fingers through it, testing the weight,
the curl. Such freedom, to touch as she wished.

He glanced down at her shoulder holster, his expression

wry. "Would you mind taking care of that yourself? I don't
like guns."

That made her laugh, and laughter made her fingers less
clumsy, so she was able to unfasten the buckle and lay her
weapon in its holster on the bedside table. Rule came up behind her then and put his arms around her waist, pulling her
to him. He'd slid off his shirt while she took care of her
weapon, and she felt the heat of his skin through the linen of
her shirt. The hard length of him nestled against the small of
her back.

Her breath caught. He bent and grazed his teeth along the
cord of her neck. A shock of pleasure vibrated through her
and wrecked her breathing. He ran his hands over her body
slowly, luxuriously, breasts to stomach, pubic mound, thighs—
and her vision hazed.

He unfastened her shorts and pushed them down. She
stepped out of them and would have turned around, but he
clasped her to him, her back to his front, and carefully unbuttoned her top. Undid the catch on her bra, and removed it.
And eased her panties down.

Then she turned and reached for his belt buckle. Her hands
weren't steady. Neither was his breathing. The heat in his eyes
made her fingers fumble, because she couldn't look away.

When he was as naked as she was, he said, "I don't think
I can go slow. I want to. I want to spend hours on your body,
but I can't. Not this time."

"Thank God." And she looped her arms around his neck,
bringing their bodies together. They touched, skin to skin, and
the world changed.

He lifted her, tumbling her onto the bed and following her
down. She wrapped herself around him, trying to touch all of
him at once while he tried to kiss her everywhere. His hand
snaked down between her legs, where he stroked the slick
folds. Her stomach went hollow. The muscles at the tops of
her thighs clenched and quivered, a kinetic percussion with
her heart pounding out the accompaniment.

She dug her fingers into his waist. *Hurry.* He slid up her
body. Instinctively, her legs opened and the head of his penis
teased her inner folds . . . the soft, silky, *bare* head of his penis.

"Wait," she gasped. "I'm on the pill, but—"

"Are you?" He had a funny look on his face, his eyebrows

all awry and his mouth pressed down. His arms quivered with strain, but he bent and kissed her gently. "You can't catch anything from me, or vice versa. Bugs don't stick around in my system."

In spite of everything, indignation pricked her. "Does that mean you've never even had a cold?"

His lips twitched. A drop of sweat drifted down the side of his face. "Afraid so. Lily . . . *now?*"

He needed her. As any man needs a woman—in a purely human way—he needed her. Something softened and opened inside her, and she answered without words, cupping his face in her hands and lifting up gently with her hips. He pushed inside.

Full. Throbbing. Complete. Sensation pinwheeled through her, a thousand little sparks like colors spun into feeling. Her eyes squeezed closed, and the colors were there in the darkness with her.

"Ahh," he said. "Ah, Lily." And he stroked her face with his hand while he stroked her, deep inside, with his cock. "Look at me, Lily. Look at me while I'm inside you."

She opened her eyes and his were right there above her, waiting to catch her as she emerged from her private darkness. His pupils were huge. Growing. Darkness bled through his irises and beyond, pooling where white should be, a black, alien rainbow overtaking the colors she knew.

The shock of fear hit instantly, an electric tremor. But it was too late to pull back, too late to reserve any portion of herself—he was already inside her, deep inside in a way beyond the physical. Fear was only another sensation, giving claws to the need in her belly.

"Now," she panted, digging her fingers into his buttocks. "Now, Rule."

He shuddered. As if some inner chain had snapped, he dug his hands into her buttocks, lifting her, putting her where he needed so he could pound into her. She cried out. Need surged—his, hers, the two swirled together in complex patterns disturbing the lines that were supposed to divide them.

Fingers gripped, bruised. Flesh smacked into flesh as sweat dripped, running over heated bodies as the great, greedy beast of passion took them both by the throat, shook them—then flung them out into a clear, crisp darkness.

* * *

"SOMEDAY I WANT to see you in colors. Green, maybe."
Lily's head was pillowed on Rule's chest. It was damp and
warm, stirring slightly with his breath. The aftershocks had
faded into drowsy bliss. Later, she knew, she would question,
wonder, try to understand. That business with his eyes . . . but
not now. Not yet.

He opened his eyes. "I must have done something wrong.
You have enough breath left to talk."

Her laugh was husky and delighted. "Blue. You'd look
good in blue."

He ran a hand over her hair. His voice was quiet, almost
sad. "I wear colors sometimes at Clanhome. Tomorrow I'll
wear blue for you."

Reality seeped back in, about as welcome as a cold trickle
of rain leaking beneath a raincoat collar. And just as impossible to ignore. She propped herself up on one elbow. "You
never did tell me why you had to see me so urgently, did you?
It's because you're finally taking me to Clanhome. Your father
is back."

"I'm taking you to Clanhome, yes. I believe my father will
see you, though he hasn't said. He . . ." Rule sighed. "He's
been back for several days."

He'd lied to her. Though she'd warned herself all along not
to believe everything he told her, learning that he had lied
stripped her of something warm and important.

"I couldn't tell you," He touched her cheek. "He directly
forbade me to tell you until . . ."

"Until what?" Hurt throbbed inside her. Honor bound Rule
to obey his Lupois, whose decisions he was pledged to uphold
with his own body. She knew that. And still it hurt. "Until I
went to bed with you?"

"He didn't want his condition known."

"What do you mean?"

"Four days ago, on his way home from meeting with another Lupois, my father was attacked by other lupi. He was
badly mauled. He nearly died."

Chapter 10

THE RAIN OF last night had vanished as if it had never been. The sky was clear and cloudless, the land around them seriously rumpled, studded with live oak, juniper, and pines. Wind blew in the open windows of Rule's Explorer, smelling of dust and living things.

Lily wondered what it smelled like to him. She would never really know what his world was like, would she?

Returning to the real world was a bitch. She'd been mostly silent ever since they left her apartment, where she'd changed into clean clothes. But the doubts and the questions—and a few uneasy answers—hadn't waited until morning to hit. They'd plagued her last night, but they hadn't kept her from making love with him a second time, or sleeping in his arms. Even now the urge to touch him rose every so often, strong and compelling. Rather like a sneeze, she thought. If she ignored it, it went away.

But it kept coming back.

He slowed and turned off the pavement onto a well-graded dirt road. "We're almost there," he said.

"Good. Your authority does extend to getting me through

the gates, I take it. Since your father doesn't know I'm coming."

"He'll see you."

"How can you be sure now, when before you wouldn't bring me to him?"

"It's complicated." He grimaced. "I lied about my father being gone because he didn't want his condition known. Everything else I told you about lupi was true. You'll need his approval to accomplish anything."

She stared at him, angry. "Everything? Are you sure?"

"Of course I . . . shit." He ran a hand over his hair. "I forgot. No, not quite everything."

"You admit, then, that you lied about being able to identify the clan of the lupus who killed Charlene Hall."

"How did you figure that out?"

She shrugged and looked out the window. He was wearing last night's clothes and a pair of wraparound sunglasses he'd had in the glove compartment, and he made her ache. "That's my job, figuring things out. Your father was attacked by a member of the Leidolf clan, wasn't he? You believed it was someone from the same clan, or the same group within that clan, who killed the others. So you lied to direct my attention that way."

"I didn't tell you it was Leidolf who attacked my father."

"You didn't have to." He'd told her enough. Leidolf hated the Citizenship Bill, and they'd very nearly killed its strongest proponent among the lupi—the leader of Nokolai. But what about Rule? He supported the bill, too. If his father was killed, he would be Lupois.

Fear balled up cold in her stomach. Surely he was a target, too. "Can you identify the killer at all?"

"Oh, yes. If I ever got close to him, I could. But the clan scents aren't quite as distinctive as I led you to believe. I could tell Leidolf from Shuntzu, but the various European clans have interbred too much. Not all Germans are blond, and not all Leidolf smell the same."

"But your father is sure it was Leidolf who tried to kill him."

"He recognized them," Rule said grimly.

"Them? How many—"

"You can ask him, but I doubt he'll tell you." He glanced

at her, then reached out and caught her hand. "What's wrong, Lily? You've a right to be angry that I deceived you, but I think there's something more bothering you."

His fingers clasping hers felt right. Absolutely right. Lily swallowed. What was she supposed to tell him? *Sorry, but I've developed an addiction to you after just one night. I have to touch you every so often, which is likely to play hell with my job.* "Things went pretty far, pretty fast with us last night. There's something I'd meant to ask you. Or tell you."

"A jealous boyfriend I don't know about?" His voice was light.

"No. That's just it. If there had been a man in my life, last night wouldn't have happened. Fidelity is very important to me. You might say it's nonnegotiable."

"I see. You don't think I can—or would want to—be faithful to you."

A little bump of hope, quickly squelched, stuck in her throat. She swallowed. "Lupi don't respect fidelity."

"Normally, that's true. We consider jealousy a sin." He drove in silence for a moment, one hand holding hers, one on the wheel, staring straight ahead. "You need to see for yourself to understand. That's one reason I'm bringing you to Clanhome. So you'll understand."

CLANHOME WAS VINEYARDS and forests, steep slopes and a long, narrow valley cradling what amounted to a village or very small town. The Nokolai held roughly seventeen thousand acres, and were jealously protective of their wilderness; only a small part of the land was used or settled.

To Lily's surprise, dogs raced the Explorer as they drove down the single main street. Modest stucco, timber-frame, or adobe houses lined the dusty street and peered out from the pines and oaks covering the slope to her left. Lily saw a gas station, a small open market, a café, a laundry, and a general store.

And children. Laughing, playing, arguing, they raced around in swirls and eddies like flocks of birds. The youngest ones, boys and girls both, wore shorts and nothing more.

So did most of the adults she saw—the men, at least. The two women standing talking in one neatly fenced yard had added skimpy halters. A teenage girl sitting in front of the store drinking a Coke wore a loose, gauzy dress. A huge, silver-coated wolf sat beside her, panting cheerfully in the heat.

The Lupois's home was set slightly apart, perched partway up the slope at the end of the street. It was larger than the others, but by no means a mansion—a sprawling stucco home with a red tile roof and a terraced yard brimming with flowers.

Rule's son came running out when they drove up.

Lily recognized who the boy was instantly. He looked so much like his father . . . but she'd thought both boys lived with their mothers.

Maybe his mother was here, too. Lily got out of the car slowly.

Rule kissed his son on the cheek, leaving his hand on the boy's shoulder when he straightened. He was tall for his age—if she hadn't known better she would have guessed him to be thirteen or fourteen instead of eleven. His eyes were darker than Rule's and shining with curiosity.

"Paul," Rule said, "I would like you to meet Lily Yu."

"Oh! Is she the one you—"

"Your mother would be unhappy with your manners," Rule interrupted gently.

"Sorry, Ms. Yu." He smiled, and some of the resemblance to Rule slipped, letting the person he was becoming shine through. "I'm happy to meet you."

"I'm glad to meet you, too, Paul." Though apparently he knew more about her than she did him. Rule had scarcely mentioned his sons.

Rule kept his hand on Paul's shoulder. The boy chattered happily all the way to the house. "Grandfather's *much* better today. He was sitting up in bed when I went to see him. He called me a nosy pup and told me to go chase rabbits. I said that wasn't much fun when I couldn't catch them, not being four-footed yet, and he chuckled. You know that chuckle of his." He glanced around his father at Lily. "You'll see what I mean. It sounds like when you turn the bass way up on the stereo. So I figured he was feeling better, if he was chuckling instead of cussing."

"I suspect you figured right," Rule said.

The entry hall was large, tiled, and ended in sliding doors, left open, that led to an atrium. Doorways opened off both sides of the entry. The woman who stepped out of a doorway on the right was fifty or sixty with gray hair hanging in frizzy clouds to her waist. She wore running shorts and an athletic bra. Her skin was coppery, probably from heritage as well as sun, and her muscle tone was excellent. She heaved a short, put-upon sigh. "Paul said that was your car. He knows the sound of the engine, I suppose. Go on in, Rule. Your father's expecting you."

"Giving you a hard time, is he, Nettie?" Rule asked sympathetically.

"He wants steak!" Her hands flew up in exasperation. "What he thinks he's going to do with it, I don't know. He doesn't have enough duodenum left to wrap around my thumb. I would have preferred to keep him in sleep another day, but you know him."

Lily stiffened. The duodenum—wasn't that part of the intestines? And he was here, at home, not in a hospital?

Rules glanced down at her. "It's not as bad as it sounds. He's regrowing the parts that are damaged, and Nettie Two Horses is a doctor. Nettie, this is Detective Lily Yu."

"Oh." The older woman looked her over thoroughly, then smiled. "I don't imagine I look the way you think a doctor should, but I assure you I am a real doctor. Trained in conventional medicine at Boston, shamanic practices with my uncle. Chalk the outfit up to too much time spent around these heathens." Her fond glance took in Rule and his son. "Lupi are the worst patients in the world. They think that because they can heal almost anything, they don't have to listen to me. Or take care of themselves."

Rule grinned. "Guilty as charged. But I'll have a talk with your worst patient. He knows very well he can't have steak yet. Paul, why don't you and Aunt Nettie see if Louvel has any coffeecake while I take Lily to meet your grandfather?"

Aunt Nettie? As Lily and Rule started down the short hall the older woman had emerged from, she asked quietly, "Is 'aunt' a courtesy title? Nettie looks Native American, and your clan is of European extraction, isn't it?"

"Yes. Nettie is Navajo. She's married to my uncle, which of course makes her Paul's great-aunt."

Married? But lupi didn't . . . only, apparently one had.

He paused just outside a heavy wood door. "I should have

warned you earlier. My father's injuries . . . lupi heal better when our wounds are left open to the air, and infection isn't normally a problem. He's not pretty to look at right now, and he won't be wearing much in the way of clothing. Probably nothing."

"Ah . . ." She gathered her scrambled wits enough to ask, "Is there any ceremony or greeting ritual I should know?"

He smiled wryly. "If he were in better shape, he'd insist on kissing your hand. But no, there's no greeting ritual that applies." He opened the door.

The bedroom was large, airy, and masculine, decorated in earth tones and forest green. The furniture looked as if it had been shifted; the king-size bed was empty and shoved against a bureau. The man she'd come to see was in a hospital bed with the head raised and an IV attached to his far arm. And yes, he was quite naked, except for the patch over one eye.

He was a lot hairier than Rule. He was also a bloody mess.

The wound running from his cheek up under the eyepatch was broad and bumpy with a heavy scab. New pink skin had formed at its edges, trailing into what was left of a grizzled, rust-colored beard. The gouges along his chest and belly had been stitched, but the abdomen dipped in oddly, as though not all of the usual pieces were under the skin. Lily thought of the missing duodenum and managed not to wince. His legs and genitals seemed undamaged, and she couldn't see his left arm. His right hand had only two fingers. The rest were marked by tiny, pinkish-white nubs, and part of the palm was gone.

Rule moved into the room and bent to kiss his father's cheek. "Paul told me you were doing better. I'm glad to see he was right."

Better? If this was what he looked like after four days of a lupus's rapid healing, what had he looked like right after the attack?

"Apparently you considered me well enough for company." The Lupois's voice was ten fathoms deep, a rumble from the bottom of that barrel chest. He gave his son a searching look. "You were right, then?"

"Yes." There was satisfaction in Rule's voice, and something Lily couldn't identify. He stood aside. "I've brought Lily to meet you. Lily, this is my father, Isen Turner."

"Come closer, Lily." The uncovered eye studied her as she

approached the bed, and the chuckle his grandson had mentioned rumbled up. "Rule. We have embarrassed your lady. She isn't accustomed to our ways." He reached out casually with the two-fingered hand and draped a corner of the sheet across his loins. "As you see, Lily, I have not postponed the pleasure of meeting you without reason."

"Yes, sir." If there was a protocol for meeting naked semiroyalty, Lily didn't know what it might be. "I was sorry to learn you'd been injured. I have some questions."

"It is a trifle awkward, Lily, your being with the police."

An odd thing to say, since that was why she was here. "Rule said you recognized your attackers."

"Did I? I have forgotten. The trauma, no doubt."

"Were you attacked while in wolf form, sir?"

"I find this difficult to express politely, but since the attack did not take place in your jurisdiction, the details are not your affair."

"Three other people have been murdered who are most definitely my affair. Their killer is almost certainly connected to those who tried to kill you."

"A like-minded soul, perhaps. I assure you that the ones who attacked me did not travel to the city the next day and kill someone else."

Lily had the unpleasant suspicion he meant that his attackers had been killed. Probably by those defending him, judging by the extent of his wounds. He wasn't going to "remember" anything about the attack, no matter what angle she took. And he was in pain. Though he hid it well, it showed around his undamaged eye.

Time to finish up. "I need to question your people, sir, about these murders. Will you ask them to cooperate with me?"

He looked at her thoughtfully for a long moment. "I will call a meeting of my Council for nine o'clock," he said at last. "We will discuss it tonight."

Anywhere else in the country, people didn't hold a meeting to discuss cooperating with the police. "I understood that you had complete authority."

His mouth crooked up on the undamaged side. "We have a saying: The Lupois who rules alone soon runs out of sons. I will bring this to Council, Lily. You go with my son, let him show you around. I must require you to pretend, for now, you are not a police detective. Ask no questions related to your investigation until after I have spoken with the Council. And I . . ." He sighed. "I must rest, unfortunately, if I am to hold Council tonight."

AS SHE AND Rule passed from the hall to the entryway, Paul raced past. "Bye, Dad! See you at lunch!" He yanked open the door, stopped, turned around, and added in a polite rush, "It was very nice to meet you, Lily. I'll see you at lunch, too. We're eating with Aunt Nettie and Uncle Conrad." Then he sped outside, leaving the door open.

A gnome trotted out of the atrium. No, not a gnome, just a tiny old man made of wrinkles stretched over bony angles. He had a little potbelly and a round, smiling face, and wore yellow biking shorts. "There you are!" he exclaimed, as if amazed to see Rule, and added apologetically, "Is it lunchtime? I lose track. The laundry, you know."

"That's fine, Louvel. We're eating with my aunt and uncle, I'm told. This is Lily Yu."

"Oh! Lily?" The old man trotted up, lifted Lily's hand, and, in a curiously graceful gesture, raised it to his face. He smelled it thoroughly, then dropped a kiss on it before releasing it. "Charming. Charming. Do you like chocolate, Lily? So many humans do."

"Louvel is my father's cook and housekeeper," Rule said. "His chocolate torte is legendary."

"I love chocolate," she said honestly.

"Good! I'll make you a torte." He beamed at her, then trotted off down another hall.

"Louvel is a little beyond taking care of the house on his own, but his baking is still not to be missed." Rule put a hand on her back. "I could use some coffee. You?"

She nodded.

A few minutes later she was seated in a sunny kitchen while Rule poured them each a cup of coffee. The back door stood open. They tended to leave doors open, she'd noticed. Perhaps because there wasn't any air conditioning. Or maybe they just liked things open.

Rule handed her a steaming mug and sat at the table beside her.

"What your father said about running out of sons . . . does that mean someone might do that challenge thing?"

He sipped his coffee. "It depends. If he says you will be allowed to ask questions, that may annoy people but is unlikely to seriously upset anyone. It wouldn't be the first time police or other law enforcement agencies poked around in clan business."

"This isn't just clan business."

"Most people here will see it that way, though. We haven't exactly been on friendly terms with the authorities—any authorities. If, on the other hand, the Lupois rules that you are to be answered honestly and completely—"

"You mean that's an option?" She shook her head, baffled. "And if their Lupois tells them to be truthful and complete, they will be? Even if they disagree with him?"

"They will, or they'll challenge. If he does so rule," he added calmly, "I'll go with you as Lu Nuntius when you ask your questions."

"Lu Nuntius? What does that mean?"

"It's my title. My presence will be official, representing the will of the Lupois. In practical terms, it means I'll be in wolf form."

"To answer any challenges," she said flatly.

"And because my sense of smell is more acute in that form. It's almost impossible for a lupus to lie in the presence of his Lu Nuntius. Rather like a devout Catholic trying to lie to a priest while hooked up to a lie detector."

She considered that in silence, sipping the truly excellent coffee. "Do you think he'll tell everyone to answer me honestly?"

"You said you don't try to predict your grandmother. I don't make predictions about my father, either. But I hope he does as you wish." His mouth tightened to a grim line. "He was betrayed by one of his own people. I want the traitor named."

Lily was only startled for a second. Her mind skipped through possibilities, sorting her few facts into a new shape. "You think someone here—someone from his own clan—set him up."

"It was an ambush. Carefully planned, and requiring knowledge that Leidolf shouldn't have had."

"Someone told them where he would be."

"Yes. And who would be with him. I'm hoping you'll be able to arrest the bastard so I don't have to kill him."

Chapter 11

⌒

DID SHE TRULY want what Rule thought she did?

Off and on for the rest of the day, Lily tried to answer that question. She knew what she needed—to stop a killer. Make an arrest. Turn up proof that would stand up in court. She'd play by the Lupois's rules for now and ask none of the questions burning in her, and hope he cooperated in turn.

But how far did she want his cooperation to go? Was she willing to let Rule put his life on the line in order to get to the truth? Because that's what that whole Lu Nuntius business amounted to.

In the normal course of things she didn't have a lupus lie detector along on interviews, and she did okay. So what if she had to handle things the hard way here? Cops dealt with lying or reluctant witnesses all the time.

But if she didn't find out who had betrayed the Lupois to the other clan, Rule's father would. Once he was well enough, he would look for the traitor himself, and his justice would be final—and administered by his son. There wasn't a thing Lily could do to stop it, either, if she couldn't find the guilty party first. Not if they fought in wolf form. Killing a lupus in wolf form wasn't murder.

Lily was really growing to hate that law.

After they finished their coffee, Rule changed clothes. He wore blue for her, as he'd promised—denim blue. A ragged pair of cutoffs. He looked magnificent in them, especially since he didn't wear a shirt. Or shoes, for that matter, but neither did most of the people she met that day. Lily felt seriously overdressed, but wasn't about to leave her gun behind. Since most people found a gun out in plain view distracting, she kept the jacket on.

Clanhome was a shock of toppled preconceptions.

Lily had pictured a patriarchal, heavily masculine society. Everyone knew lupi were always male and didn't marry. She'd expected to see a few women who were kept around to have babies, tend the children, cook, and clean. That's how men all over the world arranged things when they could, wasn't it?

By lunch, she'd met Rule's uncle and one of his brothers, his first grade teacher, three of Paul's friends, several dogs, and an assortment of lupi . . . and Nokolai. That was a surprise, though it shouldn't have been: they were all Nokolai, but only some were lupi. Because only about two-thirds of the clan was male.

When she made a rather foolish comment on the number of girls and women she saw, Rule said, "What did you think we did with our girl children? Drown them? Expose them at birth on a hillside?"

She learned that between 350 and 450 people lived at Clanhome at any given time. There wasn't enough work here to support everyone, so some officially lived here but had jobs that kept them away a lot. Others lived and worked on the clan's ranch to the north, and the rest were scattered all over— how many that might be, she didn't find out. Most Nokolai came, when they could, to the gatherings held on the winter and summer solstices. And many of those who didn't live here themselves sent their children to stay for part of the summer . . . and their adolescent boys for much longer. To learn to control the beast.

Lily saw a lot of children that day. The only wolf she saw was the one that had been sitting with the teenage girl when she and Rule first arrived.

She visited the daycare center, which was attached to the clubhouse. The center was run by an older woman in a wheelchair named Oralie Fortier, and staffed by volunteers—which meant pretty much every adult at Clanhome. These people were nuts about kids. While Lily was there Ms. Fortier had to settle an argument about whose turn it was to work in the baby room—three people wanted to, and there were only two babies there at the time.

Two of the three insisting it was their turn with the babies were men.

The clubhouse had pool tables, a weight room, a smaller room where dance and gymnastics were taught, a kitchen, and a library. It was the only place on the grounds with television. When they left it, heading for the school across a lightly wooded section, Lily quit fighting herself and tucked her hand into Rule's.

He gave her a smile of such startling sweetness that her heart turned over. A second later, the panic hit.

She was in love with him.

No. No, this wasn't love, it was some kind of physical obsession created by incredible sex. Or magic. Whatever it was, though, it couldn't be love. She'd known him less than a week. He wasn't human, for God's sake. Besides, she'd been in love before, and this—this whatever she felt was different.

Deeper. Stronger.

Lily was thoroughly shaken when they reached the school, a U-shaped building with a courtyard in the center. There Rule excused himself, saying he needed to talk to his uncle. He dropped a kiss on her lips and left her with his first grade teacher.

Arthur Madoc was another surprise—a tall, narrow man with a gentle smile and the bluest eyes she'd ever seen. He'd taught first grade for forty-seven years. The school itself reminded her of country schoolhouses she'd read about, with kindergarten in one room, grades one and two in another, and third and fourth graders sharing the third room. After fourth grade, Mr. Madoc told her, the children had to go into town.

Classes in various subjects were offered during the summer. Today twelve kids aged six to nine were there for art lessons. The wilderness studies group, she was told, had already left the building.

Lily joined the budding artists, who were experimenting with print-making. She dipped leaves, twigs, and sponges in paint and dabbed them on paper. She helped other artists dip things and admired the results. And she asked questions.

After her shock had worn off, she'd realized she had more than one investigation to make.

One of the little girls wanted to be an airline pilot like her mother when she grew up. One wanted to be a doctor. Another thought she'd do something with computers, while a third couldn't decide between building houses like her uncle or being a movie star.

More of Lily's preconceptions toppled quietly. "What about babies?" she asked casually, daubing her sponge in canary yellow paint. "Or getting married? Do you think about doing that, too?"

"That shade of yellow won't work with purple," the budding actress said critically. More patiently, the would-be physician told her, "Not everyone gets to be a mommy, so you can't *plan* on having babies. Unless you want to marry out," she added, and her expression made it clear she considered that a poor choice.

"Not always," the computer enthusiast said with the air of correcting a small logic error. "Sophie Duquesne mated with a man from Rachmanov Clan."

The future pilot rolled her eyes. "Like *that's* going to happen. We were talking about *plans*. You can't plan to mate. That's like planning to win the lottery. My dad says—"

"Time to finish up," Mr. Madoc said pleasantly. "It's past noon."

The builder's niece had been right about the yellow. It didn't look good with the purple.

When Nettie came to get her, Lily wasn't surprised to learn that Rule's uncle, not his aunt, had cooked lunch. She was surprised, though, when those she sat down to lunch with included Rule's five-year-old son, Johnny. And Johnny's mother.

"I'M NOT UPSET with him for not telling me," Lily said, handing the bright blue plate she'd just washed to Nettie, then plunging her hands back in the soapy water. "Not exactly. He doesn't owe me his life story, and besides, I knew he had children. I'd dug into his background in the course of my investigation."

"But you are upset." Nettie stacked the dried plate on top of the others in the oak cabinet. "I suppose it's one thing to know something professionally, another to unexpectedly sit down to lunch with the mother of your lover's child."

That was putting things bluntly. "It's the way he did it. Just like the way he let me arrive at his grandfather's house without telling me Paul would be there. He's putting me through some kind of tests, and I don't like it."

Nettie didn't answer.

The two of them were alone in Nettie's small, cheerful kitchen. Lily had offered to help clean up after lunch. Somewhat to her surprise, Nettie had accepted right away and delegated the washing to her. Everyone else had left after they ate, with Johnny and his mother going home with her friend, Paul to his grandfather's, and Rule's uncle back to work at the vineyard.

Rule had said he needed to talk to a few people. "You can't come with me," he'd told her. "I'm sorry, but they won't speak freely if you're there. I'll tell you what I learn."

"Will you?" She'd studied him gravely. "People hold things back. They want to protect those they care about, and tell themselves whatever they're hiding couldn't really matter." Instinct, culture, history—all would shriek at him not to reveal too much to an outsider. To human authority.

He'd hesitated. She'd had the idea he was weighing his response, making sure he could speak the truth. "I'll tell you," he'd repeated.

Nettie stacked the last of the plates. "I take it Rule hasn't told you a lot about Johnny and Paul."

"He hasn't told me anything." Lily scrubbed hard on the pot in her hand. "I didn't know they lived here. I didn't know Johnny's mother was Nokolai."

"Johnny and Belinda do live here, but Paul is just staying for the summer. In August he'll return to his mother in Washington. She's a reporter for CNN."

Good grief. Rule's former lover, the mother of one of his sons, was a reporter? "That's almost as tricky for him as having a relationship with a cop."

"Almost," Nettie agreed cheerfully. "Has it been difficult for you, balancing your professional duties with your feelings for Rule?"

Lily took a moment to think about her answer, rinsing the pot thoroughly. Nettie should have been a cop. She was alarmingly good at getting people to talk. "He and I haven't known each other long, and for most of that time our relationship was professional. It turned personal very suddenly."

"Did it? Still, I can understand if you were uncomfortable today. Our customs are different from what you're used to."

That was certainly true. Lily grinned. "I think I would have been a lot more uncomfortable if Belinda hadn't been accompanied by the gorgeous Dede." The two women had, quite obviously, been a couple.

Nettie smiled. "I'm glad you're tolerant. Not everyone is."

"Really?" She rinsed the lid, handed it to Nettie, and opened the drain. "I had the impression this was an accepted and long-standing relationship."

Nettie shrugged. "Long-standing, yes. And lupi don't consider much about sex truly sinful. But relationships such as Belinda and Dede have are discouraged."

"Why?"

"Customs usually evolve for a reason," she said vaguely, turning to put away the last of the silverware. "Dede and Belinda are good together, though, so most accept them. It's not like having a true mate, of course—but then, few are that lucky."

"True mate." Lily thought of the little girls she'd met. "Is that like true love?"

"Something like that. You seemed to enjoy yourself at the school. I thought you might like to join the group learning woodcraft for a while this afternoon. Nick is leading them. He's our woodsman."

"Sure." Lily dried her hands. She knew when she was being herded out of the way. For now, she didn't mind. It wouldn't stop her from seeking answers. "Do you mind if I ask you something personal?"

"Will it stop you if I do?"

Probably not. "I wondered how you felt about—well, the way your husband turns furry sometimes. Does it bother you?"

"Not in the way you mean. I'm a little envious. It would be wonderful to experience the world as vividly as they do." She shrugged. "But it's a guy thing, isn't it?"

A guy thing. Lily grinned and dried her hands, but her grin

soon faded. "Nettie . . . what happens if a Lu Nuntius doesn't do what he's told by his Lupois?"

"I've never heard of such a thing occurring." Nettie smoothed lotion over her hands and held out the bottle. "Want some?"

Sometimes you let a subject get away with evading the question. Sometimes you didn't. "What would happen if one did?"

Nettie sighed. "At best, he would be banished. Not allowed at Clanhome. He would cease to exist to other Nokolai."

Lily didn't have to ask what the worst would be. She could guess.

The lupi had such final concepts of discipline.

Chapter 12

ONE LAST SLIVER of sun clung to the rounded shoulder of Bole's Peak like an incandescent fingernail clipping. The moon hung low on the opposite side of the sky, looking more shadow than substance, her solidity drained by the presence of her fiery sister. Rule hurried toward his aunt and uncle's house, buzzing inside as if his skin were but a coat slipped on over a teeming hive of choices, chances, fears, and dreams.

When the moon rose tomorrow, it would be full. But the buzzing came from more than the proximity of the full moon. He was returning to Lily.

Night came earlier in the mountains than down in the city, but it was still later than he'd planned to return. There had been so much to arrange, and discussion had taken longer than he'd expected. So had the congratulations. But his plans had gone well, he thought. Extremely well.

It remained to be seen how well his other plans had worked, and whether Lily would be angry. No, he thought ruefully as he reached the front door, the real question was *how* angry she would be. Lily was not going to like learning she'd been deceived.

The second he crossed the threshold, she looked up. She'd

been playing chess with his uncle. Nettie wasn't there, of course. She'd remained at his father's to make sure he hadn't set back his healing too much.

His uncle gave him a searching look, and Rule nodded slightly.

Lily stood. "All right. I've had enough of cryptic glances. What's going on?"

He smiled. The sight of her lifted his heart, even if her expression left something to be desired. And his news was good. "The Council has agreed that you are to be allowed to ask your questions. You are to be answered as honestly as if the Lupois himself posed the questions."

Her eyebrows went up. "The Council has already met."

"I'm afraid so. You made a very good impression on them."

"How remarkable of me, when I never met them." Her voice was flat with suspicion. Or maybe hurt.

"Yes, you did." He held out his hand. "Walk with me, and let me give you the explanations you deserve."

She looked at him for a long moment. Then she took his hand.

THE SKY WAS messy with sunset when they left the little house, darkening to indigo overhead. Lily didn't speak as Rule led her away from the scattering of lights that was the little village. It felt so good to be with him. She wanted to thump him in the head—hard—but still it felt right to walk beside him.

"This path leads to the lake," he said. "Though that's a rather inflated term—it's more like an ambitious pond, but lovely by moonlight. I asked the others not to take you there today. I wanted to be the one to show it to you."

"You also wanted to explain some things," she reminded him. "Not that I haven't figured some of it out. The Council meeting was never set for nine o'clock, was it?"

"No, though you weren't the only one who believed it was. They met around six, after most of them had had a chance to meet you and form an opinion."

Lily had been passed from person to person, group to group, all afternoon—courteously, often with real friendliness, but after a while it had been obvious her time and encounters were being managed. She'd thought they were checking her out because they were curious about the cop Rule had gotten himself involved with—and that they were making sure she didn't speak to anyone she wasn't supposed to. "Why all the secrecy?" she burst out. "Why go to the trouble to trick me?"

"We are a secretive people. Too much so, perhaps, but we've had reason to be wary. My father knew his councillors wouldn't agree unless they trusted you. They in turn wanted to meet you without your knowing who they were. Didn't you wonder why everyone you met put you to work?"

"I thought it was a custom or something." She'd fixed tea and swung a hammer, helped clear away deadfalls in the woods, washed a baby, and swept an old woman's floor. "What did they learn by watching me work?"

"What did you learn by watching them while you worked together?"

It was a fair question. An excellent question, actually. "A lot. One of the biggest surprises was how familiar some of it seemed."

She'd startled him. "Familiar?"

"Sure. The respect for tradition, the importance of family, work, and honor, the duty owed to one's elders—that's all very Chinese, you know."

"I hadn't thought of it that way."

"You don't know much about my people, either." Not yet. Would he? Did he want to learn? "I also began to get a grasp of why some lupi oppose the Citizenship Bill. It will change a lot of things, won't it? Your whole governance structure is based on the challenge. Not that I like it, but it does provide a check on the Lupois's power."

"Some of my people believe the proposed law will make tyrants of our Lupois, yes. But humans evolved a system of checks and balances that doesn't necessarily involve killing each other. We can, too."

They came out from under the trees and walked for a few yards along the shore before drifting to a stop. The sky overhead was salted with stars. Ahead, moonlight spilled across water as dark as Rule's eyes had been when the Change tried to take over. "The moon is almost full."

He looked at her. "You aren't at all frightened, are you? Going for a moonlit stroll with me doesn't worry you. All of the lupi councillors who met you said you gave off no fear-scent."

"They didn't give me any reason to," she said, surprised. "Neither have you. Maybe if I'd met a young teenage boy I'd have been worried, given what you said about them."

"They live separately until they learn control."

That made sense. "So—who were they? Which of the people I met today were councillors?"

"Nettie, Nicholas Masterson, Emile Hunter, Arthur Madoc, Fera Bibiloux—"

"Fera? The blind woman? But . . ." Her voice trailed off as she remembered the odd feeling she'd had, sitting in the dimly lit cabin drinking tea while the old woman worked her loom, her hands sure in spite of her lack of sight. A prickly feeling, yet peaceful. Belatedly she understood that she'd been in the presence of power. "Okay, I guess I understand that. She's Gifted, isn't she?"

"Something like that. Fera said you made good tea and would be welcome to return—from her, that counts as approval. She also said that something you haven't told me is going to come as a big surprise. She seemed amused, so I gather whatever it is won't be too much of a shock."

"Ah. Well . . ."

"You don't have to tell me right this second." He sounded amused himself.

Her heart was beating a little too fast and her mind jittered along the surface of her thoughts like a water bug. "I'm more than a little surprised that Nettie is a councillor. I thought they would all be Nokolai."

"Nettie is Nokolai."

"Is she?" They were facing each other now, their hands clasped. "Did she become part of the clan when she married your uncle? Or does mating mean something more than marriage?"

He touched her cheek. "I should have known you would turn up a clue or two. You heard about mates."

She nodded. Hope and guesses tangled in her throat, keeping her from speaking. So much depended on the accuracy of those guesses. . . .

"There is something about my people you don't know. Something no one outside the clans knows." He took a deep breath, letting it out slowly. "Over half of all lupi never father a child. And fertility is . . . limited . . . in the rest of us."

It wasn't what she'd expected to hear. "But—you have two children—"

"By two different mothers. Few women conceive by us, and of those who do, none has ever borne more than a single child."

"It's the magic in you. It screws with the results in DNA tests, too."

"You see why only a lupus who has sired sons is able to become Lu Nuntius?"

She nodded slowly.

"The outside world considers us promiscuous. In your terms, this is true. The need for children shapes us, defines us. We are seldom fertile with women of our own people, so we seek bed partners wherever we can. Not indiscriminately. We don't want our children birthed or raised by a chance-met stranger in a bar. But our survival as a people depends on those of us who are fertile siring as many children as possible."

"And you're fertile." Lily was dazed, as she'd heard gunshot victims sometimes were in the first seconds—the blow registers, but isn't real yet. Not real enough to hurt. She remembered the men at the childcare center arguing over who got to stay with the babies. The swarms of children everywhere.

Not everyone gets to be a mommy, the little girl had told her. Not everyone—relatively few—got to be a daddy, either. "That's why lupi don't marry," she whispered. "Because to be faithful to one woman would be to betray the needs of your people."

"Yes."

Abruptly the numbness was ripped away. Pain wrenched her around to face the water, hugging herself as if something vital was leaking out, like blood from a gut wound. "I can't . . . I can't do it, Rule. It wasn't long ago I said you were going too fast, and maybe I'm doing that now. You haven't . . . but for me, this has gone too far. I can't share you."

"No!" He grabbed her shoulders, spun her around. "Lily, I didn't mean—I thought you knew about mates!"

"I thought so, too. At least, I'd made some guesses." Her voice shook and her legs weren't too steady, either. She held on to his arms. "But no one came right out and said what—"

One second she was holding him and being held. The next she was rolling on the ground where he'd thrown her.

Rule howled. The eerie, ululating cry had goose bumps popping out on her flesh even as she threw her arms out, stopping her skid toward the lake. She pushed up onto her hands and knees—and stared.

He was Changing. Flickering—no, it was as if reality itself flickered, time bending in and out of itself like a Möbius strip on speed. Impossible not to watch. Impossible to say what she saw—a shoulder, furred, or was it bare? A paw; a muzzle that was also Rule's face—a stretching, snapping disfocus, magic strobing its fancy over reality.

And then there was a wolf. Huge, black and silver furred, snarling.

And three other wolves racing at them from fifty feet up the shoreline.

Lily's gun was in her hand, though she didn't remember drawing it. The wolves moved like streaks of pure speed, impossibly fast. She pushed to her knees, aimed, and fired—just as the black and silver wolf beside her launched himself at the one in the lead.

She hit the one on the left in the haunches. It didn't stop him—he still threw himself at the snarling tangle the other two wolves made. The third wolf veered toward her and leaped—huge, beautiful, and terrifying, jaws open.

Lily shot him in that gaping mouth.

The silver-alloy bullet went into the brain. The beast convulsed in midair. Lily scrambled back, but still it fell half on top of her, pinning her, smearing her with blood. And raised that bloody head and lunged for her throat.

She rammed her gun against the wolf's skull and squeezed the trigger. Blood and brains spattered, and the big body collapsed. Lily pushed out from under the wolf and scrambled to her feet.

Ten feet away, three wolves fought. She saw them clearly in the moon-washed night. She knew which one was Rule. Though she'd only seen him in wolf form for a few seconds, she knew him. But they moved too fast, stayed too close. She circled, but couldn't get a clear shot.

Then one of the wolves—the one she'd wounded, she

thought—staggered back, whimpering in pain. Blood, black in the moonlight, poured from what was left of its face. And the black and silver wolf's jaws were clamped on the back of the neck of the other attacker. He shook the beast, then flung him away to fall, bloody and broken, one paw twitching.

Then he turned, snarling, on the one left.

"No, Rule!" Lily ran forward. "I need him alive to interrogate!"

She stopped beside the black and silver wolf, who stood with his head lowered, hackles raised, teeth bared. His shoulders reached her hipbone. One of them was gashed and bleeding. More blood dripped from his muzzle, and a deep growl rumbled from his chest.

Lily aimed her weapon at the other wolf. "Silver bullets," she said tersely. "Don't move." Then in a whisper to Rule, "He does understand me, right?"

The growl cut off. The big wolf lifted his head to look at her in what she could have sworn was surprise. Or maybe amusement.

"Oh, yeah," she muttered. "If you understand me, then he does. Okay. You, there—you have the right to remain silent—at least you will, as soon as you're back on two legs. You—oh, shit."

Four more wolves raced toward them along the shore.

A big head nudged her thigh. Rule-wolf pointed his muzzle at those who approached so quickly, then nodded, his mouth opening in a grin a great deal like Worf's.

"Those are the good guys, huh?" When he nodded again she breathed a sigh of relief. "Good. We could use some backup." And went back to informing the suspect of the rights he'd have when he wasn't furry anymore.

THE COUNTY SHERIFF'S office, while it wasn't much like headquarters outwardly, held a comforting familiarity for Lily. Cops were cops, even when they were deputies. She was finishing up a report, using one of the deputy's computers. Unlike her, the deputy had a tiny office to himself. The sounds that came from the bullpen weren't much different from those at the city's cop shop. And the coffee was just as bad.

When the report was done she'd email it to the captain. She'd spoken to him on the phone briefly. He'd told her that the leak to the press had come from the mayor's office—a secretary interested in helping the mayor's opponent in the next election, it seemed.

Lily frowned at the screen. The text was trying to blur on her. God, she was tired. She paused for another sip of awful coffee.

Of the three wolves who'd attacked them, two were back in human form and being treated for injuries. One was in critical condition; he'd lost more blood than a human could have survived and had gone into shock. The other—the one whose neck Rule had broken—was actually in better shape. Paralyzed, yes, but with lupi that was a temporary condition.

The one she'd shot would never walk on two legs again. Or four. Lily was putting off thinking about that.

She'd been able to question the one with the broken neck before the sheriff arrived and he was taken to the hospital. He'd confirmed that they were Leidolf, and claimed that the one she'd killed had been the killer she was after. According to Rule, he'd told the truth. Lily was hoping for a little hard evidence to back that up, now that they had names and faces for the conspirators.

Some of the conspirators, anyway. The man she'd questioned insisted that the three Leidolf who had attacked her and Rule were the only ones involved in the killings, that they'd acted without their Clan chief's knowledge or consent. They'd attacked because their Nokolai contact—whom he insisted wasn't involved in the killings—had told them about the Council meeting, thinking it was to be later that night.

The Nokolai traitor turned out to be a woman. No one Lily had met.

Lily was embarrassed. Unconsciously she'd kept right on equating clan interests with lupi, and lupi with male. She hadn't considered any of the women of the clan as suspects because they couldn't be the killer. Dumb. Lily had taken the woman into custody immediately, unsure that the lupi's veneration of women would protect her from their notions of justice.

So far, the woman wasn't talking. But she was scared—and not of the police. Lily figured she'd end up with a second witness if she could get the woman into the Witness Protection

Program. Which was what she was recommending to her chief right now.

Her fingers paused on the keyboard. Rule was here. She knew it without turning to look, without his having made a sound. She swiveled her chair.

He stood in the doorway. He wore tattered denim, not black. The last time she'd seen him he'd been furless, naked, and covered in blood—much of it not his, thank God—with Nettie calmly stitching the worst of the wounds. Lily had had to leave with her prisoners and the sheriff.

He looked a lot better now. Except for his eyes. He had the rest of his expression locked down tight, but his eyes told the real story.

She shoved the chair back and went to him.

His arms closed around her, hard. He buried his face in her hair. She knew he was breathing her in, just as she was him.

After a moment she said, "How do you do that thing with your clothes, anyway? They didn't rip when you turned furry. They just weren't on you anymore."

His chuckle was real, if strained. "You never run out of questions. I don't know exactly what happens, except that they aren't part of me so they aren't part of the Change. Lily." He ran both hands over her hair. "I've never been so scared in my life. They were on us so fast, and I couldn't stop them. Not all of them. I didn't think you had a chance."

"I'm pretty fast for a human." She hugged him tightly around the waist, where he didn't have any wounds. "Maybe now you'll relax when I'm driving."

"Maybe I will." A deeply held tension was easing out of him. "I was still scared, afterwards."

She swallowed. "I know what you mean. I am, too."

"I knew you'd let me hold you again. That's the nature of the mate bond. But I didn't know if you would want me to, after what you saw tonight."

She was the one who had killed someone tonight, not him. But Lily didn't have the energy to get off on side issues. Exhaustion was turning her brain to lint. "Speaking of the mate bond . . . I don't know what the hell that is. We were interrupted, remember?"

"I think you've guessed the important part." He cupped her face and smiled into her eyes. "Some say the mate bond is nature's way of apologizing for our troubles with fertility. It doesn't happen often, but once in a long while, a lupus finds his mate, the woman who is so supremely right for him that no other will do. His life-mate. I knew you before I saw you, Lily. The moment you walked into the room, your scent reached me and I knew."

She swallowed. "So it's like true love, lupus style?"

He brushed a kiss across her mouth. "Very like that."

"And it doesn't cause problems? With the clan, I mean. If you have to bow out of the fertility business—"

He laughed. "I've been out of the fertility business since I met you. There can be problems, yes, but not that way. If a lupus is lucky enough to find his mate, no one expects him to keep spreading his seed around. It would be . . . abomination. Like rape, or the worst form of prostitution."

"But it can cause problems."

He nodded slowly. "That's the other reason everyone was so curious about you. Just because a lupus finds his mate doesn't mean she'll be able to accept him, his people, and his ways. Sometimes . . ." His throat muscles worked. "Sometimes he has to choose between his clan and his mate. But you had no fear-scent." His thumbs stroked along her cheeks. "You have no idea how important that is, how everyone rejoiced for me. Women who are deeply afraid of us often can't adjust. They may try, but they can't become one of the clan."

Happiness swelled inside her, so large and grand she had to tell him. "I love you, Rule." He kissed her, and that was delightful, but after a moment she pointed out, "You're supposed to say it back to me."

His eyebrows lifted slightly. "You know how I feel."

"Wrong answer." Her lips twitched. "This mate bond doesn't make everything perfect, does it?"

"No. It just makes everything possible."

A long time later he was sitting in the visitor's chair, one of those plastic devices supposedly shaped like people but that don't really fit anyone's rump. It couldn't have been comfortable. She was, though, since she was in his lap. "So, are we engaged?"

"If you like. In the eyes of my people, we're already married."

"In the eyes of my people, we aren't. So I think engaged

is a good idea. That makes you part of *my* family. Speaking of which . . ." She thought about all she still had to tell him. To explain. Things that were known only within the family.

Maybe it was stretching a point to call him family before they married, but he had to know. They might have children. From what he'd said that was far from certain . . . but with Grandmother involved, matters often fell out quite differently than anyone expected.

And she was likely to be involved.

Some traits were passed through the male line. Some through the female. Very few of the women in Lily's family inherited Grandmother's abilities; Lily hadn't, and she didn't think anyone alive today had, either. Probably it was a recessive trait. But Lily carried that heritage in her genes. She would pass the possibility on to her daughters.

All her life she'd had issues about just who was and wasn't considered human, and here she was, more or less proposing to a werewolf. "Rule, you know that we sometimes call Grandmother 'Tiger Lady'?"

He smiled. "I can handle being related to your grandmother if you can."

"That's good. Because she's not a witch, like you thought."

"Lily, I felt her power."

"I know, but . . ." She settled herself more comfortably and began, "You see, lycanthropy isn't just a guy thing."

And now, a
special preview of
Christine Feehan's

SHADOW GAME

Now available from Jove Books!

CAPTAIN RYLAND MILLER leaned his head against the wall and closed his eyes in utter weariness. He could ignore the pain in his head, the knives shredding his skull. He could ignore the cage he was in. He could even ignore the fact that sooner or later, he was going to slip up and his enemies would kill him. But he could not ignore guilt and anger and frustration rising like a tidal wave in him as his men suffered the consequences of his decisions.

Kaden, I can't reach Russell Cowlings. Can you?

He had talked his men into the experiment that had landed them all into the laboratory cages in which they now resided. Good men. Loyal men. Men who had wanted to better serve their country and people.

We all made the decision. Kaden responded to his emotions, the words buzzing inside Ryland's mind. *No one has managed to raise Russell.*

Ryland swore aloud softly as he swept a hand over his face, trying to wipe away the pain speaking telepathically with his men cost him. The telepathic link between them had grown stronger as they all worked to build it, but only a few of them could sustain it for any length of time. Ryland had to supply the bridge, and his brain, over time, balked at the enormity of such a burden.

Don't touch the sleeping pills they gave you. Suspect any medication. He glanced at the small white pill lying in plain sight on his end table. He'd like a lab analysis of the contents. Why hadn't Cowlings listened to him? Had Cowlings accepted the sleeping pill in the hopes of a brief respite? He had to get the men out. *We have no choice, we must treat this situation as if we were behind enemy lines.* Ryland took a deep breath, let it out slowly. He no longer felt he had a choice. He had already lost too many men. His decision would brand them as traitors, deserters, but it was the only way to save their lives. He had to find a way for his men to break out of the laboratory.

The colonel has betrayed us. We have no other choice but to escape. Gather information and support one another as best you can. Wait for my word.

He became aware of the disturbance around him, the dark waves of intense dislike bordering on hatred preceding the group nearing the cage where he was kept.

Someone is approaching ... Ryland lifted his head, abruptly cutting off telepathic communication to those of his men he could reach. He remained motionless in the center of his cell, his every sense flaring out to identify the approaching individuals.

It was a small group this time, Dr. Peter Whitney, Colonel Higgens, and a security guard. It amused Ryland that Whitney and Higgens insisted on an armed guard accompanying them despite the fact that he was locked behind both bars and a thick glass barrier. He was careful to keep his features expressionless as they neared his cage.

Ryland lifted his head, his steel-gray eyes as cold as ice. Menacing. He didn't try to hide the danger he represented. They had created him, they had betrayed him, and he wanted them to be afraid. There was tremendous satisfaction in knowing they were ... and that they had reason to be.

Dr. Peter Whitney led the small group. Whitney, liar, deceiver, monster-maker. He was the creator of the Ghost-Walkers. Creator of what Captain Ryland Miller and his men had become. Ryland stood up slowly, a lethal jungle cat stretching lazily, unsheathing claws as he waited inside his cage.

His icy gaze touched on their faces, lingered, made them uncomfortable. Graveyard eyes. Eyes of death. He projected the image deliberately, wanting, even needing, them to fear for their lives. Colonel Higgens looked away, studied the cameras, the security, watched with evident apprehension as the thick barrier of glass slid away. Although Ryland remained caged behind heavy bars, Higgens was obviously uneasy without the barrier, uncertain just how powerful Miller had become.

Ryland steeled himself for the assault on his hearing, his emotions. The flood of unwanted information he couldn't control. The bombardment of thoughts and emotions. The disgusting depravity and avarice that lay behind the masks of those facing him. He kept his features carefully blank, giving nothing away, not wanting them to know what it cost him to shield his wide-open mind.

"Good morning, Captain Miller," Peter Whitney said pleasantly. "How are things with you this morning? Did you sleep at all?"

Ryland watched him without blinking, tempted to try to push through Whitney's barriers to discover the true character hidden behind the wall Whitney had in his mind. What secrets were hidden there? The one person Ryland needed to understand, to read, was protected by some natural or manmade barrier. None of the other men, not even Kaden, had managed to penetrate the scientist's mind. They couldn't get any pertinent data, shielded as Whitney was, but the heavy, swamping waves of guilt were always broadcast loudly.

"No, I didn't sleep but I suspect you already know that."

Dr. Whitney nodded. "None of your men are taking their sleeping meds. I noticed you didn't either. Is there a reason for that, Captain Miller?"

The chaotic emotions of the group hit Ryland hard as it always did. In the beginning, it used to drive him to his knees, the noise in his head so loud and aggravating his brain would rebel, punishing him for his unnatural abilities. Now he was much more disciplined. Oh, the pain was still there, like a thousand knives driving into his head at the first breach of his brain, but he hid the agony behind the façade of icy, menacing calm. And he was, after all, well trained. His people never revealed weakness to the enemy.

"Self-preservation is always a good reason," he answered,

fighting down the waves of weakness and pain from the battering of emotions. He kept his features totally expressionless, refusing to allow them to see the cost.

"What the hell does that mean?" Higgens demanded. "What are you accusing us of now, Miller?"

The door to the laboratory had been left standing open, unusual for the security-ridden company, and a woman hurried through. "I'm sorry I'm late, the meeting went longer than expected!"

At once the painful assault of thoughts and emotions lessened, muted, leaving Ryland able to breathe normally. To think without pain. The relief was instant and unexpected. Ryland focused on her immediately, realizing she was somehow trapping the more acute emotions and holding them at bay, almost as if she were a magnet for them. And she wasn't just any woman. She was so beautiful, she took his breath away. Ryland could have sworn, when he looked at her, the ground shifted and moved under his feet. He glanced at Peter Whitney, caught the man observing his reaction to the woman's presence very closely.

Ryland's first thought was embarrassment that he had been caught staring at her. Then he realized Whitney knew the woman had some kind of psychic ability. She enhanced Ryland's abilities and cleared out the garbage of stray thoughts and emotions. Did Whitney know exactly what she did? The doctor was waiting for a reaction so Ryland refused to give him the satisfaction, keeping his expression totally blank.

"Captain Miller, I'd like to present my daughter, Lily Whitney. Dr. Lily Whitney." Peter's gaze never left the captain's face. "I've asked her to join us, I hope you don't mind."

The shock couldn't have been more complete. Peter Whitney's daughter? Ryland let out his breath slowly, shrugged his broad shoulders casually, another ripple of menace. He didn't feel casual. Everything inside of him stilled. Calmed. Reached. He studied the woman. Her eyes were incredible, but wary. Intelligent. Knowledgeable. As if she recognized him, too, in some elemental way. Her eyes were a deep startling blue, like the middle of a clear, fresh pool. A man could lose his mind, his freedom in eyes like hers. She was of average height, not tall, but not exceedingly short. She had a woman's figure encased in a gray-green suit of some kind that managed to draw attention to every lush curve. She had walked with a decided limp, but when he looked her over for damage, he could see nothing to indicate injury. More than all of that, the moment he saw her face, the moment she entered the room, his soul seemed to reach for hers. To recognize hers. His breath stilled in his body and he could only stare at her.

She was looking back at him and he knew the sight wasn't very reassuring. At his best, he looked a warrior, at his worst he looked a savage fighter. There was no way to soften his expression or lessen the scars on his face or shave off the dark stubble marring his stubborn jawline. He was stocky, a fighter's compact build, carrying most of his weight in his upper body, his chest and arms, his broad shoulders. His hair was black, thick and curled when it wasn't kept tight against his skull.

"Captain Miller." Her voice was soothing, gentle, pleasant. Sexy. A blend of smoke and heat that seared him right through his belly. "How nice to meet you. My father thought I might be of some use in the research. I haven't had much time to go over the data, but I'll be happy to try to help."

He had never reacted to a voice before. The sound seemed to wrap him up in satin sheets, rubbing and caressing his skin until he felt himself break out in a sweat. The image was so vivid for a moment he could only stare at her, imagining her naked body writhing with pleasure beneath his. In the midst of his struggle to survive, his physical reaction to her was shocking.

Color crept up her neck, delicately tinged her cheeks. Her long lashes fluttered, drifted down, and she looked away from him to her father. "This room is very exposed. Who came up with the design? I would think it would be a difficult way to live, even for a short period."

"You mean like a lab rat?" Ryland asked softly, deliberately, not wanting any of them to think they were fooling him by bringing in the woman. "Because that's what I am. Dr. Whitney has his own human rats to play with."

Lily's dark gaze jumped to his face. One eyebrow shot up. "I'm sorry, Captain Miller, was I misinformed, or did you agree to volunteer for this assignment?" There was a small challenge in her voice.

"Captain Miller volunteered, Lily," Peter Whitney said. "He

was unprepared for the brutal results, as was I. I've been searching for a way to reverse the process but so far, everything I've tried has failed."

"I don't believe that's the proper way to handle this," Colonel Higgens snapped. He glared at Peter Whitney, his bushy brows drawing together in a frown of disapproval. "Captain Miller is a soldier. He volunteered for this mission and I must insist he carry it out to its conclusion. We don't need the process reversed, we need it perfected."

Ryland had no trouble reading the colonel's emotions. The man didn't want Lily Whitney anywhere near Ryland or his men. He wanted Ryland taken out behind the laboratories and shot. Better yet, dissected so they could all see what was going on in his brain. Colonel Higgens was afraid of Ryland Miller and the other men in the paranormal unit. Anything he feared, Higgens destroyed.

"Colonel Higgens, I don't think you fully understand what these men are going through, what is happening to their brains," Dr. Whitney was pursuing an obviously long-standing argument between them. "We've already lost several men . . ."

"They knew the risks," Higgens snapped, glowering at Miller. "This is an important experiment. We need these men to perform. The loss of a few men, while tragic, is an acceptable loss considering the importance of what these men can do."

Ryland didn't look at Higgens. He kept his glittering gaze fixed on Lily Whitney. But his entire mind reached out. Took hold. Closed like a vise.

Lily's head snapped up. She gasped out a soft protest. Her gaze dropped to Captain Miller's hands. She watched his fingers slowly began to curl as if around a thick throat. She shook her head, a slight protest.

Higgens coughed. A barking grunt. His mouth hung open as he gasped for air. Peter Whitney and the young guard both reached for the colonel, trying to open his stiff shirt collar, trying to help him breathe. The colonel staggered, was caught and lowered to the floor by the scientist.

Stop it. The voice in Ryland's mind was soft.

Ryland's dark brow shot up and his gleaming gaze met Lily's. The doctor's daughter was definitely telepathic. She was calm about it, her gaze steady on his, not in the least intimidated by the danger emanating from him. She appeared as cool as ice.

He's willing to sacrifice every one of my men. They aren't expendable. He was just as calm, not for a moment relenting.

He's a moron. No one is willing to sacrifice the men, no one considers them expendable, and he isn't worth branding yourself a murderer.

Ryland allowed his breath to escape in a soft, controlled stream, clearing his lungs, clearing his mind. Deliberately he turned his back on the writhing man and paced across the cell, his fingers slowly uncurling.

Higgens went into a fit of coughing, tears swimming in his eyes. He pointed a shaky finger toward Ryland Miller. "He tried to kill me, you all saw it."

Peter Whitney sighed and walked with heavy footsteps across the room to stare at the computer. "I'm tired of the melodrama, Colonel. There is always a jump on sensors in the computers when there is a surge of power. There's nothing here at all. Miller is safely locked in a cage; he didn't do anything at all. Either you're trying to sabotage my project or you have a personal vendetta against Captain Miller. In any case, I'm going to write to the general and insist they send another liaison."

Colonel Higgens swore again. "I'll have no more talk about reversing the process, Whitney, and you know what I think about bringing your daughter on board. We don't need another damn bleeding heart on this project, we need results."

"My security clearance, Colonel Higgens, is of the highest level and so is my commitment to this project. I don't have the necessary data at this time, but I can assure you I'll put in whatever time necessary to find the answers needed." Even as she spoke, Lily was looking at the computer screen.

Ryland was "reading" her. Whatever was on the screen puzzled her as much as what her father was saying, but she was willing to cover for him. She was making it up as she went along. As calm and as cool as ever. He couldn't remember the last time he had smiled, but the impulse was there. He kept his back to the group, not certain he could keep a straight face while she lied to the colonel. Lily Whitney had no idea what was going on, her father had given her very little information, and she was simply winging it. Her dislike of Higgens, compounded with her father's unusual behavior, had left her firmly in Ryland's camp for the moment.

He had no idea what Whitney's game was, but Peter Whitney was buried deep in the mire. The experiment to enhance psychic ability and bring together a fighting unit had been his project, his brainchild. Peter Whitney had been the man to persuade Ryland the experiment had merit. That his men would be safe and that they would better serve their country. Ryland couldn't read the doctor as he could most men, but whatever Whitney was up to, Ryland was certain it wasn't anything that would benefit him or his men. Donovans Corporation had a stench about it. If there was one thing Ryland knew for certain, Donovans was about money and personal profit, not national security.

"Can you read that code your father uses for his notes?" Higgens asked Lily Whitney, suddenly losing interest in Ryland. "Gibberish if you ask me. Why the hell don't you just put your work in English like a normal human being?" He snapped the question at Dr. Whitney irritably.

At once the captain swung around, his gray gaze thoughtful as it rested on the colonel. There was something there, something he couldn't get hold of. It was shifting, moving, ideas formulating and growing. Higgens's mind seemed a black ravine, twisted and curved and suddenly cunning.

Lily shrugged. "I grew up reading his codes; of course I can read it."

Ryland sensed her growing puzzlement as she stared at the combination of numbers, symbols, and letters across the computer screen.

"What the hell are you doing getting into my private computer files, Frank?" Peter Whitney demanded, glaring at the colonel. "When I want you to read a report. I'll have the data organized and the report will be finished and up-to-date, neatly typed in English. You have no business in my computer either here or at my office. My research on many projects is on my computer and you have no right invading my privacy. If your people go anywhere near my work, I'll have you locked out of Donovans so fast you won't know what hit you."

"This isn't your personal project, Peter." Higgens glowered at all of them. "This is my project too and as the head of it, you don't keep secrets from me. You don't make any sense in your reports."

Ryland watched Lily Whitney. She remained very quiet, listening, absorbing information, gathering impressions and soaking it all up like a sponge. She seemed relaxed, but he was very aware that she had glanced toward her father, waiting for some sign, for a hint of how to handle the situation. Whitney gave her nothing, didn't even look at her. Lily hid her frustration very well. She shifted her gaze back to the computer screen, ignoring the others and their obviously long-standing argument.

"I want something done about Miller," Higgens said, acting as if Ryland couldn't hear him.

I'm already dead to him. Ryland whispered the words in Lily Whitney's mind.

All the better for you and your men. He's pressing my father hard about pushing this project forward, not terminating it. He isn't satisfied with the findings and doesn't agree it is dangerous to all of you. Lily didn't look away from the computer or give away in any manner that she was communicating with him.

He doesn't know about you. Higgens has no idea you're telepathic. The knowledge burst over him like a light from a prism. Brilliant and colorful and full of possibilities. Dr. Whitney was hiding his daughter's abilities from the colonel. From the Donovans Corporation. Ryland knew he had ammunition. Information he could use to bargain with Dr. Whitney. Something that might be used to save his men. His flare of excitement must have been in his mind because Lily turned and regarded him with a cool, thoughtful gaze.

Peter Whitney glared at Colonel Higgens, clearly exasperated. "You want something done? What does that mean, Frank? What do you have in mind? A lobotomy? Captain Miller has performed every test we've asked of him. Do you have personal reasons for disliking the captain?" Dr. Whitney's voice was a whip of contempt. "Captain Miller, if you were having an affair with Colonel Higgens's wife, you should have disclosed that information to me immediately."

Lily's dark eyebrows shot up. Ryland could feel the sudden amusement in her mind. Her laughter was soft and inviting, but her features gave nothing of her inner thoughts away. *Well? Are you a Romeo?*

There was something peaceful and serene about Lily, something that spilled over into the air around them. His second-in-command, Kaden, was like that, calming the terrible static and tuning the frequencies so that they were clear and sharp and able to be used by all the men regardless of talent. Surely her father hadn't experimented on his own daughter. The idea sickened him.

"Laugh all you want, Peter," the colonel snapped, "but you won't be laughing when lawsuits are filed against Donovans Corporation and the United States government is after you for botching the job."

Ryland ignored the arguing men. He had never been so drawn to a woman, to any individual, but he wanted Lily to remain in the room. He *needed* her to remain in the room. And he didn't want her to be a part of the conspiracy that was threatening his life. She seemed unaware of it, but her father was certainly one of the puppet masters.

My father is no puppet master. Her voice was indignant and faintly haughty, a princess to an inferior being.

You don't even know what the hell is going on so how do you know what he is or isn't? He was rougher than he intended but Lily took it well, ignoring him to frown at the computer monitor.

She didn't speak to her father, but he sensed her movement toward him, a slight exchange between them. It was more felt than seen, and Ryland sensed her puzzlement deepen. Her father gave her no clue, but instead, led Colonel Higgens toward the door.

"Are you coming, Lily?" Dr. Whitney asked, pausing just inside the hall.

"I want to look things over here, sir," she said, indicating the computer, "and it will give Captain Miller a chance to fill me in on where he is in this."

Higgens swung around. "I don't think it's a good idea for you to stay alone with him. He's a dangerous man."

She looked as cool as ever, her dark brow a perfect arch. Lily stared down her aristocratic nose at the colonel. "You didn't ensure the premises were secure, Colonel?"

Colonel Higgens swore again and stomped out of the room.

As Lily's father started out of the room, she cleared her throat softly. "I think it best we discuss this project in a more thorough way if you want my input, sir."

Dr. Whitney glanced at her, his features impassive. "I'll meet you at Antonio's for dinner. We can go over everything after we eat. I want your own impressions."

"Based on . . ."

Ryland didn't hear a hint of sarcasm, but it was there in her mind. She was angry with her father but he couldn't read why. That part of her mind was closed off to him, hidden behind a thick, high wall she had erected to keep him out.

"Go over my notes, Lily, and see what you make of the process. Maybe you'll see something I didn't. I want a fresh perspective. Colonel Higgens might be right. There may be a way to continue without reversing what we've done." Peter Whitney refused to meet his daughter's direct gaze.

"Do I need to leave an armed guard in this room with my daughter, Captain?"

Ryland studied the face of the man who had opened the floodgates of his brain to receive far too much stimuli. He could detect no evil, only a genuine concern. "I'm no threat to the innocent, Dr. Whitney."

"That's good enough for me." Without looking at his daughter, the doctor left the room, closing the door to the laboratory firmly.

Ryland was so aware of Lily, he actually felt the breath leave her lungs in a slow exhale as the door to the laboratory closed and the lock snicked quietly into place. He waited a heartbeat. Two. "Aren't you afraid of me?" Ryland asked, testing his voice with her. It came out more husky than he would have liked. He had never had much luck with women, and Lily Whitney was out of his class.

She didn't look at him, but continued to stare at the symbols on the screen. "Why should I be? I'm not Colonel Higgens."

"Even the lab techs are afraid of me."

"Because you want them to be and you're projecting, deliberately enhancing their own fears." Her voice indicated a mild interest in their conversation, her mind mulling over the data on the screen. "How long have you been here?"

He swung around, stalked to the bars and gripped them. "They're bringing you on board and you don't even know how long my men and I have been locked up in this hellhole?"

She turned her head, tendrils of hair swinging around her face, loose from the tight twist at the back of her head. Her hair, even in the muted blue light of the room, was shiny and gleamed at him. "I don't know anything at all about this experiment, Captain. Not one small fact. This compound is the highest security clearance this corporation has and while I have clearance, this is not my field of expertise. Dr. Whitney, my father, asked me to consult and I was cleared to do so. Do you have a problem with that?"

He studied the classic beauty of her face. High cheekbones, long lashes, a lush mouth—they didn't come like this unless they were born rich and privileged. "You probably have an underpaid maid whose name you can't even remember, who picks up your clothes when you throw them on your bedroom floor."

That bought him her entire attention. She moved away from the computer, crossed the distance to his cage in a slow, unhurried walk that drew his attention to her limp. Even with her limp she had a flowing grace. She made every cell in his body instantly aware he was male and she was female.

Lily tilted her chin at him. "I guess you were brought up without manners, Captain Miller. I don't actually throw my clothes on the bedroom floor. I hang them in the closet." Her gaze flicked past him to rest briefly on the clothes strewn on the floor.

For the first time that he could remember, Ryland was embarrassed. He was making an ass out of himself. Even her damn high heels were classy. Sexy, but classy.

A small smile curved her mouth. "You're making a *total* ass out of yourself," she pointed out, "but fortunately for you, I'm in a forgiving mood. We elitists learn that at an early age when they put that silver spoon in our mouths."

Ryland was ashamed. He might have grown up on the wrong side of the tracks in the proverbial trailer trash park, but his mother would have boxed his ears for being so rude. "I'm sorry, there's no excuse."

"No, there isn't. There's never an excuse for rudeness." Lily paced across the distance of his cage, an unhurried examination of the length of his prison. "Who designed your quarters?"

"They constructed several cages quickly when they decided we were too powerful and posed too much danger as a group." His men had been separated and scattered throughout the facility. He knew the isolation was telling on them. Continual poking and prodding was wearing, and he worried that he could not keep them together. He had lost men already, he was not about to lose any of the others.

The cell had been specially designed out of fear of reprisal. He knew his time was limited; the fear had been growing for weeks now. They had erected the thick bulletproof barrier of glass around his cell believing that it would keep him from communicating with his men.

He had volunteered for the assignment and he had talked the other men into it. Now they were imprisoned, studied and probed and used for everything but the original premise. Several of the men were dead and had been taken apart like insects to "study and understand." Ryland had to get the others out before anything else happened to them. He knew Higgens had termination in mind for the stronger ones. Ryland was certain it would come in the form of accidents, but it would come eventually if he didn't find a way to free them. Higgens had his own agenda, wanting to use the men for personal gain that had nothing whatsoever to do with the military and the country he was supposed to serve. Higgens was afraid of what he couldn't control. Ryland wasn't about to lose his men to a traitor. His men were his responsibility.

He was more careful, speaking matter-of-factly this time, trying to keep the accusations, the blame he put squarely on her father's shoulders, from spilling over into his thoughts, in case she was reading him. Her eyelashes were ridiculously long, a heavy fringe he found fascinating. He caught himself staring, unable to be anything but a crass idiot. In the midst of being caught like a rat in a trap, with his men in danger, he was making a fool of himself over a woman. A woman who very well might be his enemy.

"Your men are all in similar cages? I wasn't given that information." Her voice was strictly neutral, but she didn't like it. He could feel the outrage she was striving to suppress.

"I haven't seem them in weeks. They don't allow us to communicate." He indicated the computer screen. "That's a constant source of irritation to Higgens. I bet his people have tried to break your father's code, even used the computer, but they must not have been able to do it. Can you really read it?"

She hesitated briefly. It was almost unnoticeable, but he sensed the sudden stillness in her and his hawklike gaze didn't leave her face. "My father has always written in codes. I see in mathematical patterns, and it was a kind of game when I was a little girl. He changed the code often to give me something to work on. My mind . . ." She hesitated, as if weighing her options carefully. She was deciding how honest to be with him. He wanted the truth and silently willed her to give it to him.

Lily was quiet for a moment more, her large eyes fixed steadily on his, then her soft mouth firmed. Her chin went up a minuscule notch but he was watching her every expression, every nuance, and he was aware of it, aware of what it cost her to tell him. "My mind requires continual stimulation. I don't know how else to explain it. Without working on something complex, I run into problems."

He caught the flash of pain in her eyes, fleeting but there. Dr. Peter Whitney was one of the richest men in the world. All the money might have given his daughter every confidence, but it didn't take away the fact that she was a freak . . . a freak like he was. Like his men were. What her father had made them into. GhostWalkers, waiting for death to strike them down.

"So tell me this, Lily Whitney, if that code is real, why can't the computer crack it?" Ryland lowered his voice so that anyone listening wouldn't hear his question, but he kept his glittering gaze fixed on hers, refusing to allow her to look away from him.

Lily's expression didn't change. She looked as serene as always. She looked impossibly elegant even there in the laboratory. She looked so far out of his reach his heart hurt. "I said he always wrote in code, I didn't say this one made any sense to me. I haven't had a chance to work with it yet."

Her mind was closed so completely to him that he knew she was lying. He arched a dark brow at her. "Really. Well, you'll have to put in for overtime because no one seems to be able to read how your father managed to enhance our psychic abilities. And they sure can't figure out how to make it go away."

She reached out, gracefully, almost casually, naturally, to grip the edge of a desk. The knuckles on her hand turned white. "He enhanced your natural abilities?" Her mind immediately began to turn that bit of information over and over as if it were the piece of a jigsaw puzzle and she was finding the proper fit.

"He really let you walk in here blind, didn't he?" Ryland challenged. "We were asked to take special tests . . ."

She held up her hand. "Who was asked and who asked you?"

"Most of my men are special forces. The men in the various branches were asked to be tested for psychic ability. There were certain criteria to be met along with the abilities. An age range, combat training, working under pressure conditions, ability to function for long periods of time cut off from the chain of command. Loyalty factors. The list was endless, but surprisingly enough, we had quite a few takers. The military issued a special invite for volunteers. From what I understand law enforcement branches did the same. They were looking for an elite group."

"And this was how long ago?"

"The first I heard of the idea was nearly four years ago. I've been here at Donovans's laboratory for a year now, but all the recruits that made it into the unit, including me, trained together at another facility. As far as I know we were always kept together. They wanted us to form a tight unit. We trained in techniques using psychic abilities in combat. The idea was a strike force that could get in and out unseen. We could be used against the drug cartels, terrorists, even an enemy army. We've been at it for over three years."

"A wild idea. And this is whose baby?"

"Your father's. He thought it up, convinced the powers that be that it could be done, and convinced me and the rest of the men that it would make the world a better place." There was a wealth of bitterness in Ryland Miller's voice.

"Obviously something went wrong."

"Greed went wrong. Donovans has the government contract. Peter Whitney practically owns this company. I guess he just doesn't have enough money with the million or two in his bank account."

She waited a heartbeat. Two. "I doubt my father needs any

more money, Captain Miller. The amount he gives to charities each year would feed a state. You don't know anything about him so I suggest you reserve your opinion until all the facts are in. And for the record, it's a billion or two or more. This corporation could disappear tomorrow and it wouldn't change his lifestyle one bit." Her voice didn't raise in the least, but it smoldered with heat and intensity.

Ryland sighed. Her vivid gaze hadn't wavered an inch. "We have no contact with our people. All communication to the outside must go through your father or the colonel. We have no say in what is happening to us at all. One of my men died a couple of months ago and they lied about how he died. He died as a direct result of this experiment and the enhancement of his abilities. His brain couldn't handle the overload, the constant battering. They claimed it was an accident in the field. That's when we were cut off from all command and separated. We've been in isolation since that time." Miller regarded her with dark, angry eyes, daring her to call him a liar. "And it wasn't the first death, but by God, it's going to be the last."

Lily pushed a hand through her perfectly smooth hair, the first real sign of agitation. The action scattered pins and left long strands falling in a cloud around her face. She was silent, allowing her brain to process the information, even as she was rejecting the accusations and implications about her father.

"Do you know precisely what killed the man in your unit? And is there the same danger to the rest of you?" She asked the questions very quietly, her voice so low it was almost in his mind rather than aloud.

Ryland answered in the same soft voice, taking no chances the unseen guards would overhear the conversation. "His brain was wide open, assaulted by everyone and everything he came into contact with. He couldn't shut it off anymore. We can function together as a group because a couple of the men are like you. They draw the noise and raw emotion away from the rest of us. Then we're powerful and we work. But without that magnet . . ." He broke off and shrugged. "It's like pieces of glass or razor blades slashing at the brain. He snapped, seizures, brain bleeds, you name it. It wasn't a pretty sight and I sure didn't like the glimpse of our future. Neither did any of the other men in the unit."

Lily pressed her fingers to her temple and for just a moment, Ryland caught the impression of throbbing pain. His face darkened, gray eyes narrowing. "Come here." He had an actual physical reaction to her being in pain. The muscles in his belly knotted, hard and aching. Everything protective and male in him rose up and flooded him with an overwhelming need to eased her discomfort.

Her enormous blue eyes instantly became wary. "I don't touch people."

"Because you don't want to know what they're really like inside, do you? You feel it too." He was horrified to think her father may have experimented on her too. *How long have you been telepathic?* More than that, he didn't want to think about never touching her. Never feeling her skin beneath his fingers, her mouth crushed to his. The image was so vivid he could almost taste her. Even her hair begged to be touched, a thick mass of shiny silk just asking for his fingers to toss away the rest of the pins and free it for his inspection.

Lily shrugged easily but a faint blush stole along her high cheekbones. *All of my life. And yes, it can be uncomfortable knowing other people's darkest secrets. I've learned to live within certain boundaries. Maybe my father became interested in psychic phenomena because he wished to help me. For whatever reason, I can assure you, it had nothing to do with personal financial gain.* She let out a slow breath. "How terrible for you, the loss of *any* of your men. You must be very close. I hope I can find a way to help all of you."

Ryland sensed her sincerity. He was suspicious of her father in spite of her protests. *Is Dr. Whitney psychic?* He knew he'd been broadcasting his sexual fantasies a little too strongly but she was unshaken, handling the intensity of the chemistry between them easily. And he knew the chemistry was on both sides. He had a sudden desire to really shake her up, get past her cool demeanor just once and see if fire burned beneath the ice. It was a hell of a thing to think about in the middle of the mess he was in.

Lily shook her head as she answered him. *We've conducted many experiments and have connected telepathically a few times under extreme conditions, but it was sustained completely on my side. I must have inherited the talent through my mother.*

"When you touch him, can you read him?" Ryland asked

curiously in a low voice. He decided men were not all that far from the caves. His attraction to her was raw and hot and beyond any experience he'd ever had. He was unable to control his body's reaction to her. And she knew it. Unlike Ryland, she appeared to be cool and unaffected, while he was shaken to his very core. She carried on their conversation as if he weren't a firestorm burning out of control. As if his blood wasn't boiling and his body hard as a rock and in desperate need. As if she didn't even notice.

"Rarely. He is one of those people who have natural barriers. I think it's because he believes so strongly in psychic talent where most people don't. Being aware of it all the time, he's probably built up a natural wall. I've found many people have barriers to varying degrees. Some seem impossible to get past and others are flimsy. What about you? Have you found the same thing? You're a very strong telepath."

"Come here to me."

Her cool blue gaze drifted over him. Dismissed him. "I don't think so, Captain Miller, I have far too much work to do."

"You're being a coward." He said it softly, his hungry gaze on her face.

She lifted her chin at him and gave him her haughty princess look. "I don't have time for your little games, Captain Miller. Whatever you think is going on here, is not."

His gaze dropped to her mouth. She had a perfect mouth. "Yes it is."

"It was interesting meeting you," Lily said and turned away from him, walking without haste away from him. As cool as ever.

Ryland didn't protest, instead watched her leave him without a single backward glance. He willed her to look back, but she didn't. And she didn't replace the glass barrier around his cage, leaving it for the guards.

About the Authors

Christine Feehan is the *New York Times* and *USA Today* best-selling author of several romances, including the "Dark" Carpathian novels. She lives in California. Visit her website at www.christinefeehan.com.

Katherine Sutcliffe is a multi–award-winning national and international bestselling author of historical romance and contemporary suspense novels. A native Texan, Katherine lives near Dallas. Visit her website at www.katherinesutcliffe.net.

Fiona Brand is a national bestselling author of contemporary romances. She lives in New Zealand. Visit her website at www.intimatemomentsauthors.com/authorpages/fionabrand.htm.

Eileen Wilks is a *USA Today* bestselling author of contemporary romances who lives in Midland, Texas. Visit her website at www.eileenwilks.com.

Christine Feehan

DARK SLAYER

The Dragonseeker Razvan is considered an enemy of both Carpathian hunters and vampires. But when Ivory, a rare female Carpathian, encounters Razvan after he has escaped from captivity, she senses that Razvan is more than what he appears to be, and she is willing to go against the entire Carpathian race to help him. But will her belief cost them their lives?